# Whispers of Excalibur: The Remains

Lennie DiFino


ISBN: 979-8-9914677-3-5
Library of Congress Control Number: 2024918603

# ACKNOWLEDGMENTS

A big thank you to: Dad for always being a source of love and knowledge; Nando & JJ, Joe & Heather, Anthony & Andrea, Anne & Matty, Mena – Carmela, Sofia, Dalia, Duke, Xander, Elizabeth, Norina, Salvatore, Santo, and BellaMia Deborah – for always surrounding me with Love and Laughter and helping me see the light when it was difficult to find.

Thank you to my amazing editor, Julie Hutchings, for her incredible attention to detail and bringing my words the power they needed. You are second-to-none. (Except in this list…then you are second…but I did my ellipses right!)

To Trevor, Brent, Mary and the Barbano & Fallico families: I would not be who I am without you all in my life. Thank you for always letting me be part of your family.

To LaShonda & Carolyn: Thank you for teaching me how to get through the hardest days with grace and compassion.

To Roger & Corey and DJK: There is no story without friendship; what I gained from you all will never be lost. May you continue to rest in peace.

To all my Adornato, DiFino, and Bonanno cousins near and far, and to the Ludingtons, Littlejohns, Pikes, Sweeneys, Proscias, Mom's Christmas Stroll Crew, PLC 5 & family, Fuleihans, Cusatos, Kearneys, Carmola, and Ralph: Your support my entire life has shaped me; thank you all for always believing in me.

To my dear friends, especially: Snot Pig (Danielle), Toxic V, Lesley, Meh, KK, Silly, Elijah "Pope" Burke, Marc Mero, Nattie, Gandalf, Al, Yosh, Jamie, Bobby Tis, Dr. Ron, Aaliyyah (is GOD), Natalie, Ditch-Bro, Piker, Emily, Llama Face, Nicole P-I-O – never mind…and Ashley, I challenge you to find yourselves in these pages.

To TP: Courage comes in many forms; thank you for sharing this gift with me.

To Desmond & Scarlet – there is no greater feeling than the love you give to me. Always remember how much I love you both. Thank you for making me believe that there is *magic inside all of us.*

And Mom—thank you for always lifting me up to reach my dreams. You are missed beyond measure. I love you.

# CONTENTS

## PART II

For Desmond & Scarlet—
and for Mom

# Prologue

Legend tells us Uther Pendragon, the king of the lands of Britain, ruled with ferocity—using his power and close relationship with Merlin the Magician to satisfy his every need, no matter the cost. Merlin, the greatest sorcerer known to the world, was beholden to the king's wishes as long as he lived, a slave to the one who possessed the weapon of the king. Uther's greed ultimately led to his downfall, as he was defeated in a bloody battle that had torn apart his people. The legend also says that before he died, Uther took his weapon—the mythological sword, Excalibur—and in his last action, drove it into a stone. The sword remained there in the stone for nearly fifteen years, until the fateful day when an unsuspecting young man searched for a weapon to help his brother, Sir Kay, during a yearly event to crown a new monarch. The boy came upon the stone and drew the mighty Excalibur from its place. He was ordained king, for he was the son of Uther—he was Arthur.

Arthur would rule the land for many years, bringing all the men of his kingdom together under the banner of Camelot. Unity, friendship, love, courage, and honor surrounded Arthur at his Round Table, while the people of the land rejoiced to have their king. However, like his father before him, the Pendragon curse passed to Arthur—who's own lust, greed, dishonor, deceit, and the ill-fated search for the Holy Grail of Jesus Christ brought his reign to an end. Some historians argue that Arthur's illegitimate son, Mordred, killed him at the Battle of Camlann. Others believe Arthur was only wounded, allowing the monarch to be taken to a mystical island known as Avalon to be healed.

Before being taken to Avalon, Arthur entrusted Sir Perceval, one of the last living Knights of the Round Table, to return the sword of the king to the mysterious Lady of the Lake. Arthur told Perceval one day the sword would return to the true king, an edict that found its way through generations of believers of the tales of Camelot. In this version of the tale, Arthur supposedly died in Avalon, succumbing to his wounds inflicted by Mordred, but some think he fathered a child before his death.

A child with Pendragon blood.

# Chapter 1 - A Secret

The usual sounds of the night were drowned out by the screams from inside the cabin. They grew louder and echoed harder as the cloaked figure moved closer to the cabin. The only light he could see was a candle burning in the window, presumably illuminated by a fire burning inside. He startled a horse that was tied to a post at the fence surrounding the cabin. It jumped in surprise, and the man pulled its reins down, placing his hand to the horse's face to quiet the animal.

"Shh…easy girl," he whispered. "It's just me."

The stranger tied his own horse to the fence post and walked a little stone path that led to the cabin and peered inside the lit window. Inside, a man nervously paced the small living area by the fire. The man's white sleeves were rolled up and his green pants loosely fell from his waist. Past him the stranger could see another room, with a candle next to the bed.

The screams from before now were clear—there was a woman in labor in the bedroom. A third figure moved across the room who the man surmised must have been a midwife. Bloody cloths were piled on the floor next to the bed as the midwife dunked a fresh one into a bowl of water beside the candle, removing the cloth and placing it on the woman's forehead. In a moment of brief silence, the stranger heard the voices from inside.

"Push, my lady," encouraged the midwife. "I can see the head."

The cloaked stranger pulled the handle up on the door and entered. As he came into the light his appearance became clear. He wore a dark maroon cloak over his clothing, which appeared to be similar in almost every detail to a cloak that hung on the wall. He removed his cloak to reveal a black tunic, grey pants and a pair of black boots that came to just below the knee. This man who had ridden his horse to the cabin was old, and the years showed on his face. His bluish-grey eyes were beady and wrinkled more so than the rest of his face; his hair was more salt than pepper, including his well-groomed full beard. Though brittle in his old age, he gave the air of commanding the respect of everyone around him.

The man who had been pacing the room was much younger, with jet-black hair, a crew cut and a black-tinted goatee. His moustache curled at the ends ever so slightly. His green eyes were very light and he was well built, standing six-foot six.

"Amra," said the younger man, "why have you come?"

"You must get this child to safety, Eldon, you're both in terrible danger."

"I won't run. I will defend this house with all I have."

Before Amra could respond, the screaming turned to a higher pitch, before silence overtook the cabin. In the next moment, the cries of a baby rang through the cabin.

"My lord, Eldon," interrupted the midwife, "it is a girl. But your wife, she has taken ill. I am afraid she may not survive the night."

As the midwife relayed the news, Amra heard frightened neighs from his horse outside. Amra hurried Eldon to the bedroom just as footsteps pounded on the roof. He jerked his head upward to follow the sounds.

"They're here!" exclaimed Amra, wide-eyed with panic. "They've come for the child!"

Eldon grabbed for an ax that he'd kept under the bed while Amra drew his sword. The midwife reached for a set of bows and arrows leaning against the wall by the table in the living area and rushed back into the bedroom.

"Eldon," called out the woman. "We're going to die, aren't we? The baby too…"

Amra walked over to the woman, her face flushed and bright red; he put his left hand to her forehead. "She's burning up. We're trapped, Eldon." He swallowed once, hard. "She will not survive, no matter what we do."

Eldon dropped his ax at the foot of the bed and embraced the woman.

"Emma, it's a baby girl," he said.

Emma's eyes squinted, her face a combination of a joyful smile and the realization people were coming for the baby. The tears flowed from her eyes, but Emma didn't blink.

"Give her this," Emma said. She opened her hand, revealing a necklace she gripped in her hand. She slowly unraveled it and winced and grunted as she tried to pull herself up in the bed before she handed Eldon the necklace. The necklace had a wooden cross on the end, something Emma had worn her entire life. Emma used what little energy she had left to give the necklace to her husband. "I'm sorry, Eldon, I thought we'd have more time with her. Please, get her to safety."

Eldon kissed Emma softly on the lips, then her forehead, hot under his lips. He moved back toward Amra and handed him the cross.

"Amra, take my daughter. Get the hell out of here."

"I won't leave you," argued Amra. "I will stay and fight."

"Dad…please...go," pleaded Emma.

Emma's eyes closed; Eldon could only watch his wife as she prepared to die, oblivious to the shadows that glided past the bedroom window.

Amra knew he could not wait any longer. He placed his forehead upon his daughter's one last time, a tear falling onto her burning skin. He hoped it would soothe her. He then gazed upon his family, knowing this would be the last time he saw them, his heart broken for the reality of the moment. He wrapped the crying baby in a fresh cloth, stepping over the bloodied ones, and rushed from the cabin. Amra rushed down the stone path to the fence to the sound of windows breaking and the *clang* of Eldon's ax fighting off the invading force; Amra's escape was unnoticed. He briskly untied his horse and mounted it. He nestled the baby safely into his lap, kicked the horse's flank, and was gone into the night, the midwife's cries and Eldon's yelling trailing behind him. He turned one last time to see the roof being set on fire.

They were being slaughtered. But the baby was his priority.

# Chapter 2 – Life and Death

Amra rode under the cover of the night sky until he came to another cabin in the woods outside of a village, larger than the first, with a second floor and a porch. The night was pitch black, but the two windows on each side of the cabin allowed for moonlight to sneak into the rooms they covered.

The smell of tobacco greeted him as he approached the porch. It came from an unidentifiable man sitting in a chair, the dim light from his pipe not strong enough to make him visible through the cloud of smoke. Amra slowly pulled off the hood of his cloak, watching the man put his pipe down on the arm of his chair, revealing his features through the haze. The man was short and stocky, with brown hair brushing his shoulders. A scar slashed across his throat, gruesome at first sight, especially to those who didn't know him or where it came from. He was barefoot, his black dirty pants rolled up to his knees. The slight twitch in the corner of his mouth made it seem as if he was always grinning.

"Is that the baby?"

"Yes, Daniel," Amra replied. "Eldon and Emma are dead. This little girl is all that's left."

"She will be safe here."

Daniel reached out to take the baby from Amra as he looked at the sleeping child with great concern. "Do they know where she is?" he asked.

"No. But they will find me. They know I was there." Amra reached into his pocket and took out the cross necklace and handed it to Daniel. "Please, take this," he insisted. "Guard this child with your life."

"Amra, I'm sorry about your daughter," Daniel said.

The two shook hands the way most men of the day would, each grabbing the inside of the other's elbow and squeezing. Amra then uncharacteristically wrapped one arm around Daniel's neck and hugged him before he left. Amra pulled the hood of his cloak back over his head and rushed to his horse, where he jumped on and once more rode off.

When the baby began to cry Daniel turned to bring her inside, but a scarlet-haired woman suddenly filled the doorway, towering over Daniel. "Whose baby is that?" she blurted out.

She had blue eyes and was also barefoot. Her skin was paler than Daniel's and her freckles seemed to outline her body from head to toe. She wore a navy-blue night garment that illuminated her eyes even more, but Daniel quickly nudged the woman inside with him. Their voices echoed in the dark room.

"Eldon and Emma are dead." Daniel paused, as he looked down at the baby again.

"Oh no," she gasped, her freckled hand flying to her mouth.

"I know, Helen." Daniel reached out to Helen and put the wooden cross necklace in her free hand, calloused from years on the farm. Helen took the necklace, blue eyes wet and shining, and placed it around her own neck.

"She needs a name," Helen pointed out, as she cupped her hand under the baby's head and gently kissed her forehead. "Let's call her Almena."

"Almena is a good name," agreed Daniel.

# Chapter 3 – Meet Allen White

"Allen," a voice yelled from a distance. "Allen!"

The young man broke from his dream about Almena and Amra and rolled over in his bed to avoid the sunshine that was sneaking in through the window. Every morning it was the same thing for Allen White. He'd wake up with the sun in his eyes as his roommate called for him from the kitchen. Like a lot of mornings, his room reeked of popcorn and half-eaten macaroni and cheese from the previous movie night—*The Final Girls* this time. Rubbing his eyes, he made his way past the horror movie posters, slipping on a comic book, to the bathroom to get cleaned up.

Allen walked into the kitchen still in his pajamas and a familiar smell wafted his way. He knew in an instant Joe had made him the breakfast of choice, which brought a smile to his face.

"Made your favorite—grilled cheese."

"Thanks, Joe. Two slices of cheese?" asked Allen.

"Of course, bro, come on, I know one slice isn't enough. Damn man, you could use a shave."

"Nah, I'm good for another day or two. We don't both have to be big man on campus every day," Allen said with a wink, though he did envy Joe Figueroa's jet-black hair with touches of grey around the ears. So distinguished. Didn't hurt that he was six-foot-seven with a face and body chiseled by the Greek gods. Not to mention he was a stand-out basketball player.

The two had met at freshman orientation four years ago and hit it off over their love for video games, sports, food, and girls. They requested then and there to be placed together in the dorms the coming year at Fordham University in the Bronx and had lived together since. Now seniors, Allen and Joe looked out for each other like brothers and everyone on campus that knew the duo also knew they were inseparable. When Joe needed help scouting an opponent, Allen offered to help. When Allen wanted to bounce assignment ideas off someone, Joe would stop everything to help. Allen and Joe shared a special bond.

"I'm gonna be late again," said Allen as he looked up at the clock. "Third time this week."

"More dreams?" Joe inquired.

"Yeah. They're just so *real*, Joe."

"Maybe it's time to switch to comedies at night? Or decaf?" Joe joked.

"Keep it up, man, and I'll tell that cheerleader where you really were Monday night," Allen threatened.

"Take it for the road," replied Joe, as he wrapped the grilled cheese in a napkin.

"All right, I'll catch up with you after class. Thanks."

Joe and Allen fist-bumped as Allen raced to his room, threw on a pair of jeans from the floor, smelled a few t-shirts before settling on the blue New York Mets shirt and grabbed his backpack before he headed out the door, eating his sandwich. Allen moved across campus as fast as he could, finding his way to Keating Hall.

"Allen," a voice said from behind him at the entrance. "Allen White?"

"Yeah," Allen responded as he tossed his napkin in a garbage can. "Who's asking?"

"My name is Mead," replied the man in a soft, high-pitched voice, bobbing his head side to side.

Allen turned to see an old man in a suit. Mead looked to be almost eighty years old, but Allen noticed the man stood strong and confident. His white beard matched his hair—hair that was parted to the left and poker straight—not long hair, but not too short either. His black eyes were covered by circular-framed glasses and his ears stuck out like half-opened car doors. Mead held a briefcase in his right hand and a cup of coffee in the other. Under his right arm was a black umbrella he always carried.

"I'm kind of in a hurry here," Allen said with one foot on the step below him. "What's this about?"

"It's a personal matter," Mead answered.

"Can we do this after class?" Allen wondered.

"I'll wait here for you if that's okay?"

"Sure," Allen replied. "I'll be back in an hour."

Allen rushed to the classroom where Professor Rogers' history class was already in session. He attempted to slide in unnoticed, but after four years in the history program, Allen and Professor Rogers had built a good relationship, even though he was the most feared professor at Fordham. Allen was the student with promise while Rogers was the professor that pushed Allen to reach his potential.

"Ah, Mr. White," interrupted Professor Rogers in his deep, bellowing voice that reminded Allen of Andre the Giant. "I see you've managed to make it to senior seminar."

"Yes sir," Allen grinned. "Not a scratch on me."

"No, Mr. White, just this morning's breakfast," Rogers retorted as he pointed to Allen's crumb-laden shirt, which got a huge laugh from the classroom.

Allen laughed along as he wiped his shirt off and pulled out his notebook and pen, waiting for Professor Rogers to continue. Rogers turned off the lights to present the day's lesson—the Crusades. Allen tuned out the professor as he surveyed the room. His classmates all furiously took notes, but Allen continued to daydream—and it wasn't long before he was asleep.

Allen heard a sound, faint at first, but enough to startle him. His eyes widened as he heard the crackling of sticks and leaves and he saw a figure, then another, until a group of shadows were running in moonlight, through the mist that lay on the ground. The scene overtook him with fear, his heart racing with nerves, until he heard a voice. A soothing one, and familiar to Allen.

"You must find him."

"Find who?" Allen asked, but silence answered him. "Who I must I find?'"

But looking around, there were no shadows anymore. He reached down to touch the ground, eager to feel anything that wasn't shadows and realized he was standing on water. He hurried in his effort to make it back to land but with each movement, Allen realized he was going in circles. His frustration turned to distress when he began to sink.

"Help me!" he shouted in desperation.

Allen yelled himself awake in class and found Professor Rogers standing above him.

"Allen," the professor whispered, "you okay?"

"Fine, sir," Allen replied.

Professor Rogers placed his hand on Allen's shoulder to calm him down. "Pretty vivid dream, I imagine?" Rogers asked.

"You have no idea." He flashed a fake smile to show the professor he was okay.

Professor Rogers returned to teaching the lesson and flipped the lights on. Allen had tuned him out completely, as he furiously wrote the details of his dream down in his notebook. He impatiently waited for class to end and bolted from the room when it did, ignoring even the professor's attempt to catch him.

As he made his way out of the door into the quad, he spotted Mead on a bench, smoking a pipe and taking in the crisp autumn day. While passing students occupied Mead's attention, Allen tried to avoid the old man, to no avail.

"Mr. White," Mead said as he chased down Allen. "Mr. White, did you forget about me?"

"I'm sorry," Allen apologized, "I just don't have time right now. I have to get back to my apartment."

"Mr. White, it is imperative I speak with you," Mead begged.

"Does this have to happen now?" Allen asked. "What's so important?"

"The sooner the better, Mr. White. This is about your parents."

"What about my parents?" asked Allen as he slowed down and turned to face Mead. "Are they okay?"

"Oh, the Whites are fine, just fine," Mead replied, waving Allen's worry off with his hand.

"Well, what's the problem then?"

"You and I both know they're not your real parents."

Allen took a step back. Who the hell *was* this man talking so bluntly about his past? His family wasn't something he kept a secret, but he didn't freely share it either. He didn't know much about his real parents outside of what he learned when he turned eighteen—they'd died when he was young. He never wanted to know more, as he was happy with the Whites. They were the only family he ever knew.

"What do you know about my parents?" Allen inquired.

"I know everything about them," Mead explained. "I was great friends with your family long before you were born. I know everything there is to know about you, Allen."

"I'm sorry, *what?* Who are you?" Allen was hesitant to respond, wary of this odd old man and unsure if he wanted to open a part of his life he had kept closed off for the past twenty-one years.

"I'm sure you have many questions," Mead said.

"I just don't have time for this right now," Allen replied. "I have a really important night ahead of me. Can you give me your number and I'll call you tomorrow?"

Mead nodded, but disappointment made his lips purse. He pulled a dark blue card out of his breast pocket and handed it to Allen.

"Take this," Mead said. "When you're ready, call me."

"Thanks," Allen took the card and began to walk away, eager to end the awkward conversation, when Mead called out to him once more.

"Oh, Mr. White, before I forget…happy birthday."

As quickly as he said the words, Mead disappeared into the crowd of coeds on campus, leaving Allen flustered and frustrated. Did this man truly know his biological family? He reached for his phone and called his mother, intent on getting to the truth.

"Hi, honey," the voice on the other end said. "How's the big birthday going?"

"Hi, Mom. I have to ask you something."

"Okay, what's up?"

"Have you ever heard of a guy named Mead?" Allen asked.

There was an uncomfortable silence on the other end of the phone.

"He was a friend of the family," Allen's mother replied after a long breath. "He knew your parents and grandparents."

Allen's entire face squeezed with anger. Why would his mother hide someone connected to his past from him? Could this old man be trusted? What was happening and why today?

"Well, he showed up here at school today," Allen said, accusation in his voice. "He said he wanted to talk to me." More silence. "Mom?" Allen pushed.

"Sorry, Allen," she softly replied. "If you want to know more about your parents, he's the one who can tell you."

"How is that even possible?" Allen barked.

Allen heard his mother take a deep breath. Whatever answer she was about to give was something he wouldn't want to hear, so he decided to just drop it.

"Forget it, Mom. I'm sorry I even asked. I'll talk to this guy and figure it out."

"Are you sure, honey?"

"Yeah. No big deal," Allen said. "I don't care that much because I trust you and Dad."

"Okay, sweetheart. Please try to enjoy the rest of your birthday. I love you!"

"I love you too, Mom. Talk to you later."

Allen returned to his apartment as quickly as he could make it across campus. Still spinning from the bombshell dropped on him earlier, he headed to the kitchen to grab a drink, absently checking his phone. Joe had texted him:

*Playing ball till 5, team dinner and then be ready to…PARTY!!!!!*

Allen had completely forgot that Joe had planned a party, and he was in no mood to be around people; he knew, however, that if he didn't let Joe throw this party, he'd never live it down. Allen shook his head with a grinning acceptance. Maybe a celebration would be good for him.

Back in his room, he tossed his phone on the bed, grabbed the remote and turned the TV on. He lifted his shirt above his head and flopped on to the end of his bed to kick off his sneakers. Allen shifted back on the bed toward his pillows, wanting nothing more than to relax after all the emotion of the day. Unable to stop wondering about Mead, but not ready to call him, he turned on his Xbox One to play NBA 2K as he listened to Spotify's '80s rock station in the background. Before Allen knew it, he was back to sleep.

# Chapter 4 – Friend or Foe?

"You must find him," the voice once again whispered.

Allen found himself in a familiar setting. He was surrounded by mist and the only light was from the moon as it reflected off what appeared to be a lake about fifty feet away. The area behind Allen was wooded and ominous, but he felt serenity as he made his way toward the water. Stepping over some fallen leaves and branches provided a harmony to the sounds of nature; the trees whistled as Allen walked, welcoming him with their song, while owls and crickets accompanied the moonlight sonata. Approaching the water, Allen spotted a shadowy figure off in the distance, standing behind a giant oak tree. Allen felt a chill in his body as he suddenly became unsettled by the figure, a terror he had felt before.

He somehow mustered the courage to continue toward the dark character when he heard more movement off to his right. He spun in that direction, and Allen realized there were figures on all sides of him, and they were getting greater in number. The fear began to overwhelm Allen, his heart trying to escape from his chest.

"What do you want from me?" Allen screamed.

Sudden silence surrounded Allen. Time stood still.

The figures that had lined his approach to the area were gone. The trees were gone. All that remained was the mist, the moon, and water in front of him—the same water he'd walked on before. Allen was sure he was alone by this lake, when the same voice from before startled him.

"You must free him now."

"Who must I free? Where is he?" pleaded Allen.

"Allen…wake up, bitch."

Allen jolted himself awake. Kimo, a good friend of Joe's, was standing over Allen, shaking him by the shoulder. Kimo had a tattoo of the word "Holoholona," emblazoned from just below his wrist to his elbow. Allen had never really gotten along with Kimo, their past littered with several misunderstandings about Kimo's ex-girlfriend that defined their uneasy relationship. Allen was always cordial for Joe's sake, no matter how much he loathed Kimo's presence.

Allen yawned, stretched, and kicked his legs over the side of the bed to sit up and talk to Kimo.

"What's up?" Allen asked.

"Sorry I woke you up, but you were thrashing," Kimo answered.

Allen stood up and shook his head clear of the dream. He moved past Kimo toward the kitchen to get water, but Kimo wasn't through talking to him.

"You're good for tonight, right?" Kimo asked.

"Yeah, man, I'll be ready to rock. Just tired as hell."

"You better man up," Kimo teased. "So many girls coming through tonight."

"Let's just make sure everyone gets along," Allen said.

"You still on that? I told you I was sorry a hundred times. I'm over her, man."

"I wasn't even talking about her…"

Without a word, Kimo turned to the door. "I'll see you tonight," Kimo said, pulling open the front door. "Be ready. You're only 21 once."

"Thank God for that," joked Allen.

The two clasped hands and half-hugged each other, the awkwardness between them evident in every movement they made and word they spoke. Kimo left and Allen sat on the arm of the couch, sipping a glass of water, remembering the reason for the coldness between he and Kimo.

It was sophomore year just before Christmas break that Kimo and Allen had their falling out. They'd all gotten very close after freshman year and decided living together would be fun for their sophomore year. Joe, Kimo, Allen, and Tommy had planned a night out to party and relax before a month away from campus and each other. Tommy Illanito was the type of guy who could bring a crowd of any size to its knees with his humor and wit, but most of the time he preferred his own company. He wasn't always comfortable being the life of the party, but when he was, it was a treat for anyone around. Even though he was about five-foot-six and 180 pounds with black hair that seemed to be slowly sliding away from his head, Tommy talked with a bravado reserved only for the most confident people.

But, despite the closeness the four had when they moved in together, things quickly changed. That first semester was treacherous for them. Tommy left Fordham Columbus Day weekend and never came back. His mother had gotten sick, and he decided to stay closer to his home in Chicago to be with her. Joe was injured at practice and was worried he'd have to redshirt and give up a year of basketball. Allen was annoyed that he was always cleaning up after his roommates, and when Tommy left it was even worse. Tension was high, and tempers flared with all the stress everyone felt.

Kimo had invited Allen and Joe out to the most popular bar near Fordham's campus, Moons over My Rammy, where a smile was all the ID a student needed—especially the athletes.

The bar was pretty empty that night for a "Thirsty Thursday," especially before a break, but it filled in a little more as the night progressed. A giant dance floor covered with the stickiness of spilled drinks was where Kimo went while Allen planted himself at the bar to people watch. Joe pulled a stool up next to Allen to watch the dance floor with him. The night was going well for all three of them and should have gotten better when Kimo's girlfriend, Stephanie, walked in with her friends.

Stephanie was the girl very comfortable in her own skin, the type that radiated confidence wherever she went. Petite, maybe five feet tall on her tip toes and 100 pounds, with strawberry blonde hair and a smattering of freckles on her fair skin. She always wore the brightest pink shades of lipstick to accentuate her full lips. Stephanie wore color contacts to make her eyes bright blue. Allen couldn't even remember if anyone knew her real eye color. Her and Kimo made an opinionated couple; one would verbally spar a point and the other was quick to defend regardless of the argument or consequence. They were both hotheaded at times but never with each other. Her reputation for never backing down, even with professors and administrators, resulted in most of the campus referring to her as "The Bitch." But Stephanie didn't even seem to care.

She waved hello to a few people and hugged Allen before she made her way over to the dance floor. Stephanie's phone hung halfway out of the back pocket of her short jean skirt–she wanted people to stare at her butt. Her chest exploded from a spaghetti-strapped tank top a size or two too small. Her friends, Jemma and Gia, both dressed in almost identical fashion to Stephanie, followed in silence and obedience, never once trying to acknowledge anyone in the bar. Kimo leaned forward and wrapped his arms around Stephanie's neck in greeting and moved in to give her a kiss as Allen turned his focus to the television in the corner of the bar, not particularly paying attention to anything other than the football game.

As Allen scrolled through his phone to read the latest Tweets, he was caught off guard by an arm resting on his shoulder. He turned to see Stephanie next to him, as Kimo passed by and down the narrow, dark hallway to the restroom.

"Having fun?" Stephanie asked.

"Not really my scene," Allen replied, "at least the game is good."

"You're always so shy," Stephanie nudged. "Loosen up, will ya."

Allen didn't know how to respond to Stephanie's comment, so he just chuckled and played with his phone to ignore her, but she persisted.

"All these girls in here and you're playing with your phone at the bar," she commented.

"Not my type of girls."

"Nobody in here catches your eye?" she said, slightly tilting her head with a smile.

"Nah," Allen said, "I'm fine with things being like this, though. Don't have time for a relationship."

"Who's talking about a relationship, Al?" Stephanie quipped, quietly near his ear.

Allen stopped scrolling as her hot breath hit his ear. "I'm not looking for a one-night stand either, Steph."

"Well, that's a shame you don't have time for anyone, Al," she replied. "You're a really good guy."

Allen hated being called Al; one of his many pet peeves. But he let it slide with a select few. Stephanie was one of the few. She hugged Allen, wrapping her arms tight around his neck. Then she pulled her head back and gave him a kiss on the cheek. Allen lowered his phone down to show his appreciation for the gesture. The two smiled at each other, sharing this tender moment between friends.

Allen never saw the punch.

Before he knew it, he was off the bar stool and on the ground with

Kimo on top of him throwing punch after punch. Kimo's strength was incredible, an expected power from an All-American Wrestler. Allen had no time to react or protect himself. He caught flickers of Stephanie behind Kimo, first with her head in her hands, then watching her boyfriend attack one of her best friends. She tried to pull Kimo off Allen but couldn't possibly match his ferocity. Her screams for help were barely audible across the bar, but Joe happened to look over and see Kimo putting a hurting on someone and walked over to casually break it up. But as Joe got closer, he saw it was Allen on the ground, bleeding, and he pushed harder through the crowd to break it up. He pulled Kimo off Allen and shoved him out the front door of Moons onto 189th Street.

"What are you *doing*, dude?" Joe screamed.

"He was hitting on Steph!" Kimo yelled, "he got what he deserved."

Stephanie ran out after them toward Kimo, wildly swinging her arms. Joe scooped her up and carried her back inside the bar, telling her to stay put while she flailed, trying to escape. Kimo attempted to walk back into the bar, but Joe and others blocked his path.

"So, this is how it's gonna be," Kimo growled.

"Don't be like that," Joe started.

"Kiss my ass," Kimo interrupted.

"You're drunk," Joe said, "you need to go walk this off."

"So, he hit on my girl, and you take his side? Forget you all, man."

Joe reached out to Kimo, but the angry Hawaiian shoved Joe out of the way and stormed off toward campus.

Stephanie didn't go after her boyfriend. She stayed at the bar and helped Allen to his feet. "I can't believe this," she moaned, looking hard at Allen's left eye. It had swollen shut.

"I'm fine," Allen bristled.

"I think your orbital bone is broken. Kimo *sucker-punched* you..." With blood dripping everywhere, the bartender threw a towel to Stephanie, who dabbed at Allen's face.

"Steph, I'm good," Allen said as he pulled away from her touch.

The rest of the bar began to clear out as it got closer to last call, and Allen could feel his eye getting puffier as the seconds passed. The manager, a short muscular man, came over to check on Allen, but Stephanie simply waved him off, assuring him everything was okay—despite the truth.

Allen would spend the next few days in bed, missing school and recuperating. Allen didn't mind the solitude too much as most of his professors had already heard what happened and went easy on Allen once he returned to classes. Kimo stayed away from his roommates and opted to spend his time with the wrestling team.

A few days later, Allen and Joe were walking on campus near the soccer field when they heard Kimo shout, "Allen, Joe, hold up!"

"Crap…here we go." Allen muttered.

"I got your back," Joe insisted.

Kimo caught up to them, making Allen cringe. "Look, guys, I'm sorry. I was drunk and out of line. I messed up and I want to make things right."

"Dude, you sucker punched me!" Allen yelled.

"I know, man, I know, I feel terrible. Please forgive me," Kimo pleaded, extending his hand. Allen took it.

Soon after that day, however, Kimo and Stephanie broke up and Kimo blamed Allen. Kimo brimmed with anger anytime the two of them were near each other, and Allen could no longer trust his former friend. When Kimo moved out, Joe decided to stay with Allen. After a lot of tense encounters, Kimo and Allen knew they'd have to see each other often, and put aside their anger, remaining on speaking terms for Joe's sake.

Allen wasn't ecstatic that Kimo would be at his party that night, but he knew that if Kimo didn't come, Joe wouldn't feel right about leaving him out. Joe was always trying to get the two of them to sincerely put their animosity to rest, so he always included both whenever the opportunity presented itself.

As Allen prepared to take a shower and get ready for the party, his phone vibrated on his bed—a text from Joe.

*Meet me at 8 – Mad River – UES*

With a sigh, Allen looked in the mirror, letting it cloud up with steam as he waited for the shower.

He was eager to get the night over with before it even began.

*****

Allen didn't particularly care for New York City's Upper East Side and the crowds they brought in, but he knew it was better than being dragged to Times Square. In his four years at Fordham, Allen couldn't remember a night where a trip to the City's famed area didn't end in disaster.

His first trip as a freshman laid the foundation for the years to come. Allen came from the small town of Clayton in Upstate New York, 350 miles north—removed from the hustle of New York City. He loved to be on the water all summer long, watching the "summer folk" come and go each year. He was used to watching tourists make fools of themselves, and while his upbringing wasn't sheltered, Allen wasn't necessarily prepared for his first few months on the rugged streets of New York. Joe had convinced him to tag along with a group that first night as a freshman. They took the Ram Van from Rose Hill's campus in the Bronx to the campus at Lincoln Center on 60th and 9th in Manhattan. They split up into two groups from there and took cabs to get to the heart of Times Square—Allen went with Joe, Kimo, and Stephanie; Tommy went off with his girlfriend, Danielle, and her friend, Brittany.

As the group pulled over to the end of the block at 49th and 8th, Allen's excitement grew. Neon lights lit up the night sky. Allen had never seen so many people in one place in his life, a chorus of voices from all over the world that hummed in unison. There were people everywhere, a sea of anonymity that splashed with the boisterousness of the crowds—it was then Allen felt at home, surrounded by the permanent "summer folk" he had grown up around. He stepped out of the cab and onto the sidewalk, awed by the colorful beauty before him. The rest of the group shared Allen's admiration for the city, all of them watching people pass as if time stood still for them alone. Intoxicated as they were by the bright lights of the Big Apple, the friends continued to move on, making their way toward Bar 54, a rooftop bar above the Hilton on West 45th. One of Joe's friends from the football team was a bouncer at the bar, so they had no trouble getting through the door. Each received a pink wristband to allow them to drink for the night before they boarded the elevator to the roof. Shuffling off the elevator, they walked past the next set of bouncers and took in the view on the roof, open-mouthed. The views of the city were even more incredible from 200 feet above the ground.

"Allen, you can see everything from up here," Danielle said, breathless.

"Yeahhhhhh," Allen exhaled in reply. "This is just awesome."

"You ever seen anything like this before?" Danielle wondered.

"No," Allen whispered, "but this is the first time since I got to New York that I can understand why people fall in love with this city. I feel like I finally get it. Like I belong here."

After a few beers and some random conversations with strangers, the group left the bar and headed back down the elevator. As they floated out the front door of the hotel, ready to head back to the pick-up point for the Ram Van, the giggling group decided to walk the fourteen blocks back. Halfway through their walk back, in the midst of the group drunkenly serenading unbothered New Yorkers, Joe got a text from some of his teammates asking him to meet them at Turtle Bay, a bar on 52nd Street and 2nd Avenue. Joe said his goodbyes and hailed a cab as the friends made it to 54th street.

The group continued to walk, Allen following a few feet behind Kimo and Stephanie, who had flirted with each other all night. Allen watched as the two began to kiss on the street—which cemented the beginning of their relationship. They were both fairly drunk, and barely noticed they were crossing a street as taxis raced through the lights.

"Look out!" Allen yelled.

Allen lunged forward, pushing his friends out of the way as horns blared through the intersection. His momentum carried all three of them to the ground in one heap, halting to a stop on the edge of the sidewalk, safe from harm. Kimo sat up and immediately vomited on the pavement, while Stephanie crawled over and checked on him; the fall had sobered her up.

Allen, however, was like a rock. He simply stood up and brushed the dirt from his clothes, ignoring the giant gash that was pouring blood from his elbow.

That moment could have been enough to keep him from ever wanting to go to the heart of the city. He tried a few more times, each as unsuccessful as the next. There was the Bike Messenger Incident of 2017, the McDonald's food poisoning, the lit cigarette to the face from the top of a balcony bar, and the unfortunate karaoke incident of 2019. Allen felt over time it wasn't in his best interests to venture far from the Bronx and the comforts of campus, but he kept going back because of that one moment on top of the world his freshman year.

Now, two years later, he thought about how much had changed since that night and where life would be next year after graduation and the need to find a job. He wondered if he and Joe would remain as close, if he would even stay in the city.

Allen's phone rang, again snapping him back to reality. It was Stephanie.

"What's up?" he asked, picking up.

"I'll be there tonight," Stephanie said. "Hope you're excited, birthday boy."

"Yeah, so excited," Allen said, rolling his eyes.

"Come on, it won't be that bad," she assured. "You might even have some fun, you know. By the way, tomorrow morning I have to go to the zoo for a bio project. You want to go?"

"Sure, as long as I can see penguins," he laughed.

"Okay, thanks. I'll see you tonight." Stephanie said.

"See you later," Allen said, as he threw his phone back down on the bed.

# Chapter 5 – Punch. Drunk. Love.

As he sat in the back seat of a taxi, Allen watched the city as everything moved in a blur. The driver was inaudible as he chattered away on his Bluetooth and sped down 3rd Avenue. At about eight o'clock they arrived at Mad River. Allen handed the cabbie twelve dollars for an eight-dollar fare and slid across the back seat of the cab to exit on the left.

Allen grinned as he approached the open black door of Mad River, the loud pop music thumping. Allen took a deep breath before he entered. The bouncer asked for his ID, so Allen pulled his wallet out of his pocket and showed the muscular, big-bearded bouncer who was in a black shirt three sizes too small. The bouncer motioned him inside and handed Allen back his license.

"Have a good night," the bouncer said.

"Thanks."

As he made his way to the bar, Allen scanned the establishment but didn't see any of his friends, so he ordered a beer and found an open stool where he could wait for his friends. He checked his phone every few minutes for any word from Joe or Stephanie to let him know they were going to be late, but no calls or texts came. The place was empty and quiet, and that was fine with Allen. He preferred the low-key nights, where he could just be with his friends and not have to shout to talk to the person next to him. Some bars in New York City were less crowded and noisy, and Mad River—at least for this night—was one of those bars. After thirty minutes passed, Allen became disheartened that none of his friends showed, and the bartender took notice of the frustrated young man.

"Everything alright?" she asked.

"I guess so," Allen huffed. "Just one of those nights; my friends are late."

"Could be worse," the bartender joked.

Allen cringed. His face must have said everything his brain wouldn't let him, because the bartender bowed her head, knowing she'd messed up. When her head raised again, her cheeks were flush with shame.

"It's your birthday, isn't it?" she asked.

"It is," Allen sheepishly murmured.

"Shit," she lamented. "I'm so sorry… I'm an idiot. Your drinks are on me."

"Totally unnecessary," Allen protested.

"No, I insist," the bartender said.

"Well, thanks. I appreciate it."

"What are you drinking?" she asked.

"I'll have a Jack and Coke," Allen answered.

The bartender smiled at him as she poured his drink. Allen noticed she threw a little extra booze into the glass, a nice gift to ease his worry. Allen continued to check his phone, but nobody had called or texted him. His shoulders slumped along with his body as he sipped his drink and stared blankly past the bar into an uncertain sadness.

"You ready for another?" the bartender asked.

Something about her was different. She had a giant grin on her face and Allen couldn't tell if she was flirting or just being nice. He nodded, and she refilled his glass, this time pouring in even more liquor. She slid the glass back to Allen, and he held it up and toasted the beautiful brunette. Her face was a little paler than most in the bar, not the type of girl who spent all day caking her face with makeup. She was naturally beautiful—inviting brown eyes, a slender, but muscular build. Subtle green streaks ran through her hair. Her shirt was a sleeveless black button-down V-neck, showing off her cleavage enough to make any man look twice. Her jeans weren't too tight, but her smile is what Allen couldn't stop admiring as he drank.

"What's your name?" she said.

"Allen," he nervously replied.

"I'm Clarissa, nice to meet you, Allen."

"You too," he responded, his naivety with the opposite sex painfully clear. Allen had tried a few dates over the years, but he never shook the feeling of worry that came from Kimo's punch. That moment made it hard for Allen to want to open up to anyone in a romantic way.

A few more minutes went by and with no friends in sight, Allen was ready to leave, dejected by his lonely birthday. As he pulled out his money to tip Clarissa, she wagged her finger.

"I won't take your money, sweetheart," Clarissa said. "Save that for this big party we have upstairs."

"I think I'm calling it a night, actually," Allen said.

"Check it out upstairs first," she suggested. "It's a fun time—Eighties Night."

Allen could only crack an awkward smile before he fumbled his money onto the bar's counter, and nearly tripped on his way to the upstairs bar. The bouncer at the top of the stairs laughed at Allen as he opened the door to the second bar. Allen walked through into a sea of neon lights and "I'm so Excited" by the Pointer Sisters blasting – his kind of place if ever there was one.

"Surprise!" screamed the sea of people waiting for him through the doors.

Allen froze, unable to believe they'd gotten this over on him.

"Dude," Joe laughed, "happy birthday!"

"How…why…I mean…" Allen stammered.

"Just enjoy it, Al," Stephanie interjected. "You're only twenty-one once."

Stephanie pulled a necklace out of a bag and cracked it to make it glow purple. She knew Allen well enough to know his favorite color. She put it around Allen's neck and gave him a big hug. Allen surveyed the room during the hug and saw Danielle, Brittany, Jemma, and Gia taking shots at the bar, while the basketball team cheered them on. Some other people from campus had come just for the open bar, because he certainly didn't know them. He felt a tap on his shoulder and turned to see Tommy.

"Pesci!" Allen screamed with joy. "What the hell are you doing here?"

"Al-Dente," Tommy joked. "I wouldn't have missed this for the world."

Allen and Tommy grasped hands and then hugged, as they hadn't seen each other in almost three years – Allen relieved to know that another person he trusted was around him.

"I missed you, man," Tommy said.

"Bro, I am so happy to see you. How is everything? How's Mom?"

"She's much better," Tommy explained, "happiest I've ever seen her."

"That's awesome," Allen said, "please give her my best."

"You know I will," Tommy replied. "Now, go get a drink and enjoy this party."

Allen's disappointment from feeling left alone on his birthday quickly transformed into excitement at seeing his friends, both old and new. As he smiled and hugged friends on his way to the bar, Allen noticed that Clarissa had moved herself upstairs to work the bar for the party. She smiled softly at Allen from behind the bar as she mixed another drink for him. Clarissa passed the drink to Allen, who turned to the other side of the room and locked eyes with Kimo. Allen's smile changed quickly into a straight face, as Kimo's eyes spoke volumes. Allen soon realized that Stephanie had rested her arm around his neck, shouting past the music.

"This is going to be so much fun!" she yelled.

"We'll see," Allen replied. "Seriously though, thank you."

"You're welcome, Al," Stephanie said.

Allen moved subtly to get out of her grip, hoping to avoid a repeat of Kimo's anger from years ago. Stephanie didn't take notice of the calculated move, she just ordered another drink and danced out into the crowd to her girls. He watched as Stephanie, Jemma, and Gia danced around Joe, making the star athlete the center of attention. Kimo had shifted his focus to Stephanie, eyes glued to his ex-girlfriend, making Allen uneasy in a variety of ways; Kimo was unstable to begin with, but the addition of alcohol made it worse. Allen wouldn't let Kimo ruin his night, so he walked the room, seeing who else had come to his party. He greeted a few acquaintances with sincere appreciation and took a shot off the tray of the scantily clad brunette that worked the room. He downed the shot, shaking his body to combat the taste, and moved toward the dance floor and his friends. Tommy and Danielle were all over each other, rekindling their lost romance from previous years, while Brittany and Joe seemed to be getting close as well. The night was everything Allen had ever imagined a big surprise could be—though it was short-lived.

It could have been the nostalgia, or the alcohol intake, but Allen watched Kimo get up from his spot at the bar and stride toward Stephanie, Jemma, and Gia. Strutting onto the dance floor, full of liquored confidence, he grabbed Stephanie from behind, putting his hands on her hips. Stephanie turned to see who it was and when she realized it was Kimo, struggled to set herself free.

Kimo wouldn't let go—which caused the other girls to start screaming at him to leave. The more they shouted at Kimo to leave them alone, the more he laughed at them and pulled Stephanie closer. Stephanie caught Allen's eyes and mouthed "help" to him.

Allen had had enough.

He pushed his way through the growing crowd toward the belligerent Kimo. "I think you should go," Allen interrupted.

"Nah, I'm good," Kimo slurred, shoving Allen away with one arm.

Kimo continued to grip Stephanie, who finally turned and threw her drink at him, soaking Kimo from his head to mid-chest. It happened in slow-motion, and Allen couldn't stop what happened next.

Angered, Kimo clenched his hand into a fist and swung, striking Stephanie in the face.

Stephanie was knocked out before she even hit the beer-soaked floor. Drunk and enraged, Kimo then kicked Stephanie as she lay motionless on the floor.

Allen slid to the floor and covered Stephanie with his whole body, taking Kimo's kicks as best he could, shielding his friend. Joe, Tommy, and a few other guys in the bar sprang into the fracas, pulling Kimo away as the bouncers pounced into action to prevent any more damage.

Three bouncers and a host of other student-athletes were no match for Kimo's rage; he would have been arrested on the spot, but instead fought his way through the would-be challengers and down the stairs into the New York City streets.

Allen cradled Stephanie's head in his hands, a gentle touch to offset the assault of her ex-boyfriend. He wiped away some tears from her eyes and looked around for help.

"She needs ice," he said.

Clarissa raced out from behind the bar to help the group attend to her, a cold cloth full of ice in her hand. Allen looked up at Joe, dumbfounded by what had just happened, but his rage was clear.

"Sorry, Joe. I'm going after him."

Allen stood up from his seated position on the ground, pushed everyone in his way aside, and ran to the doorway and down the stairs after Kimo. Slamming out the door into the same streets Kimo had, he found he was too late. He was gone.

The blunt reality was that Kimo had escaped into the darkness.

Throwing his head back in frustration, Allen screamed into the New York City night.

# Chapter 6 – No Luck at All

"What the hell just happened?" Stephanie asked, her voice muffled by a towel filled with ice on her face.

"You shouldn't talk," Clarissa answered. She'd sat Stephanie on a couch in the back room while Joe helped the bouncers clear the bar out.

"Yeah," Allen added, "just take it easy for a bit, Steph." *I wish my friends forgot my birthday*, Allen thought as he looked at Stephanie's swelling face. *Nothing good has come of this night.*

There was an awkward silence for a few moments, but Clarissa couldn't take it anymore. She jumped from the arm of the couch and went to Allen, who was in the doorway.

"You know the guy that did this?"

"It's her ex-boyfriend," Allen replied. "He used to be a friend."

"Well, is she safe to go home tonight?" Clarissa wondered, pointing to Stephanie.

"I don't know…I—"

"I'm fine," Stephanie insisted as she removed the blood-soaked towel from her face and moved her head downward, revealing the damage Kimo had done.

Stephanie's left eye was nearly shut, swollen from the vicious punch. The tip of her nose was also bleeding and her bottom lip was split where she hit the floor. Her elbows and arms were bruised and scratched from the fall.

"You know the cops will be here soon," Clarissa warned. "You better be ready for all those questions."

Allen thought it over for a minute. "I'll handle it," he said. "My party, my problem."

"Some party," Stephanie joked.

Two NYPD cops finally showed up around 2 a.m., ready to interview Stephanie, Allen, Clarissa, and the bouncers. They found Allen and Clarissa standing in the doorway. One officer smiled as he approached. He was shorter than Allen and much heavier. Allen thought he looked like a younger version of Carl Winslow from *Family Matters*. He looked around Allen to see Stephanie holding ice to her face in the background.

"I'm Officer Carroll," said the smiling cop. "This is my partner, Officer Young."

"I'm Allen," he said, shaking both cops' hands. "This is Clarissa and she's Stephanie."

"Stephanie, do you know where you are?" Officer Carroll questioned.

"In a bar in New York City," she replied.

"Okay," Officer Young said. "Can you remove that ice so we can get a look at the damage and take a few pictures?"

Stephanie pulled down the towel. Allen took in a sharp breath. The swelling had grown bright red from the cold, but the bloody lip and nose were dark purple, and Stephanie's face looked like she had been hit with a baseball bat. Officer Carroll took out his phone to take pictures of the injuries. As this happened, Officer Carroll and Stephanie went through the sequence of events that led to the incident while Officer Young spoke to Clarissa and the bar staff.

Allen walked back into the bar and sat on a stool. He folded his hands and placed his chin on them, but the immensity of the situation made everything feel heavy. He stood up and just paced back and forth as the cops interviewed witnesses that had scattered downstairs during the assault. Upstairs was eerily quiet now, with just the faint sounds of bass and excited screaming from the downstairs bar. Restless, Allen returned to the back room, just in time to hear the cops question Stephanie about Kimo.

"How long were you two together?" Officer Carroll asked.

"A few months freshman and sophomore year," Stephanie replied.

"Has he ever followed you, harassed you, or beat on you in any way before tonight?" Officer Young followed up.

"No," she responded.

"Okay, here's what's going to happen," Carroll assured. "We'll file this assault report, we'll get his photo out to all the precincts in the city, we'll alert campus security and the university. You need to go before a judge to obtain an order of protection against Kimo and you should use the buddy system everywhere from here on out, no matter how trivial you think it might be. We'll catch him; you can bet on that. To be safe, we'll bring you home and make sure the apartment is clear. Your roommates should screen anyone that comes to visit."

"So," said Officer Carroll, turning to Allen, no longer smiling, "where can we find Kimo?"

"If he isn't at his apartment, then I don't know where he'd be," Stephanie interjected.

"No idea," Allen added. "He won't have anywhere to go after this."

Officer Carroll reached into his right breast pocket for his business card and handed it to Allen.

"Thanks, Officers, for all your help," Stephanie said. It seemed a little tough for her to talk now with her fat lip.

"You just take care of that swelling," Carroll said. Nodding to his partner he said, "Let's get this young lady home."

Clarissa wiped down the bar and cleaned up after the cops left, and Allen stayed behind to help. He picked up stools and turned them upside down to place on the bar, while Clarissa grabbed a mop to clean up the floor.

"You know you don't have to help," she said.

"I don't mind, really," Allen replied.

"Well, that's incredibly nice of you. But you go home and try to salvage your birthday."

"I will. Let me just get this last stool."

Allen checked his phone for the time when he'd finished. Clarissa put down the pint glass she was cleaning and approached Allen. She took the phone from Allen's hands and punched her number in.

"Text me some time," she said.

"Absolutely!" Allen smiled.

Clarissa opened her arms for a hug and Allen obliged. It was a quick hug; Allen left and made his way outside to find a cab and head back to campus.

Allen returned to his apartment, half-defeated by the night's events, half-hopeful Clarissa might lead to something down the road, though he wasn't entirely sure she was interested. Maybe she pitied him because his birthday party was a disaster? Maybe she thought he and Stephanie were a thing? Allen's mind wouldn't shut off as he began his nightly routine before bed: brushing his teeth, washing his face, and putting on sweatpants. He threw his bloodied clothes to the floor at the foot of his bed and had just sat in his bed when his phone vibrated. He swiped to see a message from Stephanie.

*I'm alive. No zoo tomorrow, I'm just going to rest. HBD. Sorry he ruined it.* <3

Allen wasn't sure how to respond so he just put his phone back down and tried to sleep.

*****

When he opened his eyes again, Allen was laying on the floor of a room that wasn't his. The room was filled with a white light. Allen got to his feet and realized he was wearing all white clothing. The light was too bright—Allen tried to cover his eyes, but he couldn't block out the glow. Wherever he moved, the light followed him; however, there were no shadows.

Allen was blinded but not afraid. He felt a presence with him, but he couldn't see anyone in any direction. He heard a whimper to his left and he moved that way, kneeling to get closer to the source of the sound. Allen fell back onto his backside when the light cleared, revealing Stephanie in a pool of her own blood. She was choking on her own blood and slowly breathing, but Allen could do nothing to help her; she was dying. Another noise in the opposite direction made Allen's head swivel; when he turned back to where Stephanie had been on the ground, she was gone. And so was the pool of blood.

Allen walked across the room of light and suddenly found himself falling through a hole in the room. When the fall ended and Allen landed, (*Strangely, on my feet*, he thought to himself), he wasn't hurt. But he was surprised to find himself inside a cave with only one exit. A dim, orange light emanated from the distance, and Allen's curiosity peaked, so he followed it until he came to an opening.

Allen walked through the opening and into a vast area with hundreds of passages leading in and out. He inspected the wall next to him as the light glowed a little brighter from below. He stepped forward about six inches and leaned over the edge to see a fire burning fifty feet below on the ground. There were no stairs or ladders for Allen to use to descend to the ground, so he thought he'd jump down and be safe, similar to how he'd landed just moments earlier. Allen took a few big steps back, gathered himself, began to run toward the edge and jumped down—

In an instant Allen's eyes popped open and he was awake.

Allen rolled over to check the time on his phone—it was 7:45 a.m. and he could hear voices coming from the kitchen. After cleaning himself up, he texted Stephanie.

*Museum Tuesday a.m.?*

Allen put his phone down and stepped out to the kitchen. Joe, Brittany and Gia were gathered around the mahogany kitchen table—Joe eating cold pizza and the girls drinking coffee. Allen smelled the coffee and went straight to the coffee pot. He grabbed a mug from the counter and poured himself a cup.

"Good morning," Allen half-smiled.

"Hey," Gia replied.

"How are you? Have you talked to her?" Brittany asked.

"I'm okay. And no, I haven't spoken to her yet."

"You hungry, bro?" Joe asked.

"No, no," Allen said. "Coffee's good for now."

Allen stood near the sink and sipped his coffee, hoping to ignore the elephant in the room. He felt everyone's eyes on him, however, and he knew his friends wanted Allen to talk about what happened the night before. For a few moments, silence overwhelmed the room.

"Look," Allen said as he placed the coffee mug on the counter, "we all know what he did, we all know what type of guy he is, and we all can agree that something needs to be done. Either the cops will find him, or I will. That's all I am going to say. So please, just drop it now."

The trio seated at the table looked at Allen and knew to drop the subject.

"Alright," Joe said. "We're here if needed."

"Thanks."

The conversation ended and Allen refilled his coffee cup and retreated to his bedroom, closing the door behind him. He checked his phone and saw that Stephanie replied.

*I'm in. I'll see you then.*

Allen spent much of the day scouring social media from his laptop and phone as he impatiently waited for any sign of Kimo's whereabouts. Allen kept his television on in the background with the volume turned down. He texted a few friends to see if anyone heard from Kimo, but nobody had.

By the time Allen was ready for bed that night, he'd spent most of the day intermittently checking his phone for updates—but nobody had any news. Stephanie messaged a few times during the day just to let Allen know that the police had driven by to check on her. Allen was happy she was safe, but his anger continued to fester. The weekend had drained him of all motivation, so he prepped for bed and went to sleep.

Monday meant it was time for Allen to go back to Professor Rogers' class. Allen still reeled from the weekend's events and his focus wasn't on school, class, or even Stephanie, it was all on Kimo. Nobody had seen Kimo since the brutality he unleashed at the party. His phone was turned off, his apartment at school was dark—he'd become a ghost. Allen let it eat him alive that Kimo had gotten away.

"Mr. White," Rogers bellowed. "Stay with us."

"Sorry, Professor," Allen replied.

Rogers's lecture again focused on the Crusades, which Allen sat through, half-listening, half-dreaming of an encounter of his own with Kimo. Allen thought about finding his former friend, how he'd rip his heart out if given the chance. Each time Allen thought back to Friday night, his heart raced, and his body got hotter with fury. He thought about Stephanie and the scar that would undoubtedly be left on her face by the ring Kimo was wearing when he punched her. Just thinking the word "punch" made Allen's blood boil. So many questions popped into his head. What type of guy hits a girl? Why hadn't Allen reacted faster? Where could Kimo be? The most important question Allen asked himself over and over was how long did Kimo have this planned? Did he know when he stopped by the apartment earlier on Friday what he was going to do that night? Allen's thoughts were endless, but he noticed Professor Rogers glancing his way, so he did his best to pay attention.

Rogers looked Allen's way a few more times and could tell he was distracted, but he didn't push too hard today. The lecture finished and Allen prepared to leave, but Rogers stood in his path.

"Mr. White, a moment please," Rogers whispered.

The look Rogers gave Allen before he spoke again said volumes. He was aware that his student was feeling the stress of a situation too big for one person to handle. He placed his right hand over the top of his bald head and then stroked his middle finger and thumb over his temples a few times.

"Are you still planning on going to the Met this week for the project, Mr. White?" Rogers asked.

"Yes, sir. I'm going tomorrow morning."

"Good, it should be very enjoyable, Allen."

"I guess so, Professor."

"Mr. White," he began, "please take no offense to my next statement, but you seem troubled."

"I'm good, Professor," Allen said.

"You're preoccupied, Allen. I'm worried about you."

"Nothing to worry about, Professor Rogers," Allen responded.

"Please know that whenever you need to talk to anyone, my door is open."

"Thanks, Professor, but I swear I'm alright."

"I trust you, Allen. I do." He patted Allen on the shoulder a couple of times before his kindness gave way to his usual demeanor. He packed his things and abruptly left the room, Allen leaving through a different door.

Rushing past a few people in the hall, Allen didn't notice their eyes fixated on him. Allen opened the doors to the building and was outside again, ready to head back to his apartment when he noticed a familiar umbrella against the side of a bench. He knew instantly it was Mead's, and the old man was likely waiting on him. Allen tried to sneak past the bench unnoticed, but Mead was an observant old man.

"And where are we off to in such a hurry, Mr. White?" Mead questioned.

Allen stopped in his place and rotated to see Mead leaned against a tree outside of Keating Hall.

"Mr. White," Mead continued, "I'm not here to make your life difficult."

"I really don't have time today, I'm sorry."

"*Make* the time, Mr. White," Mead pleaded. "Do that, and I will give you the answer to the biggest question on your mind."

"Honestly, Mr. Mead," Allen snapped, "I don't care about my family right now."

Mead stood up, put both hands over the handle of his umbrella, and rested the point on the ground in front of him between his legs. Mead turned a serious look Allen's way.

"I can tell you where Kimo is."

Allen's heart dropped.

"How do you know where Kimo is?"

"Mr. White, I can tell you about many things," Mead answered. "You need only come with me, and we can—"

"Tell me *now*," Allen insisted. "Who are you and how do you know so much about my life? Where is he?"

Mead took his glasses off and pulled a handkerchief embroidered with the letter *M* from his right pocket. Mead rubbed the smudges off his glasses with the cloth.

"You have to keep an open mind, Mr. White," Mead said.

"I can do that," Allen agreed with a heavy sigh.

"Kimo is not here."

"I know that much, I can—"

"Mr. White, would you *please* stop interrupting!"

"Fine. Please, continue."

"Kimo has gone to a place where you—"

Both Allen and Mead's attention shifted as Gia ran across the center of campus toward them, screaming for Allen.

"Allen!" Gia panted. "You need to come with me."

"What's wrong, Gia?"

"It's Joe," she explained. "He was leaving practice and crossing the street, and someone came out of nowhere and hit him. He landed about twenty feet down the road from the impact."

"Is he okay? Is he alive? Do they know who did it?" Allen pressed.

"He's alive. They say he's lucky to only have a few bumps and bruises. The car kept going after it hit him, and the cops are trying to find leads."

"What hospital is he at?"

"They took him to Mount Sinai," Gia answered.

"I'm going now," Allen said. "Mr. Mead, I'm sorry, we'll have to put this off again."

"I understand. My thoughts are with your friend. I will find you, Mr. White, fret not."

"I have no doubt, Mr. Mead," Allen smiled.

*****

Mead stayed behind, watching Allen running off until he was out of sight. He sat on the bench again, taking in the sounds of the bustling college students crossing campus. Mead's peace was interrupted by Professor Rogers as he exited Keating Hall and caught the eye of the old man. Rogers sat down beside Mead.

"Beautiful day," Mead remarked, looking straight ahead.

"Indeed, it is," Professor Rogers replied, doing the same.

"We both know it wasn't a car that hit Mr. Figueroa," Mead commented. "We are running out of time, Thomas."

"Does he know where Kimo went?" Rogers asked.

"We were getting to that when Ms. Esposito interrupted with the news."

"Are you sure it was them?" Rogers worried.

"Yes, Thomas," Mead said.

"How much does he know?"

"Only that I knew his birth parents. He won't take any of this as gospel. He'll question everything. Do you think he's ready for the truth?"

"Were any of us ready when you found us, Mead? No. But he will grow to understand it; of this I'm certain."

*****

Allen rushed through the automatic doors at the hospital and approached the security guard at the front desk, pulling his wallet out. The guard never moved from his place in the chair, seemingly unaware of Allen's urgency.

"Can I help you?" the guard asked.

"I'm here to see Joe Figueroa," Allen replied, handing the guard his license before he even asked.

The guard ran the identification through a scanning machine and printed a sticker for Allen. "Here you go. Make sure it's on at all times."

"Thank you," Allen responded, peeling the sticker and slapping it on the pocket of his t-shirt.

"Figueroa is Room 7037, seventh floor. Just take the elevators there to the left." The Guard pointed.

"Okay, thanks," Allen said. "Have a nice day."

The guard mumbled what Allen thought might have been a thank you, but he just shrugged and hurried to the elevator, tossing the sticker wrapper of the sticker in a trash bin. He smashed the up button, impatiently waiting for the elevator doors to open and slid to the left to allow the nurses and visitors by as they exited. Allen held the door open for two older ladies getting into the elevator before him.

"What floor?" Allen asked.

"Four, please." One of the ladies smiled.

Allen pressed the buttons, holding his breath as the doors closed, willing them to move faster. The two ladies whispered to each other until finally the doors opened on the fourth floor. As soon as they stepped off, Allen jabbed the button over and over to close the doors faster, tapping his foot as he watched the floor numbers light up one at a time. He reached the seventh floor and finally, he'd have a chance to see Joe.

Following the numbers on the wall and the arrows that accompanied them. He turned right, past the nurse's station, then turned left, down the hall, three doors on the right. Joe's last name was on the door, and it looked like he didn't have a roommate judging by the nameplate.

Joe was asleep when Allen walked into the room. His arm was connected to an intravenous line of morphine, dripping slowly. The television was on at a whisper volume. The machines in the room flashed numbers that were a foreign language to most visitors. Allen moved the empty chair against the window closer to the end of the bed and kicked his feet up onto the windowsill. Allen shook his head, thinking to himself he'd never seen Joe look so weak, so vulnerable. Joe's arms were covered in scrapes from the pavement he slid across, his cheek showing the same signs of road rash and other cuts and scrapes littered his body.

A nurse walked into the room and rolled a blood pressure machine to the bed, wrapped the cuff around his arm, and took some vitals from Joe. She unwrapped the cuff and the loud noise of Velcro pulling away from itself jostled Joe awake.

"Allen, that you?" Joe croaked as the nurse left the room.

"Yes, it is."

"I'm sorry, man, how long you been here?"

"Not long, don't worry. How are you? What happened?"

"I'm okay," Joe started. "One second I was walking across the street, the next I was here. I don't remember the car hitting me, I just remember feeling like I had no control over my body... It was weird. All my muscles tightened up and I couldn't move my legs. It's like it wasn't me."

"Damn, dude; that's crazy. I'm glad you're okay, though," Allen said. "What did the doctors say?"

"That I'm lucky nothing was broken. If I wasn't an athlete, I could be dead. My weight saved me. Most likely a mild concussion and some bumps and bruises."

"Thank God," Allen said. "I'm glad you're okay. Do you need anything? Food?"

"Anything is better than whatever it is they're bringing me here."

Joe's carefree demeanor eased Allen's worries about his friend. "What can I do for you?"

"Nothing at all, just glad you're here."

"You sure I can't get you anything?" Allen asked. "Maybe a glass of water?"

"Yeah, sure, why not?"

Allen got up from the chair and poured a glass of water and placed it on the tray in front of his friend.

"Thanks, bro," Joe shifted his body to drink, wincing as he moved. "Any word on the other thing?"

"No."

"Gotcha…Sorry."

"It's all good, Joe. It's just weird all this stuff is happening. Remind me when you get out of here to tell you about this old guy that keeps showing up on campus."

"Forget about him; how's Stephanie?"

"She's supposed to go with me to the museum this week, but I think I'm just going to skip it."

"Just go to the museum like you planned, Allen. Don't worry about things here, I'm fine."

"But…"

"No, Allen. You go; I have my phone here; if I need you, I'll text you. You can't ditch Stephanie; she's been through enough already."

"Okay," Allen reluctantly agreed, his worry over his friend evident and alleviated at the same time. "I don't like leaving you alone here, dude."

"You're not, I'm sure one of the cheerleaders will be here soon enough," Joe joked. "You talk to that bartender at all?" Joe asked, lips turning up with what looked like effort.

"A few texts here and there," Allen sheepishly replied.

"You like her?"

"We haven't hung out yet. She's been talking to Steph more than me."

"That's never a good idea," Joe winced.

"I know." Allen grinned.

"How about after I'm out of here we go visit your parents and relax for a weekend?"

"I'm all for that, Joe."

Allen sat by Joe's hospital bed for some time, as Joe slipped in and out of sleep. Finally, the nurses came and told Allen it was time to leave. He headed back past the nurse's station to the elevator, the hallways dark now. As the elevator doors closed behind Allen, the neighboring elevator doors opened, and out walked Professor Rogers.

# Chapter 7 – Evil Grows

The neon lights of the city were blurred in his bloodshot eyes, the sounds of New York muffled as he ran from street to street, hoping to find a place to stop and catch his breath. He had been running for an eternity in his mind, unsure of how much time had transpired. Car horns blared as he dashed across the street in defiance of the blinking DON'T WALK signal. He ducked into an alleyway with some privacy, though there was only one way in or out; the other end was fenced off. He leaned against a wall, resting both hands on his knees, bending over to maximize his recuperation from his one-man marathon through New York. Looking down at his jeans, he saw some streaks on the right side, and he wondered where they'd come from. A drip fell to the same spot on his jeans. He raised his hand to his temple and realized it was blood. His eyes widened with fear as he slowly remembered what happened.

He'd sucker-punched his ex-girlfriend.

Kimo's stomach flopped as he hoped it was all a bad dream. He paced the alley as he figured out what to do next, but no clear answer came to him in his drunkenness. His panic quickly evolved to rage as he picked up anything in his sight—trash cans, bottles, wooden crates— and smashed them all against the walls of the alley. Strangers passed by and heard Kimo screaming at himself and throwing a fit, none brave enough to approach the young man as they hurried past the ruckus. Kimo continued thrashing wildly in the alley, unleashing his anger on the brick wall in front of him; he drew back and threw a punch toward the wall.

But his hand stopped before it hit the brick.

Dumbfounded, Kimo struggled to fight the force holding his arm back, but he wasn't nearly sober or strong enough. As Kimo attempted to hit the wall once more, he was thwarted by the outside force.

"It would be a pity if you were to break your hand over a foolish girl," a voice whispered.

Kimo froze in place. He slowly dropped his hand from its position in the air and turned his head 360 degrees, but there wasn't a person in sight. His heart raced with adrenaline as he looked everywhere for the source of the voice.

"Show yourself!" Kimo shouted.

"We have plans for you, Kimo," the voice hissed. "Come with us."

"Where?" Kimo questioned.

The voice didn't respond, but a piercing noise came from behind him. Hands on his ears, he turned to face the opening of the alley. A small black circle appeared twenty feet from where Kimo stood, blocking the exit. The noise stopped and Kimo dropped his hands to his side. The circle was outlined in a crimson color, and it began to rotate slowly as it moved toward Kimo. The rotations quickened and the circle's outline pulsated as it continued toward him, glowing brighter red as it grew larger and larger.

Kimo was both paralyzed and hypnotized by the light, anxious to know what was happening. He squinted as the reddish tones filled the alley, and suddenly, the circle enveloped Kimo in it, and then both Kimo and the circle vanished.

*****

When he opened his eyes again, Kimo was alone in a dark room, lightly illuminated by the same crimson color he'd seen moments before. He had no memory of how he traveled to this place; he only remembered the dark circle.

The room was cool, but not freezing and had only one entrance and exit, much like the alley he had just left. The walls were sticky to the touch. It appeared and felt like tar, but Kimo smelled his hand and found that it had no odor. Kimo's eyes shifted to the center of the room where a fixture made of marble was erected with a large hole at the top of the statuesque piece. A deep metallic plate filled the hole and appeared to contain water. Next to the structure was a small table with a black glass on it. Kimo approached the structure in hopes of getting a closer look.

"I wouldn't do that if I were you."

"Who's there?" Kimo pleaded.

Out of the darkness appeared a gigantic figure. It towered over Kimo; its shoulders were as wide as a mountain, its biceps alone had to be twenty inches all around, but Kimo couldn't see what color the figure's skin was because it was covered in tattoos. There wasn't a hair on the figure's head, just more tattoos. As it stepped into the dim light, the figure's eyes came into view—they were all black, without any whiteness surrounding them—and they emitted a red glow. He was a man, or as close to man as he could be, and Kimo stepped back, fearful of someone for the first time in his life.

"You smell like blood," snickered the figure. "Follow me. He's been waiting for you."

"Who's been waiting? Who are you? Where the hell am I?"

"I'm Jaxx."

Jaxx started toward the opening and Kimo followed. A narrow staircase led down into darkness and with each step, Kimo's heart beat faster. He couldn't tell if he was excited or scared, but he continued to follow the intimidating Jaxx.

They emerged from the stairs into an area that was incredibly vast. The ceilings were so high that Kimo thought for a second that they'd traveled outside; it was 200 yards between where they'd entered and the opposite side of the room. In the middle of the room, set back against a wall was an armory of weapons: there were guns, knives, grenades, C-4, Kevlar vests and even a few weapons Kimo had never seen before and couldn't name. Jaxx ignored the armory as he passed by, intent on getting Kimo to his destination.

"Are we the only people down here?" Kimo asked.

"For now," Jaxx responded.

Kimo stopped asking questions. On the other side of the room, they came upon a steel door with something that Kimo thought was a biometric scanner to its side. He'd seen these many times on TV and figured Jaxx would use a fingerprint to clear the security.

Jaxx, however, pulled a knife from his belt and sliced his hand open.

He squeezed the blood from his hand and dripped it over the scanner, grinning the whole time, his teeth crooked and yellowish, an off-putting sight for Kimo. The scanner made a few noises, then flashed green. The steel door slid to the right, and Jaxx stomped through its opening with Kimo not far behind. The door closed behind them and

Jaxx moved forward toward another staircase, this one leading up. The usually bold Kimo hesitated and Jaxx pushed him forward. Kimo didn't dare push back, his fear keeping his instincts at bay in an unknown place. They climbed the stairs into another room similar to the one from before, the only difference being the fixture in the middle of the room. It was still marble but had no opening on top. A red cloud of smoke swirled above the fixture, not rising or dissipating at all.

"What is that?" Kimo asked, his head reeling from the sight, his stomach churning from the smell of the room. The air itself felt like an added weight, Kimo's breathing labored.

"That's The Fylorn," Jaxx explained. "It can show you anything you want to see; past present, future."

Before Jaxx could explain more, Kimo activated The Fylorn.

"Show me Stephanie," he barked.

Red lights spurted out from different places in The Fylorn, which forced Kimo to slowly back away. The lights moved through the air and connected, sending off black bolts of light where they joined. The walls were masked behind the light and Kimo watched as The Fylorn expanded and connected to form an uneven circle. Kimo put his hand out and tried to touch The Fylorn, but it was as impossible as trying to shake hands with the air he breathed. Kimo stared at the floating fissure when suddenly Stephanie's laugh echoed in the room. Then she appeared in The Fylorn just as if Kimo was watching a movie. He saw the smile on Stephanie's face, the same thing that had captured his attention freshman year. She was wearing her favorite shirt, a peach-colored t-shirt with white lines; Kimo hated that shirt, but it really reflected her blue eyes in the most perfect way. Stephanie's eyes came into focus and Kimo finally saw what he had done to her. Kimo watched a bruised and healing Stephanie pick up her pace a little. Kimo started to feel the weight of what he'd done.

"Hey you!" Stephanie waved. Her voice boomed across the quad, sending echoes through Kimo's viewing room once more.

Allen came into the picture and hugged her. She hooked her arm through his and the two laughed as they walked across campus. The Fylorn shrunk back to its normal size and position, closing the window to Stephanie that had opened.

Kimo looked around the room as he took deep, deliberate breaths. His nostrils flared, the corners of his mouth twitched, and his head quivered, his fury growing and growing. Without thinking he attacked the only thing nearby—Jaxx.

Kimo charged hard, but Jaxx simply sidestepped and stuck out his right leg. Kimo tripped and fell to the ground face first; before he could turn over, Jaxx was on Kimo's back, shoving his knee between Kimo's shoulder blades, and then pulled a knife from his boot. He pulled Kimo's hair, heaving his head back and held the knife to Kimo's throat. He put his head to Kimo's ear, stuck out his tongue and licked the side of Kimo's face.

"I can taste your fear," Jaxx badgered.

"Jaxx," a voice boomed, echoing in the bare room. "Be nice to our visitor."

Jaxx slowly dismounted Kimo's back and shoved his adversary as he tried to stand. Kimo used his arms to push his body up from the floor and pulled his torn t-shirt back into place. He scowled at Jaxx and looked around to see who it was speaking, but once again, nobody appeared. A small door appeared seemingly out of nowhere, hidden before to them but now open to Kimo and Jaxx's left. Jaxx pushed Kimo through the opening.

This time they marched into a room with thirty-foot-tall ceilings. Kimo wondered if he was dreaming, feeling like he had fallen down a rabbit hole—but this was no Wonderland. Kimo froze as he noticed the walls were adorned with bones—and his stomach roiled when he realized they were human skulls. For the first time in a long time, fear gripped Kimo. His heart nearly gave out when he realized the entire room was covered like this. There was a singular path six feet wide and twenty feet long—also made of bone—that led through the room and stopped at the base of a throne. *What kind of a person would make this their throne room?* Kimo thought.

A dark red glass throne and seat wrapped itself around two green glass arms. Seated upon the throne was a figure wearing a cloak that covered its entire body with the hood pulled forward to conceal the head and face. The figure's hands were gloved, the cup of a goblet-shaped golden chalice cradled in the right hand.

"Here he is, Master," Jaxx said.

Kimo hesitated to step forward, but Jaxx grabbed his arm and walked him halfway down the bone-covered aisle until the figure held up his left hand to stop them.

"Jaxx, you know what to do," the voice encouraged.

Jaxx nodded and exited the room, leaving Kimo alone with the figure that was even more ominous than Jaxx himself.

"Kimo," the Master started. "Too long you've masked your pain, choosing instead to pretend you like those around you. Too long have you waited for her to come back; but we both know she loves him. *He* is the cause of all your pain, the reason you hurt her—the reason you wanted nothing more than to kill her that night."

"How—"

"I have seen it in the Fylorn. I can see it in your eyes as you stand here now. Why do you let these people make a fool of you? Why do you let those you call 'friend' laugh behind your back? You are strong. You are special."

The Master tapped the side of the chalice with one long finger as Kimo stood before the throne, stung by the harsh reality of the figure's words.

"Even now you worry for her," the voice teased.

"I love her," Kimo replied.

"Love is for those without the strength to live alone," the Master snapped. "Real power comes from solitude. Be more than some lovesick fool; become a warrior. This is your path, Kimo. There's no turning back now."

The one Jaxx called Master held out his left hand and The Fylorn appeared in the room. Once again it materialized before Kimo's eyes and showed him Stephanie. She was in her apartment lying in bed with an ice pack on her face. Gia walked into the room.

"Are you going to tell him today?" Gia's voice echoed.

"I don't know. He's had a bad few days," Stephanie replied.

"And you've had it easy," Gia joked.

"So true." Stephanie giggled. "I just have to find the right time."

"If you don't tell him today, it better be soon," she cautioned.

"I will. Just not easy to find the right time."

"What time are you meeting for the museum?" Gia asked.

With a wave of the hand, The Fylorn disappeared, and the Master leaned forward, now holding the chalice with both hands, almost reverently. The Master extended it to Kimo.

"If you want to know real power, Kimo, drink from this chalice. No more pain; no more worry; just power. The power at your fingertips to hurt those who have hurt you. One sip and Allen will suffer for all he has done to embarrass you."

Just the mention of Allen's name made Kimo's body quake with hatred. The images he'd just seen through The Fylorn haunted him already. He thought about how good it felt to punch Allen all those years ago and how he longed to do it again. Kimo reached out and snatched the chalice from the figure and drank all it contained.

The chalice dropped from his hands and Kimo grabbed at his stomach immediately.

"What is that?" Kimo choked out.

Kimo's body shook as he fell to his knees and doubled over, blood coursing, burning its way through his veins. Ice cold overtook him inside as he slowly became an agent of the Master. When the pain stopped and Kimo rose to his feet, he looked down at his tattoo, which now swirled and glowed with a reddish tint. The Master leaned back in his chair and watched his new recruit. Kimo looked at his hands as he folded his fingers into a fist; he flexed all his muscles and growled loudly. Kimo was stronger.

"I feel different," Kimo remarked. "What have you done to me?"

"Nothing you didn't want," the Master replied. "You did drink it after all."

"What did I drink?"

"The essence of my being. The blood that courses through my veins now runs through your body."

"Blood?!" Kimo exclaimed.

"You have been given the greatest gift one can give," the Master commented. "Nothing can kill you now."

"I'm…I…feel…different."

"No weapon can harm you. No one can kill you. You are impervious to anything man has created. You are the highest form of being."

"Thank you," Kimo said as he pounded his right fist to his heart, a sense of newfound purpose and revenge wiping away any feeling he once had for his former friends.

"Thank you?" the Master prodded.

"Thank you, *Master.*"

# Chapter 8 – The Day We MET

Allen was excited Stephanie decided to tag along for his trip to the museum. It was her first time in public since Kimo's assault and Allen knew she needed a day out to try and begin to feel normal again. Stephanie's eye was healing well and remained just slightly discolored; unless a person spent a great deal of time focused on her face, they wouldn't be able to see the damage that had been inflicted a few days earlier. She hadn't been herself emotionally—not that anyone had expected her to be stable in the aftermath of the incident. Stephanie didn't head out since the party, and when she would FaceTime Allen, she wasn't wearing makeup and had trouble holding back her tears. Allen hated seeing her so distraught, heartbroken that he knew just how deep her pain went on the inside.

When Allen suggested she come with him to the museum, she initially hesitated, but he convinced her that she'd have to start doing the things she loved again if she wanted to get back to normal. It's the same way she treated Allen after Kimo's attack sophomore year. He knew she was in pain and wouldn't tell anyone. Allen struggled with seeing his carefree friend so quiet, but he hoped this trip would help them both.

Stephanie walked across campus to meet Allen and they hopped into the Ram van heading toward Lincoln Center. It was a gorgeous day, almost seventy-five degrees, so they decided to walk the nearly two-and-a-half miles to the Metropolitan Museum of Art. Neither of them talked as they walked; they just listened to other people they passed and enjoyed the peace that came with being with a good friend. They stopped a few times so that Stephanie could catch her breath, the side effects of a still-healing broken rib. On their last stop, Allen bought Stephanie a soft pretzel from a street vendor and the two shared it as they finished their walk to the Met. When they finally arrived and entered through 82nd Street and the museum's historic Great Hall, there wasn't a line for admission; Allen walked right up to the counter, took out his school identification and money, paid the twenty-four dollars and received his admission and museum maps. Stephanie had been waiting in line behind him with her I.D. out as well.

"Why did you do that?" she asked.

"My invite, my treat." Allen smiled.

Stephanie took the maps from Allen, rolled them up and slapped him over the head playfully. The duo shared a laugh as they headed straight down a hallway to the Medieval Art exhibit. Allen was astonished by the amount of history within the walls of the museum. He smiled and took pictures as he walked around the Medieval Exhibit, drawn to the weapons of the past—each item garnering special attention from him. He had always loved history and Professor Rogers had always made him feel special for his knowledge of events, not like his peers had often made him feel. Allen admired the art and history of the exhibit; Stephanie enjoyed her friend's enthusiasm and passion for the art. She hadn't smiled in weeks but had finally found a few moments to just be herself.

"Nice to see that again," Allen remarked.

"Shut up," Stephanie said with a smirk.

"Let's head to the Historical Figures exhibit," he said.

As they entered the Special Exhibits Hall of the museum, Allen could see several topics and people he'd studied throughout his academic career; specifically, in Professor Rogers' classes. Allen intensely studied the swords, shields, trinkets, rusted keys, intricate tapestries, and all the little labels that explained each item. The sword of Richard III was the piece Allen could not take his eyes off. He was mesmerized by the intricate design and the man to whom it belonged. He explained its significance to Stephanie, telling her the detailed history of Richard III and the House of York until he realized that Stephanie wasn't by his side. Allen turned to see her talking to someone. The two embraced and as Allen approached, Clarissa turned and smiled at him.

"Oh my gosh!" he exclaimed.

"I know—me, a museum. Not a great fit," she joked.

"What are you doing here?" Allen asked.

"My sister is an assistant curator," Clarissa explained. "I was bringing her a coffee and we were going to have lunch, but I saw Steph and had to come say hello."

"That's a pretty cool job your sister has," he said. "You want to join us?"

"Let me go drop off this coffee and I'll come back down. Stay put."

"You got it," Allen said.

Allen watched Clarissa leave the room and disappear into a crowd of museum patrons. Stephanie playfully punched Allen in the arm.

"You flirt," she teased.

"It's not like that," he replied. "I don't even know the girl."

"Mhm."

"Shut up and come look at this," Allen said.

A line had formed in the corner of the room to pose for a picture with an authentic shield from the fifth century. The wooden shield had been meticulously restored over the past few years, but it was undoubtedly one of the last of its kind. Allen jumped in line and while waiting to get his picture taken with the weapon, he read a notecard that described the item.

*400-499 A.D. – The Shield of the British Warrior. This shield would have been used during Anglo-Saxon warfare of the 5th century in England. These shields varied in weight – some were as heavy as one hundred pounds!*

It was Allen's turn in line and the young lady behind the tripod motioned him over. Stephanie grabbed her phone to take her own pictures to use as a source of embarrassment later, while Allen was excited to touch an incredible piece of history. Allen took the shield by the straps on its back; he lifted it up and smiled. As the camera flashed, Allen heard someone screaming.

He whipped his head, looking around the room to see where the screams had originated, but everyone went about their business as if nothing happened. Stephanie noticed the change in his demeanor. Allen put down the shield and walked away from the photography corner with Stephanie following closely, hoping to find out what was wrong. Allen sat on a bench against the wall and ran his hands over his mouth, through his hair, trying to calm himself down. Stephanie sat beside him.

"So," she started, "You gonna tell me what the hell is going on?"

"I don't even know where to start," Allen replied.

"Just tell me the truth. You might feel better."

"I've been having these crazy dreams the past few months. They feel so real; it's like I'm there, but I'm not. Almost like I have control of some of it."

"What are they about, Al?" Stephanie pressed.

Just as Allen prepared to explain his dreams to Stephanie, Clarissa caught his attention from across the room. She was back and made her way toward the bench.

"Sorry," Allen apologized. "We'll have to finish this later."

Allen stood and faked a smile to Clarissa and Stephanie followed his lead. The trio walked around the room looking at the relics of the past as Allen tried to distract himself from the nonexistent screams. Clarissa and Stephanie stayed a few steps behind Allen as he looked over each piece in the room with such care. They were ready to go on to the next exhibit when Allen's eyes locked on an item he must have missed before because of the crowd. There, behind a pane of glass, was a small *f* on a necklace. Allen leaned in to read the description.

*5th/6th Century Christian Cross – Origin unknown. Rumored to have belonged to the Warrior-King Arturas and his Round Table Knights. Found among personal effects of the executed in 1209 A.D. after clerks in Oxford hanged.*

"That's pretty cool," Clarissa said over his shoulder. "Minus the whole 'hanged clerks' thing."

"I know!" Allen replied. "The whole story surrounding the hangings is nuts."

"You know the story?" Clarissa asked.

"Of course he does," Stephanie joked.

"Well?" Clarissa persisted.

"Okay," Allen began. "This student at Oxford killed this girl 'accidentally'," Allen said with air quotes to strengthen his point, "and then fled the scene. His friends were thrown in jail and King John ordered their deaths. After the public hangings, Oxford was a ghost town. People left in droves from the city and the school. It's how Cambridge came to be."

"Wow," Stephanie said. "That's sick."

"But why'd you say 'accidentally' like that?" Clarissa inquired.

"The truth is that girl *was* actually murdered by the group of guys," Allen said. "Not really sure why, but I read somewhere she might have been an assassin and was thwarted before she could kill a monk."

The girls looked at each other and then at Allen and just laughed.

"You sound so nerdy," Stephanie chuckled.

Allen's ears and cheeks heated up in embarrassment and he lowered his head trying not to let it show. He cracked a smile and shook his head at the girls before laughing along with them.

"I'll be back," Clarissa said. "Have to use the ladies room."

Clarissa left the room again while Allen and Stephanie continued laughing until tears streamed down their cheeks. Allen wiped a tear from his eye and wiped it on his jeans. Allen noticed his shoe was untied and knelt to fix it, but he lost his balance. He grabbed onto the podium beside him with the wooden cross displayed above.

When his hand touched the podium, Allen heard screams again.

Suddenly the ground beneath them began to shake and the room became unsteady. Allen heard cracking in the ceiling, and fear tore through him. *The museum is caving in.* Spurts of dust fell from the ceiling, and the museum went silent, everyone staring up. Then, with a great groan, the museum hall ceiling collapsed, scattering screaming people everywhere. Allen pushed Stephanie out of the way of falling debris, using his body to shield their fall. Clarissa still hadn't returned from the bathroom, but Allen hoped she was safe from harm.

Once Allen got to his feet, coughing like everyone else from the dust, he turned around and was face-to-face with Kimo, holding a knife to Stephanie's throat. His one-time-friend-turned-enemy said nothing. He just smiled, and then slit his ex-girlfriend's throat.

# Chapter 9 – The Truth

"No!" shouted Allen.

"What's going on?" Stephanie asked.

Allen looked up at Stephanie, who checked her phone while she waited for Allen to finish tying his shoes.

The room was fine.

Kimo wasn't there.

"What the hell is wrong with me?" he moaned, clutching his head.

"Al, you've *got* to level with me! What's up with you?"

"Apparently, I forgot how to tie my shoes," he replied, but sweat beaded on his forehead. He stumbled a little as he got to his feet.

"Hey guys," Clarissa called as she returned. "Do you want to go see some private collections?" she asked, holding up her phone as if they could read the text there. "My sister just invited us up."

"Absolutely," Allen answered, catching his breath from his vision, or waking nightmare, as Stephanie nodded.

"Okay, follow me," Clarissa said.

The group took the stairs up a flight to Floor 2, rounded a corner near the American Art exhibit and waited outside the office entrances for Clarissa's sister. When she opened the door and held it open for the three friends, Allen knew instantly it was Clarissa's sister; she had the same eyes and facial features. Her hair was a darker brown, however, and she was about six inches taller than Clarissa. She wore a grey skirt with a white blouse and blue sport coat. She had on three-inch heels, so she stood at eye level with Allen. As soon as they all entered the offices, she took them onto an elevator that required her to swipe a card to operate. She hit "B" and the elevator doors closed.

"Kay," Clarissa said, "this is Allen, and this is Stephanie."

Kay shook hands with Stephanie and said, "I hear you're quite the historian, Allen."

"I don't know about that," he replied.

"Don't be modest, now. Clarissa told me you were pretty knowledgeable downstairs."

Allen looked at Clarissa, who looked up at the elevator ceiling to avoid taking credit for Allen's embarrassment. Stephanie put her head down and snickered as quietly as she could. Kay grinned.

"Now listen. You can't touch some of the stuff down here," Kay warned. "There are cameras everywhere and I'd get fired on the spot. Okay?"

Allen, Stephanie, and Clarissa nodded in agreement.

The elevator reached the bottom floor and the doors opened. The group exited the elevator, but the doors remained opened. The room was filled with artifacts; there were tables separated by time period, shelves with entire civilizations' histories, and an overwhelming number of weapons and other unidentified remnants of the past. Kay handed them all rubber gloves to wear while in the basement. Allen quickly put his gloves on, thrilled to touch history.

# Chapter 10 – A Lesson in History

"Where do you get all this stuff from?" Allen asked.

"Donors, historians, other museums around the world. We find things everywhere," Kay said.

"This is incredible," he remarked.

As Allen and Kay looked over a few items on the tables in the room, Stephanie and Clarissa sat in two chairs placed near one of the tables.

"This is like Christmas for him," Stephanie joked.

"Well," Clarissa replied, "it seems like he needed this."

"Especially after the other night," Stephanie added.

"Regardless of how it ended, I'm glad you came in," Clarissa explained. "I've gained new friends because of that party."

"And?"

"And nothing." Clarissa smiled. "Just taking it as it comes."

"He's not like the rest of the jerks I've met. He's a good guy."

"I knew that from the second I started talking to him," Clarissa said. "I can smell a jerk from a mile away."

The two chuckled loudly and Allen and Kay came over. "Everything okay over here?" Kay asked with a smirk.

"We're good," Clarissa replied.

Kay showed Allen to a table with miscellaneous items scattered across it and pulled a sword from the pile with a *shing*. It was a scimitar from Persia; sharp, curved, and beautiful. Kay handed it to Allen, who held it carefully. "Look at the craftsmanship," she said to him. "This particular sword belonged to Saladin."

"Are you *kidding* me?" Allen asked, eyes wide. "This was Saladin's sword?"

"The one and only," she replied. "His brother Saphadin kept it after Saladin's death, and it was passed on for generations."

"Wow," Allen commented, holding the Scimitar up to the light, mesmerized by its gleam.

"Check this out." Kay motioned to Allen.

Kay held a small knife and sheath. He placed the scimitar down on the table and took a step toward Kay. She handed Allen the knife and he studied it intensely.

"This particular piece belonged to William the Second, son of William the Conqueror. It was a birthday gift in 1058 from his mother, Matilda of Flanders."

Allen studied the sheath and then removed the knife from its cover. He admired the blade in a way that made Kay think Allen knew this blade like it was his own. With each item he touched, Allen felt more and more like each of the items was calling to him from the past—a feeling he just couldn't shake. Allen awed with each twist of it and then abruptly returned it to its case and handed it back to Kay, eager to get to the next table over. Edging by Kay, his eyes trained on the table, one item, a small golden key—cylindrical with a rectangular bit on the end— piqued his interest; Allen reached out to touch the key, but Kay grabbed his wrist hard.

"Anything but that," she warned.

"It's just a key," Allen argued.

"That key is incredibly unique," Kay responded. "Our archeological team unearthed it in England. We don't know its exact age, but early estimates have it close to 2,000 years old."

Kay loosened her grip on Allen's wrist and his hand dropped slowly. His fingertips came to rest on the table, and instantly a burst of light filled the room and Allen was blinded. A familiar voice spoke to Allen.

"Free him."

"Who?" Allen begged. "How?"

"All you need is before you," the voice answered.

The voice and the light disappeared from the basement room and Allen was again standing with his fingertips on the table, unsure of what to do next. He tapped his index fingers against the metallic tabletop, hoping that would help him formulate a plan. He lifted his arms up and crossed them across his chest, then turned to face where Stephanie and Clarissa were seated. Kay continued to rifle through things on the table, ignorant of the other three in the room.

Allen found his way to the exit; he had to get out of there to clear his head. Allen was certain an alarm would go off, but he didn't care—he was more concerned with losing his mind. His hands were on the emergency exit's push handle when Clarissa stopped him.

"Where are you going?" she asked.

"I'm sorry," Allen replied. "Thank you for today, but I just can't stay."

"Was it my sister?"

"No, no. Nothing like that. Just dealing with some weird stuff right now."

"I understand. But I want to help," she offered.

"I appreciate it, but I just don't think anyone would understand this one. Nobody can help," Allen lamented.

"You're wrong, Allen," Clarissa said. "I can help."

"How?" Allen pleaded.

Clarissa grabbed Allen's hands and looked him straight in the eye.

"I know who you have to free."

# Chapter 11 – Lionel & Nigel

The voice was muffled and loud, but the trip had been a long eight hours and the turbulence had been unbearable, so it was a voice welcomed by all the passengers.

*"Ladies and gentlemen, welcome to New York's John F. Kennedy Airport. Local time is 12:48 pm and the temperature is seventy-three degrees. Have a nice stay in New York!"*

The plane was two-thirds empty, and most people had slept their way from London's Heathrow Airport to JFK, but the two young men in the emergency exit row were wide awake the entire time. They'd gathered admiring looks from the young ladies on the flight—as well as the flight crew. The first young man by the window was wearing a navy-blue three-piece suit with a matching vest, white button-down shirt and a navy-blue skinny necktie to match. His light brown hair, parted from right to left, was swept subtly across his forehead. He had a particularly round set of blue eyes and a thick scar shot from his lower lip down to his chin, into his well-kept goatee. He wore a gold ring with a crest etched in the center of an onyx square: the letter *G.* He watched as the plane began its descent into New York with great anticipation.

The second young man sat in the aisle seat to leave space between the two travelers. Casually dressed in a black hooded sweatshirt, jeans and brand-new, white Converse All Stars. He had on a pair of reflective Aviator sunglasses that concealed his heterochromatic eyes—one dark brown, the other a bright green. Dirty blonde hair fell a bit past his shoulders, and he had a well-groomed beard. A tattoo peeked out of the sleeve of his sweatshirt at the cuff—an old English letter *B* laid over an infinity symbol on his wrist. He tightly gripped his drink as the plane neared the ground—his first time flying had been terrible, so he ordered a rum and coke to calm his nerves.

"We're almost there, cousin," said the man in the suit. His Cockney accent was all London, while his cousin's speech was slower and more succinct.

"Good, because I need another drink," he joked.

The plane landed safely, and the man in the suit pulled out his cell phone and sent a text to someone. His cousin looked on with some interest.

"Any word from either of them yet?" asked the man in the hooded sweatshirt as he furiously wrote something on his napkin.

"Nothing yet. We'll just see 'em at the house."

The man in the suit placed his phone back into the interior pocket of his suit jacket. As people shuffled off the plane, the cousins grabbed their belongings from the overhead bin—the man in the suit had a computer, while the man in the hooded sweatshirt had a small duffle bag. As they exited the plane, one of the female flight attendants winked at the man in the hooded sweatshirt.

"Sorry, mate," he said to his cousin. "I think I'm in love."

"Bollocks, not again!" The man in the suit laughed as his cousin took the napkin scrunched into his hand and put it in her hand.

The captain and crew stood to the side laughing while the man in suit just shrugged his shoulders and pulled his cousin away from the blushing flight attendant by the hood. The duo headed to the exit as the flight attendant straightened her jacket and brushed her hair off her face and smiled at the phone number scribbled on the napkin in her hand.

"Ace move," laughed the man in the suit.

The two walked through the tunnel out into JFK's Terminal 4 and to the International Customs arrivals. The line was short as they approached, and it was just a few minutes before the desk agent signaled to the man in the suit to step forward.

"What is the purpose of your trip?" asked the agent as he grabbed the man's passport.

"On holiday."

"How long do you intend to stay?"

"Two weeks."

"Where are you staying?"

"A friend's house in Manhattan."

"First time in the United States?"

"No, sir."

"Do you have anything to declare?"

"No, sir."

"Enjoy your stay, welcome to the United States."

"Cheers."

The man in the suit leaned over to grab his laptop bag from between his legs and then passed through the checkpoint. He looked around to locate his cousin and wasn't surprised to find his cousin flirting with the giggling customs agent. He watched his cousin scribble what could only be his number on a luggage tag, then slide the paper through to the agent. His cousin blew a kiss to the customs agent before leaving her to leave with his cousin out into the terminal. A group of hired car drivers waited with signs outside of Customs and the man in the suit spotted their ride.

"I think she fancies me, Nigh!" the man in the hooded sweatshirt yelled his cousin.

"Look," Nigel pointed. "Over there, Lionel." He pointed to a man holding up a sign.

The two presented themselves to the driver—Stan—who offered to take their bags but was refused. Lionel and Nigel, both nearly six feet tall, towered over the short driver, and took their own things. In the short walk to the exit of the airport, Stan sneezed and coughed constantly and used his handkerchief to blow his nose. Once outside, Stan led them to the waiting transportation—a stretch Hummer limousine built to fit twenty-four people. Lionel didn't even wait for Stan to open the door for him. He opened the door and climbed into the limo with excitement and Nigel followed. Stan closed the door behind them and made the long walk to the driver's seat. He closed the window to the back to give Lionel and Nigel privacy and the limousine pulled out of JFK's pick-up location and onto the Van Wyck Expressway toward Manhattan.

Lionel excitedly rifled through the fully stocked bar, ready for a real drink after a flight full of alcohol shooters that were far too expensive. Nigel ran his hand over the all black leather interior of the limo, commenting to his cousin how the limo smelled brand new. "Not like home, is it, Line?" They both sat spread out in the back of the limo, with Lionel sitting at the very back middle spot in the limousine and Nigel diagonally to his left. Lionel grabbed two glasses and a bottle of Johnnie

Walker Blue Label from the bar and poured himself and Nigel a drink each. He handed one of the drinks to his cousin and they clinked their glasses together.

"To New York," Nigel toasted.

"To the next step," Lionel added.

Nigel checked his phone again, hoping maybe he'd simply overlooked a message or phone call, but once more he was disappointed to find that nobody had been in touch.

"Still no word from them?" Lionel worried.

"Nothing," Nigel replied.

"Is your mobile even working here?" Lionel wondered.

Nigel glared at his cousin.

"Okay, okay," Lionel relented. "No need to get all bent."

"Once we get to the house, we can figure out what to do next," Nigel said.

"Are we even sure it's true?" Lionel asked.

"They both said it was," Nigel replied.

Stan lowered the partition between the driver's seat and the passengers and turned the volume on the radio.

"You boys going to see any of the sites?"

"No, sir," Nigel responded. "Just to the house, please."

"Where can I meet girls?" Lionel pestered.

"Plenty of bars in New York," Stan replied. "Especially fun for you Brits used to The White Hart in London."

Lionel paused for a moment when Stan answered. Nigel paid him no attention. Lionel was always on his toes for anything, always spontaneous; Nigel, however, was the one that enjoyed planning and thinking through things before acting. They balanced each other well, and not just because of their familial link to each other—they were the best of friends beyond their roots. Lionel, however, was alarmed.

"Excuse me, Stan," Lionel began, "But I don't think either of us mentioned that bar."

Stan slammed the brakes in the middle of the West Side Highway in New York, directly parallel to the Hudson River. The limousine came to rest between 62nd Street and their destination on Riverside Drive. Stan turned to his passengers, his eyes turning crimson as he spoke.

"Consider this your warning," Stan threatened. "Leave now and you'll live. Stay and die."

"It's a Syph!" Lionel shouted.

Stan laughed as he pushed his foot to the gas pedal and spun the limousine to face the Hudson River. Lionel and Nigel couldn't open the doors of the limousine from the inside, and they struggled to get through the sunroof in time. The cousins took deep, methodic breaths as they prepared for the worst.

The limo barreled through traffic, horns blaring, as Stan continued to maniacally cackle. Then the limo plunged into the water. The impact sent the cousins flying toward the partition to the driver's seat as water filled the limo rather quickly. Lionel swam through the sunroof and popped his head out of the water. As he gasped for air, he realized Nigel hadn't come up yet. Lionel dove back down and swam as hard as he could back to the sinking limo. He grasped the sunroof and pulled himself back inside.

Nigel was being held by Stan whose eyes remained red as he took pleasure in every second of Nigel's pain. Lionel took a piece of broken glass that was floating to the surface and stabbed Stan in the right forearm, forcing Stan's grip free. Lionel grabbed Nigel—who was still holding tight to their bags—led him through the sunroof and the duo reemerged from the depths of the Hudson.

"You…have…to…get…the…driver," Nigel panted.

"Oh, piss off," Lionel grumbled.

After gulping a few more deep breaths, he dove down to the sinking limo once more. Almost a full minute later, Lionel shot up from the water, dragging Stan with him. Nigel had gathered himself and regained his strength in time to help Lionel pull Stan to one of the piers, where a crowd had gathered after seeing the "accident." Some bystanders rushed to pull the trio to safety, exclaiming how miraculously all three were still alive. Stan coughed up some water and slowly opened his eyes, which were once again nut colored.

"What happened?" Stan croaked.

"You passed out and drove off the road," Nigel answered.

"I am so sorry," Stan apologized. "Was anyone hurt?"

"No," Nigel replied, glancing at Lionel who rolled his eyes. "Everyone is okay."

An ambulance arrived and Nigel and Lionel refused medical attention, walking off the pier. They looked back at Stan who half-smiled and waved at them as the EMTs wrapped the driver in a blanket and sat him on the edge of the ambulance.

"Still don't think it's true?" Nigel remarked.

Lionel didn't answer. He simply followed Nigel as they walked for a little less than a mile and came to their destination: 3 Riverside Drive.

# Chapter 12 – Emergency Exit

Allen sat at the table, listening to the clock hands moving—the only thing to break the silence.

It had been fifteen minutes since he'd spoken to anyone in the basement of The Metropolitan Museum of Art. The shock of Clarissa's declaration was too much for him to handle. Allen searched for answers in his mind but came up empty. He knew he couldn't stay quiet forever, not with Stephanie, Kay and Clarissa waiting for him to address the situation. Allen had questions and the time had come to ask them.

"How long have you heard the voices?" Allen asked.

"I don't hear them," Clarissa admitted.

"Then how is it you know who I'm supposed to free?"

"There's a lot you need to know, Allen," Kay interrupted. "We can't stay here, though; we have to leave now."

Kay stood up, unzipped her bag on the table the group was seated around and began to gather her belongings from the basement, carefully picking through items that were property of the museum and those that belonged to her.

"Somebody please tell me what the hell is going on," Stephanie demanded.

"There's no time!" Kay yelled from across the basement.

"She's right," Clarissa agreed. "Allen can you—"

Suddenly, the elevator doors closed, and it started going up. The lights in the basement flickered, dimmed.

Kay rushed from the corner of the room to the emergency exit door and pushed as hard as she could. But the door was jammed shut—and there was a growing noise outside.

"We have to go, NOW!" Kay shouted.

Allen's stomach dropped at the panic on Kay's face. The *ding* sound drew everyone's attention to the elevator.

The doors were opening.

The room went completely dark. Out of the elevator came two security guards. Allen noticed their name tags, bright white in the dark— Terry and Tony—but something was *wrong* about them. As the guards inched closer, Allen saw their eyes—they were glowing red.

Allen backed away, stumbling, from the approaching guards, just as someone began to pound on the emergency door behind them.

They were trapped.

"Come out and play," taunted the tallest guard, Tony, as he tapped his flashlight on the metal tables.

"There's nowhere to go," the other added. "Just give us the boy and we'll let you live."

Allen's heart outraced his mind. *Why do they want me? What is happening to me? Who are these guards? Why do they have red eyes?* Allen instinctively spread his arms out to shield Kay, Clarissa and Stephanie from the two guards, but Kay pushed her way out from behind him.

"They can't get that key," she whispered.

"I'll get it," Allen offered.

"No," Kay insisted. "You find a way out of here. I'll get the key."

"I can't let you do that," Allen said.

"I'm not asking."

Kay crouched herself in half as she maneuvered toward the table in the center of the room with the key on it; Allen turned to the emergency exit door behind them, hoping to force it open. He could hear very little from the other side of the thick, steel door, but he knew someone was trying to get in because the door was still being jostled. Kay reached the table, grabbed the key and spun to return to the group but came face-to-face with Security Guard Terry. He drew back his right arm and struck Kay hard across her jaw. She crumbled to the ground in a heap. Clarissa heard the commotion and rushed to Kay, but the guards pushed her to the ground, where she came to rest right beside her sister.

"You two by the door," yelled the other guard, Tony. "Come out."

Stephanie and Allen stopped trying to open the door. They walked to the middle of the room where Clarissa locked eyes with her sister on the ground and watched as Kay regained consciousness and spit the blood from her mouth. Terry yanked Kay up by her hair and held a knife to her throat, while the other held Clarissa down with a black baton. Kay struggled to loosen the guard's grip, but she was no match for his strength.

"You either come with us," snarled Terry, shoving the knife closer to Kay's throat, making her yelp, "or we kill her right here."

"Don't listen to him, Allen," Kay pleaded.

"Shut up, bitch," the guard snapped. "Don't think we won't do this."

The emergency exit door flew open from the outside, and something buzzed past Allen's head, right next to Kay's, and into Terry's skull, killing him instantly, the knife falling away from Kay's throat with his body.

The opening was all Kay needed—she swept the other guard's leg, forcing him to the ground, grabbed the knife from the dead guard's hand and stabbed the second in the heart.

"Everyone okay?" demanded the voice from outside.

"Eli, is that you?" Kay shouted.

"Bonjour, *jeune fille*," he answered.

Eli walked through the door he'd just ripped open from the outside. He was a very dark-skinned man with a distinctly different dialect – a byproduct of his upbringing in New Orleans' French Quarter. Eli loved three things in his life: his caber, New Orleans, and fighting.

"Allen, what is going on?" Stephanie whispered as they backed away. "Look at this guy, Al. He's huge!"

"I see it, Steph," Allen responded. "He can't be all that bad, he's wearing a fedora."

"He reminds me of Joe..."

"I bet y'all a whole mess of King cakes yous happy to see ol' Eli!"

"Thanks, Eli," Kay said.

Eli helped Clarissa and Kay to their feet and collect their belongings. He reached down and pulled the caber out of the security guards' skull and wiped the blades on the recently deceased guard's shirt. Eli gave Kay a smile and then ran back to the opening he'd made, tipping his fedora to Stephanie as he exited and raced back into the busy New York streets.

Handing her bag to her sister, Kay said to Allen and Stephanie, "I have to go after him. Clarissa will take you to the house."

"You sure you don't want help finding him?" Clarissa asked.

"No, thanks," Kay replied, running after Eli.

"What house?" Allen yelled, but Kay had gone.

Allen and Stephanie stood dumbstruck in the basement, trying to make sense of what just transpired.

"Don't ask," Clarissa said. She put the bag over her shoulder, stepped over the dead guards, and pulled Allen and Stephanie outside with her.

She pulled them along, grumbling, "Hurry up" now and again, to the corner of 82nd Street. She hailed a taxi and whipped the door open for Allen and Stephanie.

"Hurry *up*, you two!" she yelled.

Allen and Stephanie moved faster and got into the cab, with Clarissa piling in behind them.

"Where to?" the cab driver asked.

"Riverside Drive," Clarissa said.

# Chapter 13 – 3 Riverside Drive

Allen took out his money and handed fifteen dollars to the cab driver as the girls got out of the cab at 3 Riverside Drive.

The sprawling mansion was gorgeous from the outside, nearly forty feet tall and made of French Renaissance-styled limestone. The windows that faced the river reached out and welcomed the visitors. The steps leading to the front landing and main entrance were pristine and ready to swallow the group to safety. Vines spread across the front of the house like strands of hair that had fallen over a face. Allen marveled at the sight of the house, thinking that it was likely fake. These places didn't exist in the world Allen knew, but here he was face to face with a house that seemed alive. It wasn't that the house was part of the vast city, it's that Allen felt the house perfectly belonged. The view of the Hudson River from the property was second-to-none in New York. As the three approached the house, stained-glass paneled double doors welcomed them. Allen rang the doorbell and was shocked to see a familiar face open the door.

"Mr. White," Mead greeted him. "Welcome to Riverside."

"Mr. Mead…" Allen questioned the appearance of the cheery old man that had started this whole ordeal.

"I know you have many questions, Mr. White. Come on in and let's see if we can't answer them for you."

As Allen entered with Clarissa and Stephanie beside him, their eyes were treated to the green-and-gold tiled ceiling in the main entrance hallway. Looking up, Allen counted four more floors above them. Clarissa pushed past Allen and made her way upstairs.

"I'll be back," she said.

"Where are you going?" Stephanie asked.

"To my room. Want to come with me?"

Stephanie nodded and the duo climbed the staircase and moved out of Allen's sight.

"What happened at the museum?" Mead inquired.

"I can't even explain it, Mr. Mead. There were two…things. I can't say 'people' because I'm not so sure they were human."

"Those would be Syphs," Lionel remarked as he entered the doorway. "Name's Lionel, mate."

"I'm Allen."

"I know who you are," Lionel laughed.

"What the hell is a Syph?" Allen pressed.

"Follow me, Mr. White," Mead interjected.

Allen and Lionel followed Mead up the expansive marble staircase to a shining cherry wood landing where they faced two mahogany doors. Mead opened the doors.

Inside the room on the left was a set of four bay windows that overlooked the Hudson River and historic Riverside Park. Against the back wall was a fireplace with two bookshelves—one on each side that connected to the mantle and curved above the fireplace. There were at least fifteen different chairs spread out across the room and walls were a calming green tint. The paint was fresh, and a hint of the odor still filled the room, blending with the smell of Mead's pipe tobacco. On their right was a bar with eight glass shelves stocked full of every imaginable type of alcohol; from Absinth to Zima, there was something for everyone. On the uppermost shelf was an unlabeled bottle covered in dust.

Nigel was seated in one of the four stools in front of the bar, his back turned to the group as he worked on a vodka sour. Allen moved to the bay windows and looked out over New York—the rain had stopped but it was still overcast, making the city very gloomy and quiet. Allen turned back to the right side of the room where he spotted a leather couch and breathed a sigh of relief as he sunk into it.

"That's Nigel," Mead whispered.

"I can hear you just fine," Nigel replied.

"Nigel, mate, you've got to slow down," Lionel warned.

"Slow, schmo. Limos in rivers, Syphs all over the city. We're doomed," Nigel slurred.

"Nigel," Mead began, "This is Allen."

Nigel stopped pouring his next drink. He dropped his glass on the bar, got up and made his way toward Allen. The three-piece suit Nigel had worn earlier was replaced by a white t-shirt and khaki pants. His hair wasn't neatly parted but sticking up in every direction. Nigel's hands were cold and wet from the glass, but he extended his right hand to Allen. As they shook hands, Clarissa and Stephanie entered the room laughing. Nigel situated himself on the armrest of Lionel's chair. Lionel caught a glimpse of Stephanie as she and Clarissa found seats on a leather couch.

"I'm in love," he whispered to Nigel.

"Piss off," Nigel admonished Lionel.

"Where is everyone else?" Clarissa asked.

"My hope is that they're all on their way to New York," Mead answered. "Where is your sister?"

"Kay said she was going to find Eli," Clarissa replied. "He's in New York somewhere."

Mead pulled some wood from a basket next to the hearth and tossed a few pieces into the fireplace to start a fire. He went to the windows and closed the curtains, then returned to the fireplace. He leaned against it and waited. Allen looked at Stephanie and shrugged to show his confusion. She returned the motion and the two laughed.

"Mr. White, while we wait for another friend to make it here, why don't you and Stephanie look around the house. Clarissa, would you show them around?"

"Absolutely." Clarissa smiled.

Clarissa led them to an elevator rather than the stairs to the basement, where she showed them a massive gym, bigger than theirs at school. Through the next set of glass doors, Allen was hit with the smell of chlorine as they came upon an indoor infinity pool surrounded by a marble deck. A projection screen hung on one wall, doors on either side led to a sauna and a laundry room.

"Come on, you have to see this," Clarissa invited, pulling them next to the fifth floor, to a staircase that led to the roof. Standing on top of 3 Riverside Drive, enjoying the views of the river and park, Allen had only felt so in love with the city once before—that night freshman year at the rooftop bar.

"Amazing," he mumbled to himself. "This place is just incredible," Allen commented. "I didn't know houses like this existed in the city."

"Unreal," Stephanie added.

Clarissa said they should make themselves at home, but for now they should get back to the others.

"How was it, Mr. White?" Mead wondered when they returned to the lounge.

"Incredible, Mr. Mead. You have an amazing home. But WHO the hell are you? I'm tired of waiting for answers. Come on, Stephanie, let's go home."

"Just a few more minutes?" she begged.

Mead only laughed and shook his head. "You are certainly persistent, Mr. White. As I said, we're waiting on one more," Mead continued. "But let's see if we can make sense of today for you, Mr. White."

"Yes, please," Allen replied. "First, who the hell are you? And what the hell is a Syph?"

"Syphs, Mr. White, are parasites, for lack of a better term. They attach themselves to a human host and can take over the body and brain of anyone they choose. They're smart, they're dangerous and they share one purpose—to kill everyone in this house. Please, have a seat."

Mead reached into his front pocket and pulled out a single pearl. With one tap of his finger, it projected out a screen that all in the room could see. On it, was a picture of a beast with red eyes and long, sharp claws. Mead swiped through the screen to show different angles of the beast.

"These are Syphs in their purest form. The claws are the most vicious part of these monsters; one scratch and your body's poisoned by a venom so terrible you'll lose your mind and life within minutes. They can transform into these beasts whenever they choose and when their human host dies, they just move on to their next victim."

"Come on!" Allen laughed. "You're just messing with me, right?"

"No, Allen, he's telling you the truth," Clarissa said.

"Almost got me and Nigel today," Lionel added.

"Nasty, vulgar things," Nigel mumbled.

"Everyone realizes that this is impossible, no? This isn't some fantasy world where things like this happen," Allen said.

"Explain today then, Allen," Clarissa challenged. "Those guards just happened to have glowing red eyes, I suppose? They just *happened* to know where we were and who you were, right?"

"You have to admit, Al," Stephanie chimed in, "things have been weird the past couple weeks. Something isn't normal. Maybe there's a good reason."

"You too, Steph?" Allen said. "None of this is normal…none of this makes sense. I need to leave."

"It just makes sense. Too many unbelievable things have happened."

"So, I'm just supposed to believe all this because you all tell me to?" Allen questioned.

"No, Allen, believe Mead because he's been through this all before," a voice said from the doorway.

"*Professor Rogers?*" Allen gasped.

"I'm sorry, Allen," Rogers replied. "There's a lot I wanted to tell you and couldn't. Your parents made sure I watched over you until you found your way to all of us."

"You're *sorry?*" Allen shouted. "I've been in your classes the past four years, and you choose now to tell me this? You've known this whole time about my parents and thought keeping it to yourself was best? How could you, Professor? How dare you."

Allen jumped to his feet and paced for a few moments when someone else made their way into the room. It was Kay, and she was alone.

"Eli is nowhere to be found," Kay lamented.

"How many are here?" Rogers asked.

"Most are in New York or on their way," Mead assured.

"Good, maybe we can—"

"Good?" Allen yelled. "What's so good about any of this? People are trying to *kill* us. You tell me to accept this, and nobody can tell me why. The people in this room know more about my dead parents than me. Is that fair? Is that by design? I want to trust what you're saying, but you drag me to some multimillion-dollar house and expect me to just believe every word you speak. What about me? What about my feelings? What about my life? I'm sorry, but I can't stay here."

Allen headed for the doorway, but Rogers stepped in his path and put his hands on Allen's shoulders.

"Please listen to me, Allen. Your parents and I we were as close as family. They were my responsibility—and it's my fault they're both dead."

"How is it your fault?" Allen asked, eyes blazing with anger.

"I wasn't able to protect them." Rogers' head dropped.

"Why did nobody tell me this?"

"Nobody told you because we had to be sure you were ready," Mead said, coming to stand by Rogers.

"Ready for what?" Allen persisted.

"The truth," Rogers answered.

Rogers released his hands from Allen's shoulders and Allen turned around and looked upon the faces of those in the room. Lionel, Nigel, Clarissa, Kay, and Stephanie appeared eager to see what Allen would do next. Allen returned to his chair and sat as the rest of the people in the room pulled their chairs closer to him and formed a small circle.

"So," Allen began, "what happens now?"

"We have to wait for everyone else to get here," Mead explained.

Groaning, rubbing his hands over his face, Allen barked, "And *then* what?"

"Then, Mr. White, you can save us all."

# Chapter 14 – London's Calling



*2008 – London Eye, South Bank, London*

"Why are we here in this damn pod, Nigel?" Lionel demanded. "Met a bird I wanted to go see. Little ginger firecracker. Instead, I'm here in this bloody thing."

"I had another dream last night, Lionel. We were in this pod with our parents, laughing and dancing."

"Look around, Nigel. Just an old fool here to take pictures at the top of a giant Ferris wheel. Want to know why there's no laughing or dancing? Because your parents are dead; my parents are dead. I'm getting tired of these dreams of yours."

Nigel looked around the pod and the reality that Lionel was right sunk into his chest. While his intentions were always pure, Nigel learned in that moment that he could no longer be impulsive. He decided as the pod reached the top of its rotation that he would give up on the things his dreams unveiled.

"I'm sorry, Lionel," he said quietly. "No more of this, I promise."

"Ugh, why do you have to be so damn nice?" Lionel screamed. "It's okay to lose your shit, mate! We're fifteen years old, not thirty. Have some damn fun for once, would you?"

"I agree, Mr. Wren."

Nigel and Lionel turned to see Mead seated in the pod.

"Who are you?" Lionel pressed.

"I'm a friend, Mr. Wren," Mead replied.

"I don't know you," Lionel hissed.

"Hi, I'm Ni—" Nigel extended his hand before Lionel pushed him backwards.

"Shut up, I'll handle this. What do you want, old man?"

"What I want is for you and Mr. Bellgraves to give me ten minutes of your time, please."

Nigel and Lionel turned their backs to Mead and huddled. The old man took his glasses off, pulled out his handkerchief and wiped them clean as he waited. The pod had nearly reached the ground on their ride, and Mead watched as Nigel shook his head, seemingly frustrated by his cousin's antics.

"Fifty quid," Lionel said.

"Pardon?"

"Pay us fifty quid and we'll give you ten minutes of our time," Lionel clarified.

"I'll go with you," Nigel declared to Mead.

"Wonderful, Mr. Bellgraves. Mr. Wren?"

"He would've paid us, Nigel," Lionel quipped. "Count me in, I guess."

The three walked along The Queen's Walk of the South Bank east toward the Millennium Bridge.

"So, you're telling me that Nigel's dreams were some sort of message?" Lionel asked.

"Exactly," Mead said.

"Bollocks."

"No, Mr. Wren, it's true."

"I'm sorry, Nigel." Lionel turned to his cousin. "I shouldn't have gone on about it all."

"It's okay," Nigel said. "How could either of us have known? But, Mr. Mead, who was the little boy in the dreams then?"

"What do you mean, Mr. Bellgraves?"

"In the dream last night, there was a little boy in the pod with our family. Probably seven or eight years old. He was holding a wooden cross."

"That's impossible," Mead muttered.

Nigel leaned forward, brows knitted. "What is it?"

"Nothing, nothing at all to worry about. Come, gentlemen, let's go grab a bite to eat and discuss your shared future."

The trio turned left at Shakespeare's Globe and walked across the Millennium Bridge and into London's North End.

# Chapter 15 – A Palace and a Promise

*June 2012 – Buckingham Palace, 11 AM*

The pomp and circumstance of the changing of the Queen's Guard and Buckingham Palace was something to which Londoners were well accustomed. Nigel pressed up against the fence, eager to catch any glimpse of the Royal Family through the palace windows. He gripped the fence spindle, his ripped jeans catching the fence and stretching a little.

"Shit!" he yelled at himself.

"You know, if you stare hard enough, the whole thing will just fall to the ground," Lionel laughed.

"You followed me," Nigel said.

"Well, mate, you took off from breakfast like Batman. I know the Irish goodbye is your thing, but, Christ, man, we're Brits."

As the guards went through the motions on the palace grounds and tourists snapped pictures feverishly, Lionel convinced Nigel to walk away.

"It should be ours, I know," Lionel assured, putting an arm around Nigel's shoulder. "Someday, mate, someday."

"It's not that, Line," Nigel responded. "It just feels like…all of that," he said, waving his arm at the palace, "is a lie when the truth is so much better."

"Just have some faith, mate."

"It's not the faith that bothers me, Line; it's the secrets."

As the duo continued to walk from Buckingham Palace near Hyde Park, Lionel's arm was still around his cousin's shoulder. It was then

Lionel realized they were being followed.

"Stay cool, coz," Lionel whispered.

"What are you talking about?"

"Oy, Lionel Wren, that you?" the man behind them shouted.

"We want to have a word with you," another man added.

Lionel turned to see a group of four people had trailed them. Three men and a redheaded woman.

"Ah, shit, Robbie, not now," Lionel complained.

Robbie dressed like summer would never end. He had on white shorts and a forest green V-neck cotton t-shirt with a backwards white Polo hat and white Vans. His shiny red hair was unmistakable, and the freckles on his face seemed to dance as his mouth moved. Robbie's dark brown eyes were hidden under his sunglasses. Robbie's right-hand-man, Gregory, wore black jeans and a light grey t-shirt. His left arm was covered in a sleeve tattoo of a serpent eating an apple with Bible verses on his forearm. Gregory had hazel eyes and gelled-back black hair and was much tanner than his best friend. Jared was a tall, built Black kid with glasses and a high fade, spinning a skateboard to his side. The last of the group was Robbie's sister, Lyla. She was pale-skinned, redheaded, doe-eyed and immensely attractive. Lyla wore a light pink sundress with little cherries on it, and her figure blossomed through the outfit. The long-running joke amongst those who knew her was Lyla's nickname— Goldie. She looked at Lionel and mouthed an apology and hung her head low. Robbie approached Lionel and stopped about a foot away from him.

"You disrespected my sister," Robbie growled. "Nobody disrespects my sister."

"I didn't disrespect her, Robbie, I swear."

"Well maybe we got our story all wrong, Line," Robbie backed off. "Goldie, you said—"

"—I mean I *did* sleep with her, a few times," Lionel blurted.

"What did you just say?" Robbie screamed.

"Come to think of it, more than a few times," Lionel announced.

"Oh, God," Nigel groaned.

"That's what she said!" Lionel joked.

Lionel smiled and then headbutted Robbie, the force sending Robbie to the ground with a broken nose. Gregory and Jared charged Nigel, throwing punches to his face. Lionel picked up Jared's skateboard off the ground, tapped Gregory on the shoulder and swung the skateboard to Gregory's face; in less than a second it connected and shattered Gregory's orbital bone. Jared stopped his attack on Nigel and retreated into Hyde Park. Lionel grabbed Lyla by the waist and pulled her to him. She looked at her brother on the ground and realized he would be okay, then grabbed Lionel's face and kissed him.

"See you soon, love," he said with a smile.

"Love you, Line," she whispered.

Their hands separated and Lionel and Nigel bolted out of sight.

"Remember when you said no more of my dreams?" Nigel yelled. "No more of *your* escapades!"

"But, mate, I think I'm in love."

Lionel hailed a cab and the cousins jumped in; Nigel could only shake his head as an out-of-breath Lionel uncontrollably laughed.

# Chapter 16 – An American in London



*2018 – Heathrow Airport, London*

Lionel and Nigel stood outside the Arrivals gate past Customs as they waited on Rayna. Both were dressed smartly in button-downs and dress pants, with Lionel in a light and navy with slip-on brown dress shoes. Nigel, the shorter man, though still almost six feet tall, was wearing a black button-down with the sleeves rolled to his elbows, grey dress pants and black wing tips. He kept looking at his watch, a 24-karat gold Rolex.

"Ten quid she's a looker, mate," Lionel proposed.

"You're on," Nigel accepted.

Rayna stepped through the Customs doors into the waiting area. She pulled a rolling suitcase in her right hand and was furiously texting with her left.

"Oy, love, over here," Lionel shouted.

"Lionel?" Rayna wondered.

"Yeah, it's me. This ugly thing to my right is my cousin, Nigel."

Nigel extended his hand to Rayna, who accepted and offered hers.

"It's nice to meet you in person, Rayna," Nigel said. "Welcome to London."

"Thanks for meeting me here, guys."

"Did you check in with Mead to let him know you're here?" Nigel wondered.

"Actually, he doesn't know I'm here yet. Needed a couple days head start."

"Bit of a wild one," Lionel remarked.

"You have no clue," Rayna laughed. "Be right back, have to pee."

Rayna left her suitcase with Lionel and Nigel and walked a few feet through the terminal before turning into the women's room. Lionel looked at his cousin, who stopped him from doing anything stupid.

"Not this one, Lionel," Nigel warned.

"Come on, mate, where's your sense of adventure?"

"You do value your life, right? Mead and Rogers would kill you for even thinking it."

"You're not wrong there," Lionel chuckled.

*****

*Later that night – The White Hart, Waterloo*

Amongst the crowd in the pub, Nigel, Lionel, and Rayna each held a glass in the air and toasted their friendship at a table in the corner. Rayna leaned against the wall with her feet sprawled across the leg of the chair next to her. Nigel and Lionel sat across from her and appreciated the chance to talk to someone else about their lives. They'd consumed a few rounds apiece as they chatted, and Lionel went to the bar to get another round for them.

"How long you been at Riverside then?" Nigel asked.

"Too long," Rayna joked.

"That bad?"

"No, it's not that bad. It's just…I've been there since I was a baby, and I love my dads. But I needed to do something for myself."

"I don't think I've ever thought of things that way," Nigel said. "Must be pretty tough to always be in the thick of it."

"For a long time, they kept me in the dark about this life and what it all means. You know what I mean. Once they told me the truth, it just led to more questions. I guess that's why I'm here, Nigel. I'm *tired* of questions. I want answers."

Lionel came back with three more pints and retook his seat at the table. He pushed drinks toward his companions.

"To our ancestors," he pledged.

The trio clanked glasses and then sipped their drinks. After a few minutes of silence, Lionel spoke.

"So, Rayna, where are we off to first?"

"I can't let you come with me," she replied.

"What? Why not?" Lionel pushed.

"Line, let it go, man," Nigel said. "This is something she has to do on her own."

Nigel smiled at Rayna and patted his cousin on the back as the eternally lovestruck Lionel chugged the rest of his beer.

"Just couldn't stay away, could you?" a voice threatened from behind Lionel and Nigel.

"Bloody hell… Robbie?"

Lionel turned to see Robbie, Gregory, Jared, and others gathered around the table. Since their brawl outside of Buckingham in 2012, the years had not been kind. Jared was now as rotund as he was muscular six years ago. Robbie looked nearly identical to his past self, wearing a black V-neck with his white shorts and black Vans. Gregory traded his luxurious locks for a British buzzcut, and his sleeve tattoo now extended all the way up his neck to the back of his ear.

"These two pieces of trash jumped us a few years ago," Robbie explained to his entourage. "Had to use a skateboard and everything."

"You smell that?" Lionel asked.

"What? Smell what?" Robbie sniffed.

"I smell pig; I think someone is telling porkies," Lionel cracked.

"Here we go again," Nigel mumbled to Rayna.

"I suggest you all go to another pub," Robbie said with a sneer. "Or else—"

"Or else what?" Rayna shouted.

"A Yank? Why am I not surprised the bird's a Yank?" Robbie reacted.

"Hey, piggy-piggy," Lionel snapped his fingers. "Focus."

Lionel stood up and covertly held his drink in hand. Robbie stepped right to him and readied to throw a punch. Before Robbie could attack, Rayna smashed her pint glass to the side of his face and Lionel followed that with a headbutt that sent Robbie to the sticky floor, covered in blood from a broken nose. Rayna jumped over the table and stood beside Lionel and challenged Robbie's friends.

"Who's next?" she questioned.

Gregory picked Robbie up off the ground and moved him toward the exit.

"I'm sorry, Line," Gregory said. "We're gonna head to another pub."

As the group cleared out, the pub manager came out from the office behind the bar, having witnessed the whole thing on surveillance video. Her hair was longer and pulled back behind her head in a high ponytail, but it was unmistakably Lyla.

"Okay, everyone, show's over. Next round is on the house!" Lyla hollered. As the pub patrons celebrated the news, she turned her attention to Lionel, Nigel, and Rayna. She walked up and warmly embraced Nigel, shook hands with Rayna, and stopped in front of Lionel, who could only let out a sideways smile.

"How you been, Goldie?" he asked.

Lyla hauled off and slapped Lionel across the cheek.

"I probably dese—"

Lyla slapped Lionel across the other cheek.

"Now that was a bit mu—"

Lyla slapped Lionel six more times in succession before she pulled him by the shirt and kissed him.

"This happen often?" Rayna asked Nigel.

"No…this is a first, even for him."

"Five months, not a single call," Lyla admonished. "I thought you loved me."

"I do, love. It's just…we had to disappear for a bit."

"Right. Nigel?"

"He's not lying this time, Goldie," Nigel intervened. "We had some trouble and needed to lay low."

"Who's she?" Lyla demanded, nodding at Rayna, who frowned back.

"She's a friend from the States," Lionel answered. "She's just here for the night and then off on holiday tomorrow."

"Nigel?"

"Two truths in a night, Goldie, it's a record."

"You don't say," Lyla smirked. "And how many other women have there been, Line?"

"None, love, I swear." Lionel swiped his arms to further his point.

"Nigel?"

"Two out of three isn't bad," Nigel reluctantly said with a shrug.

Lyla slapped Lionel a few more times and then kissed him again. "God, I love you," she said breathily.

*****

*2020 – The White Hart, Waterloo*

Lionel carefully walked through the pub as the charred remnants of his favorite table turned to ash. The windows were all blown out from the blast, and it took almost three hours for the London Fire Brigade to tamp down the blaze. When Lionel heard the news, he rushed to The White Hart as fast as he could.

*Ten Minutes Ago – Hotel Lobby*
*"We have reports coming out of London of a possible explosion at The White Hart, a well- known pub in the Waterloo section of the city. Sources are telling us that there were a few people inside the bar at the time, including both patrons and staff. Authorities are asking anyone with information to please come forward by calling 112 or 999."*

*2020 – The White Hart, Waterloo*
Nigel ignored the protests of the firefighters and chased them inside after his cousin. He spotted Lionel and ran to his side.

"She's not here, mate!" Lionel cried. "She's not here."

"Maybe she got out, Line."

"How did this happen, Nigel?"

"I don't know, but we have to get out of here, it's not safe."

"I'm not leaving until I find her."

"She's not here!" someone shouted.

"Robbie?" Lionel marveled.

"I've searched everywhere, Lionel. She isn't in this pub."

Nigel looked around as Robbie and Lionel spoke to each other. He turned over burnt tables, knocked on floorboards and rummaged through the rubble. He went next to the manager's office.

Robbie's bloody body was laid across the desk. A letter opener was lodged in his neck.

Nigel stumbled from the office and back into the pub where Lionel knelt close to the ground in the distance, with Robbie standing over him. Time slowed as Nigel watched Robbie raise his arm up in the air.

Nigel swiftly reacted. He pulled his gun from behind his jacket and let loose a single shot. The bullet pierced the back of the fake ginger's head—and Robbie didn't fall to the ground covered in blood, he didn't gasp or cough…he disappeared into a cloud of black smoke.

Lionel, eyes wide, mouth opening and closing, got to his feet and faced his cousin. "You saved my life, mate."

Nigel ignored his cousin and pulled Lionel toward the back exit. "There's no time for this, we have to get out of here."

"What about Goldie?"

"We can't do anything for her if we're both dead."
"Where can we hide?"
"There's only one place we can go that's safe for us now."
"Riverside," the cousins said in unison.

# Chapter 17 – Eli

*July 1, 2000 – 3 Riverside Drive*

A skinny, timid ten-year-old boy sank into the couch in the lounge at Riverside. Mead had excused himself to the other side of the room to answer the phone. The boy smiled and kicked his legs back and forth while he anticipated his first baseball game in New York. He wore a New York Yankees hat, a white Yankees t-shirt with a picture of Derek Jeter on it, and a pair of blue Champion mesh shorts. His lanky legs were covered to mid-calf by a pair of white socks pulled high, with black high-top Nike sneakers on his feet. A brand-new baseball glove rested on his lap.

"Hello?" Mead greeted.

That was all Mead said before he slowly hung the phone back on its receiver. He took his glasses off, set them on the end table, and rubbed his temples with his thumbs. The young boy left the couch and went to Mead's side.

"Mr. Mead, are you okay?"

"Eli let's have a seat," Mead directed.

"Are we still going to the Yankees game?" Eli asked.

"No, Eli, I'm afraid we won't be going to the game tonight."

"Hmpf," the boy groaned. "Alright…"

Mead and Eli seated themselves on the couch and Mead gathered himself. "Eli, there's been an accident." Mead hesitated. "It's your father."

"What happened to my father?" Eli asked. "Is he hurt? Can we go see him?"

"No, Eli." Mead choked up. "Your father is…gone."

The boy's lip quivered before he narrowed his eyes. "No! Liar! I don't believe you!" Eli wrestled away from the couch and Mead's grasp.

"Eli, I'm sorry—"

"It isn't real, it can't be real," Eli sobbed. "It's not fair."

Mead kneeled and gently took Eli's face into his hands. The boy quaked with shock and pain; a feeling Mead had seen too many times before today. Mead offered whatever comfort he could to the young boy.

"Why…is…this…happening?" Eli hyperventilated, his tears falling onto Mead's hands.

"I don't know, Eli. I just don't know."

*July 1, 2010 – My Cup Overflowith Tea Room, French Quarter, New Orleans, 10 pm*

"You'z the psychic, you tell me," Eli joked.

The black marble table offered privacy to Eli and the psychic. Though he had lived in New Orleans his entire life, Eli never ventured into any of the shops in the city that many believed connected to the supernatural. Eli preferred to frequent piano and jazz bars, always in search of a good time and a strong drink. The young psychic was dressed casually, with a teal blouse, a pair of jean shorts that showed off her tanned legs, and black sandals on her feet. She was strikingly attractive with long, blonde curly hair and deep, dark eyes.

"Have a seat," the young psychic said, flashing her smile. Her extraordinarily white teeth brightened the sparsely lit room. "Would you prefer a Tarot, Tea Leaves, or Palm reading?"

Eli smelled the hint of peaches in the room, an aroma that gave him a laid-back feeling in his heart.

"Dealer's choice, *mon ami*."

"Adelaide. The name's Adelaide."

"Pleasure, Adelaide. I'm—"

"—Eli. Yes, I know."

"Whoa, how did you know that?"

"You booked the appointment under your name," Adelaide said, her dark eyes glittering at him.

"Oh, you are slick, *mon ami*." Eli wagged a finger and squinted his eyes.

"Shall we start?

"Yes," Eli implored. "Let's go with the palm reading."

Adelaide held out her hand and motioned for Eli to give his right hand to her. She flipped his hand over and rested it in hers with his palm facing up. Adelaide circled her left hand clockwise above his palm.

"This is to get a reading of your energy," she explained. "It helps me to build a baseline for your emotions."

"What's my energy tell you?" Eli asked, leaning in.

"It tells me you're troubled, Eli. Something weighs heavy on your mind, all the time."

"That's not hard to see, *mon ami*."

"I'm going to need you to shut up and let me do my thing, Eli," Adelaide demanded. Adelaide closed her eyes and continued to move her hand in a circular motion above Eli's and stopped momentarily. "Interesting," she said.

"What? What is it?" Eli asked.

She shot him a stern look. "You really don't understand patience, Eli."

"Sorry," he mumbled.

"Today is a day of great pain for you, I'm sorry," her eyes tightened shut with empathy, her teeth biting her lip.

"It's okay," Eli answered.

"I wasn't talking to you, Eli. The spirit *attached* to you refuses to leave your side. He says today is the day he died."

"What the hell?" Eli shot back from the table and recoiled his hand.

"His name is Terrence. Does that mean something to you?"

"That was my father's name," Eli whispered. "He's been gone for—"

"Ten years today," her shoulders lifted, and she watched as Eli's face went from disbelief to anguish.

"Who have you been talking to?" Eli pressed, his gut turning with her words, realizing she wasn't a fraud.

"He says…he's sorry you didn't get to the Yankees game."

Eli teared up as Adelaide closed her eyes to commune with Terrence.

"Take my hands, Eli," Adelaide invited. "Don't be afraid."

Eli reached out his hands and slowly interlocked his fingers with Adelaide's. She gently pushed her hands into his and the lights in the room went out. A single candle on the left side of the table lit itself and supplied a tiny bit of light in the room.

"Eli…" a voice echoed. "My boy… Open your eyes…"

The young man gradually unsealed his eyes and to his surprise, before him and Adelaide was the specter of his long-dead father. Sparks of light swirled around Terrence as he smiled at his son; upon the ghost's head sat a fedora. Eli could smell his father's cologne and hear his voice as if he was alive in the room. He wore shadows of the same black suit, white shirt. and black tie he was buried in, like a black and white movie but grainy, dustier somehow.

"You have grieved for me long enough, Eli," Terrence began, his voice a soft boom. "The time has come for you to live for *you*, son."

"I can't do that, Pop."

"Why, son?"

"You know why, Pop."

"Eli, I'm sorry. I never meant for you to carry this burden. I hoped we would've finished all this before you were born."

"But you didn't, Pop. And now I'm left with two burdens. What do you want me to do?"

"Fight, son," Terrence's specter glowed with strength in the moment and the apparition looked directly into his son's soul. "I want you to *fight*. Stop hiding in piano bars and the French Quarter. You have to go to New York. To Mead."

Eli pursed his lips, stubborn anger making him breathe out hard. "No. I won't ever go back to that place. They're on their own, Pop."

Terrence turned his attention to the girl. "Adelaide, tell him what you see."

Adelaide stared into Eli's eyes and then slowly closed her eyes again. Her forehead scrunched against her vision, the message clear. "You're in New York…I see a giant rock…you're surrounded by darkness…but there are lights flashing ahead…" Then Adelaide winced.

"What is it?" Eli demanded.

"There's a man standing on top of the rock and he's pointing toward the lights, but he has no voice…I'm sorry, Eli, that's where the vision ends."

"What does it mean?" Eli fretted. "Pop?"

But the specter disappeared as soon as Eli addressed him again, and the lights in the room came back on. Adelaide opened her eyes and Eli pulled his hands back to his lap and shot to his feet, head whirling with all that transpired in the shop.

"I know you don't know me," Adelaide soothed as she stood up. "But what just happened is something I've never experienced. *You*…are special, Eli."

"Special?" he shouted. "A dead father, a mother I never knew, and all the secrets worth dying for a man could ever want. 'Special' you say. No, *mon ami*, you mean cursed. *Je crache sur vous.*"

Eli kicked over the chair at his feet and stalked out of the room, through the shop, out the front door, and back toward the banks of the Mississippi River.

*****

*February 2014 – Preservation Hall – New Orleans, Adelaide on the move*
The blonde girl at the bar twisted a curl in her fingers as she listened to Eli argue with Kay. She grew annoyed with each passing moment as Eli continued to reprimand Kay. She watched Eli move to the dance floor, while Kay turned and ran to the bathroom. The blonde girl jumped up and chased after Kay into the bathroom where Kay stood over the sink berating herself.

"He isn't going to listen to you," Kay mumbled. "He doesn't want anything to do with you…stupid, stupid, girl."

"There's no use in blaming yourself for Eli," Adelaide said, looking at Kay in the mirror. "His path is complicated."

"Who are you?" Kay asked, not turning but using the mirror to reflect her anger at Adelaide.

"My name is Adelaide de Fontaine," she explained.

"I'm—"

"Kay," Adelaide stated. "I knew you'd be here tonight; it's why I came out."

"How could you know that?" Kay whipped her body around and looked Adelaide up and down with wonder and disgust. "Who are *you*, really?"

"I'm here to help you," Adelaide stepped closer to a retreating Kay. "I'm…well, there's no right way to describe what I am. I'm—"

"She's the crazy psychic from My Cup Overflowith," a woman at the next sink over interrupted. "At it again, Batty Addy?" The woman walked between them, shaking her hands and laughing her way out of the bathroom.

"Don't listen to her," Adelaide said. "People fear what they don't comprehend. In her case, that's everything."

"You're a psychic?"

89

"I know, weird, right?"

"Actually, not really. But…are you a friend of Eli's, or…?"

"Kind of. We met a few years ago and I've stayed in touch with him here and there. We shared a moment."

"You did what, now?"

"Oh, shit, sorry, he came to me for a reading once, and something weird happened."

"What happened?" Kay asked.

The bathroom door pushed open and Eli stormed in. "It's time for you *both* to go," he announced. "Go back to New York, Kay."

"Eli, I can explain—" Kay started.

"Don't want to hear it, Kay. Go home—and don't ever come back here."

"Eli, please, she deserves to know," Adelaide begged. "Tell her the truth."

"Damn it, *go*! Both of you." Eli banged his closed fist against the wall before he walked out.

*****

*October 7, 2020 – Desire Oyster Bar, New Orleans, Louisiana – Mead's Warning*
At the corner of Bourbon and Bienville Streets in the French Quarter is the Desire Oyster Bar, one of New Orleans' most famous establishments. The tiled floor seemed like a painting, white with a black and red pattern, and candy red chairs surrounded black dining room tables. The light brown high-top tables with beige stools hosted collections of friends with drinks. The long bar matched the high-top tables and the brown backed stools fit perfectly into the atmosphere. The restaurant never had a lull in business, tonight being no exception, full of people as music spilled out the front door. Seated at the oyster bar in a black Henley shirt and a pair of jeans, his fedora rested on his knee, Eli scooped up his final oyster on the plate. He signaled to the exceedingly tall bartender.

"Another plate on the half shell, and a Sazerac, *mon ami*," he ordered as he handed the bartender a fifty-dollar bill.

The bartender took the money, nodded and turned his back to Eli to enter the order into the computer at the bar. He curved back around and extended his hand toward Eli.

"Keep it, *mon ami*."

"Wow, thank you," the bartender said.

"Mighty kind of you, Eli," Mead said, approaching from behind. He gestured to an empty stool. "May I?"

"I knew it would be you this time, Mr. Mead."

"Why's that, Eli?"

"I wasn't so gracious last time someone visited."

"You were a jerk is what you meant to say."

"*Oui.*" Eli slumped in his chair. "I know she cares, Mr. Mead, but I wasn't ready."

"And now? Are you ready now?"

"No. I'm sorry, but I'm not coming back. This fight has cost my family too much."

"As it has many others, Eli. I understand your reluctance. I've watched countless friends disappear over the years. But this time is different, I promise you. We have watched over this boy for some time—he's smart, he's strong, he's kind. He can *do* this, but he needs us all."

A stunned Eli thought for a minute before he answered Mead. He took another oyster off the plate and ate it and washed it down with his drink. He let out a quiet burp and finally answered. "He'll have to do it without me."

There was a long pause as the bartender returned with Eli's food and drink. He looked to Mead next.

"Coffee, please. Black."

Mead hummed and smoothed out a bar napkin, watching the bartender's back as he poured the coffee. Eli looked back and forth anxiously between the two of them, waiting impatiently to finish their conversation when clearly Mead was enjoying drawing it out. Eli pulled out a five-dollar bill, but the bartender waved it away. Mead lifted the cup to his nose, inhaled the aroma and smiled. Eli pursed his lips as Mead rotated the cup a tiny bit and sipped on the dark blend. Mead brought the cup back down to the bar and shifted his body so that he was almost completely sideways on the stool.

"I know you love her."

"Who?" Eli asked.

"Ms. Blakemore. I see the way you two look at each other. It's love."

"Is it, *mon ami?*"

"Don't get wise with me, young man."

"I'm sorry, Mr. Mead," Eli relented. "The truth is—"

"—The only truth that matters is this, Eli," Mead said, taking a sharp breath, his eyes boring into Eli's. "Kay will be dead in less than a month unless you come back to New York. You want to run away from this life, that's fine. You can stay down here and eat oysters and drink until you're old and grey. That's your choice."

"You're right, it is *my* choice."

"But could you live knowing that people you care about are dead and you could have prevented it? Can you sit here and tell me you'll feel no guilt if Kay dies? Clarissa? *Me?* Your choice affects us all, whether you like it or not." He straightened his back, gathered himself. "I'm headed back to New York tonight; you can come with me, or you can stay here and do whatever it is that makes you happy. I believe in you, Eli. Your father believed in you. The time has come for *you* to believe in something."

Mead stood up and hovered above Eli. He placed his hand on Eli's shoulder and patted it twice before holding it in place.

"You're not the only one who's made hard choices, Eli. But if I knew I could save the woman I love from dying, there would be no choice." He stood and turned toward the entrance leading to Bourbon Street and sighed. "In four days, we meet at Riverside. If you change your mind, we'll be there. *Au revoir*, Eli."

Eli defeatedly slid downwards in the stool. After fifteen minutes of playing with the plate of oysters in front of him, out of the corner of his eye, he noticed Adelaide as she approached, pale-faced and scared.

"I need to talk to you," she begged. "It's really important, Eli."

"Leave me the hell alone, Adelaide, this ain't the time."

"It is *the* time, Eli." Adelaide begged. Her hair was a disheveled mess and her long black dress a wrinkled mess; something she might have slept in the night before. "Your time has come. There's nothing left for you in New Orleans."

Eli maneuvered his way off the stool, grabbed his fedora and pulled it down over his head, and stomped past Adelaide.

"I said, leave me alone."

"Terrence visited me again!" Adelaide shouted. "He gave me a message to give to you."

"I'm done listening to dead men," Eli said as he walked out of Desire and blended into the crowd on Bourbon Street.

# Chapter 18 – Sasha



*January 2002, Bran, Brașov, Romania*

In the far countryside, Petrov and Svetlana Radu sat at the kitchen table. Petrov was wearing a white crewneck t-shirt and jeans with his bare feet crossed right foot over left. His light brown hair was parted from left to right on top of his head and the sides of his head were buzzed in tight. Svetlana's black curls hung off the back of her chair. She wore an eggplant-colored romper with a gold belt around her waist as she smiled and caressed her stomach. The natural wood of the chairs perfectly matched the table and cabinets, and the kitchen walls were painted white from the ceiling to mid-wall and tiled in grey from that point to floor. The warm, welcoming atmosphere of the house was undeniable, but Petrov and Svetlana knew that their lives had just changed.

"*Acest lucru este atât de interesant!*" Petrov kissed his wife's hands.

"No more Romanian, Petrov. English now, we speak."

"My hope for a boy," Petrov struggled in broken English.

"You're getting so good, love."

"I am full for joy, my wife."

"If we are to work for Cousin Antonia, we must be speak well English; or we will not be having jobs."

"You no more work the job," Petrov declared. "I will take the care of our family."

Svetlana smiled and her and Petrov shared a tender kiss. "I think a girl it will be."

"No shit?" Petrov said.

*October 25, 2015, Bran Castle, Bran, Brașov, Romania*

Tourists flocked to Bran for one purpose: the majestic Bran Castle. It had belonged to King Ferdinand I and his wife, Queen Marie, before socialism became the accepted rule of Romania. They were the last of the monarchy to inhabit the castle, and the tours that were offered brought a lot of money to the region of Bran each year.

However, most people didn't come to Bran Castle for the political tours and background on King Ferdinand I and Queen Marie. People came to see "Dracula's Castle," an unfortunate nickname given to the mistaken notion that Vlad III, who many believed Bram Stoker based his Count character upon, inhabited the castle once. Petrov took pride in his job as a guide at the castle, and genuinely appreciated all that he was given by Svetlana's cousin Antonia. As he completed his final tour of the day, Antonia walked into the museum where the tour ended and pulled Petrov aside.

"Petrov, you have done an amazing job for us the past thirteen years, bu—"

"Are you firing me?" Petrov interrupted.

"God, no, are you crazy? You're the best we have! I'm here with an opportunity. Come to my office after you wrap up your shift."

"Okay." Petrov smiled. "I see you in a few minutes."

Petrov hiked back to the castle and entered the men's room. He picked up a paper towel that had missed the trash and tossed it in the bin, washed his hands and stopped, doing what he'd really come there for—to get himself together. To ready himself for change and accept that everything he'd worked for might be coming to fruition. He made his way out into the main entryway of the castle and across the hall to Antonia's office, where his wife and daughter were already seated. The room smelled like a mixture of cigarette smoke, disinfectant wipes, and oranges. Petrov greeted his wife with a kiss and then hugged his daughter.

"Happy birthday, Sasha," he murmured.

"Petrov, please have a seat," Antonia instructed from behind her desk. "I invited my cousin here because this is for all of us."

"What's this about?" Petrov asked as he slid down into a cherry wooden chair.

"We had a visit recently from someone who works at one of the museums in the United States. They went on one of your tours and emailed me shortly after their visit. They want to hire you to do tours in English and record tours in Romanian for visitors from here."

Petrov's heart jumped in his chest, and he glanced at Svetlana, whose eyes were lit up with pride before answering his boss. "But Antonia, this is my home, this is my job," Petrov said. "I can't just leave."

"Fine…you're fired, Petrov," Antonia declared. "Now you can go anywhere you want."

"I…I…don't know what to say," Petrov replied.

"Honey, we should go," Svetlana interjected.

"Oh my GOD!" Sasha squealed, jumping to the edge of her seat. "This is the best birthday ever, let's get the hell out of this place."

Petrov, Svetlana, and Antonia stopped their conversation and stared at Sasha in unison.

"I mean, this is wonderful for your career, Dad. I think we should try this."

"Thirteen years old and she's ready to see the world," Antonia remarked. "I agree with Sasha. Get out of this place."

"And where is it we're meant to go?" Petrov wondered.

"The woman's name is…" Antonia rummaged through paper on her desk. "…Katherine Blakemore; she signed her email 'Kay.' She's in New York City."

"Jesus Christ!" Sasha screamed. "Best. Birthday. Ever!"

*October 25, 2017 – The Metropolitan Museum of Art, New York City*

In the basement of the museum, Kay and Petrov sat on opposite ends of a large table with a fluorescent light above them. Both had on white cloth gloves and glasses to protect their eyes, and clean suits. All the other artifacts that were normally laid on the table were placed on other tables in the dark. On the table in front of Kay and Petrov was a single item carefully wrapped in a cloth.

"Ready?" Kay asked.

"Yes, I'm ready."

As Kay unwrapped the cloth, a voice echoed over the speaker in the basement.

"Ms. Blakemore, it's Harold at the front desk. Mr. Radu's daughter is here."

"That's okay, Harold, send her down, please," Kay answered.

"Sorry, Kay, it's her birthday. First one without Svetlana."

"Petrov, there's nothing to be sorry for; we've all been where she is now. The difference is she still has you."

"Not for much longer, Kay," Petrov announced.

"What do you mean, Petrov?"

He sighed. "I've decided to go back to Romania," he explained. "I know Sasha will never leave, but I must. I miss Svetlana, and I miss my home."

"When are you going to tell her?" Kay wondered.

"I think he just did," Sasha cried. "Dad?"

"I'm sorry, honey. There was no good time to tell you after Mom."

"Dad, look at me."

Petrov lifted his head up as Sasha walked over to him from the dark of the basement.

"It's okay, Dad," she said. "I knew this day would come. I thought you would've stayed in Romania after the funeral."

"I had to make sure you were okay."

"I know, Dad, I know. It's going to be okay. *I'm* going to be okay."

"Promise?"

"I promise."

Petrov hugged Sasha and Kay removed her glasses to wipe her eyes on her sleeve, touched by the love and understanding between the two. She thought back to her father's final words on the computer and the warmth she felt in letting go the right way; that chance she had to see him one more time before she moved to New York. She gathered herself and turned back to the table as Sasha kept her arm around her father. Kay removed the rest of the cloth and revealed a small golden key. Petrov leaned in closer, and Sasha moved to a chair on the far end of the table. Kay and Petrov took turns looking over the key, neither one touching the artifact. After thirty minutes of note taking, they reconvened as Sasha swiped away at her phone.

"It's incredible," Kay stated. "What do you think, Petrov?"

"I think this key has more to it than meets the eye," he replied. "There's something wildly different about this piece."

"I've never seen anything like this, Petrov. The texture alone is different than anything else I have ever encountered. Do you feel those etches in the side? The smell of it makes me think it's older than we thought. How old do you think it is?"

"Hmmm…my best guess, based on the construction alone, is at least one thousand years, if not more."

"I know that key." Sasha placed her phone down on the table.

Both Petrov and Kay's heads snapped around to look at the girl. "What do you mean, sweetheart?" Petrov asked. "*How?*"

"I have seen that exact key before," Sasha answered, her eyes squinting as her mind worked to remember the details. "I know I have."

"I believe you, Sasha. Think, honey, where have you seen it?"

"I can't...I can't remember...damn."

"Sasha," Kay offered with a concerned glance to Petrov. "Please try and remember. Is it the color, the size, the smell? It'll come to you."

"Can I see it?" Sasha requested.

Petrov glanced at Kay, who slid the cloth down the table to Sasha. The young girl reached down and grabbed the key from the cloth as Kay and her father were too late to stop her.

Sasha slowly unshielded her eyes from blinding light in the place she now stood. In front of her was a body of water and at the mouth of the water was a young man she had never seen before. As she approached the figure, she was shocked to see he had no features on his face but could sense her movement. He held a finger to where his mouth should have been, and implored Sasha to quiet herself. He pointed to a structure in the distance, but the light blocked Sasha's view. Sasha walked with her hands in front of her eyes to keep the light off her face as she navigated the mysterious terrain. The road was unpaved, but Sasha couldn't feel the rocks under her feet; the only thing she felt was the immense heat from the sun.

Unexpectedly, the heat from the sun disappeared and was replaced with a wintry wonderland. The faceless young man appeared again to Sasha, this time atop a giant slab of rock. His head tilted down at her, he pointed—this time to a variety of flashing lights in the distance. Sasha tried to run toward the lights but was stuck in place. The young man shook his finger and shushed Sasha, which sent her to the cold ground, and suddenly, Sasha was back in the basement of the museum with Kay and her father. Kay had ripped the key from Sasha's hand and placed it back in the middle of the table on the cloth.

"Sasha, are you okay?" Petrov shouted as he held her tight on the floor.

"I'm fine, Dad. What *was* that?"

"What did you see?" Kay asked.

"Just a lot of light and a young guy with no face," Sasha replied.

"We have to get Mead," Kay ordered.

Petrov forcibly smiled at his bewildered daughter. "Happy birthday?"

*December 24, 2017 – 3 Riverside Drive*

Sasha seated herself at the dining room table next to Clarissa. On the other side of Clarissa was Professor Rogers and to his left, Mako, a handsome young man dressed in all black with a small smile that danced across his face. Across from Mako were Kay, Rayna, Mead, and an empty chair. Christmas Eve at Riverside was a somber affair through the years, as the circle of friends continually changed with gains and loss. Anna wasn't at Riverside for Christmas Eve, back in Chicago with a woman she met years ago. The only constants over the past ten years had been Mead, Rogers, and Rayna. Kay and Rayna prepared the meal for the group, and Rogers had bought a dessert plate from a local bakery. The plate rested on the serving hatch, loaded with half-moon cookies, chocolate chips cookies with candy cane bits, and a fruitcake that nobody in the room was likely to eat. Sasha perused the faces of her friends at the table.

"Does anyone care if I put on some music?" she asked.

Nobody objected to her request, so Sasha stood up from the table and went to the receiver that was embedded in the wall, unraveled her USB cable and plugged her phone in and placed it on the serving hatch. She swiped to the Holiday favorites station and returned to the table. "Rudolph the Red-nosed Reindeer" quietly played over the speakers in the room and the group's spirits seemed to lift.

"I love this song," Rayna said.

"Me too." Mako smiled.

"It brings me back to years ago in New Jersey," Rogers added. "Our family used to have some wild gatherings. We'd play cards, play piano, sing together; those were the—"

"—days, yes, we know, Dad," Rayna mocked as the group shared a laugh.

Kay and Clarissa rose up and walked toward the kitchen. Kay went into the kitchen and Clarissa stood on the opposite side of the serving hatch. The oven door screeched as Kay opened it to pull out the ham and scalloped potatoes. As the sisters prepared the meal, they smiled at each other and listened to the laughter coming from the table. Kay always loved the smells of the holiday—a collection of candles, ham, fish, bread, and cookies, while Clarissa just wanted to get through things with as much happiness as possible. Kay leaned toward the ham and took a huge smell of the dinner, a wide smile on her face. Clarissa opened and closed a few drawers in the kitchen looking for a can opener, a clanking cacophony of silverware, swearing with each fruitless search. Kay jabbed the top of the ham with a carving fork and Clarissa finally spoke to her.

"You might've outdone yourself on this one," Clarissa said. "It looks great."

"After a few years of trying it was bound to happen," Kay laughed. She pulled the ham out of the glass dish and placed it in a serving tray. She put the tray on the serving hatch and Clarissa carried it to the table, where Rogers commenced cutting the ham. Clarissa returned to the serving hatch where the scalloped potatoes, green beans, roasted spaghetti squash, and Caesar salad awaited. The symphony of sound and smell was sensational to everyone, each plate placed on the table prepping their collective palettes.

"Let's eat!" Kay beamed.

"Thank fucking God, I'm starving," Sasha muttered.

The noise of dishes being passed and silverware clanging around the table stopped as "Silent Night" murmured over the speakers. Everyone turned toward Sasha.

"What? What'd I say?" she wondered with a mouth half-full of bread.

Mead chuckled and the rest of the group joined him in a roar of laughter at Sasha's bravado.

"I do have a gift for you, Sasha," Mead announced.

"Another of Rogers' stories? Please, I can't take more New Jersey memory lane."

"How about Romanian memory lane?" Petrov strolled into the room. "How's that sit with you and your 'fucking God'?"

"Dad! Holy—"

"Shit? Sasha, when did you get such a mouth? Come here and give me a hug."

Sasha hurried over to her father and he wrapped his arms around her and hugged her hard. Kay started to cry, and Rayna leaned her head over to Rogers' shoulder and hooked under his right arm. He took his hands and patted her hand.

"It's only been two months and it feels like forever," Sasha sobbed. "I've missed you, Dad."

"No shit," Petrov replied.

*October 10, 2020 – Ellis Island, Top of the Statue of Liberty*

Sasha admired New York City from the crown of the Statue of Liberty. She had spent the morning hours alone, something she'd grown accustomed to since her father left the United States, but she talked to him almost daily. Sasha was truly happy for the first time since her mother died. Her dyed-red hair flapped in the gusts of wind that snuck through Lady Liberty's crown. Goosebumps ran up and down her body under the cut-up jeans and long-sleeved cotton shirt. She was anxious for her eighteenth birthday, just two weeks from today.

"It was nice of you to keep your distance on the ferry," Sasha said. "I've lived here almost five years, and this is my first trip here—you're gonna come here and cut it short, aren't you?"

Thomas Rogers, dressed in the blue sweatshirt and jeans with New Balance sneakers, climbed the last of the 393 steps to the apex of Lady Liberty.

"I wouldn't dream of it, Sasha. I just thought you could use a friend today."

"Thanks. You didn't have to do that."

"Yes…I did," Rogers answered.

Sasha soaked in the moment at the top of the beacon of freedom, thankful for the friendship Thomas and the others had shown her since she arrived in New York. They banded together when her father left to make sure she was taken care of and happy, a gesture Sasha would not soon forget. As she turned to head back down the steps, Rogers stayed and regarded the city.

"Coming?"

"Just soaking it all in." He smiled.

"Just tell me, please."

"There's six of you in the city right now," he warned. "You need to get home, *now*. It's the safest place for you to be."

"And what about you?"

"I have to make sure everyone who's not there already gets to Riverside as soon as possible."

"Be careful, Thomas," Sasha instructed.

"You be careful, too," Rogers answered as he hugged her goodbye. "I'll see you later tonight."

# Chapter 19 – Mako Young



*September 2003 – New York City PS 130, Baxter Street, Chinatown*
The young boy was nervous for his first day of school in his new surroundings. He'd lived in Seattle for the first eleven years of his life. The Pacific Northwest was home, but when his father died, his mother inexplicably decided to move across the U.S. to New York City. They'd found acceptance in Seattle—people in their community looked out for the boy and his mother. Now, however, they were exposed to the ugliness of the world. Because his mother was white, they were shunned immediately. Chinatown wouldn't protect them, and his mother grew increasingly paranoid that they were being followed everywhere they went. But the boy was a rarity in the Asian community—an Asian with blue eyes was a rare sight, and one that people in Chinatown clamored to see to believe. One restaurant owner, Mr. Shuko Yang, decided to protect the mother and child if he could, offering the mother a job and apartment that she accepted. When the boy's mother allowed her thoughts to overwhelm her and transform into paranoid schizophrenia, the little boy had to grow up fast to take care of them both. One summer day, the boy returned home to find EMTs loading a black body bag onto a gurney; he immediately knew his mother was dead. Mr. Yang refused to let the boy fall into the system, so he took him in and let him live in a small apartment above his restaurant. At eleven years old, Mako Young learned to live as a man.

Over time, Mr. Yang revealed his own upbringing to Mako. He detailed the punishment and shame he withstood for having the name Shuko—a name normally attributed to the Japanese—which could be what he and Mako shared the most. He promised the boy he would look out for him and teach him the ways of *their* people. He taught Mako about traditions, respect, honor, and enrolled Mako into a martial arts training program so that he could learn to defend himself—and Mako would need that as he progressed through school.

"Mako Young?" the teacher called.

"Present, ma'am," Mako answered.

As soon as the teacher said his name, he knew that he'd be in a fight that day. Mako waited and surveyed the room when he felt a kick at the back of his chair.

"What kind of name is Mako?" his classmate asked.

"My mother loved a Japanese actor with the name, I guess."

"Your mom sounds stupid and so does your name, *gweilo.*"

Mako shoved his desk forward and stood up. He turned to the desk behind him and grabbed the kid by the hair and slammed his face into the desk. The teacher rushed over and pulled Mako away from the other student, dragging him into the hallway.

"We don't do that here, Mako," she scolded.

"Yeah, but he—"

"No buts, mister. The only butt you should be concerned with is yours. Do you want Principal Hong to call Mr. Yang?"

"No, Ms. Lee," Mako answered. "But he called me *gweilo.*"

Offended by the revelation, Ms. Lee returned Mako to the room and had him sit at his desk. She helped the other student to his feet, only to grab him by the ear and force him from the room as the rest of the class laughed. When she reentered the room, Ms. Lee scolded the class in her native tongue.

"*Wǒ yǒngyuǎn dōu bùxiǎng zài tīng dào nǐmen zhōng de rènhé yīgè rén shuō zhège dāncí.*" (I don't EVER want to hear any of you say that word again.)

From time-to-time Mako would hear it in elementary school, but when he got to PACE High School, it all but disappeared for good. Mako knew that was a byproduct of the size and strength his body accumulated during his teen years. By the time he graduated high school, Mako was six-foot-three and 210 pounds with roughly six percent body fat. He spent all the time he wasn't working at Yang's inside Rhee's Martial Arts Academy. Master Rhee had watched Mako grow from a quiet, scrawny kid into a confident young man; he often remarked to Mako that he was special, but Mako refused to believe it.

*March 2009 – Róngyù Chinese Restaurant, NYC*

The décor of Róngyù was what most people in Chinatown loved most about the restaurant. It wasn't the stereotypical New York City eatery; it was authentic in every sense of the word. No flashy neon lights or gaudy decorations, just rather tasteful touches around the room. The vaulted ceilings made it feel spacious and the dimmed lights added a sense of calm to the restaurant. The male staff all wore tuxedos, and the female staff wore black dresses. Shuko Yang wanted his customers to be the focus and his employees as classy and unnoticeable as possible. The Imperial dining tables set about the room were spaced perfectly and to Yang's exact measurements. He knew that people wanted to enjoy dinner and conversation with their friends—not with every other person dining. Róngyù had become one of the premier restaurants on the East Coast, not just in New York. Yang's vision, management style, and demand for perfection made him as caring as he was shrewd.

Master Rhee entered the front of the restaurant and waited for the hostess to receive him. Mako was bussing tables and saw Rhee hold up three fingers to indicate how many in the party. The hostess led him to a table and offered him a chair. Rhee sat alone for a few moments until an old man with an umbrella entered the restaurant. He spoke to the hostess and was brought to Rhee's table. To Mako Young's surprise, Mr. Yang joined them at the table. It was rare for Mr. Yang to sit and converse with anyone during business hours, so Mako knew this meeting was very important. As he moved back into the dining room to clean another table, Mr. Yang motioned for Mako to come his way, which of course, Mako did.

"Mako, this is Mr. Mead," Yang introduced.

"It's a pleasure to meet you, Mr. Young," Mead stated.

"You as well." Mako bowed his head.

"Mr. Mead knew your parents," Yang enlightened. "Mead goes back to your family's time in China."

"Did you have business with my parents, Mr. Mead? Or did you know them from some humanitarian missions?"

"How much do you know about your parents, Mr. Young?"

"Just the things my mother told me, sir."

"Well, Mr. Young, I'm here to tell you a few more things if you'll let me," Mead said. "Mr. Yang has agreed to give you the rest of the afternoon off, so why don't you have a seat?"

Mako glanced at Mr. Yang who stood up and gestured for Mako to sit at the table in his place.

*June 24, 2010 – Róngyù Chinese Restaurant, NYC*

It was after hours on a Saturday night and the staff trickled out of the restaurant after another busy shift. Mako had graduated earlier in the day but went to the restaurant after the ceremony and parties he attended. He smiled at the hostess as she passed him on her way out. He held the door open for her and realized he was the only one left in the place, but the light was on in the kitchen. Mako crossed the dining room and pushed through the swinging doors to find his friend. Mr. Yang was seated on a stool looking over receipts on the impeccably cleaned industrial grade table, the sleeves on his shirt rolled to the middle of his forearms.

"Thank you for coming today, Mr. Yang," Mako began. "And thank you for everything you've done for me over the years. I owe this all to you."

Yang stopped the work and lifted his head to Mako.

"You owe all this to *you*, Mako," Yang reassured. "I gave you a roof and a job. The hard things you conquered on your own. You went through a hell nobody can comprehend."

"I…I don't know what to say…"

"Say you'll go to John Jay and finish what you started when you took that Police Exam."

"You knew about that?"

"Mako, you think I don't know what goes on under my roof? This is Chinatown, son," he laughed. "We take care of our own, and I take care of you like you are my own. College is paid for—you've worked too hard to have to worry about money."

"I can't let you do that, Mr. Yang," Mako resisted, head hung humbly.

"Mr. Mead and I are splitting the cost. This is final." Yang rose to his feet and placed his hand over Mako's heart. "Remember where you come from. We were both given names that would shame most Chinese. But not me, and certainly not you. You are not *gweilo*; you are True Chinese."

*June 25, 2010 – Master Rhee's Martial Arts Academy*

Mako kneeled on the mat with his eyes closed as he meditated his worries away. Master Rhee stood against the wall that had a large mural of Bruce Lee with Rhee's favorite quote from the famous martial artist written in large white letters on a black background: *"Real living is living for others."* The image on the mural was of Lee in his famous yellow jumpsuit with a black stripe on the arms with his hands lifted above his head, and the smile that helped Lee gain superstardom around the world. Chinese characters written in black were centered on each of the other sparsely decorated white walls. One for eternity, another for strength, and a final symbol for courage. Rhee liked to keep the focus on the mind, body, and spirit of training. On the floor of the academy were ten-foot by ten-foot, two-inch thick blue mats that were normally full of students, but Master Rhee trained Mako every day after Young's shift ended at 11 pm.

Rhee was in his mid-fifties with spiky black hair and a slightly crooked nose from his teen years. He'd been illegally kicked in the face during a tournament in the eighties and even after having his nose set by a doctor, it never looked the same. Rhee idolized Bruce Lee, and had studied with martial arts experts during his youth, but he learned to dislike the martial arts scene in the eighties, mostly because overzealous students and ignorant opponents carelessly utilized the crane kick seen in the movie *The Karate Kid.* Rhee, however, never lost his cool, as he elected to live his life in the realm of peace and balance. It was that approach that most influenced Mako Young.

Being a cop in New York City was hard work; being a *minority* cop in New York City was harder. But Mako Young had his sights set on making his dream come true. He wanted to be a cop to help others, to protect the weak as he was protected, and to advocate for those who suffered with mental health. He planned to get an associate degree in criminal justice and then start on the force.

"See your life, Mako," Master Rhee guided. "Feel your purpose in this world. Channel all the energy into your mind and see what power you hold."

As Mako concentrated on Master Rhee's words, the walls of the dojo slowly dissipated and revealed a mysterious underground world.

"What is it you see?" Rhee asked.

"I'm in a large, open area that's empty. It's dark, cold, and quiet," Mako described. "There are columns throughout the room and…I feel like someone is watching."

"Mako, wrffvbhewr rfsfbvsdbksgfh," Rhee's words distorted. "Wfbnafgjnbldgb."

"Master? Are you there?"

"Master?" two voices shouted in unison.

Jaxx came into Mako's line of sight.

"What is it, Jaxx?" The Master demanded.

"There are seven of them in New York now," Jaxx reported.

"Excellent, old friend. Carry out the plan; kill them all."

"Shouldn't we wait for all twelve, Master?"

"We're going to find one together right now, old friend."

"Master you should stay here, let me handle this for you."

"Do as I say, Jaxx."

"It shall be done, Master. I will mak—"

"Mako!" Master Rhee yelled as he shook his pupil. "Mako, say something."

Master Rhee softly set Mako's head down on the mats and ran to grab his cell phone.

"Jaxx…" he mumbled, before he passed back into the shadow world.

The Master and Jaxx exited the Fylorn inside an abandoned space in Seattle's Chinatown district. There were cardboard boxes stacked around the room, some labeled with words in Chinese and others blank. The space had been used as a shoe store the previous three years, but the owners returned to China. All the shelves were cleared of shoes and some shelves were stacked on the ground by the main entrance. The lights in the office were off, but a light in the back room was on. The Master and Jaxx creeped closer, hoping they were in the right place.

"This whole street will be lined with the pride of our people, Zhang," a young Master Rhee explained. "One day, when our children grow, this will be the legacy we leave them."

Rhee and Zhang walked into the dark room where The Master and Jaxx awaited. The Master nodded to his underling and watched as Jaxx used the butt of his gun to knock Rhee unconscious. Jaxx then lifted his gun and pointed it at Zhang.

"No. He is mine," The Master ordered. "Kill the other one."

Jaxx looked to the ground where he had just knocked Rhee out and saw a dust outline where the body should have been.

"Master, he's gone."

Mako jolted up from the mats, struggling to catch his breath. Mead kneeled next to him and put an arm around him as the Rhee paced around the room. Mako looked up at Mead, and Mead bowed his head.

"You…you were there with him?" Mako spat. "How could you leave him there to die? How could you let your friend die?"

"It's what he told me to do, Mako," Rhee confessed. "I'm sorry; you were the one he told me to protect."

"I trusted you!" Mako cried.

There, in Master Rhee's hands was a piece of paper with some writing on it:

蜂蜜酒 纽约市,3滨江. (Mead. New York City, 3 Riverside.)

"This is what your father gave me shortly after you were born, Mako. He explained I was only to open this if he died. I opened it that night and convinced your mother to get her stuff together and get out of Seattle."

"It's true, Mr. Young," Mead added.

Sorrow, anger, guilt, all flashed across Mako's face. "I'm sorry, Master." Mako rose to his feet. "It is wrong to blame you."

"Please don't apologize, Mako," Rhee said. "I wish every day that the past could be undone, but I am thankful to have you in my life; *Nǐ jiù xiàng wǒ érzi.*"

"*Shīfu, wǒ ài nǐ.*"

*October 11, 2020 – 12 AM*

The echoes of the city were still loud after a breathtaking thunderstorm rolled through. Mako Young and his partner, Charles Carroll, admired the clearing night sky as they patrolled the Upper East Side on foot. As they came upon a 24-hour Duane Reade Pharmacy and Grocery store, Carroll hastily moved toward the door.

"I think that second hot dog is catching up to me," Carroll announced. "Be right back."

Young stayed outside as the cool air left behind by the storm eased the mood of the city. As he paced up the sidewalk, he turned to see a familiar face, dressed more casually than he had ever seen.

"Officer," Thomas Rogers greeted. "Lovely evening, isn't it?"

"Yes, it sure is, Thomas," Officer Mako Young responded. "What's the good word?"

"There are six of you in the city right now, Mako," Rogers revealed.

"Does he know?"

"No, but we have to prepare him. With six of you here, *they* won't be far behind."

"You don't have to remind me, Thomas," Mako said.

"Can you come to Riverside tomorrow after your shift has ended?" Rogers asked.

"I'll be there, Thomas."

Officer Carroll returned from inside the store as Rogers walked away. "Did I miss anything?" Carroll wondered.

"Three hookers and a rabbi," Mako joked.

The pair laughed at Mako Young's quick wit, then continued up 82nd Street.

"Can I ask you something, partner?" Carroll requested.

"Anything, Chuck."

"How'd you get a name like Mako?"

"Oh God, it's not a big deal," Mako laughed. "My parents' first date was *Conan the Barbarian* back when it came out in the early eighties, and there was a Japanese actor named Mako who played a wizard in the movie. Well, my mother fell in love with the name because of the actor and my father didn't have the heart to tell her that naming a half-Chinese, half-white baby something Japanese could be problematic."

"How bad was it?"

"It was here-and-there thing; it never got bad because I grew so fast most people were afraid of me. If it wasn't for Master Rhee, I probably would have killed someone in my teens."

"Well, that wasn't nearly as bad as I imagined it being," Carroll said. "Oh, no, round two. Excuse me!"

Carroll turned back toward Duane Reade and ran down 82nd Street. Mako Young shook his head and slowly followed.

# Chapter 20 – Cooper Craven

*October 10, 2020 – Hard Rock Casino, Atlantic City, New Jersey*

The handcuffs were tight around his wrists, but he couldn't complain. It was his own fault for letting himself be restrained. Resisting wasn't an option either, as the crowd was stunned at what they saw before them. Just minutes ago, he walked back and forth, pointing at people and shouting. The crowd cheered when he was finally cuffed, and now silently gawked. His bleach-blonde hair was purposely unkempt—his preferred hairstyle—meticulously held in place by hair wax. He was clean shaven and impeccably dressed in a white dress shirt with ace of diamonds cufflinks on each arm and black pinstripe suit pants. The suit jacket was thrown on the ground in front of him. The handcuffs clanked against the cufflinks a few times, a rhythmic tone while everything else was eerily quiet. Even cuffed, a giant smile was painted his face, seemingly unafraid of his current predicament. The light blasted into his blue eyes, but he didn't look away. He just stared straight ahead. After thirty seconds, the man held his hands up in the air, waved to the crowd and crossed his hands left over right; the handcuffs fell to the ground, and he showed everyone that he was free. The crowd applauded and cheered as the music started again in the entertainment center at The Hard Rock Casino in Atlantic City, New Jersey.

Cooper Craven had worked The Hard Rock for less than a year with his assistant, Selena Craven, who also happened to be his wife. The Cravens worked dinner theaters, senior homes, and small clubs for a few years prior, while Cooper honed his craft and became even more adept at sleight of hand and other tricks. He was thirty-five years old and just reaching his stride in the world of magical performance. Selena Craven was a gorgeous young woman with a seductive pair of deep brown eyes, voluptuous body with the perfect curves, and a smile befitting a queen of the stage. She met Cooper ten years ago when he miserably failed during a show in a small New Jersey club—a night Cooper often thought about.

"Hell of a show." Cooper hugged his wife. "Did you feel that energy? That could be the best crowd we've had since we got here, Mrs. Craven."

"You had them in the palm of your hands the whole time, babe. God, that was great."

The two embraced and kissed but were interrupted by a knock at the door.

"Never fails." Cooper smirked. "Who's there?"

When no one answered, Cooper swung open the door and standing before him was an old friend wearing a black suit and white dress shirt with a black tie. His glasses hung low on his nose as he looked up at Cooper.

"Mr. Mead," a shocked Cooper said. "Please, come in."

"Thank you, Mr. Craven." Mead entered the dressing room. "Lovely to see you again, Ms.—"

"—Mrs. Craven," Cooper interrupted, holding up Selena's left hand as she smiled.

"Mrs. Craven," Mead said through a smile. "Such great news, when did this happen?"

"I'm so happy to see you, Mr. Mead." Selena hugged him. "We just did it last night, spur of the moment."

"Yeah, we figured, why not?" Cooper laughed. "We aren't getting any younger. Please, sit."

Mead lowered himself onto the dressing room's white couch and Selena joined him, seated at his left. Cooper spun a stool around and slid onto the top of it to face Mead and his new bride. The lights around the mirrors blared on Cooper's back and created shadows that danced between Mead and Selena.

"What brings you here, Mead?" Cooper questioned.

"It's time, Cooper," Mead pointedly replied.

"When?" Cooper asked.

"Rogers has started gathering everyone else. We'll meet tomorrow at Riverside. Come with me tonight—both of you."

"When do we leave?" Selena asked.

"As soon as possible," Mead responded. "There's a car outside waiting for us."

"I'll go get my things," Selena said as she stood up, kissed her husband, and left the room.

"Are you ready for this, Mr. Craven?"

"I've been ready for quite some time, old friend."

*April 15, 2010 – Club Magik, Clifton Commons, Clifton, New Jersey*

"And for my next trick, I'm going to—" Cooper began.

"—make us all disappear from this shitty show!" an audience member shouted.

Club Magik was a perfect storm of terrible for Cooper Craven on the warm April night. It was his first time performing magic for a crowd and he lucked into the gig through the owner of the club, a family friend. Every trick had failed, even the easy ones. Cooper's nervousness was evident as he sweated through his shirt in the first five minutes of the show. His deck of cards splattered the stage when he asked an audience member to pick a card because of the wetness of his hands. Cooper's doubt seeped into his mind early in the show and everything snowballed from there. The crowd was there for a magical celebrity—Ferdinando Fantoccini, the Pride of Point Pleasant as he was commonly known in entertainment. Fantoccini took his name from a Ray Bradbury story, something Fantoccini loved since college. Fantoccini was in his fifties, with a shaved head and a full beard. His beard was greying, as was the little hair that remained on his head. A tall and burly man, Fantoccini was an intimidating presence on and off the stage. His eyes, however, gave him away often to those that knew him best; they were warm blue eyes.

"Thanks…" Cooper defeatedly said through the microphone. "Appreciate the support. Enjoy Mr. Fantoccini."

Cooper abruptly exited stage left and passed Fantoccini on the way off the stage.

"Chin up, kid," Fantoccini encouraged.

As Cooper rushed down the stairs that led from backstage to the hallway, he bumped into a young woman in a short black dress that showed off every edge of her body, but Cooper couldn't take his eyes off her face. Even in the dark her smile shone, and Cooper was immediately smitten.

"It gets better," she comforted. "I promise."

"It certainly can't get worse," Cooper half-joked. "I'm Cooper."

"I know," she said. "Your name is on the marquee outside."

"Right…"

"I'm sorry you bombed out tonight. I remember his bad shows too," she said, pointing at Fantoccini.

"Are you his assistant?"

"God, no," she chuckled. "I'm his daughter, Selena."

"Nice to meet you, Selena."

The two silently watched Fantoccini's show, with the famed magician wowing the crowd with his tricks and bravado. His larger-than-life stature and persona were everything Cooper wanted for himself, and the young upstart looked on with awe. When the show ended, Fantoccini made his way off stage with Selena directing him to the steps leading to the hallway.

"You coming, kid?" Fantoccini beckoned to Cooper.

Stunned, Cooper ran down the stairs and into the hallway with the famed magician and his daughter.

*November 3, 2000 – Philadelphia Museum of Art, Philadelphia, Pennsylvania*

The young man walked along the top of the stairs at the Philadelphia Museum of Art in a red crewneck sweatshirt and black sweatpants tucked in at the ankle to a pair of black boots. His hands were softly clasped behind his back as he moved around the perimeter square of the upper landing in front of the museum. A subtle wind blew through the landing, tossing his long, dark brown hair around as it blustered through.

Across the landing were two Philadelphia police officers on patrol, both in identical police issue black leather jackets over their black uniforms. The first one whistled, twirling his hat around his black-gloved index finger, whistling melodically. He looked sturdy and strong from a distance.

"What are you doing here at this hour?" The police officer approached with his partner by his side as he placed his hat back on his head.

"Just walking and thinking, sir," the young man replied.

"What's your name, kid?" the cop pressed.

"John."

"John what?"

"Craven, sir."

"Got any I.D., kid?"

"I'm fifteen, sir."

"Seems a bit weird for a fifteen-year-old to be walking alone at this hour," the cop responded.

"I'm sorry, sir, what makes walking at night weird, exactly?"

"Plenty of places to do that other than here."

"Nobody blinked an eye when Rocky was running here at this hour," the young man quipped.

"You got jokes, I see."

"No, sir, just trying to point out that people can freely walk or run whenever they'd like."

"Oh, great," the cop lamented. "You hear this, Russ? A freedom fighter right before our eyes."

"Leave him be, Kurt," the second cop advised, pulling his partner's arm toward him. "Sorry, kid, he's just joking."

"The hell I am," Kurt swung his arm. "It's punks like this that have ruined this city. Smart-mouthed little shits who think they're better than everyone else."

"Not everyone else," John countered. "Just old men who have been doing their jobs too long, so they harass and bully random people to feel better about themselves."

"You stupid son of a bitch!" Kurt attacked, grabbing John by the hair and pulling his head down to one side.

"Jesus, Kurt, let him go!" Russ shouted.

Kurt threw the young man to the ground and turned his attention to Russ. He reached to his holster, drew his gun out, and raised it at his partner.

"What are you doing, Kurt?"

"Whatever I have to," Kurt responded, cracking his neck from side to side.

Kurt stalked over to the young man and grabbed his hair again. He dragged John toward the top of the stairs and started punching him in the face. The force of one of the punches cut open John's left eye, and blood started seeping between his eyelids as his head hung sideways. Kurt placed John's head on the edge of the landing before the first step and prepared to stomp his head against the pavement with his black boots when Russ quickly pressed his two-way walkie talkie on his shoulder to call for help.

"Dispatch, code 20, code 20, officer needs assistance. I'm on the upper land—"

Kurt pulled the trigger four times, hitting Russ four times in the chest. His partner fell to the ground and took a few short breaths before he died on the landing.

"Nothing quite like spilling a little blood," Kurt laughed. "Your turn, boy."

Kurt's body began to turn to ash. The outer layer of his skin blew away in the early morning winds, as Jaxx arrived on the landing of the Museum of Art. He breathed in the cold air as deeply as he could and then turned to a nearly unconscious John.

"Time for you to die, Remain."

Jaxx spread his legs as he towered over John's weakened body at the top of the landing. Jaxx's feet were to the side of each of John's shoulders and he pointed his gun to the back of John's head.

"Please…don't…" John begged. "I'll do anything…please."

"You're already doing something," Jaxx coldly replied as he pulled the trigger, instantly killing John.

Jaxx leaned down and placed the gun next to John. He wiped his right hand in the pool of blood and lifted his fingers to his mouth to taste it. He paused only for a second before backing up, as The Fylorn spun in the center of the landing.

*November 3, 2010 – Club Magik, Clifton Commons, Clifton, New Jersey*

The club was empty in the early afternoon, but Cooper was already inside the venue sitting at one of the dark cherry wooden tables with a white coffee cup in front of him, half-filled with black coffee. Selena was seated across from him. Cooper's mind was elsewhere, but Selena brought him back to the moment when she reached toward him and massaged the top of his hand with hers.

"What's wrong, Cooper?" she asked. "This is your night! My father says you're more than ready. You've done a lot of hard work with him."

"I know, it's just a rough day today."

"Why, babe?"

"I've…never told this to anyone, so you have to promise you'll never tell *anyone*, not even your father."

"I promise, babe. Talk to me."

"Ten years ago, today, my twin brother was killed," Cooper started. "He was out walking around Philly and he and a cop ended up dead."

"I am so, so sorry," Selena consoled.

"There's more; it won't be easy to understand, because I still don't understand it myself."

"Try your best, sweetheart. I will do my best to understand."

"There's a high possibility I'll be dead before I'm thirty. It goes back so many generations and something that happened thousands of years ago will be the death of me. I can't run from it. I don't even know how I've avoided death this long."

"I know how you've managed," Ferdinando Fantoccini interrupted. "It was me."

"Dad?" Selena shouted. "What the hell?"

"I'm sorry, Lena, I should have told you sooner, but I was sworn to secrecy. Telling anyone could have put you and Cooper in danger."

"What's going on here, Mr. Fantoccini?" Cooper demanded.

Fantoccini was dressed in a tuxedo with his bow tie untied and dangling around his collar. He sat himself at the table to Cooper's right and his daughter's left. He folded his hands together and leaned into the table, softly speaking to the two.

"Years ago, after your parents died, I was approached after a show and told that the magic I *didn't* use was the real power I held."

"You mean to say that the magic we do…it's real?"

"Yes, Cooper," Fantoccini nodded, "this man explained to me that magic was real, and that my gift could save lives. He asked me to use an old spell to protect a baby from harm. Because of the power of the spell, I could only perform it on one of the two twin boys. I agreed to help but didn't realize or understand at the time how much magical energy would be used to complete the spell. After it was over, I was drained for weeks—but the baby was safe."

"It was Mead, wasn't it?" Cooper rhetorically asked. "I know he has to be the one who approached you."

"We had a terrible choice to make—protect one of the boys and know that the other would be hunted and killed. We did all we could. We shielded you from *them*. We couldn't save you both and for that I am truly sorry."

"Don't be sorry, Mr. Fantoccini. You saved my life, didn't you?"

"Yes, I suppose I did, Cooper."

"So, you know who I am? *What* I am?" Cooper asked.

"Your secret is safe with me, Cooper."

"Can someone please tell me what is happening?" Selena interrupted.

Fantoccini looked back and forth between Cooper and his daughter until Cooper nodded affirmatively.

"Come on, Lena." Fantoccini motioned for her to join him. "Let me buy you a drink so Cooper can get ready for the show."

# Chapter 21 – Rayna



*2007 – Belleville, New Jersey*

The speed limit on Joralemon Avenue was posted as thirty miles per hour, but the red Porsche 944 whizzed past the crosswalk and through the red light at closer to seventy. The driver was unbothered by the motorcade of police cars that followed as the sounds of sirens filled the small town like a symphony. People lined the streets to catch a glimpse of the chase, and as they did, they witnessed cops from four neighboring towns and cities join in. Newark, Nutley, Bloomfield, and Verona cops all followed the speeding car as it barreled toward Route 3 and New York City's Lincoln Tunnel.

As the car entered the four-lane highway that led toward the tunnel, one cop pulled alongside the driver's side of the vehicle and was met by an unexpected sight—a young girl, no more than twelve or thirteen years old behind the wheel. The girl looked to the police car, smiled and waved at the cop, and placed her foot down harder on the gas pedal, heading to the shoulder of the road to bypass the traffic and attempt to escape the caravan of police.

The car was abandoned in the center of the Lincoln Tunnel ten minutes later. As news of the chase was carried by the television stations in New York, Rayna was unsurprised to see Mead waiting for her outside of 3 Riverside Drive when she returned.

"Shit," she mumbled to herself.

"Indeed," Mead agreed.

"I forgot you hear everything," Rayna conceded.

"Rayna, I'll only say this once…" Mead started.

"Let me guess, the behavior has to stop, am I right?" she interrupted.

"No, I was just going to say be careful you don't hit anyone." Mead smiled.

"You're…not mad?"

"I understand your need for rebellion, young lady. I was your age once, too. Just be careful, promise?"

"I promise."

Rayna hugged Mead and ran back inside as Rogers approached the house. "What was that all about?" he asked.

"Just making sure that she stays safe," Mead responded.

"She's become quite wild."

"We were all wild once, Thomas."

"Hard to believe that we were, my friend. I have to go across the river to Passaic, do you need anything?"

"No, thank you."

"I should be back in a couple of hours if there isn't much traffic," Rogers stated. "I'll just grab my car keys."

"Eh, Thomas…about your car…maybe you should come inside." Mead motioned toward the front door.

*Three Days Ago – Barrière d'Enfer (Gates of Hell), Paris, France, 10 am*

"What do you mean I can't go in?" Rayna snapped.

"I am sorry, young lady. The gates are closed for the rest of the week," the guard explained.

"I have to get in there," Rayna pleaded.

"Unless you're the President of France, which you are clearly not, you cannot enter."

Rayna stared at the guard for a moment before reaching into the pocket of her grey Adidas track pants. The guard moved his hand slowly to his holstered weapon.

"You're kidding, right?" Rayna insisted.

"I am sorry, miss, but it's time you go."

Rayna didn't heed the warnings of the guard and pulled out a wad of cash, held together by a rubber band.

"How's 5,000 Euros sound?"

"It sounds like I need to check for a noise I heard…over there." The guard pointed, turning his head far away from the door.

Rayna handed him the money and the guard walked away for a quick moment.

Rayna entered the catacombs and into the vast metropolis of the dead.

What few people knew about the Catacombs of Paris was that the underground home to over seven million people was constructed with more than one purpose.

While the world believed the catacombs existed to rid Paris of an eternal stench during the eighteenth century, to the educated and trained mind and eye, respectively, the tunnels opened a door to history. Napoleon knew that when he made it a tourist attraction. He hoped by enticing the adventurous they would do the hard work and find the long-rumored remains of Merlin. Merlin's skeleton would bring Napoleon a great fortune and cement his place in history. However, when he grew closer to the truth of Merlin's whereabouts, the universe planted thoughts of war into his mind, and Napoleon refocused his efforts into the failed invasion of Russia.

Rayna found herself surrounded by the carefully designed walls of the catacombs—bones and skulls of the dead from floor to ceiling. She scoured the skulls and scanned the walls as if she was looking for a library book, and then she came upon it.

On a curved path, Rayna found a skull with a small red *N* carved into the base. She knew Napoleon had been at this exact spot centuries ago and marked the skull to make it easier to find when he returned. After his failure and subsequent exile, the diminutive leader never made it back to the Catacombs of Paris. Rayna closed her eyes and stuck her index and middle finger into the eyes of the skull directly next to the marked one and pulled. The mouth on the skull dropped and quickly closed again and Rayna waited for what seemed like an eternity before the wall started to move. It slid backwards just enough for Rayna to squeeze through the opening and pushed back out as soon as she was through.

The area was surprisingly well-lit and ventilated, but the tunnel Rayna had just stumbled upon seemed to stretch forever. When she came to a wooden sign, the rein of a horse was still tied to the marker, with the bones of the horse scattered on the ground below it. Rayna leaned down to examine the bones and found a small piece of paper with them.

"Clearly, he meant to come back," Rayna said out loud to herself.

Rayna rose to her feet and opened the paper. *Brocéliande.*

The nearly five-hour drive from Paris to *Ille-et-Vilaine* relaxed Rayna's racing thoughts after leaving the Catacombs. Rayna had investigated a number of places in Europe for the better part of two years, hoping to find any hint of Merlin's existence. The young woman had spent an even greater amount of time learning all she could about the mythological magician's life and apparent death. *Brocéliande* was the mythical name given to Paimpont Forest in *Ille-et-Vilaine*, a place Rayna had searched her first days in Europe in 2018 and come up empty.

"What changed between 2018 and now?" she wondered aloud.

Rayna went to check her phone but remembered she'd lost it three weeks ago in Brussels. She hadn't spoken to anyone in that time and remained unaware of everything in New York City. Her one saving grace was the rental car had a GPS, so she didn't have to read a map. With nothing but time to spare, Rayna thought about Mead and Rogers.

*December 8, 2012 – Rockefeller Plaza, New York City*

Rayna's birthday tradition was to go ice skating every year with her friends and take a picture by the giant Christmas tree with Rogers and Mead. It was silly to her when she was in her rebellious phase, but she never missed the chance to take that picture. And now that she neared adulthood, the tradition—no matter how silly—was something she looked forward to all year. The only parents she'd ever known as a young woman were the two men that had raised her at 3 Riverside Drive. After the camera flash blinded the three companions, Rayna took her camera back from the stranger that offered to take their traditional picture. Rayna looked at the pictures and smiled.

"Thank you so much!" Rayna exclaimed.

"You're welcome," the woman said. "They make a cute couple."

"Oh, they're not... Yes, yes they do," Rayna said.

"Merry Christmas to you!" the woman shouted.

"To you, too!"

A sea of people crowded around the tree as it illuminated the plaza in multi-colored lights. Rayna joined them, her arm hooked in Rogers'.

"Thanks," she beamed.

Rogers smiled down at Rayna as Mead caught up to them.

"A cute couple, eh?" Mead joked.

"You really do hear everything," Rayna laughed. "Come on, let's go have cake."

The night air was warmer than usual for December in New York, with the temperature approaching fifty degrees, prompting the trio to walk back to Riverside from the plaza. The two-mile walk would take about forty minutes if they cut across the side of Central Park, which is what they planned.

On the southwest side, they passed behind Columbus Circle, and

Mead's disgust for the famed adventurer couldn't be contained.

"Columbus, what a disgraceful human being," Mead yelled, drawing attention from some other New Yorkers.

"Tell me how you really feel, geez," Rayna said.

"I'm sorry, I just do not like that man."

Rayna detoured them through Columbus Circle and down 60th Street. They headed north on 11th Avenue until they hit 72nd Street, where they turned west toward the Hudson River and home. Rayna stopped momentarily to take her sneaker off and bang a pebble out of it onto the sidewalk. Mead and Rogers strolled ahead, knowing she'd catch up to them. As Rayna put her sneaker back on, when suddenly she felt a hand grab her side.

"Hey, mama," the voice whispered in her ear.

Rayna heard other voices in the noisy city background, but her fear made it impossible to decipher what they were saying. She could only smell his cologne, which sickened her. She felt the hot breath of the man as he rubbed up against her in a most vile way.

"What's a pretty little thaaaang like you doin' out all by yourself?" he groaned.

Rayna shoved the hand off her waist and turned around to confront the person. "Look, dickhead, leave me alone."

The man and his friends looked like carbon copies of each other. The six white males each had on something preppy and expensive. They all had blonde hair, light eyes and each of them wore stonewashed jeans with button-down shirts or V-neck sweaters. They quickly grabbed Rayna into a secluded, wooded area of the park.

"Aww, come on, baby, six for the price of one," he snarled.

Rayna reeled her hand back to slap the man, but he grabbed her wrist with his giant hand and squeezed with all his strength. Rayna crumbled in pain, and the man continued his assault.

"If you think that hurts, just wait until we're done with you," he hissed into her ear.

Rayna opened her mouth to scream, the man punched her in the face, only his grip keeping her from falling to the ground. Two of his friends held her arms behind her back. Rayna spit the pooled blood from her mouth in the man's face.

"You'll pay for that, bitch."

"Fuck you," Rayna responded.

"No. Fuck *you*," the man threatened.

"I think the young lady was right," Mead emerged from behind a tree, his senior citizen stature no threat to the group of attackers.

"Go away, old man," the attacker ordered.

"It's time for you to go," Mead said calmly, "before something bad happens to you and your friends."

"What are you gonna do about it, gramps?"

The leader of the group of men turned his focus to Mead. The two men restraining Rayna laughed, pulling her closer to them—until they were hoisted in the air by Rogers, who grabbed them from behind and lifted them each at least one foot off the ground—enough for them to loosen their grips on Rayna.

"I think you mean what are *we* going to do about it," Rogers barked.

Mead grabbed the ringleader by his shirt and slowly lifted him off the ground. As the assailant's feet kicked in the air, the three other would-be attackers standing by turned tail to run, just as the newest member of the New York Police Department stepped into their sight.

"Help us!" one of them shouted.

"They're attacking us!" the other stammered, pointing.

Mako Young stepped into the streetlight and blocked their path.

"Now why do I feel like that's a lie?" Mako remarked.

Mead tossed the lead attacker, who crashed into a tree and slammed onto the ground, as Rogers and Mako pummeled Rayna's attackers. Mead rushed to Rayna's side and pulled her close to him to protect her while Rogers came to their side. Mako pulled the lead attacker to his feet.

"And what should we do with this one?" Officer Young asked.

"I'd say you just made your first arrest," Rogers answered.

"Okay, get out of here, I've got this," Young directed. "Central this is Officer Mako Young on the eastern edge of Central Park with six men incapacitated and ready for pick up. Requesting backup."

"Copy. Backup dispatched to your location."

"No," Rayna demanded. "It's not that easy."

She walked over to her assailant. She stared him up and down, debating internally what to do as he shook. Every fiber of Rayna's being wanted to kill this man for what he did, for what he planned to and probably had done before. Rogers and Mead sensed it. Each man put a hand on one of Rayna's shoulders.

"I know what you want to do," Mead reasoned. "And you'd have every right to kill him right now; but you would never be the same."

"He's right, Rayna," Rogers added. "Let's go home and clean you up and have that cake."

Rayna pondered their words for a few moments as the lead attacker squirmed in Mako's grasp. She looked at Mako and tilted her head down to his left side. He followed her eyes down and laughed before he took his taser out and handed it to her. Rayna took a few steps back as Young tightened his grip on the assailant.

"Just aim and fire it like you see in the movies," Young instructed.

"You're hurting me," the man whined.

"If you think that hurts, just wait until we're done with you," Rayna mocked.

She fired the taser at the man's crotch and watched him writhe before handing Mako Young back his taser.

"Thank you, Officer," Rayna said over her shoulder as she walked away.

Mead and Rogers each hooked an arm of Rayna's as they finished their way home. As they got to the front of 3 Riverside Drive, Rayna stopped them outside the front door.

"Thanks, Dad—and Dad—for saving my life."

"I'll never get used to that," Mead said.

"I know the feeling," Rogers added.

"Also, whatever it is you haven't told me all these years, that can be my birthday gift," Rayna insisted. "I saw what happened tonight. There's no way either of you should be able to toss people around like that. No use in trying to deny whatever you're hiding."

Rogers and Mead nodded to each other in agreement.

"Okay," Rogers whispered. "But let's get inside."

Rayna gave Rogers a kiss on the cheek as he opened the front door and entered the house. As Mead followed, Rayna grabbed his arm and extended a kiss to his cheek as well. The kind warmth in his eyes made Rayna start to cry, her emotions flooding out.

"You really do hear everything," she said.

*Three Days Ago – Forêt de Paimpont (Paimpont Forest – also known as Brocéliande) Ille-et-Vilaine, Brittany*

Rayna climbed out of the car and readied herself to enter the forest's northwest portion. She remembered bits of her previous visit and hoped that would be enough to guide her back to Merlin's supposed burial site. When she had first visited two years earlier, she never found Merlin's

Tomb, but in that time, she learned of other mystical sites in the forest, specifically *Fontaine de Barenton*—the Fountain of Barenton. Rayna was so focused on Merlin's whereabouts her first visit to France she overlooked how the forest all connected to the history she was now living. The fountain, the oak tree where Merlin first met Viviane, and the *Val sans Retour*—the famed Vale of No Return, all were within the area of the forest, and all held significance in the history of the lives of the Britons. The water from Barenton, however, was what Rayna needed to open Merlin's Tomb. Just a few drops of that water would be powerful enough to give her access to the ancient wizard.

Rayna advanced toward the fountain with an empty plastic water bottle in her hand. The path was flat and wide, but as she drew closer to her destination, the path began to wind around. Tree roots seemed to crawl out of the ground and grab at her feet while red mushrooms grew out of the ground around the trees. The trees were all but bare, as autumn had shed the leaves in the forest. Rayna delicately moved on the path, careful not to lose her way. The sun slowly creeped toward the ground as Rayna rushed to maximize daylight in the forest. Without a phone, the clunky flashlight in the other hand would be her only guide when night absorbed the area.

Through the trees, in a barely cleared nook of the woods, a circlet of grey rocks emerged. "The Fountain of Barenton," Rayna whispered, and Rayna glided toward the stones. From a distance, the fountain appeared to be heart shaped with a crack at the bottom. This is where Merlin had met, fallen in love with, and taught Vivian the deep magic. Rayna envisioned two young lovers in the forest, their immense love bursting with magic and mysticism as the world was so innocent and free. Rayna knew this was sacred ground for so many reasons. She could feel the past around her, as if the wind whispered in these woods to whoever visited them.

Rayna bent down at the opening of the fountain and submerged the whole bottle into the water. She returned to her feet, twisted the cap back on the bottle and prepared to walk back toward the path she had taken to get to the fountain. Before she hiked away, a few droplets from the bottle fell onto a slab of stone situated to side of the fountain.

The skies immediately darkened. The downpour happened before Rayna had time to react, and she sprinted as fast as she could back to the car and the thunder rolled and the sky lit up with bolts of lightning. Drenched, shaking with the sudden chill of rain, Rayna started the car and sped away east, to Merlin's Tomb.

*****

In the twenty minutes it took for Rayna to get to the other side of the forest, the storm had ended, and the sky returned to its intertwined pink and purple hue. Rayna, however, was soaked and angry as she got out of the car again. Despite the raging storm, Rayna's feet didn't sink into the ground with each step. Whatever this forest protected, Rayna knew she had found something special. All the searching and struggle finally paid off. Rayna arrived at a small, dark wooden fence that encircled the perimeter of Merlin's Tomb. The site itself was two large boulders that barely pressed against each other and a circle of rocks on the outside of the mound where the boulders stood. As Rayna twisted the cap off the plastic bottle to pour the magical water over the grave, the roar of a lion echoed throughout the forest, making Rayna gasp and stumble. She fell to her butt and when she looked up, a lion stood in front of her.

"Do not spill that water on the grave," the voice instructed. "It will not bring him back."

"How do you know this?"

"Because others have tried and failed. You have spilled water onto Merlin's Step and summoned me. Turn, young warrior, and face me...or take you can take your chances with the lion."

Rayna slowly spun herself and into her view came a knight dressed in black armor. His sword was drawn, and he held it up parallel to his arm and glided it slowly toward Rayna's throat. Unarmed and afraid of something for the first time in a while, Rayna raised her arms in surrender.

"You scavengers are all the same," the man in black lectured. "You come here to this place seeking only to take that which is not yours."

"I've taken noth—"

"You have stolen water from Barenton!"

"I can explain," Rayna insisted.

The knight relaxed the sword and slammed it down into the grass. He slowly removed the helmet and revealed himself.

"I have heard many explanations from travelers through the years, young lady. There is nothing you can say to convince me to let you leave here with that bottle."

Rayna took a deep breath and closed her eyes.
"I know who you are, Yvain."

# Chapter 22 - Anna

*February 12, 2006 – Social Services, Las Vegas, Nevada*

Less than five miles away from the noise and hustle of the Las Vegas Strip, Emory Gallagher sat in his office at Social Services. He was in his late fifties, wearing a yellow, short-sleeved button-down shirt with blue dress pants and a brown belt. He wore brown shoes and, rather unfashionably, white socks. He looked across his desk to the silent little girl seated in front of him. Dirt covered the little girl's face, except for under her eyes to her chin, where her tears had cleaned her skin. She had on a tank top with a glitter unicorn in the middle of shirt, a pair of pink shorts, and was barefoot. Her clothes were covered in the filth of the streets and on the corners of her mouth were crusted bits of garbage she had eaten overnight.

Emory had been a social worker for thirty-five years, and his office walls were adorned with framed pictures of happy people he'd helped throughout his decades of service. The little girl had been in Emory's office for almost an hour and refused to speak. Instead of pressing her to talk, Emory went on about his work, making phone calls and answering emails as the child stared at the unopened McDonald's Cheeseburger Happy Meal on the edge of Emory's slate-grey desk. The desk was covered in paper and clutter, Emory's personal brand of organization.

"No, Bob, I haven't had lunch yet," Emory said into the phone as he shuffled some papers, "but I have a Happy Meal right here."

Emory reached over his stacks of clutter and to the golden arch handles of the Happy Meal.

"No!" Anna jumped up from her chair.

"Bob, I'll call you later." Emory placed the phone back on the receiver. "So…you *can* talk."

"Yeah," Anna sheepishly replied.

"Go on and eat, Susie."

"Hey, that's not my name!" Anna yelled.

"Hmmm…Charlotte?"

"Nope," Anna grinned as she chomped on her French fries.

"I know," Emory clapped. "Your name is Cinderella!"

"No," the girl laughed. "Anna."

"Banana? What kind of name is that?"

"Anna, silly."

"Ohhhh…Anna; I'm Emory."

"Hi, Emory." Anna smiled at the man with one front tooth missing and another just coming in.

"Anna, can you tell me where your parents are?"

"Miss Gina says they're in Heaven."

"And who is Miss Gina?"

"She takes care of me." Anna devoured her cheeseburger in three bites.

"Where does Miss Gina live?"

"I don't know," Anna shrugged. "Can I keep the prize?"

"Of course you can," Emory answered. "Anna, I have a very important question for you, now. Don't be afraid to answer me, okay?"

"Okay," Anna agreed.

"Does Miss Gina bring you Happy Meals?"

Anna stopped eating her fries and drooped her chin into her chest.

"Anna?"

"No…" she meekly replied. "Miss Gina doesn't have food for me."

"Explains why you were eating out of the dumpster," Emory mumbled.

Emory jotted things down on a notepad and placed the pad back on his desk. He leaned back in his chair as Anna finished the last of her food. Emory raised his arms above his head and pulled himself forward with a giant breath.

"Are you going to send me back to Miss Gina's?" Anna said meekly.

"No, Anna. You won't ever be going back to Miss Gina again."

*March 15, 2013 – Penn Station, New York City*

Tucked underneath Madison Square Garden in Manhattan, thousands of commuters briskly moved through the concourse of Pennsylvania Station. The air in Penn Station always felt different, even to New Yorkers. For a fresh-faced thirteen-year-old runaway from the West Coast—even one from Las Vegas—New York's Penn Station was an intimidating structure, despite being buried underground. Twenty-one tracks hosted over half-a-million travelers daily. Penn Station acts as the epicenter of the Northern Corridor, connecting New York to all the major cities of the Northeast: Boston, Philadelphia, and Washington D.C.

Anna stepped off the Amtrak train on track fifteen with nothing more than the bright red backpack over her shoulder. She followed the throng of people that headed to the stairs to the concourse. Nothing prepared Anna for the incredible noise of the main concourse. Hundreds of people stood and stared at the departure board hanging in the center of the concourse; others ran past Anna as they attempted to get to departing trains on time. Anna's face was hidden under the hat on her head, a solid black hat with a Velcro band on the back. She had on an oversized hooded sweatshirt and her jeans were three sizes too big— clothes she stole from her latest foster home when she left. Earphones in, she strode past the restaurants and shops to the escalators at the exit to 7th Avenue and 33rd Street. Armed National Guardsmen and NYPD patrolled the station, the Guardsmen a security measure put in place after the events of 9/11. Scared and a tinge excited, Anna grabbed hold of the escalator railing and was lifted into New York City.

In that first moment when the streets of New York came into her sight, Anna froze with amazement. And with the change in temperature from the warmth of Penn Station to the biting cold of blustery New York, she froze another minute longer.

"Move," an agitated man shouted.

"Sorry!" Anna yelled back.

Anna didn't know where to go from the spot she currently stood, but she knew she couldn't stand in the middle of the gigantic sidewalk any longer. She decided to go left, which carried her into the craziness of Times Square and Pedestrian Plaza. She found her way to a bistro table and sat, throwing her backpack onto the table and rummaged through it to find the bag of potato chips she purchased on the train. Anna decided one chip at a time was all she would allow herself. She unraveled the bag, pulled out one chip, and repacked her backpack. Anna briefly admired her dinner as the little bit of sunlight that had escorted her to Times Square vanished into the night and gave way to cold, whipping winds. Anna raised her hood over her hat and head and devoured the chip. Turning up the volume up on her music, she walked out of Pedestrian Plaza with no idea where she was headed.

Anna wandered the city for hours, as it bustled with people coming and going to and from Broadway, restaurants, bars, and other sights. She may have been in the city that never sleeps, but Anna was exhausted with nowhere to spend the night. The young runaway was cold, sad, and desperate—but most of all she was alone. The farther she got from Times Square, the less secure she felt; solitude had always brought back into her mind the abuse she suffered at Miss Gina's, but this loneliness was necessary for her survival after the hell she escaped days ago.

She found a secluded alleyway and leaned against a wall, using a broken box crate as a nightstand for her backpack. Her eyes closed as a quiet whisper hummed through the alleyway.

*2 Days Ago – Chicago, Illinois*

It had been two years since Anna had arrived in Chicago—a visit that started at her mother's cousin's house and ended back in the system, until she was ultimately placed in the Popp house. Frank and Ashley Popp were wealthy, respected in the community, and good to Anna. She finally started to put behind her the hell of Miss Gina and Las Vegas as she acclimated to the Windy City. Their biological son, Patrick, was three years older than Anna. He was a high school hero; an All-State quarterback with Division I promise and a "cannon" right arm. Patrick Popp's flowing blonde hair was always pulled back under a headband. Patrick was six foot, five inches of solid muscle, with warm blue eyes and a smile that sent young classmates into a frenzy. His late grandmother would tell him all the time when he was younger that he was chiseled by the gods. He loved his parents very much but disagreed with their decision to invite Anna to live with them. He still showed her flashes of kindness when the mood struck him, though.

The walls of Anna's bedroom were bright white and ten feet high, reaching to a ceiling designed with swirls and a lighted fan hanged hanging from the center, slowly circulating air around the room. The queen bed was piled with three pillows all her own, and a voluminous grey comforter. A stuffed elephant sat at the foot of the bed. Anna lived comfortably at the Popps over the past two years, and her bedroom was a large reason why. Across the room from her bed was her closet, which was almost always open. Anna despised closed closet doors, as Miss Gina used to lock her in a closet for days at a time when she complained about not being fed. Some of Patrick's old clothes were still folded on the floor of the closet; a hooded sweatshirt, football jerseys, and a box of his things from when Anna's bedroom was his trophy room. The window to the left of her bed on the other side of the nightstand faced the street, with a big tree whose branches stretched close to the house. Under the window, fifteen feet down, a row of bushes lined the house and around a bay window on the ground floor. A charger cube was plugged in next to the whitewashed wooden nightstand, but the cord wasn't attached. The lamp that normally stood on the table was smashed into pieces on the floor, its heavy, metallic base dented. The mirror Anna used each morning before school was completely shattered, and giant shards of glass sprawled across the bedroom floor.

Anna kneeled in the center of the room as she looked down at her hands, wide-eyed and terrified. Everything happened too quickly to recount the details. She coughed hard as she reached up to her neck and unraveled the charger cord from her throat and breathed as deep as she could. The lightheadedness subsided and the floor came into Anna's focus.

Patrick's lifeless body was crumpled on the carpet in front of her. The dented lamp base was covered in blood; the same crimson that poured from Patrick's cranium.

Patrick had been suspended from school earlier in the day and been sent home. He slapped another student across the face when the student made a crude remark about Patrick's girlfriend. Alone all afternoon at home, Patrick decided to drink his worries away, consuming half a dozen beers in a little under an hour, and he ended up in Anna's room, digging through his forgotten things in the closet. Little by little Patrick relived his years of accomplishments, while anger grew inside him. Sitting at the opening of the closet, he looked around the room, until he focused his ire on Anna. He punched her mirror and slammed it to ground, shards flying around the room. Patrick was too drunk to hear Anna when she came in.

"Patrick, what are you doing?"

"You…" He jumped to his feet, blood oozing from his hand. "This is all your fault."

He took long strides toward his foster sister and twisted the front of

Anna's shirt in his bloodied hand.

"Patrick, you're bleeding, what the hell? Get your hands off me."

"From the day you got here, everything changed," he frothed. "My life, my room, this family. You ruined *everything*."

"You're hurting me, Patrick!" she cried. "Please, let me go."

Patrick shoved his hand against Anna's chest, and she stumbled backward, falling onto her backside. He paced around the side of the bed, hitting himself in the head repeatedly to calm himself down. Anna carefully stood up and backed herself away from Patrick, quaking with fear, but Patrick crossed the room, grabbed her by the hair and dragged her back to the middle of the room.

"This isn't over, you little shit."

"Please…please, leave me alone," Anna begged. "You're drunk."

"You don't belong here, Nava-HOE," he taunted. "This is *my* room, *my* house; go back to hell where you came from."

Anna wildly swung her fists as Patrick laughed, until her left hand connected with his groin. Patrick fell to his knees from the forceful blow and grabbed at this crotch. Anna quickly moved to grab her phone off the ground, but Patrick recovered, and before Anna dialed 9-1-1, Patrick took her phone and smashed it against a wall. Then he reached for the first thing he could get his hands on—a charger cord—and pulled it from the cube on the wall. He punched Anna in the back of the head— a punch that knocked her forward against the side of her bed. And then from behind, he wrapped the cord around her neck and started to pull back. Anna's left hand was caught between the cord and her neck, giving her just enough space to sneak some breaths before Patrick noticed. He moved closer to her and put his head on her left side.

"They won't even miss you, Pocahontas."

Patrick yanked Anna's left arm down, removing the barrier she had built between the cord and her neck. Anna felt for the lamp on the nightstand, while Patrick was distracted by her left arm. He squeezed his hands together as Anna's focus of the room blurred little by little. Gasping for whatever air she could, Anna inched her neck to Patrick's hand and bit down with all the strength she could muster. Patrick screamed in agony as Anna turned, raised the lamp and brought it down against the side of his face. The metal base cracked Patrick's jaw in two places and forced him to his knees. As he tried to speak, Anna raised the lamp a second time and brought it down on the back of Patrick's head. The impact crushed his skull and caved in a portion of his head. Anna dropped the lamp at her feet.

Anna panicked; she knew nobody would ever believe that Patrick, the hero, the heartthrob, could ever do what he just did to her. She ran to the closet, took her bloodied shirt off, slung it over her shoulder, and reached down for the red hooded sweatshirt. She leaped over Patrick's body and grabbed her backpack off the ground. She opened it and shoved in the bloody shirt and then pulled the hooded sweatshirt over her head. She ran to the stairs but heard someone opening the garage door. As quietly as she could, Anna raced back to her room and opened her window. She crawled through the opening and steadied herself on the roof of the house. She softly lowered herself as best she could, dropping into the bushes below.

Anna heard the gasps, and then screams of Ashley Popp.

Frightened, Anna sprinted up the street with only one thought in mind—get the hell out of Chicago.

When she arrived at Union Station, Anna pushed through the Canal Street Entrance on the South Side to the group of thirty-two stairs— five of them at the top made of grey Tennessee marble, and the remaining twenty-seven stairs made of cream-colored Italian travertine. There were two landings between the twenty-seven lower-level stairs, but Anna didn't care about the colors or count of steps. She rushed into the Great Hall of Union Station and heard an announcement over the speaker:

*"Last call for Amtrak Passengers traveling to New York's Pennsylvania Station, Gate A. New York's Pennsylvania Station, Gate A."*

Anna hustled to Gate A, slipped past the ticket agent, and hopped aboard the train. She immediately turned left and found herself in business class, a place she could not blend in. The train started its exit from Union Station and Anna's paranoia was apparent. An older woman in brown and black from head to toe noticed Anna from the back row in business class, noticed Anna's wide eyes and quickened breath as the ticket taker headed through the dining car. The woman smiled at Anna and motioned for her to come to the back row. Her face was subtly wrinkled, and the bright lipstick she wore nearly matched Anna's hooded sweatshirt.

"Nobody is sitting there but they forgot to collect the tag," she whispered. "Sit down and shut up."

Anna hastily complied without asking any questions.

"Close your eyes, dear," the woman advised.

The ticket taker walked into business class and glared at Anna, who was curled into the fetal position with her backpack between her legs. He approached the back row of business class.

"Sir," the woman beckoned. "My granddaughter fell asleep before Chicago and missed the chance to go and get me aspirin for my headache. Do you happen to have any?"

"Yes, ma'am, I do." He smiled as he reached into his jacket's interior breast pocket and pulled out some aspirin. "How many would you like?"

"Four would be great if you can spare them," she stated.

"Here you are, ma'am."

"Thank you, sir; very kind of you."

"You're welcome, ma'am. If you need anything else, let me know."

"Can my granddaughter get one of those free waters for business class passengers?"

"Of course, ma'am," he said, signaling to the dining car attendant to bring a water.

The dining car attendant brought over a cold bottled water with a napkin under it and handed it to the ticket taker. The ticket taker rotated back to the old woman and gave her the drink.

"Thank you, sweetheart."

The man smiled, turned, and moved back through the dining car and toward the coach class cars. Anna peeked through one eye and then sat up in her chair.

"These are for you," the older woman handed Anna the aspirin. "Should help with that swelling. Two now, two later."

Anna extended her hand, and the old woman dropped the caplets. The old woman untwisted the cap on the water bottle and handed it to Anna. The young girl opened her mouth and tossed two of the aspirin in and then chugged half the water from the bottle.

"Take this, too." The old woman removed her warm brown shawl and handed it to Anna. "It will cover the bruises."

"Thank you," Anna hoarsely replied. "Why are you helping me?"

"My dear, you look awful. You needed the help, or you'd have been off this train before we started moving. Lucky for you, they change crews in Chicago. What's your name?"

"Anna," she answered.

"Where are you traveling to?"

"Wherever this train ends."

"And what brought you here today, Anna? Why are you on this

train?”

"It's a long story."

"Well, if we are truly going to New York, we have nothing but time to kill."

Anna froze when she heard that last word and the old woman sensed the worry.

"You're safe with me," she comforted, patting Anna's hand. "But a word of advice—until you are wherever you're going, your name is not your name, young lady."

Anna nodded in agreement and turned her body sideways to face the old woman.

"Now, young lady," the old woman insisted. "Tell me everything."

*March 16, 2013*

Anna's body ached when she woke up against the cold wall. She gathered her bearings and stretched what she could as morning crept into the sky. When she fully opened her eyes, an old man with an umbrella entered the alleyway. Anna snatched up her bag and jumped to her feet, startled by the appearance.

"Anna," he calmly began, reaching out his right hand. "You're safe now."

# Chapter 23 - Jabberwocky

"Save the world?" Allen laughed. "No, thanks. Not my thing."

"Mr. White, you have to under—"

"With all due respect, Mr. Mead, I don't have to do anything. You bring me here, go all Jarvis on me, and my teacher is telling me he let my parents die. By all means, tell me what I *have* to do. I think I'm good on whatever it is you're selling; and if you say the words 'destiny' or 'prophecy', I will burn this house to the ground."

"I hate to stop the party," Anna said, "but it would seem we haven't yet covered the one thing we should."

"What's that?" Allen asked.

"Can you fight? Have you ever held a weapon in your hands?"

"My father taught me how to shoot when I was younger…" Allen shrugged.

"How about an actual fistfight? Ever been in one of those?"

"No," Allen admitted.

"Have you ever punched anyone? Have you ever hurt anyone? Have you done anything to prepare for what's ahead?"

"No," Allen replied.

"This is no game, Allen. You didn't stumble into this world by accident. You were marked; you better start preparing for what's ahead."

"Anna, that's enough," Kay scolded. "You've known this world your whole life. He's known about this world for a week, cut him some slack."

"Some slack, Kay? We are out of time. He's had no training, we have no magic, we're short an army, and we don't know where we are supposed to go next. Sound about right?"

"You're right, Anna," Allen said. "I didn't ask for any of this. My life was fine without any of this—any of *you*. What have you done to help me? Nothing. You asking me if I've been in a fight isn't helping me, it's you worrying about your own ass."

Anna took a deep breath and clenched her fists. "I'm sorry, Allen," she said.

"Al," Stephanie interjected, "you're being a jerk."

"I'm sorry, this is just too much. I need to get out of here." Allen stomped around the room.

After some glances between the group, Mead pulled Allen toward the doorway. He took a small silver key from his pocket and handed it to Allen. "When you get in the elevator, use this key. It will get you to the tunnels."

"What tunnels?" Allen asked.

"You'll see." Mead smiled.

Stephanie walked over to the two.  "Can I go with you, Al?" she requested.

"Sure," he agreed. "Good night, Mr. Mead."

"Good night, Mr. White."

Allen held the elevator door for Stephanie and then walked in behind her. "Going down?" he said in a fake fancy voice to get a giggle from her. Allen turned the tiny key in the lock by the number panel, and the elevator began to descend. When the doors opened, the light from inside the elevator slightly illuminated the area. Allen's anger from earlier dissipated as his curiosity took over. His nose caught a whiff of the cleanest place in New York City—the seldom-used tunnels. Allen and Stephanie slowly exited the elevator, and she reached up, gripping Allen's arm with a little trepidation. Allen led the way into the darkened tunnel as the elevator doors closed behind them. Allen noticed a small switch next to the elevator and he walked over and flipped it up, lights coming on in succession and leading the way to an infinite labyrinth under the city.

"It's like a dream," Stephanie said.

Allen noticed under the light switch a map that showed the layout of the tunnels.

"Steph…these tunnels don't just go for a few blocks."

"How far do they go?" Stephanie asked.

"The map there makes it look like the *entire city*, but there's only one way to know for sure," he said.

"Are you sure you want to follow this? What if it just leads to a sewer? I'm not dressed for literal shit."

"Do you see the walls around us, Steph? Solid brick...no deterioration. There's no way we are going toward the sewers."

"Ok, Al...I trust you."

"Let's go," Allen said.

"Right behind you," Stephanie added.

Allen and Stephanie worked their way through the tunnels beneath 3 Riverside Drive. The passages that covered the entirety of Manhattan were a secret Allen and Stephanie were both amazed to discover. The tunnels were cylindrical in shape, virtually untouched by the outside world. The concrete ground of the tunnels was so intact, it appeared as if it had been poured the day before. Along the walls every hundred yards were dim lights that illuminated the area for easy navigation.

For Allen, it was nice to get out of the confines of the house after all he had heard in the past two days. Allen wasn't sure what to make of anything that had happened over the past couple of weeks, but he did his best to stay open-minded, despite his doubt, until he couldn't handle any more. Stephanie was happy to accompany him as they hadn't had any moments to just hang out together in a long time. She knew Allen was confused and just wanted to offer her friendship, even if that meant following him in silence through the tunnels as he cleared his head.

"No more cabs!" Allen exclaimed.

"No more subways, either," she added.

"I wonder where these tunnels come out in the city."

"Guess we'll see. I feel like Michelangelo," Allen said.

"This *is* a beautiful area. Maybe he inspired it?"

"I meant the ninja turtle," Allen laughed.

"I'm an idiot," Stephanie said.

"Where do you think we're going?"

"There's your answer." Stephanie pointed.

The two approached an opening on their left in the tunnels to find a small copper plate with black print screwed into the base of the wall.

*Central Park* ← *3 Miles* ∞ *Upper East Side* ↑ *2 Miles*

"Which way we headed?" Allen asked.

"The park," Stephanie answered with a big smile. "I love the park."

"You got it."

They turned left and began their walk to Central Park. Stephanie felt nostalgic.

"This reminds me of that time sophomore year that we went to the park at night," she said.

"*That* was a long night," Allen said with a smirk.

"I still can't believe we didn't get killed by that horse!"

"Vodka and sledding are not a good combo," he laughed.

"Like me and Kimo," she said.

"That's not on you," Allen turned to face his friend, placing a hand on her forearm. "He's always been a jerk; you just didn't want to see it. But it's not on you."

"I saw it when he punched you freshman year."

"You were the only one who saw *that*." Allen nervously laughed.

Stephanie laughed along with him as they continued down the path toward Central Park. They came to a steel ladder attached to the wall in the tunnel. The only way to go was up, so Allen scaled the ladder first; it was about seventy-five feet from the ground to the top.

"This climb feels like forever," Allen complained.

"I'm glad I didn't wear heels today."

Ten minutes later, Allen reached the top of the ladder and noticed the cover that acted as the entrance above wasn't circular like he'd seen in movies, but a rectangle big enough for just one person to fit through. It was heavy, but Allen pushed with his left shoulder and forced it open. He slightly rose through the opening and looked around but didn't see anyone. He also didn't hear any noise, something he thought was odd for New York City, but he cautiously moved through the opening and found himself in an eerily quiet Central Park, directly next to the statue dedicated to *Alice in Wonderland*. Allen made sure the area was clear and then helped Stephanie through the opening; he quickly closed the cover to the tunnel. When Allen looked down at it, he could see letters but couldn't make out what it said in the darkness. Stephanie pulled her cell phone out and shone a light on the plaque.

*'TWAS BRILLIG AND THE SLYTHY TOVES*
*DID GYRE AND GIMBLE IN THE WABE:*
*ALL MIMSY WERE THE BOROGROVES,*
*AND THE MOME RATHS OUTGRABE.*

"Spooky poem," Stephanie commented.

"Spooky week," Allen stated.

The two sat on the edge of the wall that surrounded the Alice statue and stared at the night sky. Clouds obscured the stars, but the moon was bright enough for them to enjoy the view.

"Did you *ever* think this is where you'd be senior year?" Stephanie wondered.

"Oh, sure. I always thought crazy things with red eyes would be chasing me around New York," Allen joked. "I hope tomorrow a peanut vendor turns into a robot and eats me."

"Wise ass!"

"Seriously, though…never would've thought anything like this was even possible if I hadn't seen it with my own eyes."

"It's a lot to take in, for sure. But you're not alone, remember that, Al."

"I know," he replied. "Thanks for always having my back."

"I always will. You mean a lot to me."

"And you to me."

"And you both mean *so* much to me," a voice said.

Kimo appeared through the night from around a corner and Allen and Stephanie jumped to their feet, Allen positioning himself in front of Stephanie to shield her from harm. Allen noticed Kimo had a weapon to his side, a blade of some type, about three feet long with a handle composed of bone. Kimo lifted his arm and twirled the handle.

"Sorry to interrupt your little lovefest," Kimo snarled.

"What do you want?" Stephanie shouted from behind Allen.

"I'll deal with you in a second, whore," Kimo said.

Four years of frustration were ready to spill over in Central Park. All the anger Allen carried since freshman year was about to erupt in this moment. Allen and Kimo circled each other down the steps from the Alice statue, and Allen finally charged after his enemy, but as he ran toward Kimo, someone speared him to the ground. All Allen could hear was Kimo's laughter. Allen couldn't break free and when he was pulled to his feet, Jaxx shoved a gun to his forehead. Allen stopped struggling and held his hands up.

"Did you really think I was going to fight you?" Kimo said with a snicker.

"You're a coward!" Allen shouted.

"Shhh," Jaxx said. "Don't make me pull this trigger."

Kimo stalked his way toward Stephanie, who was frozen in fear. She trembled as he ran the back of his hand across her left cheek—the same spot he had punched her. Tilting his head to the side of Stephanie's neck, Kimo smelled her; it was seductive to him and sickened Stephanie. She gathered her courage and spit in Kimo's face. He cackled as he wiped the spit from his eyelid. It only angered him more.

"Enough playing around," Jaxx encouraged him. "Finish this."

"Kimo, don't do this," Allen begged.

"Kimo is dead," Jaxx growled. "*You* killed him; and now, you've sentenced *her* to death."

"We might not have ever been friends, Kimo," Allen said. "But you loved this girl at one point. If you want revenge for something, take it out on me."

"Shut up," Kimo snapped.

"Do it!" Jaxx ordered.

Kimo grabbed Stephanie by the hair on the back of her head; he moved his face toward hers and forced a kiss on her. She fought all she could to push him away, but he was too strong. When he was done with her, Kimo pulled his lips away with a smacking sound, and spun her around to face Allen just as Jaxx moved behind Allen and pressed the gun to the back of his head.

"Goodbye, lover," Kimo whispered.

"Kill her!" Jaxx screamed.

Allen tried to find an opening to escape, but as he moved forward Jaxx shot at the ground and jerked Allen back into place.

"Look at me," Allen pleaded. "Stephanie…"

Stephanie's eyes opened wide, and she looked directly at Allen. She took a deep breath, closed her eyes and angled her head upwards. She clasped her hands together and tears flowed down her cheeks and onto her shirt.

"Stephanie!" Allen yelled.

Kimo pulled the blade from his side, raised it up and thrust the blade through Stephanie's back; Allen could hear the blade as it cracked bones through her chest. Kimo pulled the blade back out with a squelching sound, and Allen watched Stephanie slump to the ground, blood pouring out of her and pooling on the ground. Kimo stood over Stephanie's lifeless body, laughing as he rubbed his boot on her chest. Her blood dripped down his hand—he wiped it across his chest, then licked his hand to taste it. Kimo stepped over the blood and got into Allen's face. "This is *your* fault," he spat. "She'd be alive if she hadn't placed her trust in you."

"I'm going to kill you!" Allen cried.

"You're about to die and you say I'm dead?" Kimo said as he and Jaxx laughed.

Kimo closed his eyes and inhaled the air in Central Park and then drew his blade back once again.

Allen closed his eyes for a moment, letting memories of his life flood his mind as he knew this was the end. He thought about his parents, his friends, Stephanie, Joe, and all the people he had met the past few weeks. He smelled the air one last time with a giant breath, taking in the scent of the city—a crisp fall night mixed with coffee and hot dogs.

"Central Park is your last memory, Allen. The hot dogs, the popcorn, the horse shit. It's all yours now. I'll see you in Hell," Kimo said, as he prepared to impale Allen with his blade. "I guess you'll never get to kiss her after all."

A single gunshot rang out from forty feet away, piercing Kimo's forearm and exiting through his elbow. Kimo dropped his blade and fell to his knees, howling. Jaxx pistol-whipped Allen in the back of the head, knocking Allen down for a second until his head cracked the ground. Momentarily dazed, Allen almost immediately regained consciousness, and Stephanie's body was just a few feet away; Kimo and Jaxx, however, were nowhere in sight.

Allen crawled over to Stephanie and knelt by her side. He gently lifted Stephanie into his lap, and she gasped for air. Allen cried out her name with a wet sob of relief—but there wasn't much to be done. Tears flowed from Stephanie's eyes, onto his arm, while he put pressure on her wound. Allen welled up as he watched his friend struggle to stay alive.

"I'm sorry," Stephanie sobbed.

"Don't talk," Allen instructed. "Help is coming, but you have to stay still."

"I'm so sorry," she repeated.

Someone approached from the distance, footsteps loud on the pavement, radio noise coming closer with the figure. Allen realized it was one of the cops who'd come the night Kimo hit Stephanie—Officer Young.

"We've got to get her to a hospital," Allen said.

"No," Stephanie coughed. "There's no time, Al."

"Don't say that, Steph, you're going to be fine."

Officer Young took his peaked cap off and rubbed his arm across his forehead to clear the sweat. He tossed his hat to the ground in anger and then knelt and tried to help Stephanie.

"Al, don't let him hurt anyone else," Stephanie choked out, red spittle staining her lips. "P—promise me."

Her breathing became labored, rattled, and Officer Young checked her pulse. He locked eyes with Allen and shook his head. Allen turned his attention back to his friend.

"I promise," Allen replied. "It's okay, Stephanie," he assured. "You're going to make it, you'll be fine."

"Al," she struggled. "I—"

Stephanie stopped speaking and breathed one last time. Her body went limp and slumped into Allen's lap as she held his hand—a final moment between friends.

# Chapter 24 – Anguish

Allen carefully picked Stephanie's body up over his shoulder and moved toward the plaques around the Alice statue. Officer Young followed behind and made sure nobody approached, his gun still drawn, his head on a swivel. It was late at night so not too many people would be out in the park, but Officer Young didn't take any chances. Allen placed Stephanie on the ground next to the plaque that had opened before to let them out of the tunnels and tried to open it back up, but he failed with every attempt. Allen tried everything he could think of to open the entrance but grew frustrated. Officer Young continued to play the part of a lookout, but he was getting more and more worried as each minute passed. Young finally put his gun down, moved to the Alice statue and gripped Alice's left index finger. He twisted it in a circular motion. The plaque opened. Allen stared at Officer Young in great surprise.

"I thought Mead would've told you how to get back in," Young said.

"No, he didn't. Thanks, though," Allen replied. "So…you're one of them too?"

"If by 'them' you mean the others, then yes, I'm one of 'them'," Young responded.

"I didn't mean it like that," Allen explained.

"I know you didn't. And for what it's worth, Allen…I'm sorry."

"Thanks."

"But you gotta get out of here. They could be back any second."

Allen looked down at Stephanie's body. The blood on her shirt soaked through and his hands were covered with her blood. *It was her favorite shirt,* Allen thought. He nodded to Officer Young and then he leaned down and lifted Stephanie over his shoulder once again. Allen painstakingly maneuvered himself down into the tunnels as he carried his dead friend on his shoulder. This would be the longest walk of his life. Just moments ago, their combined laughter had echoed through these tunnels. Now it was just a mausoleum for Allen's pain and Stephanie's blood. He refused to take a break, each rung of the ladder with Stephanie's lifeless body a reminder of the hatred he had for Kimo. 75 rungs gave Allen a chance to think through 1000 ways to kill Kimo. Slow and determined, Allen returned to 3 Riverside Drive.

When Allen finally reached the elevator, he put Stephanie down on the ground to get the key from his pocket. Before he opened the elevator, Allen leaned against the wall and allowed his exhausted body to slowly slump to the ground next to Stephanie. He wouldn't let anyone see him cry, not today. His eyes moistened, and he wiped at them with his blood-soaked hands, spreading her blood across his cheek. Allen gathered himself and stood back up. He put the key into the lock and turned it again and the elevator doors opened. He gently lifted Stephanie's body into his arms and entered the elevator—and the doors closed to return Allen to the second floor.

As the doors opened, Allen carried his best friend off the elevator. He carried her down the hall and into the lounge, where Clarissa was engrossed in a book. She looked up and dropped the book when she saw Allen enter. Her hands instinctively rose to her mouth and covered her face in shock.

Allen's appearance was jarring—his hair, his hands, his face, and clothes were all covered in blood. Clarissa jumped up from her chair to help him place Stephanie on the couch. Allen moved to one knee and continued to hold Stephanie's hand as she lay motionless on the couch.

"What happened?" Clarissa asked from over his shoulder.

"Kimo happened."

"I'm so sorry, Allen."

"She didn't deserve this. She shouldn't have come with me."

"Then you'd be dead, too," Clarissa reminded.

Allen kept his gaze focused on Stephanie as tears clouded his eyes. He'd never lost anyone except his parents, and he was too young then to know. He still didn't fully grasp their deaths.

"I'm sorry, so sorry," he mumbled into Stephanie's ear.

Clarissa left the room to alert the others, leaving Allen grieving over Stephanie's body. He knew he was alone now—and he felt it more than ever. He held Stephanie's face as he attempted to wipe the blood from her cheeks. Allen's mind was in a vicious cycle; he envisioned Kimo stabbing Stephanie over and over. The despair in Allen's heart grew as his thirst for vengeance became insurmountable.

"I will find him, Stephanie, I promise. And when I do, I'll kill him."

Mead walked into the room with Clarissa and Lionel.

"Oh no, mate," Lionel lamented.

"This is *my* fault!" Allen cried.

"You can't blame yourself," Mead advised.

"I had a vision of her death…" Allen said softly.

"What happened?" Lionel pressed.

"Kimo came out of nowhere. We'd just left the tunnels and he showed up. It was like he'd forgotten who he was, who she was to him before. He stabbed her and…"

Allen broke down and Lionel tried to change the subject as fast as he could.

"How did you escape?" Lionel asked.

"A cop—Officer Young—shot at Kimo when he was about to kill me. I think he hit him, but it scared him and the other guy off."

"What other guy?" Lionel demanded.

"I don't know. He held me down and yelled at Kimo to kill Stephanie. I didn't hear his name."

"It had to be Jaxx," Lionel said. "Mead, you know what this means, right?"

"Yes," Mead agreed. "But now is not the time."

Mead placed his hand on Allen's shoulder. "Mr. White," Mead whispered. "Let's go."

Allen let go of Stephanie's hand and followed Mead out of the room toward the elevator.

*****

Lionel and Clarissa remained in the room, moving away from the couch but staying close to Stephanie's body to keep guard. Lionel poured them each a drink from behind the bar.

"To Stephanie," he said, pounding his drink. "Are we going to talk about this, love?" he asked.

"We both know who it was that helped him," Clarissa answered.

"Why are we waiting here? Let's go find the son of a bitch."

"If it *was* Jaxx and he's helping Kimo, that means all hell's gonna break loose in New York soon. We can't do this without him."

"He just watched his best friend die."

"I don't mean Allen," she said.

"*Him?* Where do we even start?"

"I don't know. But eventually, Allen will have to know what he's up against. The Syphs in the museum were nothing compared to what's coming. Jaxx is just the dawn of this evil."

Mead waited outside the master bedroom while Allen showered and changed his clothes. He put on a black t-shirt and a pair of grey sweatpants and disposed of his blood-soaked outfit in the trash. After a few minutes, Allen unlocked and opened the door and Mead entered. He sat in a chair against the wall while Allen sat on the edge of the bed, staring at the floor, unsure what to say.

"I know what you're feeling, Mr. White," Mead started.

"No, you don't," Allen snapped. "Nobody does. I should have never come here, I should have never stopped and talked to you that day on campus. None of this would've happened."

"This isn't your fault, Mr. White."

"I saw this happen," Allen repeated.

"What do you mean, Mr. White?"

"At the museum…I had a vision that Kimo would…would…kill her."

"Mr. White, there's no chance you could have known this would happen—vision or not."

"Maybe not; but did *you?*"

"No, Mr. White, I didn't. But I am sorry it did."

"What happens now?"

"Let me worry about that tonight. I think you should sleep, Mr. White. The room is yours."

Mead rose to his feet and crossed the room to the door. He exited the room and closed the door behind him. Allen slid back to the middle of the bed, grabbed a pillow and squeezed it under his head. He closed his eyes and finally was able to sleep.

Professor Rogers walked past Allen's room and trailed Mead to the lounge. Clarissa had gone to bed, but Lionel was still at the bar, nursing another drink. Lionel pulled two more glasses out from under the bar and poured Rogers and Mead each a drink.

"He's pretty hurt," Lionel commented.

"This could take longer than we thought, Lionel," Rogers said.

"Gentlemen," Mead interrupted, "We don't have time. Syphs are here; Jaxx is here. The city is just the beginning."

"What can we do?" Lionel asked.

"First, we have to let Allen bury his friend," Mead replied. "Lionel, can you and Nigel handle that tonight?"

"We can. I'll go get him and we'll handle it."

Lionel finished his drink quickly and put his glass into the sink behind the bar before leaving the lounge to get Nigel. Lionel was determined to help Mead in any way he could.

Mead and Rogers walked past the couch that Stephanie was on, and they both took a hard look at the stark reality of the evil they faced.

"Let him grieve tomorrow, Thomas," Mead began. "Then we have to tell him."

"You focus on Allen; I'll focus on finding and gathering the rest of the group. I'll be back here in three days, Mr. Mead."

The two men finished their drinks. Mead left first and Rogers knelt at Stephanie's side. "I'm sorry, Stephanie. I promise you he will pay for what he's done." Rogers prayed over her body before exiting the lounge. Rogers walked to the landing, down the stairs into the main hallway and out the front door. "We're coming for you, Jaxx."

# Chapter 25 – Eli & Kay

Kay checked all the jazz clubs she could think of as she searched New York City for her friend Eli. She imagined she would find him inside of one, smiling, dancing and drinking as he usually was, but she'd come up empty in her search. She didn't even think she would ever see him again after the last time they were together, almost nine months earlier. Kay walked the streets of Greenwich Village as she reminisced about the sometimes awkward and tumultuous friendship she had with Eli.

*February 2014 – New Orleans, Louisiana*
It was February and the streets were packed with drunk revelers as Mardi Gras was in full swing in New Orleans French Quarter. People fought off those around them to get the attention of the bead-throwers on the passing floats. Kay slipped through the crowd and made her way to New Orleans' most famous jazz venue—Preservation Hall.

Inside, the clamor of partying outside melted away to the sweet sounds of trumpets and pianos in harmony. While most people in the club were engaged by the music, Kay was focused on getting through the throng to the bar. A man in a black fedora, black button-down shirt, white suspenders and white pants leaned against the bar with a brown drink in his hand. He twirled the glass in circles, not drinking or paying attention to the woman who had clearly come there to find him. He put the glass down on the bar and slid the glass out of his hand and to Kay, who picked up the glass, chugged its contents and slammed it back on the bar.

"*Bonjour, jeune fille,*" Eli said.

"*Bonjour,* Eli," Kay replied. "It's been a while."

The two hugged warmly and kissed each other on their respective cheeks. It had been a few years since they'd seen each other, and Eli couldn't help flashing a big smile upon seeing his old friend.

"New Orleans seems to be treating you well," Kay commented.

"Oh, absolutely," he agreed. "Mardi Gras is my kind of party, dawlin'."

Kay held up two fingers to the bartender to grab his attention.

"What can I get you?" the bartender shouted.

"Two Beam shots," she said.

"Oh, it's that kind of night?" Eli laughed.

Eli put a twenty-dollar bill down for the shots, picked them both up and handed one to Kay. The two clanked their glasses together and drank their shots, then slammed their glasses down on the bar as Kay winced from the taste. Eli continued to look toward the stage, tapping his foot to match the beat of the music. Kay watched as Eli smiled and subtly danced in place. She hated to stop his fun, but she had to reveal why she had come to Mardi Gras.

"Mead sent me," she whispered. "We found him."

Eli's smile disappeared. He glared over at Kay without saying a word.

"Eli, are you listening to me?"

"I heard you, but why'd you come down here now to tell me all this?"

"We need you to come back to New York with me," Kay explained. "Mead and Rogers are going tomorrow."

"I don't care," Eli started. "It's not my life anymore; I'm happy here."

"You swore you would never turn your back on us, that you would always fight by our side."

"I didn't turn my back on y'all, remember?"

"Let's forget that incident, Eli. It hurt us all. Please come back to New York."

"Y'all are mistaken to think I still want to do this," Eli responded. "Just tell them you didn't find me."

"You know I can't do that, Eli."

"Looka here! Nobody tells me who or what my life is for. Now I'm sorry you got sent down here—"

"I volunteered," she interrupted.

"I'm sorry you wasted a trip, *jeune fille*. You're welcome to crash at the apartment, but I won't be going back to New York. Find him on your own."

Eli vanished into the crowd on the dance floor. She knew it was no use to argue with him—he wasn't going to budge. When Eli turned around from the dance floor, Kay had already disappeared from Preservation Hall.

*Present Day – New York City*

As Kay roamed the streets of New York wondering where Eli could be, she found herself in Washington Square Park, seated on one of the stone benches that surrounded the circular water fountain in the middle of the park. She'd just left the Blue Note Jazz Club empty-handed and was discouraged from continuing her search. She thought hard about where Eli could be, and why he chose to return to New York. He was adamant in New Orleans that whatever life he was tied to was one he didn't want, so what changed? How long would he stay in New York? Would Eli help her? Would he help *them*? Kay had too many questions to calm her mind, but the serenity of the fountain at least gave her something to focus on. As Kay looked at the water, Eli approached from behind her.

"I knew I'd find you eventually," she greeted.

"You been following me long enough."

"I'm sorry, Eli, I had to find you."

"I'm the one who needs to apologize, *jeune fille*; I was wrong. I'm sorry for not being here until now, I'm sorry for the way I treated you in New Orleans. I lost faith."

Kay stood up and hugged Eli hard. He was a bit taken back by the sentiment and hesitated to hug back, instead letting his arms hang outward from his body. She grabbed both sides of his face in her hands.

"You have nothing to apologize for, Eli. Thank you for being here. For saving us."

"Is Clarissa okay?" Eli worried.

"She's fine, thanks to you. All of us are."

"What about *him*? Is he safe?"

"We don't know. Mead is working on it. We have so much left to do."

"How many of us are here?"

"Enough of us to make a difference. Everyone is gathered at Riverside. Will you come?"

Eli nodded and followed Kay to the edge of the park entrance to hail a taxi. They were headed to 3 Riverside Drive, unaware of all that happened during the night.

As the duo left in a cab, a woman stepped out of the darkness and into the park. She skipped around the water fountain a few times, humming louder and louder. Her waist-length hair was bright silver and looked as if it had been ironed, it was so incredibly straight. Even as she moved around the fountain her hair didn't seem to budge. She wore a form-fitting, long-sleeve black jumpsuit with a zipper down the front to the waist that she had unzipped about one-fourth of the way down her chest. When she looked down into the fountain, her eyes reflected a dark black.

The volume of her humming annoyed a few people in the park, and someone pointed the cops to her location. Two patrol officers parked their car and approached the woman. She immediately grew silent.

"Miss…Miss…are you okay?" the first cop asked.

"Excuse me, ma'am," the second cop added. "You have a name?"

Before he could say anything else, the woman interrupted him by singing "Wondrous Boat Ride" from the Willy Wonka movie.

"Ma'am, have you been drinking tonight?" the second cop said.

The woman looked up at him and her eyes changed from dark black to red in an instant. The cops jumped at seeing this, swearing, and backing up, their hands at the ready on their holsters.

"What in God's name?"

"What the hell was that?"

"I don't know."

"Run along boys," the woman ordered.

"Ma'am, we're going to have to—"

"Is it raining, is it snowing?"

"Call it in," Gary suggested.

"Central, requesting backup for an EDP in Washington Square Park."

"Oh, more friends!" The woman beamed. "Fun, fun, fun for me!"

"Miss, if you'd just tell us your name, we can all be on our way tonight," Frank reasoned.

"A rose by any other name would smell so sweet," she recited.

"Ma'am, please," Frank persisted.

The woman ignored the cops as they devised a way to deal with her. She mumbled incoherently to herself, splashing them with water from the fountain.

"Last chance, boys," the woman sang.

The cops drew their tasers and ordered the woman to the ground, but she only laughed.

"Put your hands in the air!"

The woman looked at her hands as she held them up to the fading night sky, waving them and laughing menacingly. She knelt and placed her left index finger in the fountain; the water that filled the fountain rose up and swirled in the air like a free-standing maelstrom. It sprayed water all around, while the two cops stood dumbfounded. Then the water slowly froze and turned into ice. With a flick of her wrist, two icicles broke away from the block and zipped through the air. The woman controlled them and kept them spinning at the two officers' foreheads.

"Leave now," the woman warned.

The two cops looked at each other, holstered their weapons and slowly backed away from the woman. They turned and ran toward their patrol car as they warned arriving cops to stand down.

The woman smiled and the skin around her eyes changed to black. She restarted her humming and returned the ice to its natural form in the fountain.

"New York, New York." The woman grinned. "It's a hell of a town."

# Chapter 26 – The Remains

He hadn't been to a funeral before, but he stood before a shallow grave in the backyard garden of 3 Riverside Drive long after everyone else had gone inside.

Four years of memories overtook him, but it was Stephanie's last moments that still lived in his mind—the look on her face just before Kimo murdered her invaded his every breath. Allen's pain was very fresh and real, and he cried for the first time since he was a young boy. He was thankful to those at Riverside for their support, but he'd never felt so isolated. What would life be like without his best friend? Allen gripped the red rose in his hand tightly as he stared at Stephanie's grave.

"I'm sorry, Allen," a familiar voice said.

Joe put a hand on Allen's shoulder. Allen spun around, excited and surprised to see his roommate in the garden. Joe was wearing sweatpants and a hospital gown, apparently discharged just moments earlier from the hospital.

"Joe, what are you doing here? How did you know what happened?"

"Professor Rogers told me. I rushed right over."

"Rogers visited you in the hospital?"

"He said you needed me and told me what happened to Stephanie. I can't imagine what you're feeling, bro. What can I do?"

"Help me find Kimo. He's going to pay for this."

"I'm in. I'll leave you alone out here, let you have some time; I need to find some clothes."

"No," Allen insisted. "Stay for a few."

The two friends stood in silence in the garden for some time as Mead looked out from the window above. Joe walked back toward the entrance to the house and Allen squatted down and put the flower on top of the grave.

"Goodbye, Stephanie."

Allen went back inside and took the elevator to the lounge floor, where the group awaited. Lionel, Nigel, and Joe were seated at the bar. Officer Young stood by the bay windows flanked by Eli and Kay. Allen sat beside Clarissa on the couch. Mead paced back and forth while the others around the room whispered to one another within their groups. Allen was ready to speak to Clarissa when he heard more people coming up the stairs. Rogers entered the room and moved to his left to give way to two more people.

"Everyone," Rogers announced. "Sasha and Anna."

Anna stood five-foot-seven, a bronze-skinned half-Native American, half-Puerto Rican young woman. Anna's medium-length black hair was tied back in a single braid with bright brown eyes. A distinct scar ran from the inside of her wrist to her shoulder, a souvenir from her teen years when her arm caught the top of the chain link fence she was jumping and tore the entire appendage open. Anna never hid the scar, opting instead to wear it as a badge of honor.

Sasha couldn't have been more opposite of anyone in that room if she tried, though she was used to standing out in a crowd. Her dyed-red hair and pale complexion complemented her dark blue eyes. She was dwarfed by most of the room at only five-foot-three inches. Sasha wasn't flashy, instead always comfortable. She had on a solid black hooded sweatshirt, jeans and black sneakers.

"Welcome home," Mead greeted.

While the others all said their hellos to the two new arrivals, Allen waited, anxious to hear what Mead had to say.

"And what of the others, Thomas?" Mead asked.

"I'm sorry. I couldn't find them," Rogers replied.

"An incomplete circle is a broken circle," Mead muttered. "No matter, Thomas, we can do this and find them later."

"Mr. White…" Mead turned his attention to Allen.

The focus of everyone in the room was on Allen.

"I know by now you have many questions so here it is: Each person in this room is special, Mr. White. All have come from near and far to gather here at Riverside with one common purpose—to save the world from destruction."

"Who exactly are you?" Allen interjected.

"We are The Remains, Mr. White."

"The Remains? The Remains of what?"

"Well…Some of us are friends to the group, while others are direct descendants of the Knights of the Round Table. For centuries, families before us have protected this secret, protected the world from the growing threats of a group that calls themselves The Nimayrd—an evil that has been around for just as long as any of us can remember. Their thirst for blood makes them very dangerous. Their leader is known only as The Master; and those who serve him are strong. They believe that The Master is the most powerful being to ever live; and they follow him without question. His army is endless, as you encountered in the museum—they can come and go as they please with what can best be described as magic. They show their loyalty to him by drinking his blood when they are embraced by evil. The Master and his followers truly believe that the only things standing in the way of their total domination of the world are the people in this room. Throughout history, The Remains have carried out the mission of maintaining peace in the face of that threat; and now we have a chance to end their way of terror, forever."

"The Knights of the Round Table?" Allen asked. "You expect me to believe this?"

"He speaks the truth, *mon ami*," Eli said.

"He's not lying," Clarissa added.

"Hear him out, Allen," Rogers suggested.

"Professor, how can you of all people expect me to believe this? You were the one who told us we didn't study that part of history because it never happened."

"Whoa!" Lionel yelled. "Thom-ass, you bad, bad boy."

"Next you'll tell us Santa isn't real, Rogers," Nigel added.

"Stop it, you morons," Officer Young laughed.

Nigel and Lionel looked at each other and started laughing uncontrollably. The room erupted and joined in the laughter and the mood immediately lightened. Even Allen managed to loosen up momentarily and crack a smile before Mead returned to explaining.

"Mr. White, there are forces gathering in this city outside the realm of your wildest imagination. Things you've already seen this week with your own eyes. The Nimayrd will not stop until we're all dead. Syphs will keep coming, Jaxx will return with Kimo, and your former friend will want nothing more than to kill you. Now is the time to ask questions.

I'll help you understand whatever I can."

"Okay…What exactly is a Syph? Where did this Nimayrd come from? What does The Master want with me?"

"A Syph is a demon of The Nimayrd; they can take many forms, human or beast, but it's their claws that pose the biggest threat. One touch from one of those and you will die in minutes; the poison is instantaneous. The Nimayrd isn't as easy to explain because nobody is certain when they came to be in the shadows where they live. They, quite simply, are a collection of evil that has amassed over a long time—and they're not of this world. Their ruthlessness is only matched by their power and their numbers are far greater than ours.

"And The Master?"

"Some say he is born from blood."

"Blood?"

"Yes, Mr. White. Blood spilled on sacred land centuries ago; and when the dark sorceress Morgana escaped defeat, she used the blood of the fallen to create a powerful sorcerer capable of unthinkable evil."

"Is he the one that was with Kimo?"

"No. That was Jaxx. He's the right hand of The Master, twisted by his loyalty to the being. Jaxx is the weapon that carries out the orders. The Master is the gun…Jaxx is the bullet."

"Morgana is real?"

"Quite real—and just as dangerous as The Master, if not more. If he is the gun, she is a grenade; unpredictable, powerful, and explosive.

"Jaxx is dangerous," Nigel pointed to his scar. "If Kimo is with him that's extremely unnerving."

"What can we do to fight them?" Allen asked.

"Our greatest strength is when The Twelve are reunited," Kay explained.

"The Twelve?" Allen wondered.

"The Twelve Remains of the Knights of the Round Table, Allen," she answered.

"Well…how many are here now?"

Clarissa raised her hand first and Allen looked around the room to see Young, Eli and Kay by the windows with their hands raised. Sasha raised her hand and Anna followed with her hand in the air. Allen looked over to the bar where Lionel and Nigel raised their hands as well.

"Nine," Kay said.

"That's eight," Allen counted.

"That's not important right now," Mead said. "What is important is that you realize you are in danger. Stephanie's death was just the spark for this war; it's up to everyone in this room to defeat The Nimayrd."

"And it starts with you, Allen," Rogers added.

"Me?"

"You are meant to lead this group of warriors," Mead said.

"Please don't feed me some crap about destiny," Allen begged.

"It's not destiny, Mr. White, it's your birthright. The people in this room will fight beside you, they will protect you with their lives. Lead them; lead them and destroy The Nimayrd for good."

"I don't think I'm ready for all this." Allen shook his head, regretted it when he got dizzy. "I'm sorry Mead; I'm sorry everyone. I just don't know how to help."

Allen stood up and prepared to walk out of the room, but Joe blocked him in the center of the room. Bowing his head, Joe grabbed Allen by the shoulders and looked at Allen eye-to-eye.

"I know this is all crazy, brother. But you gotta do this, Allen. If not for the people in this room, for the one who isn't. Stephanie would tell you to get out there and fight. I know you feel alone, but make no mistake about it, I'll be right here by your side the whole time. She was my friend too and I don't care about Remains, Nimayrd or anything else—I want to help you kill Kimo."

"As do I," Clarissa joined.

"We all do, *mon ami*," Eli said.

Allen surveyed the room and realized all eyes were on him.

"Fine," he submitted. "Tell me what I have to do."

"Free him," Clarissa said.

"Will someone please tell me who 'he' is?" Allen pleaded.

A collective pause and deafening silence filled the room. The group waited for the one thing none of them was prepared to tell Allen to come from the one person who could. "Merlin," Mead said.

Allen swallowed hard and he felt a chill through his entire body; the hairs on his arms stood up on end. Allen had heard the name Merlin many times. Merlin was a character in books, movies, television shows, and video games. It was impossible to think that Merlin existed outside of the confines of fiction, a struggle that Allen felt when Mead spoke Merlin's name.

"How is that even possible?" Allen asked. "None of this makes sense."

"It makes sense to everyone in this room, Mr. White," Mead asserted.

"If all this is true, what's next? Where do we go from here?"

"That's a good question," Mead replied. "Kay?"

Kay moved toward the middle of the room, reached into her pants pocket and took out a small piece of cloth. Sasha let out a little gasp from across the room. Kay unwrapped it to reveal the little key she'd prevented Allen from grabbing in the basement of the museum, but now she extended her arm to Allen.

"There's no going back once you take this," Kay warned.

Allen hesitated for a second. "For Stephanie."

# Chapter 27 – Dark Magic

Deep in the darkness, echoes could be heard in the throne room.

"A fine job, Kimo." The Master clapped. "She deserved to die for all the suffering she caused you."

"Thank you, Master," Kimo replied.

The Master took his goblet and poured its contents over Kimo's elbow. The gunshot wound disappeared and Kimo stretched his arm out a couple of times, rocking his elbow back and forth to test its full strength. The Master then turned his attention to Jaxx.

"Jaxx," The Master scolded. "The boy was supposed to die and yet, he lives."

"I'm sorry, Master," Jaxx said. "It was that cop. He's one of them."

"Mead is foolish to think his precious Remains have a chance at fighting us. They're weak and stupid, just like him."

"Send me back, Master," Jaxx begged.

"It's too late now, Jaxx. I will do it myself," The Master calmly said.

"Master?"

"Tonight, we will put a stop to Mead and his little friends."

"Allen is mine," Kimo growled.

"There will be plenty of blood to go around," The Master laughed. "Jaxx, gather the others. Meet me in the Great Hall. I must find Morgana."

"Yes, Master," Jaxx responded.

"And me?" Kimo asked.

"Go with him, Kimo."

"Yes, Master."

Jaxx and Kimo exited as The Master worked his way to the Viewing Room and The Fylorn. He watched as Morgana's memories filled throughout the room—like a giant 360-degree projector showing a movie with perfect sound.

The man was in his late forties, his beard greying but trimmed short and close to his face. His eyes were a deep brown, and his hair was buzzed short all the way around. He wore a long, black robe with red silk inside, and on his right index finger was a silver ring, tapping against the four-foot-tall silver staff he clutched. The girl by his side was a teenager, with blonde hair that reached to her waist. Her eyes were ocean blue, a beautiful, pure color that reflected as she stared down at the object in front of her—a goblet.

"This goblet is like no other," the man said.

"What can it do?" the girl asked.

"This, my dear Morgana, can give you the gift of immortality."

"But Merlin, you told me only the cup of Christ could make one immortal."

"You misunderstood, child. The cup of Christ can only be touched and drank from by the purest of this world. The Holy Grail chooses its seekers and finders."

"And Arthur is the one it will choose, I'm sure of it."

"Morgana, nothing in all my years surprises me more than the will of the Grail. Men have died just trying to catch a glimpse of it. That type of power corrupts even the purest who seek the cup."

"Would it corrupt you, Merlin?"

Merlin envisioned touching the Holy Grail, drinking from it, and wondered if he could be considered pure after all the things he had seen and done. "I do not know, Morgana. There is no way to know until you come face-to-face with the relic."

"And what of this cup?" Morgana asked, leaning closer and closer to the goblet before them.

"That is for another day," Merlin answered.

Morgana was frustrated with Merlin's answer but didn't let it show. She'd learned from him that showing the ugly sides of yourself allowed enemies to know all your weaknesses, all your fears. She trained with Merlin from the day she turned ten years old, eight long years on and off with the wizard. He taught her to control her magic, to use her gifts and powers only when necessary and to always remain even-tempered.

"Merlin, I have an important question," Morgana said.

"What is it, child?"

"What happens if we use my magic for purposes outside of what you've taught me?"

"A sorcerer who uses magic for their own good will suffer the ill-effects of the greed in their heart."

"What ill-effects?" Morgana pressed.

"What have you done, child?" Merlin asked, his eyes piercing through Morgana with an intensity she had never seen from him.

"I…I don't know," she stammered.

Merlin took a deep breath and his shoulders dropped. He knew whatever Morgana had done was catastrophic. He'd never seen her this upset or scared in all their time together. Merlin had tried to keep Morgana from the darkness that young sorceresses often faced because it could only lead to terrible things.

Morgana waved her hand to stop The Fylorn, defiant of her past and the consequences that came from it. She never had to tell Merlin what she'd done, but she realized he knew at that moment, that she had killed a man. It was her first.

The pig farmer had harassed her time and time again over the death of her father and the fall of his reign. Morgana had always taken things in stride and shook them off, but when the man cornered her in the town market and dragged her into an alley, she had enough. As he pressed his lips against her neck, forcing himself on Morgana, she unleashed her inner fury and killed him by snapping his neck with magic. Morgana was just a young girl and had no idea the power she possessed. Merlin couldn't have known she would become his nemesis because she didn't even know at the time. Morgana waved her hand again at The Fylorn. This time it skipped ten years into the future.

"Merlin, where is Arthur?" Morgana asked.

"He is off with Gawain and Galahad attempting to find a new knight, a young man by the name of Lancelot."

"I have seen this Lancelot in my dreams, Merlin. He will bring down Camelot with his lust for her."

"I have seen it too, Morgana. But we cannot interfere in this. Fate has spoken."

Ten years older, enchantingly beautiful, intelligent, and confident, Morgana saw an opening for an overture to her mentor. "We are more powerful than fate, Merlin. We can change the future. We can save Arthur from this pain."

Merlin looked at Morgana with reluctance. This was not the same girl he had trained and watched over all these years. The woman she had become was angry, vengeful and obsessive over Arthur.

"Don't look at me like that, Merlin," she snapped. "What good are all these gifts we have if we don't use them? What good are we to the King if we don't help him when he needs us?"

"Dear child, I—"

"I am not a child anymore, Merlin. When will you see I am your equal? When will you see I can do things you can only hope to achieve? Stop treating me like I'm a little girl. See me as the woman I am."

"I see you as a woman, Morgana. However," he took her hand, thinking better of it the moment he did, "I see the way you feel, and I cannot return your affections, Morgana. To do so would be against the code by which we all live."

"Why can't you see past the silly code and look into your heart? We could rule the world forever!"

"I am sorry, Morgana. I cannot be what you would want from me. My heart belongs to someone else."

Morgana moved in and tried to kiss Merlin, hoping once again to make him change his feelings for her, but Merlin gently moved to one side, leaving Morgana embarrassed.

"You will regret this one day, Merlin," she said, her face growing red with fury and her head shaking.

As Morgana's heart broke, the trees on the bridge in the courtyard caught fire and burned.

The Fylorn closed again, and Morgana laughed at the past. She rolled her eyes at the thought of Merlin's naivety and his lack of faith in her powers.

"We could've ruled the universe together, Merlin, you fool. Instead, you chose the side of light. You tried to stop me. You saw right through my seduction for what it was—maybe my eyes betrayed me, maybe you're smarter than I ever gave you credit for? You knew that day with the goblet what I wanted. Despite all my hatred for you, I would have stood with you."

The Fylorn opened back up and fixed on the moment that led to the great duel between the two conjurers. They were deep in Brocéliande Forest.

"Why have you summoned me here, Merlin?"

"What have you done, Morgana?" Merlin pleaded.

"I challenged fate, and I saved this kingdom," she answered.

"You…you bore a child with your half-brother! You deceived us all! You disguised yourself as his queen to lay with him."

"Camelot needed to be protected. My Mordred is saving it as we speak."

"I'm sorry, Morgana," Merlin began, "but your son will be dead before the night is done."

"You will not touch my son, Merlin!" Morgana shouted and the entire sky darkened.

"I will not have to, Morgana. You forget that every king is tied to me and I to them. The dragon's breath has already been cast to help Arthur and his knights defeat your son's army."

"How could you, Merlin?"

"You chose this path, Morgana. Your *bastard* is cursed."

Merlin's insult was enough for Morgana. She took two steps back.

*"Ignis et aqua pluvia composita inducam super vos ardebit!"*

The skies darkened and fire shot from the ground toward the heavens and met with falling rain, bringing down deadly, blazing showers.

*"Protege me a malo,"* Merlin chanted.

A force field appeared around the great sorcerer and sheltered him from the dark magic that fell from the sky into the forest.

"You are no match for the darkness, Merlin," Morgana taunted.

Merlin drew circles on the ground with the bottom of his staff. *"Sub pedibus tuis Infernum, et absorbebunt, ut sint in mugit non receperit vos, sicut vos."*

The earth shook below where Morgana stood and slowly opened beneath her feet. The fires of Hell lit up the Brocéliande Forest. Merlin waited to watch the underworld bring her down, but Morgana levitated above the opened ground and continued to laugh.

"You thought the fires of Hell would engulf me, old teacher. You were wrong."

Morgana waved her hand and the ground closed again. Merlin was dumbfounded at the power of his pupil. She laughed as she directed her fury at Merlin once again.

*"Elementa mundi illam tenebrosus inebriasti me; da mihi potestatem habente occidendi Merlinus!"* Lightning shot from the ground and into Morgana, who held her arms open to receive the power she craved. As the bolts coursed through her body, Merlin watched as whatever good was left in his former student died. Merlin watched as lights shot out of Morgana's body and landed on the ground in the forest. Her body convulsed as the

voltage continued to infiltrate every cell of her body. She screamed in pain, her brain rattling from the vibration. Her hair changed colors instantly, becoming the silver it would remain all her days. The lightning stopped and Morgana fell to her knees in a cloud of smoke.

Merlin stepped forward to see if she could be helped. "Morgana?"

Morgana looked up and her eyes and the skin that extended to her hairline cycled through every color of the imagination. Her eyes finally stopped when they turned white, and she laughed at her former mentor.

"Don't do this, Morgana," Merlin pleaded. "There is still hope for you, for the kingdom."

Morgana stomped her foot on the ground as she rose to her feet. A white tiger appeared beside her and lunged at Merlin. The old sorcerer slapped the beast away with his staff and stabbed it in the chest where it fell. Morgana stomped again and a king cobra squeezed around Merlin's neck, dripping fangs poised to bite him. Merlin waved his hand and the cobra disappeared. Merlin then felt a terrible pain in his chest.

"Arthur…" Merlin cried, his hand grasping at his chest at the same moment Arthur was stabbed in Camlann.

"My son's blade has pierced your King's heart. Now, you will join Arthur."

Morgana reached forward, and like a hand through water, moved her hand through Merlin's chest and squeezed his heart. As Merlin gasped for air, Morgana felt a terrible pain in her own heart, and she released the hold on Merlin's chest.

"Mordred…my boy."

"Your plan has failed, child. Mordred is dead," he taunted Morgana. "Excalibur has pierced his heart."

Morgana looked at the former object of her childhood teachings and sneered. "*Ut mortem laudi tibi, Magister.*"

She pursed her lips together and blew subzero air toward Merlin, a dangerous spell meant to incapacitate her adversary. While he tried his best to protect himself, he was no longer any match for his student, weakened by Arthur's pain. Merlin felt the deep freeze take hold—it started with his fingers and toes and moved through his body. He was paralyzed by the cold and stopped fighting the inevitable. Merlin was frozen solid.

Morgana used her magic to create a grave there in the forest for him. The electricity she had absorbed moments before was all the power she needed to put Merlin's cold, stiff body into the ground and sealed the tomb of the once-great sorcerer with her newfound skills. The smell of smoke filled the forest, a cloudy farewell to the great sorcerer.

Morgana clapped her hands together and summoned the crimson Fylorn. She released her hands from around the orb and took a few steps back. The orb grew and shot toward her and soon she disappeared from Brocéliande Forest.

The Fylorn reappeared at Camlann, the final battle site between Arthur and Mordred. Morgana emerged from the orb onto the battlefield, searching for her beloved son through the sea of warriors and corpses, smoke, and screams. With each body she stepped over, Morgana's failed coup became painfully clear. The blood spilled at Camlann was on her hands, but she didn't care—she just needed to see Mordred. She soon spotted his familiar gold armor as it reflected the light of the sun and rushed to Mordred's side.

"My beautiful Mordred, what have they done to you?"

Holding Mordred's torso in her lap, she held her hand to try and heal him with magic, pouring all her energy into him. Mordred breathed slowly, his death a certainty.

"No use…the sword…" Mordred struggled.

Mordred's eyes rolled to the back of his head, and he went limp in his mother's arms, dead, his war to overthrow Arthur a failure.

Morgana's ferocity was uncontrollable as she screamed in agony over her dead son. Any warrior still left on that field was killed instantly by the shrieks of the grieving mother. Soldiers of Camelot and Mordred's forces collapsed on the field, blood pouring from their eyes, ears, and noses.

Morgana stood over her fallen son and called upon The Fylorn to return. She left her son there on the field, and the orb took her away.

The Fylorn closed and Morgana uncontrollably sobbed and trashed as her body was carried to its destination. Each moment an eternity of pain over her son's death.

*****

"It does you no favors to relive that moment," The Master consoled.

"Almost 1500 years later and it still is unanswered," Morgana responded.

"The time has come to end that pain, Morgana. They have gathered in New York. Tonight, we will end this nonsense once and for all."

"All of them are there?" Morgana asked breathlessly, her pain dwindling in her surprise.

"Nine of them."

"Then what are we waiting for? Let's go kill them all," she growled.

The sorceress followed him out of the throne room and down the stairs into the open hall; the same hall Kimo had seen when he first entered the fortress. The room was no longer quiet as it was before. The walls were lit up and a small group had assembled with Jaxx and Kimo in front of the warriors. As The Master and Morgana approached, Jaxx went to one knee and the rest of the party followed his lead, bowing to the dangerous duo.

"Rise," The Master motioned. "Tonight, my friends, we end a battle that has raged on for centuries. These *Remains* think they have the advantage; they are fools to think they can defeat us. For generations, we have suffered the fate of these Remains. Tonight, we change our destiny. We are the strength in this world, and it is time for us to rule the world. When this night is done every man, woman, and child will know the true power of The Nimayrd. Go now, my warriors! Go to New York and kill The Remains. And if any of those mortals helping them are foolish enough to stand in your way—kill them."

# Chapter 28 – Journey to the Past

"If you take this key, you better be prepared for everything that comes with it," Kay warned.

"I am," Allen assured.

Allen took the key from Kay's hand and immediately thousands of visions assaulted him at once. Voices were scattered and he could hear people talking and the *clang* of swords as they slammed together, but he couldn't keep his focus on one moment. Allen's body shook as he increased his grip on the key. The pictures in his vision began to take shape and he explained them to whoever was listening.

"There's a man with a baby; he's running away from a cabin that's on fire; I can feel the flames warming my face."

"That is Amra," Mead said.

The visions slowed as Allen focused on one moment at a time, gripping the key tightly in his hand. Kay, Clarissa, Mead, and Rogers stayed in the room with Allen while everyone else vacated the lounge.

"Almena is dead—Jaxx is laughing at her. Just how old is he?"

"He's been killing for a long time."

"Now I'm on a field but can't see much; there's fog everywhere."

"That's Camlann. What can you see?"

"I see…King Arthur fighting someone in gold armor…Mordred?"

"Yes."

It was The Battle of Camlann, and Allen viewed the fight between Arthur and Mordred. He watched Mordred stab Arthur through the chest and marveled at Arthur using his legendary sword to end Mordred's usurpation attempt. Allen knew that story well, he had heard it many times. But to *see* it? It was incredible to him.

"There's a knight. He's throwing a sword to the water. Now a woman is on the battlefield; she just killed everyone."

The scene flashed away from Allen's eyes and when things came back into focus, he stood inside Eldon and Emma's cabin. Helpless and horrified, Allen watched The Nimayrd execute the couple and their midwife. Allen's consciousness was transported to the moment Amra handed the baby girl to Daniel. He heard their conversation as if he was standing next to them in the past. Allen wasn't focused on the baby, however; he couldn't take his eyes off Amra. The mystery of the man intoxicated Allen.

"Who's Amra?" Allen asked as he loosened the grip on the key and opened his eyes.

"Keep going," Kay implored.

Allen closed his eyes and returned to the past. Amra was in the flashback, his face still covered by a hood. He sat in an empty, dimly lit pub with a man seated across from him at a long wooden table.

"Henry, we cannot delay," Amra argued.

"What can we do, Amra? Your own daughter is dead."

"We have to fight, dammit!" Amra slammed his hands on the table.

"We're all that's left, Amra."

"Something has to stop them."

Henry reached into the breast pocket of his mud-stained shirt and pulled out the very key that Allen currently held in the present.

"Here, Amra. Take it," Henry said, passing the key to the hooded man.

Amra held the key in his right hand and twisted it in the light of the pub. "What's this, Henry? What does this open?"

"You know what it opens."

Time skipped again for Allen as he followed Amra's movements in the night, as the hooded man led someone through Brocéliande Forest.

"We have to stay together," Amra whispered.

"Where are we going?" a young woman asked.

"To Merlin's tomb," Amra answered. "The time has come to free him. You have the key, right?"

The young, red-haired woman in a light blue dress that stretched to the ground reached into her bosom, pulled the key from between her breasts and handed it to Amra.

"It was the safest place," she joked.

As Amra and the young lady approached the wizard's tomb, whispers filled the wind. Amra knew who waited for them beyond the trees.

"Spread out!" Jaxx shouted. "Find her!"

"I'm going after him," the young woman said.

"No, Elizabeth!" Amra pleaded.

It was too late. Elizabeth charged out of the forest into the opening that led to Merlin's tomb. There she saw Jaxx standing in her way with Morgana by his side. Jaxx held an axe with both hands while Morgana fiendishly grinned at the approaching woman. Morgana moved her hand in an upward, twisting motion, freezing Elizabeth in place. Jaxx took three steps forward and swung the axe with all his might; the force of the axe ripped through the ice, striking Elizabeth in the head, killing her instantly.

Time jumped again for Allen, and he was suddenly in the middle of a street somewhere he'd never been. Allen heard the cries of a baby nearby, so he ran around a corner and saw Amra with a baby boy in his arms. The hooded Amra stood on the steps of a cathedral and handed the baby to a waiting priest. The priest reached around his neck with his free hand and removed a wooden cross that he then placed around the baby's body. Allen immediately recognized the cross as the same one he had viewed in the museum—the same necklace that enthralled him that day in the Met.

"The cross…from the museum?" he half-questioned.

"It is the same," Mead answered.

"But how?" Allen pressed.

"The Oxford students," Clarissa reminded him.

"What about them? The one's who killed the girl. Who is Elizabeth?"

"Elizabeth is your cousin," Kay began. "She was one of us."

"I just don't get it," Allen replied.

"Just keep going," Rogers suggested.

Allen reluctantly shut his eyes again. He was transported to the lounge of 3 Riverside Drive not far from where he was seated at that very moment in the present day.

"This is a gorgeous house," a voice said as people entered the lounge.

"Yes, it is," replied another voice that Allen recognized as Mead's.

"It's expensive, but it's perfect," the unknown voice offered before he came into Allen's focus. "How is this *ours*?"

"We have amassed more than enough money through the years, Terrence," Mead replied.

"It's not the money I'm worried about, it's our safety," Terrence said, pacing the room and smoking a cigar. Terrence's roundness stood out on first impression. His hair was black and greying on the sides with a flat top, the soul patch on his chin already completely grey. Terrence's brown eyes lit up along with his wide smile, when he wasn't as worried as he was now. He wore a navy-blue bow tie with his short-sleeved white button-down shirt, khaki pants, and light brown alligator skin shoes.

"There's tunnels under the house that spread through the entire city," Mead explained. "And there are access points in the city to help us disappear quickly if needed."

Terrence took a minute to think as he chomped on the end of his cigar.

"Okay. I'm in."

The scene in Allen's mind flashed to Times Square and Terrence running as fast as he could through a rainstorm, glancing over his shoulder. When he turned forward again, he collided with a group of tourists and fell to the pavement. Sweating through his rain-soaked shirt, Terrence finally made it to a pay phone on the corner of Broadway and 47th. He fumbled for change in his pocket and placed a dime into the slot. He breathed heavy as he turned to face the throngs of people in the city as the phone rang.

"Come on, come on," Terrence said to himself.

"Hello?" Mead answered at Riverside.

"They're here! Get out!" He looked down to see the blood pouring from his shirt. He collapsed on the sidewalk as people screamed in horror and his assailant escaped into a sea of New Yorkers.

The scene faded and gave way to a hospital. The floors were being polished by a janitor, while the night nurses readied to go home as their shift ended. It was very early and most of the patients on the floor were sleeping. The elevator door near the nurses' station opened and Mead stepped out with a stuffed animal in one hand and a bottle of champagne in the other. Allen followed Mead down the hall until he found his destination and entered the room.

A man in the chair at the end of the bed stretched his arms and then rose to his feet to greet Mead. His shoulder-length hair was a mess, flying off his head in every direction. His face was freshly shaven, his lone attempt to try and look refreshed. The buttons on his plaid shirt were buttoned wrong, and his wrinkled jeans told Mead the man had not slept. The blonde, green-eyed woman in the bed held a sleeping baby in her arms; the baby was wrapped tightly in a blanket. She'd spent the previous twelve hours in labor. Mead leaned over to kiss her on the cheek and then pulled another chair up to the end of the bed and sat down.

"Congratulations to you both," Mead whispered. "He looks great. You've done well, Melanie."

"Thank you, Mead," she replied.

"Have you come up with a name yet?" Mead wondered.

"Nothing yet," Melanie said.

"We are thinking of Samuel, however," the man said.

"No; *you're* thinking of Samuel, dear. I can only deal with one of you though," Melanie joked.

"This is true," Sam laughed.

"We're all so happy for you both, really," Mead gushed.

"Would you like to hold him?" Melanie asked.

She extended her arms carefully and handed the baby to Mead, who rocked slowly back and forth and softly cooed as the baby began to cry.

The hospital disappeared and the baby's screams became loud. Allen's view shifted to an apartment that had been the site of a struggle. There was debris all over the hardwood floors of the room Allen was in, and the walls had holes in them that appeared to be caused by bodies hitting against them. Mead cradled the baby as he checked the pulse of a few men on the ground. They were all dead. Mead moved through the large room and toward a closed door that led to a bedroom. He kicked the door down and saw two bodies—one on the bed, and one on the floor.

It was Samuel and Melanie, and their hands were connected.

Mead knelt and checked Samuel for a pulse; there was no sign of life. Samuel's eyes were bloodshot, his face strained from trying to breathe through being choked to death. Melanie had a deep gash across her stomach, and as Mead went to check for life, he winced to see Melanie's throat had been cut. He used his free hand to close Melanie's eyelids.

"I'm so sorry, Melanie," Mead said.

As the baby quieted, Mead heard a noise down the hallway and ran from the bedroom toward it. He swung open the door to the spare bedroom and found a young Professor Rogers, bloodied and struggling to get to his feet.

"Thomas, what the hell happened?"

"They attacked so fast. Sam and Melanie, did they get out?"

"I'm sorry, Thomas. They didn't make it."

"I tried to hold them off, but there were too many. We've got to get the baby out of here, Mead," Rogers said.

Mead said, "We'll take him together to Samuel's family. It's the only way to keep him safe."

"Do they know?" Rogers asked.

"They will."

"And Samuel and Melanie? Are we just going to leave them here?"

"We have to, Thomas. Melanie wouldn't want anything to happen to their son."

"How will he find us when he's older?"

"We will find him."

The next flash brought Allen to his childhood home. The sounds of the St. Lawrence River—the freighter ship horn echoing in the distance, the waves softly slapping against the dock—they were recognizable even in Allen's visions. He had spent so much time on the water it had become part of his identity. Mead walked the red brick walkway to the front door of the colonial home. The house was white with a brick façade around the bay windows that faced the entranceway, and the main door was wide open as was customary, with the screen door keeping the bugs of summer outside. Rogers walked behind Mead by five or six paces, continually looking over his shoulder to make sure they hadn't been followed. The driveway led to an opened garage door with a 1983 XLH-61 Harley-Davidson motorcycle that had been kept in pristine condition over the past fourteen years, proudly displayed. It had only been ridden a handful of times since it was purchased. To the right of the driveway and attached to the garage on the outside was a cold-frame greenhouse that was about three feet tall, housing several growing vegetables inside.

Mead knocked lightly on the screen door and a beautiful young woman with dark black hair, full eyebrows to match and brown eyes answered. She wore jean shorts and an unbuttoned long-sleeved shirt over a black bathing suit. She had flip flops on her feet and was holding a vegetable peeler in her hand. Her subtle dimples on each cheek showed as she reached the door.

"Mom?" Allen whispered in the present. He quieted again to keep watching.

"Hi there," she welcomed. "How can I help you?"

"Lisa?" Mead asked.

"Yes, that's me," she answered. "Who are you?"

"My name is Mr. Mead, and this is my associate, Thomas Rogers."

"Pleasure to meet you both. What can I do for you?"

"Is your husband home? We would like to speak to you both."

"Yes, he's home. What's this about?"

Mead unveiled the baby under his arms.

"What are you doing with my nephew?" Lisa hurried them inside.

Lisa opened the door and led Mead and Rogers into the house. It was rustic on the inside, with lots of country flavor. The enormous windows facing the water gave a panoramic view of the St. Lawrence. The inside of the house was wide open and let the natural light flow through every room. The windows on either side of the kitchen were open to let the country breeze blow through at ease and a wooden high-top table was situated just in the corner near the great views. There were six stools around the table, but placemats were set for two, with a tall vase full of freshly picked sunflowers between them. The refrigerator to the right of the entrance was old and hummed a bit. As they progressed toward the table, Allen noticed all the things he had grown up around—the house phone with the rotary dial, the table full of books and magazines, the fishing poles in the corner, the life jackets in a trunk of water toys. The stairs to the left that led upstairs to his bedrooms were still the same—the carpet hadn't changed, the way the light hit each step was exactly as Allen recalled.

"Jamie!" Lisa shouted out the sliding door. "Jamie, we have company."

"On my way, Mrs. White," Jamie replied from the water as he maneuvered the jet-ski onto the lift in the water.

Jamie had on a yellow t-shirt with the sleeves manually cut off and a black and white pair of bathing trunks. He was tan from long days in the sun and his hair was short, dirty blonde and wet from the river. Jamie's eyes were hazel-blue, and his face was baby smooth. Jamie wasn't overly built, but he was stronger than most people would think at first glance. Jamie twirled the jet-ski key in circles as he walked to the house, not a care in the world. He kicked off his water shoes on the grass, grabbed a towel off the hook to the right of the door and wiped his feet dry before he stepped inside. Mead and Rogers introduced themselves to Jamie, and he motioned for them to sit on the stools around the table.

"So, Mr. Mead, what can we do for you?" Jamie wondered.

"There is no easy way to say this," Mead started as the baby cooed. "Samuel and Melanie are dead."

"Mel is dead?" Lisa gasped. "But how? When?"

"I…I couldn't protect them," Rogers admitted.

Lisa placed her head on the table and cried as Jamie did his best to calm and console her.

"We just saw them," Jamie fretted. "We were just there for the baptism."

"How did my sister die?" Lisa demanded.

"They were murdered," Mead answered. "Thomas did all he could, but there were too many of them."

"What did these people want?" Lisa persisted.

"As you know, Mrs. White, your sister was adopted. As was her father before her and his mother before him. It's a pattern that goes back more generations than you could know. Your sister was the offspring of some very powerful people, and there are those who want nothing more than to eradicate that bloodline."

"She told me once she had a family secret," Lisa recalled. "But I never imagined it was something she'd be killed over."

"That secret didn't die with her," Rogers interjected. "This baby now carries that same burden."

"What do we have to do?" Jamie inquired.

"Keep him safe," Mead explained. "We'll take care of the rest. One of our associates will be close always to keep an eye on you all, but he will never reveal himself to you. Most importantly, however, is that you never tell the boy what happened to his parents."

"Why?" Jamie asked.

"If he knows the truth before he's ready, he'll go looking for answers and end up vulnerable to the same people that did this to Sam and Melanie."

"Won't they know he's here? Don't they know about Mel's family?" Jamie worried.

"They know of you, Mr. White, I can assure you of that. Their senses are connected to the bloodlines. We can protect you for some time, but there's no definitive answer on how long."

Lisa wiped the tears from her eyes and slid off the stool. She extended her arms to Mead who handed the baby to her. Hugs and handshakes ended the difficult conversation.

"Goodbye, Mr. White. Goodbye, Mrs. White," Mead said.

"Goodbye, Mr. Mead," Lisa replied, bouncing the baby gently.

Jamie and Lisa stood at the screen door and waved as Mead and

Rogers drove away. Lisa looked down at the baby and smiled.

"You'll be safe here, Allen," she said.

In the present, Allen let go of the key and opened his eyes in the lounge at 3 Riverside Drive. He couldn't find the right words, unsure of how to react. The surreal continued to happen despite his resistance and the glimpses into the past seemed too much for him to handle.

"So, The Nimayrd killed my parents and pretty much any family I've ever had?" Nobody answered Allen's question because even Allen knew the answer was simple. "How do we stop them?"

"That's the hard part, Allen," Rogers answered.

"Why?" Allen demanded.

"Without Merlin by our side, we don't stand a chance."

"Morgana?" Allen wondered.

"You saw for yourself," Clarissa said. "She's an animal and she's dangerous beyond measure. If you see her, run. She won't think twice of killing anyone—especially you, Allen."

"Merlin is the only one who can defeat her," Mead said.

"Where is Merlin? How do I free him?"

"The key in your hand, it will guide you," Mead offered. "We have to leave New York tomorrow night."

"Where are we going?"

"England, Mr. White."

# Chapter 29 – Trick or Treat?

Allen walked out of the Starbucks in Times Square with a coffee in his hand. He made his way to Pedestrian Plaza with one hand in his hooded sweatshirt pocket until he found an outdoor café table and sat down. Allen sipped the coffee while he soaked in the sounds and smells of the city. Kids and adults alike walked past him, Halloween excitement at a fever pitch in the city.

This time tomorrow, he would be a world away. Clarissa came to join Allen but chose not to bother him as he enjoyed the last moments of New York City he would experience for some time. Normally during visits to Times Square, Allen would send his mother a picture or text friends and extend the invitation to join him. Today, however, Allen just loved being in the midst of the city.

"You know you can talk, right?" Allen said.

"Nervous about the trip?" Clarissa finally asked.

"I've never been anywhere other than New York and Canada," Allen replied. "It's not nerves, it's not excitement…I can't describe it, really."

"I'm sure none of this is easy, but you're doing a good job of holding it together."

"Thanks, Clarissa," Allen said.

"Is there anything else you want to do before we go?"

"I wish I had time to go home and see my parents. I haven't talked to them much since my birthday."

"Why not?"

"Mead just kind of showed up at school on my birthday and my mother got nervous when I mentioned his name. She's been much quieter since then. I think she feels guilty for not telling me the truth about my birth parents; but I saw what happened. She shouldn't feel bad at all, she protected me and raised me like I was her own."

"At least you had that," Clarissa lamented.

"I'm sorry, I didn't mean to make you——"

"There's nothing to apologize for," Clarissa said with a sad smile. "We've all sacrificed a lot to get to this point, including you. It's about making this all worth it in the end."

"You all knew when you were younger about all The Nimayrd and The Master?"

"We were taught by Mead when he brought us to New York. It took a long time for some of us to come to grips with it; Eli more than most."

"It's just surreal. To think I'm part of some ancient war is ridiculous."

"That's what I thought when Mead first tried explaining it to me. But you're luckier than the rest of us, Allen. You've seen some of the moments we all wished we could've when we got told about who we are—you've *felt* it; the fire on your face, the Battle of Camlann. Eli left when he couldn't take anything more at face value."

"But if everything about The Master and the power they have is true, if all of these terrible things happened—if death follows wherever they go, if they have this giant army, if they can kill us a will, how can we even hope to stand up to them?"

"That's where you come in, Allen. You don't realize it, but you are the only one of us who can free Merlin."

"Me?"

"Yes, Allen...You."

"How? I don't know half of what you all know."

"I don't know that I am the one to answer that for you. But I will see this through with you all the way."

"Thanks, Clarissa."

"You're welcome."

Clarissa moved her hand over Allen's to offer encouragement and Allen closed his fingers and clasped her hand. He smiled at her and for a split second could see nothing else; the sounds of the city were gone, the craziness of Times Square replaced with an eerie calmness. There was peace in this moment, short-lived as it would be.

"I hope we aren't interrupting anything," Kay said.

"I couldn't have said it better myself, love," Lionel said.

Allen laughed and quickly recoiled his hand. Nigel, Eli, Anna, and Sasha arrived and each of them took chairs from other tables and set them up to sit as a group around Allen.

"Mead thought it'd be a good idea to keep an eye on you," Nigel said.

"But who's keeping an eye on you?" Clarissa joked.

"That's what I'm here for, love," Lionel chirped.

"And so, the blind lead the blind," Nigel retorted.

"Room for a couple more?" Joe asked as he and Young made their way over.

The group was almost whole again; nine of The Twelve Remains were together and ready to take the next step to protecting the future and keeping each other, and the world, safe from the threat of the Nimayrd.

"I hope you know you aren't going without me," Joe said to the group.

"Joe, are you sure you're up for a fight?" Kay asked.

"I'm as good as I will be," Joe answered. "Besides, I can't leave my best friend to do this alone. I have a promise to keep."

"So, what's the plan then?" Nigel wondered.

"The plan, *mon ami*, is simple. Hop a plane, free the wizard, destroy the evil and be on with our lives," Eli responded.

"I'm with Eli on this one," Sasha said.

"Bollocks!" Nigel shouted. "It won't be as easy as we hope, Allen with us or not. They know we're coming. They know what we want, what we're after. They'll protect what they think is theirs with all they have. Why are we all pretending this will change overnight? Every person at this table has lost everything to the Nimayrd. All of us have a lifetime of pain because of our so-called destiny. Our parents, our siblings, entire families wiped out by the likes of Jaxx and Morgana— and what do we have to show for it? Nothing. I'm willing to give my life if it means they're stopped, but I won't pretend to think we can just *stop* them because we believe in ourselves."

The mood around the table immediately changed. Nigel's dose of reality was too much for many in the group to handle. They all knew the truth, but Nigel made it a brutal reality. While most of them had spent at least some time training, The Master and Morgana alone could be enough to defeat them without Merlin. Especially Allen.

"What do you suggest?" Clarissa questioned.

"I think some of us should go right now. The rest should meet us in London. They expect us to be together, so if we split up, they could be thrown off guard."

"No," Lionel disagreed. "Our best bet is to stay together. If we split up, we are vulnerable."

"It's foolish to think we're any safer together," Nigel replied.

The group began to argue amongst themselves while Allen silently sat and listened to the heated discussion.

"Let him decide," Lionel pointed to Allen.

"Me? Why me?" Allen said.

"You're meant to lead us, you decide," Nigel answered.

Allen looked around at the faces of his new friends, each eager to see what he would choose.

"We stay," Allen decided. "Everything Mead talked about included us being together. We'll go to England together."

Nigel dramatically threw his arms in the air and slammed them down onto his lap. "Fine," he said. "We go together." He got up and stomped off.

"Where you going, *mon ami?*" Eli called after him.

"To get pre-flight drunk," Nigel answered over his shoulder.

Lionel and Eli jumped up from the table to follow Nigel. "We'll be back!" Lionel shouted.

"Wound a bit tight, that one, Jesus Christ," Sasha commented.

"She speaks," Joe said with a laugh.

Sasha pulled a switchblade from her back pocket and flipped it open, quickly pointing it at Joe's crotch. Joe tightened in the chair as Sasha ran the blade along his leg and tapped it on his thigh.

"You're a funny man, Joseph," Sasha said, grinning through her thick fake accent. "I'm a funny lady. Ready for a joke? Knock, knock."

Joe had no choice but to play along.

"Who's...who's there?" he asked.

"Knife."

"Sasha, behave," Kay interjected.

"You shut the hell up!" she yelled. "Joseph...focus; Knife."

"Kn...kn...knife who?"

"Knife to meet you!" Sasha took the knife and lifted it into the air. Joe jumped back with his eyes closed and Sasha roared with laughter as she closed the blade and put it back in her pocket.

"I like you, Joseph. We'll be friends."

Joe slid back into the chair uncomfortably as the rest of the group heckled him. Even Allen joined in the laughter. "You had that one coming, bro," he said.

As the sun began to set in Times Square and night was upon the city, Allen was mesmerized by the laughter and joy around him. "It's such a beautiful city," he said.

"We're probably missing one hell of a Halloween party right now," Joe said.

"The girls are probably pre-gaming and wondering where the hell we are. Where Stephanie *could* be," Allen added.

"They'll be okay without us," Joe assured.

Officer Young approached the group as Officer Carroll trailed not too far behind.

"Mako, what's going on?" Kay asked.

"Just checking in, Kay. Is everyone ready to go?"

"Yeah, everything is ready. We'll meet back at Riverside tonight. Mead is making the arrangements."

"I'll see you there," Young said, stopping his conversation with Kay just in time, as Officer Carroll approached.

"You ready to roll, partner?" Carroll asked.

"How do you get a name like Mako?" Allen wondered.

"It's a long story," Kay chuckled.

For some time, the remaining members of the group sat and watched as the younger kids ran and skipped around Times Square in costume, basking in the delight of the sunset. It was by far Allen's favorite holiday. He loved autumn, it meant Halloween season was here. He could remember the pillowcases full of candy he would get when he was younger. The North Country of New York was a small but generous community, and Halloween was the holiday where a neighbor's generosity was most apparent. Allen remembered how his father would help him create a better costume every year. All the kids would gather after trick-or-treating at Farmer Miller's barn. The old farmer would rearrange his barn for a Halloween party with dancing, games, and contests. Allen won the costume contest when he was ten for his Ninja Turtle costume. As he got older, the novelty wore off for Allen and the other kids, but he still went to that party every year until he went to college.

Nigel, Lionel, and Eli returned from their jaunt to the bar looking relaxed after a few drinks.

"Do they drink *all* the time?" Allen whispered to Clarissa.

"It's more than usual, that's for sure," she said. "But don't let it fool you, the three of them are equal to 1000 men."

"They're that good?"

"Better than you can imagine; just wait until we get to London, they'll teach you."

"Why haven't they taught me already?"

"What do you mean?"

"We kinda just sat around and held keys when I could have been learning to fight; I could've saved Stephanie."

Clarissa didn't have time to answer because Lionel's antics caught everyone's attention.

Lionel's head kept turning as the young ladies' outfits became increasingly revealing. He then saw a woman alone in Times Square wearing a dark cape and a Venetian mask to cover her face. Her dress was tight, silver, and flowed elegantly as she paced back and forth by the red stairs of the TKTS booth. She didn't fit in, and she enthralled Lionel, who couldn't resist the urge to talk to her.

"Not now," Nigel whined.

"I'm in love, mate!" Lionel announced. "She's a silver fox!"

"He's right, *mon ami*. Now's not the time," Eli added.

Lionel ignored their protests and made his way toward the attractive young woman.

"Nice night, isn't it?" Lionel opened.

"It just got better, handsome," she replied.

"What's a beautiful woman like you doing all alone tonight?"

"Waiting for you, of course," she quipped.

"The wait is over, love."

"I couldn't have said it better myself…love," she said.

The others watched as the woman pulled Lionel into a kiss. His arms flailed at his sides as he attempted to gain his composure. The sexy stranger released her lips from Lionel and his friends all stood and clapped for him. Some laughed, some pointed, but they all took joy in Lionel's embarrassment.

"I'm definitely in love," Lionel whispered. "I don't even know your name, but can I call you sometime?"

The woman smiled at Lionel and pulled him toward her again, this time whispering into his ear. As she tightened her grip on him, Nigel jumped out of his chair from across the pavement and rushed to his cousin.

The woman's body began to slowly transform into her true form.

"Oh, you can call me anytime…Lionel."

Lionel's heart dropped into his stomach. The stranger cackled and drew back her right hand. A ball of fire filled her palm and she focused on Lionel. She threw the fireball at him just as Nigel tackled his cousin to the ground. The duo ran for cover behind a trash can.

"Is this burning, an eternal flame," Morgana screamed loudly as she prepared another fireball.

"It's Morgana!" Lionel screamed to the others.

The Nimayrd had arrived.

# Chapter 30 – Fight Night

The Remains hurried to their feet as Morgana climbed the red stairs in Pedestrian Plaza until she reached the very top. Lionel remained ducked behind a trash can, waiting for the right moment to rejoin the others. Whatever light the sky had offered before disappeared as Morgana prepared her magic to terrorize The Remains. The group huddled at the bottom of the red stairs as New Yorkers and tourists alike gathered around, murmuring to each other that it was another it was another of several street performances to which they'd grown accustomed.

Morgana waved her hands in an hourglass shape through the air from her head to her waist and her black jumpsuit and silver hair reappeared. Her eyes and the skin that stretched to her ears glowed the color of her hair. The Remains formed a semi-circle near the base of the stairs, their only true defense against the psychotic sorceress. Weaponless and afraid, The Remains gathered close to protect each other by any means necessary.

"Allen, get behind me," Eli said. "The rest of you, get ready."

As they readied for a fight, the manhole over the adjacent street opened and Rogers emerged with a katana in one hand and a duffle bag in the other. Morgana watched as Rogers rallied to The Remains.

"Stay close to each other!" Rogers shouted.

He dropped the bag on the ground behind the group and Kay and Clarissa dug in first. Kay pulled out a small ax with a wooden handle and sharp blade at the tip, while Clarissa dragged a machete out from the duffle.

"You!" Morgana exclaimed.

"Your evil has no place here, Morgana," Rogers retorted. "Go back to the fires of Hell."

"A long time ago, Thomas, someone tried to send me back to the fires of Hell," Morgana said. "We all know what happened to *him.*"

"Leave now, Morgana," Rogers insisted.

"I'll only say this once," Morgana warned. "Give me the boy and the key and you'll all be spared. Don't, and you'll all die."

"We aren't afraid of you," Kay shouted.

"You should be, Kay. You should be," Morgana responded.

"If you want him," Clarissa started as she raised the machete, "come get him."

"You fools! You're all dead."

"It's you who will die, witch!" Sasha yelled.

Tilting her head to the baby of the bunch, the foul-mouthed Romanian, Morgana laughed. "Little Sasha, all grown up. Amazing you lived this long. Your mother here to help you? Oh, wait, that's right."

Morgana raised her hands to the sky and looked up. She mumbled incoherently to herself and slowly lowered her head down to stare at The Remains. The Fylorn appeared beside the sorceress and dozens of Syphs floated through the portal.

The Syphs were in their purest form—beasts with red eyes, grey skin, pointed ears and sharp teeth like a shark. Their hands had only one thumb and two fingers, and each appendage was a dangerous claw with venom dripping, waiting to poison the next victim.

"Kill them all!" ordered Morgana.

"You'll have to do better than Syphs," Lionel stated, leaning against the railing.

"Is that so? Well…try these, lover. *Fortitudo et vento certamen, da mihi potestatem bestiae fugam!*"

The Syphs all contorted backward in a disturbing harmony as Morgana sent lightning from her palms into their spines. When she stopped, the Syphs convulsed as the skin on their backs opened and wings protruded from their bodies—grey and veiny, the wings looked like giant bat signals flapping in the sky. Allen had never experienced anything like this. Now he knew, this was all very real.

"What the hell are those?" Allen said, voice high-pitched and anxious.

"Bloody hell," Lionel complained.

"Just had to kiss her, didn't you?" Nigel mocked.

Nigel rummaged through the duffle bag completely and pulled out a dagger which he placed on the ground next to him. He then shoved his hand into his pants pocket, pulled out a black glove and slid it on his hand. Nigel slammed his fist into his open hand and squeezed them both into fists while Lionel reached into the bag, shuffled his hands around and pulled out a chrome Smith & Wesson 9-millimeter gun.

"A gun?" Nigel asked, eyebrows raised.

"No bow and arrows," Lionel huffed.

"Well, Mr. Bond, are you ready?" Nigel joked in a Sean Connery voice.

"Let's do this."

"Y'all can't have all the fun," Eli interrupted.

Eli took off his jacket and tossed it to the ground. Underneath his coat, he wore a white tank top that showed off his muscular physique and chest tattoos. Eli reached behind his back and pulled his caber from between his lower back and his track pants. The uncanny Cajun's fedora never budged from his head.

"*Laissez les bons temps rouler!*" Eli shouted.

"Finally, we fight." Sasha beamed as she reached into the bag and pulled out a sickle, swinging the weapon in her hand a few times, then gripping it tightly. "This thing is shit." She dropped the sickle and grabbed her switchblade.

Morgana watched, amused, from the top of the red stairs, intent to let her minions kill their prey. The Syphs jumped into the air, testing their new power for the first time. They climbed higher and higher through the air, leering down on The Remains from nearly thirty feet above the ground. Eli threw his caber and it lodged into the chest of one Syph. The creature went limp and fell from the sky, then slammed into the pavement of Times Square.

The remaining Syphs dived down into The Remains. Outnumbered, The Remains were overwhelmed by the flying fiends, each of The Remains wildly swinging or shooting at the beasts—they tried to stay close to each other, but they'd be dead if they didn't spread out to fight. One Syph managed to grip Eli's tank top and started to fly upward, but gunshots rang out and hit the Syph in the back, sending both the Syph and Eli plummeting to the pavement. Eli used the creature to break his fall. Officers Young and Carroll ran into the melee as they fired numerous times at the Syphs, killing six, while Lionel killed four more with his gun.

"Uh, Mako…What the hell?" Carroll said.

"I'll fill you in later; kill anything that looks like it wants to eat you."

Morgana looked to the orb again. More winged Syphs zoomed into New York. The Remains stood ready, but nothing prepared them for the other creatures that exited the orb. And worse, Jaxx came through first, with Kimo following behind. With a glance at each other, Allen and Joe rushed the red stairs. Morgana stopped Joe before he climbed the stairs, as she let the invading Syphs attack Allen.

Joe suddenly stopped, held in place by Morgana's magic; he thrashed and punched but couldn't break free from whatever she had done to him. Allen was swarmed by three Syphs. Clarissa threw Allen her machete; Allen caught the weapon and plunged the blade deep into the chest of the closest Syph while Clarissa weaved through the battle, striking and slicing until she managed to get back to the bag. She retrieved a spiked battle club; the weapon was wooden with twenty-one metallic spikes protruding from its length. Clarissa joined Allen at the base of the stairs—Allen's priority was to protect Joe, trapped in Morgana's thrall.

Joe continued the struggle to move his body through the power of Morgana's spell while Allen and Clarissa stood back-to-back, facing a Syph swinging its claws at them. Five more Syphs circled Allen and Clarissa as they fought with all they had. Allen killed another Syph as Lionel and Nigel came to their aid. The four of them fought off the attacking beasts, but the winged army kept coming. Allen was surrounded but still fought to keep Joe safe and as he stabbed through one monster's chest and pulled the machete out of the Syph, another wildly swung its arms and pierced Allen's skin before Lionel could kill it; Allen fell forward to the pavement as Lionel angrily finished the monster off.

"No!" Joe screamed.

"Allen, stay with me, mate," Lionel encouraged.

"Allen," Clarissa cried. "Allen, can you hear me?"

Morgana invited Jaxx and Kimo to her side, and released the hold over Joe, who ran to Allen's side. He gaped up at the trio, shaking in anger. Kimo turned his head to Morgana.

"Don't look at me, Kimo, he's your friend," Morgana said.

"Do it, Kimo!" Jaxx said.

Kimo descended the red stairs as Joe picked up Allen's machete and charged his old friend. Kimo met Joe at the base of the stairs, brandishing the same blade he used to kill Stephanie. He wildly heaved the blade at Joe with a vicious growl. Their blades met and sparks flew as the noise of metal on metal got louder with each swing from each combatant. Kimo pulled back his left arm and clenched his fist. He threw a punch at Joe; however, Joe was stronger than Kimo and caught his opponent's fist with his hand.

"You never could throw a punch that mattered," Joe insulted.

Joe punched Kimo with the handle of the machete, sending his old roommate to the ground. Joe kicked Kimo's blade out of his hand and stabbed his former friend through the heart with the machete. Morgana stomped her foot and a thunderous noise reverberated through Times Square, forcing the machete out of Joe's hand as she snickered at him. Joe spun to the sorceress and Morgana kept his attention as she watched Kimo rise to his feet.

"Something funny?" Joe asked.

"You thinking you could hurt me is funny," Kimo snarled.

Joe turned around and was face-to-face with his old roommate and friend. The wound Joe inflicted healed itself and closed on Kimo's chest as if nothing happened. Joe tried to throw another punch but found himself stuck under Morgana's power again; his body stiff and motionless this time—frozen and vulnerable in what appeared to be an invisible energy that encapsulated his body. Kimo bent over and picked his blade up off the ground. He violently swung it a few times through the air as he circled the frozen former friend.

"You always thought you were better than me! You always favored him." Kimo pointed to Allen. "You're both going to die tonight, but I want *him* to suffer."

"Kimo, you don't have to do this!" Allen shouted from the ground.

"I'll get to you soon enough," Kimo spat.

Kimo grabbed Joe by the back of the neck. "All the time I wasted trying to impress you, trying to be your friend. You're like the rest of them. You're a liar. You *betrayed* me."

"I never betrayed you, Kimo. You did this to yourself, time and time again," Joe said.

"Your time is up, Joe. Any last words?"

Kimo leaned toward Joe and cupped his hand to his ear to feign listening before he placed it back on the nape of Joe's neck.

"Stephanie was right," Joe stated. "You are a piece of shit."

Kimo grinned. "Tell her I said hey."

Kimo thrust his weapon into Joe's chest and in one motion pulled the bloodied blade back out. He repeated the action four or five more times as tears welled in Joe's eyes and blood escaped Joe's body through his chest and mouth. Kimo rubbed his hand in the blood and wiped it across his chest in a ceremony of celebration. He pounded his fist to his chest and screamed. Allen's heart broke once more as he watched his friend being stabbed. Morgana waved her hand in a shooing motion and Joe collapsed into the pool of his own blood.

"No!" Allen cried. "How could you do this, Kimo? Why?"

"Your turn," Kimo snarled. "I've been waiting for this moment since freshman year. You stole my girl and turned my friends against me. It felt good to punch you then, so I can imagine how good this is going to feel—for me at least."

"Leave him alone!" Clarissa shouted as she shielded Allen.

The Remains rallied to Allen, but they were quickly thwarted by Morgana's magic. Kimo continued to stalk Allen as the venom of the Syph claw coursed through Allen's body, slowly paralyzing him. Kimo looked over his shoulder to Morgana and the evil enchantress simply nodded her head—and slowed the venom from overtaking Allen's body.

Kimo hissed at Allen, voice trembling with fury, "I wanted her to take that poison away so that you could feel everything I'm about to do to you. This won't be a fast death, Allen. I'm going to savor every cut, every drop of blood. Before I'm done, you will beg me to slit your throat and end this. One cut for every single time you hurt me."

Allen's strength returned to him slowly, but he managed to get to one knee and tried to throw a punch at Kimo—who laughed and sidestepped the fist. Allen breathed heavy as he struggled to get his hands on Kimo, wildly throwing his fists at the murdering maniac.

"You are pathetic," Kimo mocked. *"Poor me, all my friends are dead."*

"You'll pay for this, Kimo," Allen assured.

"You say that so often and yet, here I am. Maybe after I'm done with you, I'll take a trip to see Tommy. Or even better, I'll look up your parents and pay them a visit."

Allen jumped up off the ground and grabbed Kimo by the throat. Kimo raised his arm and pounded down on Allen's forearm and elbow, breaking the hold. A weakened Allen stumbled back a few feet and as he moved forward again to attack, Kimo took out a knife and thrust it deep into Allen's lower abdomen. As blood sprayed out from the wound, Allen became dizzy and disoriented; the combination of blood loss and the pain overwhelmed him. Kimo kicked the back of Allen's legs, forcing him to kneel, and held the knife to Allen's throat, ready to slice.

"Goodbye, Allen," Kimo whispered.

"STOP!" a voice shouted. "The boy is *mine*."

A shadowy figure emerged from the glowing crimson orb as Allen struggled to get back to his feet. Morgana bowed her head as The Master appeared in Times Square. He made his way down the red stairs to where Allen struggled to stay alive.

"Step aside, Kimo," commanded The Master.

"Yes, Master."

The Master surveyed Allen and the other Remains, all standing solid under the hold of Morgana.

"I heard nine of you had convened, yet I count ten… Morgana?"

"The fat cop," she said.

"I thought I told you there were to be no witnesses, Morgana. Erase it all from their minds and shield us." The Master's voice was full of rage and Morgana quickly realized her mistake.

Morgana closed her eyes and focused on the people in Times Square. She erased thousands of people's memories and stopped all of New York at that moment—people were stuck in time, cell phones wiped clean, all of them unaware of what was happening. The Master passed by The Remains and tormented the group of friends.

"For years, I've watched those before you come and go, some unaware of their importance, some with the knowledge that has been passed on to you. The same thing is always true, however," The Master sneered, "you all scream just before you die. It's music to my ears, really. Anna, your parents didn't scream; Jaxx cut their throats before they died, so I guess they…gurgled? Ah, Officer Mako Young. I'm genuinely happy to see you, I told your parents I'd keep an eye on you. In fact, *Officer*, here you go…your father's eyes. How's Mom? Still dead tired?"

The Master unfolded his hands and two eyeballs dropped from his grip. He wiped his hands together a few times and then rubbed them on Young's chest.

A strangled cry escaped Young's lips, a sound so inhumanly sad that it seemed to echo through New York City, piercing the eerie silence. It was a sound born of shock, an agony that rose from the depths of Mako's soul. The Master paid no heed to Young's anguish, his movements deliberate as he wiped his hands together, the sickening sound of flesh against flesh filling the air.

"Eli," The Master started. "You're not quite as plump as your father. Think you could run away from Jaxx? We all know Daddy couldn't, isn't that right, Jaxx?"

"Certainly was the easiest hunt I've had," Jaxx snickered.

"Maybe your fastest. Morgana, thoughts?"

"Sweet little Sasha's mother," Morgana gloated. "Chug-a-chug-a-choo-choo."

"I could go on and on with the past," The Master said. "Tonight, however, is about the future. The Nimayrd's time has come. Look at these people. New York—one example of all that's wrong in the world. But we will change all that. There's no room in our new world for any of these people, especially all of *you*."

The Master pulled a curved dagger out from under his cloak and sunk the knife into Officer Carroll's neck. Morgana released her hold on Carroll, and he dropped to the ground with the knife still in his neck as blood poured from the wound.

"Now it's just us again," The Master mocked. "Kay, Clarissa, ready for some real fun? How about you Nigel, Lionel? I remember the night we killed your families. It was very much just like this. Kneel."

Morgana forced all The Remains to kneel, each of them still under her control. The Master turned his attention to Professor Rogers. The sweat dripped off Rogers' bald head and onto the ground as he struggled to break free of the magic of Morgana.

"Who…are…you?" Rogers asked.

"I haven't forgotten you, Thomas. All these years you held on to this belief that you could defeat us, that we were somehow vulnerable. Tonight, we are stronger than ever. Watch, Thomas, as your grand scheme goes up in flames."

The Master bent down and pulled the knife from Officer Carroll's neck. He wiped the blood on the dead officer's uniform and turned his attention to the would-be-hero, Allen. The Master strutted over to Allen, hovered above him and grasped his knife in both hands above his head.

"You failed, Remains, much like those before you. And look at you, Allen White, the savior. I don't know why they thought you'd be different. You can't fight, you have nothing special about you. Thomas, are you sure he's a king?"

"Show us who you are before you kill us," Rogers said.

"Another time, Thomas," The Master said.

The Master thrust the dagger downward and a sonic boom of white light filled Times Square. The dagger flew from The Master's hands and hit the ground as he hunched over to shelter his eyes from the light. When the light faded, The Master reopened his eyes to see Mead standing across from him, holding a staff.

"Impossible," The Master said. "Why, that staff belonged to—"

"Merlin," Morgana finished.

"Quite right, witch," Mead said with a smile.

Mead swung the staff around his head with such ferocity and power that The Master and Morgana both flinched. He slammed the staff against the ground, delivering another boom that knocked down The Master, Morgana, Jaxx, and Kimo.

The power of the staff crackled in the air as Mead unleashed its raw energy; a force that was both awe-inspiring to his friends and terrifying to The Nimayrd. The remaining Syphs stood no chance, their twisted forms writhing in agony as they were consumed by the searing light. With a flick of his wrist, Mead sent forth a wave of energy that tore through the ranks of the Syphs like a scythe through wheat, leaving nothing but dust and ash in its wake. The air was filled with the sickening sound of the Syphs' final screams.

Morgana's hold over The Remains shattered like glass as the power of Merlin's staff flowed, an energy and force that was uncontrollable. As the group rushed to protect Allen, Mead raised the staff high, its magic glowing with intensity. With another tap on the ground, a blurred prism of light shot forth and the pavement trembled beneath their feet—the unleashed power delivering an eruption like an earthquake. Chunks and sheets of asphalt projected into the air, then rained back down, sending The Remains into panic.

But the debris never hit them.

A force field had formed around them, and between The Remains and The Nimayrd, crackling with energy and humming like a generator.

Angered, Morgana let out a blood-curdling scream that darkened the sky and gave The Fylorn more power, the orb spinning at speeds nobody had ever witnessed. The orb created a funnel that began to engulf the ashes of the Syphs and lifted Joe's corpse off the ground and sucked it into the abyss of The Nimayrd. The Master picked up his dagger and hurried toward the force field where Allen lay on the ground, losing more and more blood.

"Master, we must go," Jaxx implored.

"No. We wait one more minute," The Master ordered.

"Jaxx, Kimo, back through the orb," Morgana said.

The Master turned away from the vessel of his escape after meeting Morgana's eyes. Jaxx jumped into the orb and disappeared. Kimo wasn't far behind.

"You really have no idea what you're meddling with," The Master barked at The Remains. "You are all doomed."

"You're the hopeless one," Allen coughed out.

"Tsk, tsk, Allen. Let me guess. You think if Merlin lives that all of this will just end? You think the power of The Nimayrd can be stopped by the likes of him? You are a fool."

"We will find him, and we will end this fight," Rogers said.

The Master laughed as he walked over and stood with his hand against the force field. Beams of red light radiated around The Master's hand as he tried to find a weakness in the barrier.

"You may have escaped death today, Remains, but all of you will die before this war is over."

"We will kill you," Clarissa promised.

"Silly girl, you will try, and you will fail. I am eternal. There's nothing in this world that can harm me."

"Exc—" Mead began.

"Even that cannot harm me, old man. For all your insight into the past, Mead, I thought you'd know this by now."

"I don't understand," Allen mumbled.

Allen attempted to rise to his feet, but his agony forced him quickly back to his knees. He pressed his hand over the wound to control the bleeding but was slipping farther away from consciousness.

"Morgana, come!" The Master summoned.

Morgana floated from the top of the red stairs to be at the side of her Master. The Fylorn followed her down and spun next to them.

"The barrier is too strong, we need to get out of here," Morgana said. "As long as Mead has the staff, they are protected."

"You can't defeat me," The Master warned. "The sword won't help you. It belongs to me and me alone."

"The sword chooses its wielder; you will never hold it," Rogers said.

"The sword will answer to me," The Master insisted. "You see, Allen, you can't beat me; I am immortal. I am forever."

The Master knelt to face Allen and slowly removed the hood of his cloak and bowed his head. His wavy salt-and-pepper hair was pushed back from his forehead and face. His beard was just as multi-colored as the hair on his head. The Master's eyes weren't red like his followers, but a deep green color that were warm and inviting, not imposing. Allen was shocked at how kind The Master's eyes looked. The Master grinned as he lifted his head upward, showing the long scar that covered his neck to his chest.

"I…am…Arthur."

Arthur pulled the hood of the cloak over his head. He and Morgana walked through the glowing orb and both villains disappeared., leaving The Remains to deal with a wounded Allen and the terrifying truth. Mead tapped the staff to the ground and The Remains disappeared as Allen surrendered his consciousness to the pain.

PART I – THE END

PART II

# Chapter 1 – Home at Last

Allen's eyes slowly opened in his bedroom at home in Clayton, New York. He'd left his window open during the night and the crisp morning breeze intoxicated him as he rolled over to look out the window. The sunlight trickled in and shined into the center of his room, but Allen was just happy to be home. Everything in his room was as he'd left before he returned to school for his senior year. The dresser across from Allen's bed had a few framed pictures on top of it, while a mirror was fixed to the wall behind the dresser. The walls were the same light beige, littered with thumbtack holes where the posters he took to school used to hang.

Allen let out a sigh of relief that the nightmare was over; the dream was so real he was sure he'd experienced everything. He shook it off, kicked off the bed sheets and got up.

"Mom, Dad?" Allen called, heading down the stairs after he'd cleaned up.

But nobody answered. Instead, just a faint breathing sound Allen thought was coming from outside. As he moved toward the doors that led to the river, Allen stopped in his tracks.

He saw the lifeless bodies of his parents on the floor with Kimo standing over them. With a guttural cry, Allen moved to attack Kimo, but searing pain made him grab at his stomach. His wound from Times Square was oozing more blood. Kimo laughed as Allen fell to the ground and left the bodies on the floor to hover over the fallen Allen. Kimo raised an ax above his head. As the ax came down, Allen instantly awoke.

Allen was still in his childhood bedroom, but he could hear the echoes of people talking from downstairs, though nothing was clear. As

Allen attempted to sit up in bed, a hand gripped his shoulder to keep him from moving.

"You shouldn't move," Clarissa said. "You have a pretty nasty wound."

"What happened?" Allen wondered.

"After the attack in Times Square, you collapsed. Kimo stabbed you deep. Some of us traveled through the night to get here to your parents' house, but others decided to head to London last night."

"Is everyone okay?" Allen worried.

"Everyone is shaken, but ready to do whatever needs to be done next."

"And what about Joe?"

Clarissa breathed heavy and told Allen the truth.

"I'm sorry, Allen. He's gone."

The news defeated Allen. He'd hoped Joe's death was part of the hallucinations brought about by the venom of the Syph scratch, but he realized both his best friends were dead. Clarissa's presence was a welcome one—but there was little comfort in all the new friends he'd made. The reality was Joe and Stephanie were irreplaceable and Allen was crushed to lose them. Allen's need for vengeance filled him and fueled him past the pain.

"Who's here?" Allen asked as he clutched at his abdomen.

"Me, Lionel, Sasha, Mead, and Rogers. The rest are probably in London by now. Do you want to see your parents? They've been sick worrying about you."

"We both know they aren't my parents. They could leave today and never look back again and they'd finally have their own lives—not someone else's problems.

Allen nodded and Clarissa leaned over to help him to his feet. The pain in his abdomen was excruciating as Allen struggled to his feet and hooked his arm around Clarissa's shoulder and neck. Clarissa helped him downstairs and into the living area, where the others had gathered around the high-top table.

"Allen!" Lisa shouted.

"Son!" Jamie added.

His parents jumped up from the table and ran toward Allen. As Clarissa released Allen, his mother embraced him gently, while his father put his hand on Allen's back. Lisa kissed Allen's forehead and cupped his head in her hands as she took a step back.

"How are you feeling?" she asked.

"I'm okay, just really sore. Not every day someone stabs you in the stomach," Allen joked.

"That's not funny," Lisa said.

"Sorry, Mom. Just trying to show you I'm fine."

"We are sorry, Allen," Jamie explained. "We wanted to tell—"

"Dad, it's okay," Allen interrupted. "I know why you couldn't tell me. I get it, trust me."

"Well, your mother and I just want you to know we never wanted this to happen to you," Jamie assured. "We knew this day might come, and we did what we could to shield you from all this pain."

"I know, Dad. I know."

Lisa looked Allen in the eyes and stroked his face a little. "Your parents would be proud of you," she said.

"Thanks, Mom."

Allen's parents helped him to the couch and gingerly placed him on the middle cushion as his mother sat on one side and Clarissa sat on the other. Lisa placed her hand over Allen's, softening the quiet tension in the room for the next few minutes before Mead finally had something to say.

"We all know what has to happen next," Mead began. "We have to free him."

"We can't get there with Allen," Rogers warned. "They'll know."

"Then we only have one option," Clarissa stated, "and you know what that means."

"That's a dangerous journey," Mead said. "Are you up for that, Mr. White?"

"Yes," Allen responded. "Whatever it takes."

"Are you sure you're up for this, honey?" Lisa asked.

"I have to be, Mom. I gotta do this. I can't watch anyone else I care about die."

"Let me go with you," Jamie begged.

"No, Dad, you have to stay here. Mom needs you. What if they come here for her?"

"And what about you?" Jamie moved toward Allen from the table. "She needs you to be okay, too."

Allen looked at his parents, the pain in their eyes, and their tired faces from days of worrying, and he took a deep breath. He got to his feet on his own and put a hand on his father's shoulder as he turned and locked eyes with his mother.

"I promise you that I'll be back."

"You'll watch over him?" Lisa asked the group.

"With our lives," Lionel assured.

Allen violently jerked forward and the pain in his stomach was uncontrollable. Blood poured from his stomach as Clarissa applied pressure to the wound.

"Allen! Can you hear me? Allen?" Clarissa shouted.

"Mom...help me," Allen garbled.

Allen's body jerked as he snapped back to reality. Gone was the hallucination of the life he left behind in Clayton. Allen's mind twisted in and out of New York City and the imminent danger of death.

"The poison from the Syph is in his blood," Mead said, "we have to get him back to Riverside."

Clarissa looked around as people riding the subway crowded around to see the commotion. Allen's body jerked as his body was ravaged and his mind slipped in and out of delusions. The other companions tried to shield Allen from prying eyes as the subway car came to a stop.

When they stepped off the car onto the platform, Allen's eyes opened, and he was on his feet. The usually filthy station was clean, odorless, and full of light. The pain subsided momentarily, and Allen heard a soft voice reverberate through the station.

"*Allen...*"

"Who's there?" Allen asked.

"*...Free me...*"

"Who are you?" Allen shouted. "What do you want from me?"

The sound of a voice over the intercom echoed throughout the empty station: "*FREE ME.*"

The lights strobed and Allen shielded his eyes from the brightness—and then, the station blackened. Allen could feel the breeze of the underground station moving a little faster, and then the wind blew forcefully through the station. The gusts swirled in front of Allen, and they began to form a figure.

*This is it*, Allen thought. *This will get me closer to learning who I need to free.*

But as the figure became clearer, he realized he was wrong—it was the former king, The Master.

"I...am... Arthur..." The Master had said. "I...am...Arthur."

It was a memory from earlier in the night, and the three words repeated in Allen's head over and over—those kind green eyes piercing his mind like the Syph wound.

"I am Arthur…" Allen mumbled.

"Oh, this can't be good," Lionel said.

The tranquil subway station disappeared, and the terrible reality returned; Allen spit up blood as Clarissa and Lionel supported his weight. They struggled, pulling and carrying Allen up the stairs. When they finally reached the top, Allen collapsed.

"I am Arthur…" Allen repeated.

Allen's eyes opened and rolled into the back of his head, and he once again lost consciousness—this time into a vision of Arthur after Camlann.

The wound was deep, and the young man was certain to die. His body was sprawled across a wooden table as the Sisters of Avalon's healers gathered to try and keep him alive. The room was quiet and dimly lit by the sun that teased through the small window. The mood was somber as worry grew. Arthur could feel hands all over him, his pain increased each time they came to the wound on his chest. Death pressed in closer on him, and his mind began to give in to the reality of dying.

Several women shuffled around the table, some bringing clean cloths, others removing blood-soaked towels. The smell of blood and death filled the room, each moment a race against Death. One of the healers, Sarah, grabbed a handful of cloths and tied them together to make a tourniquet for Arthur's wound. She gently lifted his head and tied the cloths around his shoulder as another healer frantically tried to sew the wound shut with a small needle and makeshift thread. He was surrounded by people that hoped to save his life. The Avalonian women were all wearing white robes with a small red stripe across the collar, each garment hand woven by the woman as proof of their skill as healers. Their healing tools were nothing more than their hands and the needle and thread for sewing wounds closed.

"If he truly is the king we've waited for all these years, he has to be saved," Sarah said, though they all knew it.

"He will not survive the night if this continues," another healer whispered.

"We can't let him die," Sarah added.

"There is no way we can save him," a voice lamented. "We need Merlin; we need magic."

"I am Arthur…" the young man whispered.

"Leave us," a woman in the darkest corner of the room demanded.

Her face was shielded by the darkness, her intent just as hidden.

The room cleared out and the young woman approached the table. She leaned over the wooden table Arthur had been placed upon. His entire chest was covered in blood, the table dripping bits of blood off the side and to the floor. The wound was ripping through the stitches, a dam that would kill him if it broke. The mysterious woman reached out and softly stroked his face with her hand. She touched Arthur's hands, the coldness telling her death was imminent. She bowed her head and bent over to kiss his forehead.

"Who…who's there?" Arthur asked hoarsely.

"You're safe, that's all that matters," she responded.

The young man opened his eyes and fear coursed through his body. "Morgana?"

A flash of red light filled the room, and the Sisters of Avalon pushed back into the room as Morgana revealed herself. The young witch stood over her half-brother and one-time lover and began chanting.

"*Libera mortis limine daret regi vitam. Libera mortis limine daret regi vitam. Libera mortis limine daret regi vitam. Libera mortis limine daret regi vitam. Libera mortis limine daret regi vitam.*"

Arthur gasped for air to fill his lungs as Morgana backed away from the table.

The King had been brought back to life.

The Sisters of Avalon all clasped their hands together and looked to the heavens in praise of the miracle they'd witnessed.

"Leave us," Morgana ordered.

The Avalonian women bowed their heads to Morgana and exited the room one by one, each one showing respect and love to Arthur and Morgana.

A newly healed Arthur sat up on the wooden table, confused.

"Why are you helping me, Morgana?" Arthur asked.

"Shhh," she replied. "You mustn't speak. Save your energy, brother."

The wound at Arthur's neck was healed; the wound at his chest disappeared as if it never happened, leaving only a scar from neck to bellybutton as a reminder of the day Arthur confronted death. Morgana wanted Arthur to fail and their bastard son, Mordred, to take the throne, but her real anger was with Merlin, not her brother. It was Merlin who set all of this in motion when he tricked Morgana's mother; the same seductive ruse Morgana used with Arthur.

"Mordred lost his focus, Arthur," she explained. "It was always about the wizard, never about you."

"Merlin—where is he?" Arthur asked.

"He is gone forever." Morgana smiled. "Now you can rule these lands forever."

"The Grail is gone, Morgana," Arthur revealed.

"You don't need that stupid trinket anymore, brother. You have my magic to keep you alive forever."

Arthur's eyes opened wide upon hearing this. "How is that even possible, Morgana?"

"The dark magic has given me a power beyond compare—a power the wizard only wished he had. I can create life, Arthur; I just brought you back from the dead. I am almighty."

"But why spare me?"

"You are my blood; what courses through your veins gives you strength. I would not waste another drop of our blood for their wars."

"What will this cost me, Morgana?"

"It will not cost you a thing, my King."

"Why the change of heart…sister?"

"All I ever wanted was to see the wizard burn for what he and your father did to Igraine. Our *mother*. You're only alive because of that deceit—something I never held against you."

"What Uther did all those years was unthinkable—but remember, you did the same to me," Arthur answered. "He is the one who tricked our mother that night. But Merlin didn't have a choice. You know he is bound to that sword."

"Where *is* Excalibur?" Morgana asked.

"Lady Nimuë. The Lady of the Lake."

Morgana closed her eyes, and her forehead wrinkled as she squinted in her vision to find the sword. "It has passed beyond my sight," she said. "Nimuë will never give the sword back to you after all that has happened. There is only one hope—the child you put in Guinevere before she left. Nimuë will make certain that child is pure and incorruptible. She will find a way to protect Guinevere and that baby, and when that child grows strong enough, she will present it with Excalibur, and they shall be king…or queen."

Arthur slammed his hand on the wooden table. "No! Excalibur is mine! Nobody shall wield that sword but me!"

"You speak the words of Uther Pendragon, my brother," Morgana taunted.

"I am the King. I am the land, and the land is me," Arthur boasted. "I am not my father!"

"Then you will do what needs to be done?"

"I will," Arthur proclaimed.

Morgana grinned widely, knowing she had turned the infallible Arthur to her side, her vision. She motioned Arthur to lay back down on the table and readied to complete the young monarch's transformation. She pulled a small knife from the table and cut open her left arm, then did the same to Arthur's. Morgana squeezed her blood and the blood of Arthur into the same golden chalice Kimo would drink from years later—the same cup that gave life to The Nimayrd.

"Cheers, brother," Morgana said, and took a gulp from the chalice.

Morgana handed the chalice to Arthur, who held it in his hands and looked it over. This was his last chance to do what was right after all he had done to destroy his kingdom.

"The moment I pulled Excalibur from the stone, I knew my life had changed. All I wanted was to do good, to make this land peaceful and vibrant. Instead, it's stained with the blood of *my* people. How did it come to this? Guinevere…Lancelot…Merlin. You were all supposed to help me be the best of us, and instead we failed each other. I know I've made mistakes, but would drinking this make me any less of a king? Or is this the answer? Being a king was about leaving a mark, creating a legacy—it was about destiny. I see now that legacy is always about nobility; that greatness is measured by others…but in the end, if this is destiny, do the thoughts of others mater?"

"These people don't deserve you," Morgana encouraged.

Arthur looked at Morgana, then to the chalice. He closed his eyes and lifted the chalice to his lips, then drank all that was left of the Pendragon siblings' blood. The skies darkened, and from the chalice, shot out red lights. Arthur could feel the unbridled power work its way through his body, giving him the supremacy he felt he deserved. His eyes flashed red for a moment…The Master was born, and under Morgana's protection.

"*Ex Pendragon sanguinis, vitam immortalem,*" Morgana chanted.

"From Pendragon blood, immortal life," Arthur said.

The Fylorn spun as Morgana moved her hands to control it—and in an instant, Arthur, King of the Britons, and his sister, Morgana, disappeared.

*****

"Morgana, where are we?" Arthur asked. All he could see what a red light all around them, the sensation of movement like a bird taking flight with the wind at its back as they whizzed through a vast unknown. "How is this happening?"

"We are traveling through the world, brother. I told you my magic was the ultimate power."

"It certainly is sister. Where are we going?"

"We are going to build a *new* world, Arthur," Morgana claimed. "Camelot was out in the open, too boisterous. The shadows are the safest place for us, brother."

"Then to the shadows we go, sister. It is time for you to teach me all you know about the darkness."

"With pleasure," Morgana cackled.

# Chapter 2 – The Blakemores

Mead sat next to Allen's bed at Riverside, closely watching for any signs of renewed life in the young man. Clarissa entered the room and locked eyes with Mead.

"He seems to be breathing much easier," she noticed.

"You need to rest, Ms. Blakemore," Mead said.

"Not until he's safe."

"It would appear that Mr. White is on the path to recovery," Mead whispered.

"How did this happen, Mead?" she asked.

"I've never seen Syphs do that before, Ms. Blakemore. Everything I know about them indicated that couldn't happen. Something is different…I think Allen scared them."

"You mean *him*…Arthur."

"I still don't believe it either."

"What can we do?" Clarissa worried.

"The same thing we have always done, Ms. Blakemore. Fight."

"Will we win? Will Merlin help us if Arthur is alive?"

Mead wiped his glasses with his handkerchief and left both on his lap, his mind stuck on Arthur. Hearing the name was a bullet to the heart, his chest tightening with each mention of the former king. "Not without him," Mead pointed to Allen.

The two sat silent watch over Allen, but Clarissa couldn't clear the thoughts of losing someone else she cared about. Her mind wandered to her past, and to what brought her and Kay to New York City.

*August 6, 2008 – Los Angeles, California,*

The two closed caskets were situated at the front of the room, surrounded by an array of flowers. The lights were dim, and the room was nearly silent, with some whispers coming from the chairs that faced the deceased. The soft instrumental music that played in the room was no comfort to those that had come to mourn. The line of grievers had steadily flowed for most of the early afternoon, as the California sun came and went as it pleased outside. A young, blonde girl sat in a corner and cried as her older sister greeted family and friends that had come to pay their respects. The younger girl's eyes were puffy and red from the crying, and her older sister excused herself as the line stopped and pulled her sister to her feet.

"I can't do this alone, Clarissa," Kay begged. "I know this sucks, but I need you next to me."

"I'm sorry, Kay," Clarissa replied.

Clarissa joined her sister in the receiving line, the only two members of their family that remained. Hundreds of mourners waited in line while the girls readied to repeat "thank you for being here" and "we are okay" over and over. People from all walks of life hoped to offer condolences to Kay and Clarissa, but the girls didn't want platitudes, they wanted their parents.

Los Angeles was used to crime, but the grisly nature of the murders of Howard and Johanna Blakemore was disturbing news. Howard was the District Attorney of Los Angeles and Johanna was an actress, having won an Emmy Award for a guest starring role on a television series a few years before they met. The couple attended a police fundraiser in Los Angeles and when the night was over headed to the valet. Per the news reports, after they retrieved their car, something went terribly wrong. The bodies were found in Santa Monica the next day, bound and gagged with acid burns through the skin and straight to the bone. There were no suspects, and all public tips led to dead ends. The couple had left behind the two girls—Kay was sixteen years old, and Clarissa had just turned thirteen years old. While Kay comprehended the full horror of the situation, Clarissa was still too young.

The limousine followed the hearses and navigated the streets of Los Angeles, but Clarissa just stared out the window and let the fading sunlight dance around her face. The cemetery was crowded and overwhelmed the girls, but they interlocked their arms and made it through together. They watched as people tossed roses onto the caskets; they stood and cried together as the caskets were lowered into the ground. The girls watched the cemetery workers fill the holes with dirt.

By then, it was just the two of them in the cemetery. Kay knew that from that moment on, it was just the two of them in the world.

"I don't know what we're going to do, Clarissa," Kay said.

"We can stay together, right?" Clarissa worried.

"I hope so," Kay answered.

However, Kay knew the reality of the situation was much different than the optimistic reassurance she gave to her sister. Kay wondered how long it would be before two newly orphaned children with no family would be taken into Child Protective Services and split up into the foster system. Clarissa was already scared enough, and Kay didn't want to add to that fear, so she kept a smile on her face in the days following the funeral. Clarissa returned to school about a week after her parents were buried, while Kay stayed at home and cleaned out her parents' belongings. Box after box was filled with memories of her parents, until only the items that remained resided in her father's home office. Neither Kay nor Clarissa had entered the office since the murders. A rush of trepidation fell over Kay as she opened the sliding door that blocked the office off; it felt wrong to her, as if she were disrupting her father's eternal rest. She flipped up the light switch, illuminating this space that had solely been her father's. The office had a subtle cigar scent, a reminder of the nights Howard Blakemore had spent looking over cases. The forest green curtains were still drawn, keeping the outside world from watching Kay's moment of grief. Her eyes welled with tears, but she had to stay strong for herself, and more importantly, her sister; if she broke down now, they'd come take her sister right then and there. Kay surveyed the room, blinking the tears away. Her father's diplomas and degrees were framed and hanging to the right of the room entrance. Howard's desk was toward the back right of the room, and to the left was a bookcase full of law books, journals, and an entire shelf of pictures of Johanna and the girls. Next to the pictures was Johanna's Emmy award. Kay remembered that her father used to call it "the best shelf in the world." Now, it was a painful reminder of what would never be again.

Kay slowly plodded across the office and maneuvered herself into the chair behind the desk. She opened the top drawer and rifled through the pens and other miscellaneous items—paper clips, rubber bands, post-it notes and tacks. She closed the drawer and turned her attention to the bottom left drawer of the desk; it was the largest of the drawers. As she pulled the drawer toward her, she noticed a small black safe inside the drawer with a lock. She pulled it out of the drawer and softly dropped it onto the desk. Kay tried to wedge it open with a letter opener, but she was unsuccessful. Kay frantically searched the rest of the drawers for a key, but to no avail. She leaned back in the chair, defeated, angry, and her eyes fell on a frame on the "best shelf in the world" that read "the key to happiness is family." Kay jumped up, flipped the frame over and pulled out the backing, but there was no key to be found. She shook every single book from the bookcase and still came up empty-handed. Kay wondered where the key could be hidden, and if the contents of the safe were that important.

The doorbell rang, meaning Kay's search would have to be put on hold. Kay feared that CPS had finally come to collect her and Clarissa; she wondered if a lost family member would show up and save her and her sister from a doomed future. She approached the door, unlocked the deadbolt, and opened the door.

"Ms. Blakemore, I presume?" the man said.

"Yes," Kay replied. "How can I help you?"

The man smiled. "Actually, I'm here to help you. May I come in?"

The man began to push his way into the house, but Kay lightly placed her hand on his chest to prevent him from moving forward.

"How can you help me, exactly?" Kay pressed.

As he reached into his coat's breast pocket, Kay worried this might have been the man that murdered her parents. She jumped back, eyes darting to the man's hand movements.

"I assure you, Ms. Blakemore, I am not here to harm you. I was friends with your parents."

Kay composed herself momentarily as the man opened his hand to reveal a small key in his palm. Kay grabbed the key and choked up again.

"Where did you get this key?"

"Your father gave it to me. As I was saying, my name is Mead and I am here to make sure you are safe, Ms. Blakemore."

"I'm so sorry," Kay said. "Please, come in."

Mead walked through the doorway and into the house. Kay closed the door and locked the deadbolt.

"Please, Mr. Mead, follow me," she said, walking toward the office again.

With Mead a couple of paces behind, Kay entered the office and sat down at the desk. She placed the key into the safe and unlocked it. The safe opened, the smell of money wafting to her nose. Kay started to pull things out, not sure what she would find. There were a ton of envelopes inside, some thick, some lighter, each written on in Howard's chicken scratch. A Last Will and Testament, an envelope labeled $$ that Kay unsealed to find $50,000, and an envelope marked, "if anything happens." Kay forced open the envelope and out fell a flash drive, along with a letter. Kay unfolded the paper and began to read.

*Johanna,*

*If you're reading this, then I am gone. I'm sorry this happened, but please know I loved you with all that I had, and that Kay and Clarissa meant the world to me. Eventually, they will have questions. Please give this to them when they are ready.*

*Love,*

*Howard*

"I'll be right back," Kay said.

Mead nodded and waited for Kay to return. She quickly came back with a laptop in her hands and sat at the desk and plugged the flash drive into the USB port on her computer. Kay navigated the files on the drive, looking for the right one to open. She saw an .mp4 file and immediately clicked the video. Mead intently listened from the entrance to the office. The video was old, and a young Howard was smiling as he spoke directly to the camera.

"Hi, girls. I know you have questions about what happened to me. I know you're hurt and confused and wondering why anyone would want to hurt your father. Before you start speculating, I want to set the record straight. There are forces in this world out of my control. Our family is part of something unexplainable, something beyond understanding. It took your grandfather and it's come back to take me. I'm sorry, girls. I love you both very much. Please know that if this could have been stopped, I would have done whatever it took. More importantly, if you're watching this, you're not safe. You must leave the house as soon as possible. Get to New York City with Mead—he can and will answer all your questions about me, our family, and your future. Mead will protect you and your mother. I love you, Kay. I love you, Clarissa. I will always love you both and will never be far from your hearts. Stay together, never separate. Have each other's backs. Goodbye, my darlings. I love you." The video faded to black, and Kay sat in silence, arms crossed, as she attempted to make sense of what she just saw. "So," Kay started. "What happens now?"

Mead took a deep breath and moved across the office to sit in an empty chair facing Kay. "That's all up to you. You can stay here and take care of Clarissa; take her and travel the world and pretend you never saw that video. Or you can convince her to join you and come to New York and stay with me. You won't have to worry about people taking her from you. You heard your father…I will protect you both. I will make sure you both survive."

"But this is where we grew up, Mr. Mead. Clarissa won't like leaving this house, it's all we've ever known."

"It's not an easy decision," Mead reassured. "I will promise that if you come to New York, you'll never have to worry again. Not about her or money or your future—it will all be provided."

Kay couldn't hide a small look of reluctance that ran across her face. Kay eyeballed this little old man and wondered how such a frail thing could take care of them. An odd feeling of being rescued, a princess in a tower being taken away, came over her, but she realized that nothing was holding her here. No one had locked her away. She was drifting and Mead was the only thing that offered to tether her. "When do you go back to New York?" Kay asked.

"I need to be back in New York tomorrow night to welcome another old friend to the house. If you have any other questions, I'm staying at the Los Angeles Burbank Marriot at the Burbank Airport. The plane takes off at 8:30."

"One day? You're asking me to throw aside my life here in one day?"

"I'm sorry, Ms. Blakemore. I know this whole situation is not easy. Think about it carefully, talk to your sister."

Mead sprung to his feet, left the room and walked to the front door. Kay grabbed her laptop, followed Mead, and unlocked the door to let him out.

"Be well, Ms. Blakemore," Mead said. "I hope to see you in the morning at the airport."

"Thank you, Mead."

Breathing heavily, Kay paced up the narrow hallway into the kitchen and back toward the front door over and over. She had always wanted to follow in her father's footsteps and go to Stanford University to become a lawyer. Clarissa had always been closer to their mother, though neither sister was jealous in the least; they were a happy family. That had ended so quickly, nothing was certain anymore, but leaving meant she would give up her place at Stanford. Conflicted, Kay slowed herself down.

Kay stopped in the kitchen, surrounded by open cardboard boxes full of her parents' things. She placed her laptop on the table and went to the sink. In the empty house, every little sound became a *noise*, something to focus on. The *click* of the cupboard opening, the slight scratching sound when she took out a glass. The rush of water when she turned the faucet on, and she stared at her left hand under the water to make sure it was cold before filling the glass. She pushed one of the boxes away from the kitchen table with her leg, the scraping sound deafening, and placed the glass of water on the table with a little *thud* before she sat down. The silence of the house overwhelmed Kay, and she was happy to hear the bolt of the front door unlock as Clarissa returned home from school.

"Kay, you here?"

"In the kitchen," Kay replied.

Clarissa dropped her backpack in the front hallway and went to the kitchen. Kay was seated at the table and looked directly at her sister. Clarissa knew something serious was on her mind.

"You may as well just tell me, Kay," Clarissa blurted. "I can't take any more surprises."

Kay could see that Clarissa was exhausted, the sleepless circles under her eyes had deepened. How did her sister make it through a day of middle school? Dealing with all they were, how did this petit teenage girl deal with the craziness of school and all the kids who probably treated her like a fragile *thing*? Kay couldn't even leave the house yet, and she admired her sister for the resilience. She almost didn't tell Clarissa the truth because she didn't want to knock her down again.

"I don't even know where to start," Kay responded.

"Is this about Mom and Dad?"

"Kind of…"

"Just tell me!"

"I was just visited by an old man named Mead. He had answers about Mom and Dad; and he had the key that opened a safe in Dad's office."

"What was in the safe?" Clarissa asked.

Kay breathed deep and composed herself. She could feel the tear fall from her eyes.

"It was a video Dad ma—"

"Show me," Clarissa demanded.

Kay opened her laptop and played the video for Clarissa. The younger of the Blakemore girls sobbed as she listened to her father. When the video ended, an emotional Clarissa slammed shut the laptop.

She wiped the tears from her face with her hands and then wiped her hand on her shorts.

"So, when do we leave for New York?" Clarissa asked.

"If we do this, we have to meet this Mead guy tomorrow."

"Then I guess we better start packing."

"Ris, this isn't an easy decision," Kay said, sounding more like an adult than she felt. "This is our home. We can't just leave like that."

"Why the hell not? You heard Dad, get to New York City, find Mead. Looks like he found us and knows how to keep us safe."

"What about school?"

"Seriously, Kay? Maybe a fresh start is what we need. I don't want CPS coming here and splitting us up."

"How did you—"

"I'm the daughter of a lawyer. I'm not an idiot. I'm going to pack a bag and I hope you do the same. I won't go unless you come with me, but we both know this is the only way to stay safe. What if the people that killed Mom and Dad come after us? Let's get the hell out of here and go to New York."

Clarissa stood up, resolved, ready to head upstairs. Kay grabbed her sister's hands and rose to her feet.

"Together. That's the only way this works," Kay said.

"Together," Clarissa echoed.

The sisters embraced and as Kay headed upstairs to pack a bag, Clarissa stepped into her father's office and grabbed her mother's Emmy award. With one last look around the room, she turned off the lights and walked out. She closed the door behind her and made her way upstairs.

Clarissa felt a hand on her shoulder and returned her mind to the present day. She looked up to see Kay behind her. Clarissa placed her hand over the one on her shoulder and squeezed to let her sister know she was okay.

"Mom and Dad?" Kay asked.

"You already know," Clarissa responded.

"Come on, Ris, time for bed."

Clarissa looked to Mead and before she could speak the old man assured her, "If anything changes, I will let you know, Ms. Blakemore."

"Thanks, Mead," Clarissa said. "Good night."

Mead pulled a tattered book with a gold-plated fountain pen hooked over the cover from a black leather bag at his feet; much like most of what he owned, it was engraved with a letter M in the center. Mead held the pen with his left hand, opened the book with his right and scribbled some thoughts before he placed the cap back on the pen and reattached it to the front cover. He ran his left hand across the inside cover of the book and flipped through the pages until he came to the middle; it was there, in his own words. He reminisced about everything that had brought them to this point.

# Chapter 3 – Plan A

*October 11, 2020 – 3 Riverside Drive, Manhattan, New York*

The lounge was eerily quiet for a room full of friends. Mead sat on the left side of the couch while Rogers, Anna, Sasha, and Mako took the stools at the bar. Cooper and Selena stayed closed to Mead on the couch, while Kay and Clarissa moved a couple of chairs to the middle of the room to join the conversation. Mako was still in uniform after his night shift, Cooper and Selena were still in the outfits they wore the day before at Club Magik in Clifton. Anna was wearing ripped jeans and a white tee-shirt that was tied off to show her stomach. A long silver necklace with an arrowhead pendant was situated around her neck. Sasha was in a black tank top that was tucked into her jeans and had the words "Filthy Animal" across the chest of the shirt in neon green script. Kay and Clarissa both wore ripped blue jeans, Kay wearing an off-the-shoulder grey sweatshirt and Clarissa a forest green plaid button-down over a simple black tank top. Mead had on a white button-down and over it a baby-blue V-neck sweater and a pair of khaki pants. Rogers was still donning the sweatshirt and jeans he'd worn all over the city the previous day.

"We all knew this day would come," Mead commenced. "In this room right now are six of you. The last time this many of us were together in the city we weren't ready, and we all know what happened. The time has come again, and this time we can't afford to be caught off guard."

"We won't be, Mr. Mead," Mako encouraged. "We're ready."

"Mako, you sure about that?" Anna asked.

"If he's not, I am," Rogers interrupted. "You all know Allen's been under my watch for as long as I can remember. He's had visions; he thinks they're dreams of course, but he will learn how to use what he sees to help us. He's smart, compassionate, kind, witty, and loyal. He's also well-liked and respected by his friends and people on campus. He's had his fair share of ups and downs since getting to the city, but I've watched him rush into danger to save his friends—and enemies. His selflessness is one of his best qualities; he puts everyone else first. I would stake my life that *he* will do what hasn't been done."

"What do we have to do?" Mako requested.

"His twenty-first birthday is coming," Mead replied. "It's time for him to know the truth. I'll try to persuade him by visiting the campus. If that doesn't work, we have some other options. Thomas?" He nodded to his partner.

"His friends are throwing him a party," Rogers announced. "Mad River on the Upper East Side. We need someone there that can get him to come back to Riverside in the days after that party, if Mead can't convince him."

"I'll do it," Clarissa offered. "I'll go tomorrow and see if they need bartenders."

"Excellent." Mead beamed. "We do have one possible problem, however."

"What problem?" Anna wondered.

"One of the people at this party is the one who sucker punched him at the bar," Rogers said. "He's jealous, angry, and dangerous. If he's there, trouble is sure to follow."

"I'll stick close to that area," Mako assured the group.

"What can the rest of us do?" Sasha asked.

"Yeah, we want to help, too," Cooper added.

"Cooper; you and Selena will head to New Orleans," Mead instructed, noticing that Kay couldn't hide her disappointment. "Call your father, Mrs. Craven; he's going with you. Ms. Blakemore, you will stay here in New York and get the key ready. For now, leave it in the museum; nobody knows the key's true power. Sasha, Anna—you two will shadow. Sasha, you follow the troublesome friend; Anna, you follow Allen and his friends. Don't get noticed."

"No shit, Sherlock," Sasha blurted. "We've got this."

"What do we do if they attack, Mead?" Anna questioned.

Everyone in the room was silenced by Anna's worried ponderance.

"You fight like your life depended on it," Rogers warned. "Because it will.”

*October 18, 2020 – 3 Riverside Drive, Manhattan, New York*

In the main hallway, Rogers, Mead, Sasha, and Clarissa stood in a small circle as they discussed the night's events.

“What the hell happened?” Rogers demanded.

“He's gone,” Sasha answered. “He ran out of the bar, ducked into an alley, I saw a flash of red, and he was gone when I looked again.”

“Fylorn…” Mead mumbled. “They'll use Kimo against Allen, no doubt about it.”

“It gets worse,” Clarissa added. “He punched this Stephanie girl in a bar full of people without a second thought or any remorse. He's daring *and* delusional.”

“We have to get Mr. White inside this house as soon as possible,” Mead cautioned. “We all know this is the safest place in the world for him right now.”

“You up to try again, Clarissa?” Rogers asked.

“I am,” she quickly answered.

“He's going to the museum this week for my class; that's the perfect time to give it another go,” Rogers said.

“Kay's museum?” Clarissa wondered.

“Yes,” Rogers affirmed. “Go talk to your sister, make sure she's up for this.”

“Why wouldn't she be up for this?”

“Eli not coming has really hurt her,” Sasha interjected. “She hasn't been herself and you know it.”

“I'll talk to her,” Clarissa assured everyone. “She'll be ready.” Clarissa walked up the stairs to the second floor as the others stayed behind. When Clarissa disappeared down the second-floor hallway, Mead and Rogers both turned and faced Sasha.

“There's something else, isn't there, Sasha?” Mead said quietly.

“Yes…” She hesitated.

“It's okay, Sasha, just tell us,” Rogers said.

Sasha looked around the room, her paranoia bubbling to the surface. “I think someone's been following me.”

*October 19, 2020 – New Orleans, Louisiana – My Cup Overflowith Tea Room*

Adelaide laid on the ground, determined to hide from whatever had barged into the shop, seemingly from nowhere. While she had seen many unreal things in her life, mostly connected to spirits and ghosts, a Syph was a different kind of sight to behold. Syphs came in a few different forms that people had seen: the Parasite, like the one that attacked Nigel & Lionel the day they arrived in New York City. The Pure Formed; from the land of Morgana and Arthur, these beasts were created from the blood of those the Nimayrd had used over the years – the blood of both those drawn to the dark and The Remains. Finally, the Winged Syphs, the newest breed like the army Morgana created in Times Square during the fight with The Remains.

"What are they?" Adelaide whispered.

"Syphs," Cooper explained. "They're here for me."

The wooden door to Adelaide's back room shattered as if it was glass, and chunks of wood flew everywhere. The Syphs entered the room, their glowing crimson eyes and sharp claws and teeth glowing at Adelaide, Cooper, Selena, and Fantoccini.

"You three stay low. It's me they're after," Cooper instructed.

"No, babe, you can't." Selena pulled at his hand and brought him back to the group.

"I have to. Get your father and the girl and get the hell out of here," he hissed, eyebrows knit with worry.

Selena nodded at Cooper once, picked up a chair and sent it flying out the window and into the street. The opening was all she needed—she led her father and Adelaide out of My Cup Overflowith to safety. Three Syphs had surrounded Cooper when a voice echoed from the hallway.

"Wait," Jaxx said as he entered the room. "He's mine."

A flash of light followed Jaxx's words and immediately Adelaide's eyes shot open, her vision ended.

"We have to get out of here, now," she said to the group.

"What's wrong?" Cooper asked.

"These *things* are coming here now. If we don't leave, you'll die."

"How do you—"

"Just trust me. We gotta go now."

Cooper, Selena, Fantoccini, and Adelaide slipped out a back entrance and flirted around shadows in the French Quarter. They safely made it to Adelaide's apartment after a fifteen-minute walk, where a familiar face was seated on the curb at the entrance to Adelaide's building.

"Well, I'll be damned," Eli said as he rose to his feet and approached Cooper. "I come to see Adelaide and instead I find my brother here in the Bayou."

"It's been a long time, Eli," Cooper answered back, embracing Eli. "You look good, man."

"Hate to break up the bromance," Adelaide interrupted. "We really need to get inside."

"What for, *jeune fille?*" Eli wondered.

"They're coming," Adelaide said. "These Syphs and this…monster."

"What's he look like?"

"Gigantic. Dark eyes, tons of tattoos."

"Jaxx? Here? When?" Eli demanded.

"Soon, if they aren't here already," Adelaide cautioned as she reached into her pocket, pulled out her car keys and handed them to Eli. "Take my car and go. Get as far from here as possible."

"Adelaide," Selena hesitated. "You can't stay here. It's not safe."

"She's right, *jeune fille,*" Eli added. "Go with them."

"Them?" Adelaide confirmed. "You aren't going?"

"That thing killed my father. If he's here, I'm going after him."

"Then I am, too," Cooper stated.

"Count me in," Selena said. "If he goes, I go."

"You can't do this alone anymore, Eli," Adelaide offered. "I'll fight for you, too."

"Y'all are *killing* me," Eli frustratedly stomped. "I'm fixin' to kill him."

"You want Jaxx, come with us to New York and he's yours," Cooper said.

"I won't." Eli shook his head, lips pursed.

"You have to, Eli," Adelaide said. "She'll die if you aren't there in the next three weeks."

Mead's warning about Kay's fate replayed in Eli's head. "Ah, shit; you just gotta go and make this harder," Eli responded.

*October 30, 2020 – Devil's Night – Newark, New Jersey*

The apartment was cold and dirty from years of not being used, though it recently had seen new life. The walls were covered in gaudy wallpaper from the 1970s, and the furnishing in the space were just as old. The floors were covered in beige carpeting that complemented the walls, and the kitchen had blue and white linoleum tiling. The place had been magically secured with Merlin's staff years earlier and used as a safehouse where the only way to enter was unknown to anyone outside

The Remains. As throngs of people were on the streets of Newark, celebrating Mischief Night—a night of toilet papering houses and trees and tossing eggs at buildings and people alike—Eli paced back and forth, thinking about what to do next. Eli's impatience was evident in his every move, sweat gathered in his armpits and wetting his black tank top. He removed the royal-blue baseball hat—he hadn't worn his signature fedora in days—and wiped his brow. Adelaide sat in an old metal folding chair, her back pressed against the seat rest. She was calm and collected, a stark contrast to Eli, with a pink sweater and dark blue jeans with light brown boots. Eli stopped moving in front of Adelaide and leaned against the wall parallel to her chair.

"How did it go?" Eli wondered.

"I've been following them for almost two weeks. She's safe, Eli. I think the Sasha girl has seen me a couple of times near the museum, but I can't be sure."

"Are you still having the same visions?"

"Kay's in the museum basement with three other people and two security guards with red eyes attack her and kill her."

"So yes, then," he said. "And the other one?"

"The same as when we were in New Orleans. You're looking up at a guy on a rock, tons of light in the distance and snow falling from the sky."

"We have to find that place, Adelaide, and soon."

"I can try again now if you want me to?" she offered.

"You need rest, *jeune fille*. You look terrible."

Adelaide's stuck her tongue out at Eli. "And you're such a looker right now."

Eli tried to think of a witty comeback but instead he opened his mouth and then stopped. Adelaide got him; he let out a guttural laugh that shook the room.

"You try to sleep when your mind is flooded with images you can't control and tell me how that goes."

"Yous right. I'm sorry. I meant no off—"

"Shhh, quiet," Adelaide said as she slowly rose to her feet and covered Eli's mouth with her hand. "Someone's coming."

Eli reached behind his back, but his caber was in the bedroom. Before he could move to get the weapon, a flash of smoke popped in the middle of the apartment and Ferdinando Fantoccini appeared, bloodied and battered, his suit jacket ripped in the front lapel and his shirt torn in two underneath the jacket.

"Help!" Fantoccini yelled.

Eli and Adelaide rushed to their friend when another flash of smoke popped next to them. It was Cooper, also bloodied and weak, with Selena's lifeless body in his arms.

"Eli, help…" Cooper begged.

Eli flipped his body toward Selena and Cooper as Adelaide ran to the bathroom to grab some towels. Fantoccini frantically stomped around the room, distraught over his daughter's condition.

"What happened?" Eli asked.

"I don't know," Cooper answered.

"Those things attacked us," Fantoccini explained. "One second we're walking on the sidewalk, the next we were surrounded."

"Selena, can you hear me?" Eli said close to her face, voice squeaky. "Selena?"

"It's no use, Eli," Cooper said. He turned Selena to her side and revealed a giant gash on her back.

"No!" Eli cried as he shook Selena's body.

Suddenly, the apartment was clear, Adelaide's eyes pure white as the pupils were rolled to the back of her head.

"Wake up, Adelaide." Eli tried to break the vision. "Come on, *mon ami.*"

Adelaide's body shot forward on the chair as she started to come back to reality. Her eyes returned to their normal hues, filled with tears.

"Adelaide, you in there?"

"I'm sorry, Eli. Halloween week. It's when the spirit world is closest to ours."

"Don't apologize, you," Eli gently touched her shoulder. "What happened?"

"Another vision—this one ended here in this apartment."

"What was it?"

"Selena. I think she's in trouble."

*****

Sixty miles south of Newark and the safehouse, Selena strolled along the boardwalk as she waited for Cooper and her father to meet up with her. Cooper and Fantoccini had been gone all day, working on Cooper's growing skill set—something the group would need as the threat grew.

Cooper could no longer be just a stage act—his magic had to become part of his identity—just as Selena had become an extension of him. In the two weeks since they'd returned from New Orleans, Selena encouraged Cooper to prepare himself for whatever threat was coming for them, knowing it meant her days would be a little less lively.

The salty smell of the Atlantic Ocean danced under her nose as she took slow, deliberate steps to waste the time. Selena appreciated the small things, and a quiet night on the boardwalk with no crowds to fight was something she loved. She was dressed smartly for the relatively cool October night: black leggings, black knee-high boots and a dark purple three-quarter zip-up hoodie. In one hand was the strap of her purse that stretched over her shoulder and in the other was a Styrofoam coffee cup with a little steam rising off the top. She sipped the coffee as she made her way from the empty end of the boardwalk toward the iconic boardwalk train. During summer months, the train chugged around the perimeter of the kiddie rides at a snail's pace.

Selena smiled as she remembered summers of her past and the rides on the train. Her favorite memories were all from Point Pleasant with her parents and grandparents. Selena finished her coffee and tossed the cup in a garbage can. Just down the boardwalk, Selena could see Cooper's car pull into the parking lot. Selena started to walk across the train tracks when the train's whistle screeched and startled her. Selena turned around and was immediately confronted with the appearance of an old woman just two feet away from her. Her straggly white hair tossed in the light breeze, and her small, grey eyes reflected the moon. Her wrinkled face sagged a little under the eyes, and her nose was tilted slightly upwards, showing bristly hair in her nostrils.

"You scared me half to death," Selena gasped.

"I'm so sorry," the woman replied. "What a lovely sweatshirt."

"It's okay, it happens. And thank you, it was a gift from my husband."

"How sweet to be in love." The old woman smiled, showing yellowed teeth. "I remember those days well."

"I'm sorry," Selena started. "Did you lose someone?"

"The great love of my life," the old woman answered. "But that's okay. It makes it easier to do what must be done. Love is so painful, but death is even worse."

"What are you talking about?" Selena backed away. "What are you—"

The old woman's eyes flashed crimson as she stuck two knives into

Selena's abdomen, lifted her off the ground, and slammed her down across the train tracks with the knives still in her chest. Selena's purse went flying.

The old woman kneeled and pulled the knives out simultaneously from Selena's body. She wiped the blood from one blade on Selena's leggings. The old woman caressed the second blade barehanded and brought her blood-soaked hand to her mouth. She stuck out her tongue and licked her hand from the bottom of her palm to the tip of her middle finger. In an instant, the old woman's outer layer of skin shed and Jaxx revealed himself to Selena as she fought for her last breaths. The Fylorn appeared while Jaxx tasted the blood of another victim.

"Hmmm…interesting." Jaxx disappeared into The Fylorn.

Cooper and Fantoccini came up from the parking lot on a ramp to the little train area of the boardwalk. Cooper immediately noticed Selena's purse on the edge of the tracks and started running, with Fantoccini not far behind. Cooper got to the tracks and found his wife dead. Her face had turned a subtle blueish-white from the combination of the blood loss and the cold boardwalk planks. He fell to his knees and cradled Selena's head against his forearm.

"No, baby, no… Selena, Selena," Cooper screamed as he shook her in his arms. "Why, babe, why? It's not fair, this wasn't your fight! It's not fair…"

"Help!" Fantoccini yelled in the middle of the boardwalk.

"Help! Help! Anyone…Eli, Adelaide, can you hear me? Eli, help!" Cooper begged.

The few people on the boardwalk raced to help, but it was too late for Selena. Fantoccini picked up her purse and wrapped the strap around the purse five or six times with senseless care, as if it would keep it safe. When he looked down, Cooper ran his hand across Selena's hair. When the police and EMTs arrived, Fantoccini bent down to his daughter and gently kissed her forehead and closed her eyelids. Cooper cried and quivered as he caressed Selena's cheek. He held her face and gave her one last kiss before Fantoccini pulled Cooper to his feet as the paramedics arrived.

"You have to go, Cooper," Fantoccini said as he pushed Selena's purse into Cooper's blood-covered hands.

"I can't just leave you," Cooper moaned.

"You can, and you will. Now *go*."

Cooper turned and ran down toward the parking lot, leaving

Fantoccini behind to say goodbye to his daughter. Fantoccini slouched against a wall and slid down until he was sitting on the boardwalk.

"My poor Lena, what did they do to you?" he thought out loud.

Fantoccini couldn't keep his emotions in check anymore, and he sobbed for his daughter.

# Chapter 4 – Mead's Farewell

One hand reached to the sink and then another as the man pulled himself up. The young man stared into the mirror as if it was the first time he'd seen himself. His olive-toned skin, dark eyes and dark hair were accented by his muscular frame and trimmed beard. He stood naked in the bathroom as he studied himself—a figure he no longer recognized.

*7 Days Ago*

"This arguing will get us nowhere," Mead stated. "Allen needs time to rest; the Syph poison has left him weak and vulnerable."

"I agree with Mead," Rogers said. "We wait."

"How long, *mon ami?*" Eli asked.

"Yeah, mate," Lionel interjected, "just how long do we wait?"

"Clarissa, Rogers, Lionel, and I will stay here and take turns watching over Allen," Mead instructed. "The rest of you will go and try to find the only thing that can put this evil away for good."

"Mead, that sword has been gone for centuries," Kay said.

"It's a good thing we have a historical artifact expert in the room then, isn't it, Kay?" Mead quipped.

Cooper stood up and the room got quiet. He looked around the room and smiled.

"Last I checked, we all knew what we were signing up for when we came here. Now, we can sit here and bicker all day, or we can go find the weapon that will put an end to The Master and The Nimayrd."

"And what of the others we are missing here? Mead said an incomplete circle would leave us vulnerable," Young argued.

"Boys, I have an idea," Sasha offered. "Eli, Kay, and Nigel follow the trail of the sword; Cooper, me, and Young will follow anything we can find about the others. Who's missing, Mead?"

"Anna, Rayna…" Mead hesitated.

"Who else, Mead?" Clarissa asked.

Mead looked at Rogers. The room was silent again as the group waited for an answer. Rogers breathed out a heavy sigh.

"Just tell them," Rogers said.

"We don't even know if it's true," Mead argued.

"I want to hear this," Allen said, as he staggered into the lounge. Clarissa and Lionel helped him take a seat at the bar.

"There are rumors that one of the original Knights of the Round Table is still alive," Mead explained. "But these are just rumors."

"I think," Allen interrupted, "that seeing Arthur alive should mean that anything is possible. Who is it?"

"Perceval," Rogers said.

"If that's true, that would mean the Grail is real," Allen replied. "What are we waiting for?"

"Yes, very well, Mr. White. S-Sasha—it's up to you now," Mead stuttered.

Sasha saw Mead stammer for the first time in her life. She could see he was afraid and wanted to make sure he knew she could handle things. "Mead, I will not let you down," Sasha said.

The friends wished each other luck as two groups embarked on uncertain journeys. Allen watched as they left and waited for the room to go quiet again. He remembered the stories of the Knights of the Round Table from his childhood and from school. But he needed to hear it from the man he trusted and respected most in New York City.

"So, Professor," Allen started, "what can you tell me about Perceval?"

"Allen, you know the stories," Rogers said.

"I sure do. But I want to hear it from you."

"Fair enough, Allen. As you know, Perceval had been the last to see Arthur before he was taken to Avalon. He was the youngest knight and always considered the purest of heart, and so he was entrusted to return Excalibur to the Nimuë…Lady of the Lake…and to be the great protector of the Holy Grail. When Perceval resisted the temptation of Excalibur, his nobility was rewarded by Nimuë, who shielded Perceval's existence from Morgana, and as we have learned in the past twenty-four hours, from Arthur. Nimuë knew what had happened in Avalon, but she was powerless to stop the blood union of Uther and Igraine's children, just as she had been helpless when Uther deceived Igraine and conceived Arthur. Nimuë retreated to the depths of the water when Arthur betrayed the kingdom, never to be seen again."

"How is it then, that Perceval has lived all this time?" Allen asked.

"Why, the Grail, of course," Rogers answered.

"We *have* to find that Grail," Clarissa insisted. "If this is true and Perceval lives, he's the only one that can find Excalibur."

"No, Clarissa, we don't have to find the Grail," Rogers responded.

"How can—"

"It's here, Clarissa," Mead interrupted.

"It's in New York?" Allen questioned.

"No, Mr. White," Mead said. "The Grail is in this house."

Lionel couldn't contain himself. "Holy shit, mate."

*3 Days Ago*

"What of Rayna?" Mead wondered.

"Nothing yet," Rogers replied. "Don't worry, we'd know if something happened."

"It's been two years, Thomas. Not to mention it's been almost three weeks since we last heard from her."

"I promise nothing has happened to her," Rogers said.

"Very well, Thomas."

The two men sat in silence in the lounge. There was a tangible tension in the air, but it wasn't animosity between them, it was concern.

"I know what you are asking of me, Thomas."

"The time has come, Mead. We must find Perceval."

"I know, Thomas."

*Two Days Ago*

"Where have you been?" Rogers asked, cross-armed and relieved in the same moment.

The mocha-skinned young woman with sparkling white teeth and short curly hair stood at the entrance to 3 Riverside. She was wearing a pair of jean shorts up to her mid-thigh and a white, off-the-shoulder ripped t-shirt with an image of Tupac Shakur on the front over her black sports bra. Her sneakers were bright yellow low top Converse, and her hair moved with the wind, and streaks of purple danced in the sunlight.

Rayna was vastly different than the rest of The Remains. She'd been at Riverside for as long as she could remember and had seen all the loss and pain her friends endured, more than anyone else had. She also was arguably the freest-spirited of the group, coming and going as she wanted, and always on her own terms. This trait made her a bit of a loose cannon, and her outspoken nature only magnified the affect to people who didn't know her well enough to see her deeply rooted love of humanity.

"As you're well aware, I went looking for Merlin about two years ago," Rayna explained. "Each time I thought I was close, I was wrong. He wasn't in London, Oxford, Scotland, or Ireland. I struck out in Italy and Greece. When I got to Germany, I had a promising lead, but it turned out to be nothing. Lost my phone in Belgium, which was fun. From there, I followed things to France—and I found it."

"It?" Rogers asked.

"His grave, or tomb, whatever you want to call it."

"What did you find?"

"Nothing," Rayna said. She sighed and let out a little whimper of frustration. "He wasn't there, either. Just more mysteries."

"Morgana attacked us last week. Without Merlin, we can't defeat the witch."

"How did you survive?" Rayna questioned.

"Mead used Merlin's staff to protect us—but we lost a couple of friends."

"Dad, if the staff was that powerful in Mead's hands, that can mean only one thing."

"What's that, Rayna?"

"Merlin has to be in New York."

"That's impossible," Rogers said.

"No, Dad, it's not. There's no way Mead could give off that kind of power without Merlin being close."

*Yesterday*

Eleven of the twelve Remains sat in the lounge. Anna stood in the center of the room, explaining to the group what had happened to her over the past few years. She was wearing a long-sleeved red crewneck t-shirt with the ends stretched and clutched over her hands, a pair of black leggings and black ankle-high boots. Anna's shirt showed off her muscular frame; she arguably was the strongest person in the room, next to only Eli.

The room was quiet. Allen wasn't completely healed yet from the Syph wound—or the loss of his closest friends. He spent most of the past few days at Riverside with AirPods in his ears to shut out the noise that grew with each arrival. Allen's body and spirit had been wounded deeply by everything: Stephanie's death, Joe's death, learning about his *true* lineage, Professor Rogers' connection to his parents, that Merlin was real, and that he was now part of some great war. Clarissa and the others knew that they needed to get Allen ready for the long days ahead, both mentally and physically. Even in the lounge, Allen separated himself from the conversation, putting his music on as loud as it would go to drown out the others.

"We can't expect to do much when he's like this," Kay whispered.

"What do you want us to do, Kay? Look at everything he's lost in the past two weeks," Clarissa defended.

"Who in this room hasn't lost people because of this war?" Kay argued.

"It's not the same and you know it, Kay," her younger sister said.

Kay looked ready to erupt with anger at her sister. She started to stand to get in her sister's face, but a light pull on her arm stopped her.

"Let it go, *jeune fille*," Eli said. "Let it go."

Kay breathed deeply and looked at her younger sister across the room as her eyes welled with tears.

"I'm sorry, Clarissa. I'm just frustrated. "We are more together than The Remains have ever been, and we are still wildly outgunned. We don't have Merlin, Allen's nowhere near ready, Selena's dead, Perceval is somehow alive, the Holy Grail is in this house and nobody bothered to tell us…it's just too much."

Clarissa moved across the lounge and hugged her sister as the group watched.

"Pay up, mate," Lionel whispered. Nigel reached into his front pocket and pulled out a hundred-dollar bill and handed it over to Lionel. The motion caught Kay's eye.

"Did you two idiots take bets on us fighting?" she asked.

Lionel and Nigel looked around the room, took a shot of vodka each as they sat at the bar and then at each other and spoke in unison.

"Nahhhhhhh…not us!"

Everyone in the room exploded with laughter.

"What's so funny?" Allen interrupted, taking one earbud out.

"The Cockney twins are at it again," Clarissa joked.

"Is *everything* a joke to you all?" Allen yelled. "My friends are dead. *I* almost died. The most powerful evil in the world is being run by my great-great-great-great-whatever grandfather, who somehow is alive 1500 years after he was killed. Mead keeps telling us we're doomed without a full twelve members and all you do is drink and argue and joke. I—"

"Mate, rela—"

"Don't tell me to relax, Lionel," he snapped, pointing at him. "You all are here for a reason. You've been trained and taught since way before I came into the picture. I've been sitting here all week trying to feel normal, trying to come up with a way to help us all. You all assumed I was just hiding from what's happening. That's bullshit. I'm all in on this fight, we're not going to let the Nimayrd take over. I want to make sure that none of us have to worry about *our* kids taking up the same fight, and I will die to make sure that never happens if I have to; are you?"

Silence filled the room again as everyone lowered their heads to the ground. Allen looked around the room, and nobody would look back at him. Allen put his AirPods back into his ears and stomped out of the room.

"Finally," Lionel said.

The rest of the group lifted their heads with renewed hope.


*Last Night*

Rogers and Mead sat in the dimly lit lounge after everyone else had scattered to bed. Rogers paced back and forth slowly behind the chair Mead was sitting in as he observed the relic on the bar top.

"How long has it been since we locked this thing away?" Mead asked.

"Twenty years, I think," Rogers answered.

"Not a day goes by I don't think of the loss we have endured, Thomas."

"I am with you there, old friend. But all this happening now, feels different. I think he can do it; or, at least, I hope he can."

"Allen can't do it alone, though," Mead reminded him. "Without Perceval, this will end like all the rest. With everyone dead."

"So, old friend, let's help them find Perceval."

Rogers grabbed the Holy Grail off the bar top and reached it out to Mead.

"I'm sorry, Thomas, I dare not touch that relic. The last time I did was the night Allen's parents were killed."

Rogers placed the Grail back on the bar and turned to his oldest friend.

"Good night, Mead," he said.

"Good night, Thomas."

Mead grabbed a port glass and a bottle of Cooper's Vintage Port 1985 from the shelf and came around the bar to sit on a stool. Mead placed the glass down, opened the bottle, poured himself a full glass of the rich dessert wine. He sipped the port, swiveled the half-full glass in his hand. Mead's mind was tormented by the past. All he wanted was to help those around him.

*November 1, 1963*

Mead sat on an off-white couch surrounded by the portraits of the past. It was nearly sixty years ago, and Mead was unchanged from the way he looked in 2020. He seemed unfazed by the room in which he sat. The carpet was a deep navy-blue and the seal of the President was embossed into it. To Mead's right was a wooden rocking chair with the Presidential seal on both the back and seat cushions. A variety of nautical paintings adorned the white walls of the Oval Office, with model ships atop end tables in the room. John Fitzgerald Kennedy, the 35th President of the United States, sat across from Mead on an identical couch, and a cherry-colored coffee table was between them. Kennedy's light blue crewneck sweater fit cleanly and smoothly over his white button-down shirt, the collar of which rested neatly on the top of the crewneck. JFK had on khaki pants and a pair of brown dock-style shoes. He was leaned back into the couch, arms folded, and legs crossed.

"Mr. President, I urge caution in the days ahead."

"Mr. Mead, I know what you wish of me," the President said. "After this trip, if nothing comes of it, I will retreat with you to Riverside. But, Mead, imagine if this plan works."

"It's a big risk, Mr. President, too many things at play. I told you from the start that letting people call your presidency 'Camelot' was dangerous. I cautioned against it then and still do now," Mead lectured. "Even your ancestors knew the power in hiding the truth from the world."

"And where did that get them?" the President interjected. "Nowhere, Mead. It got them nowhere. If we're going to find out what the world is up against, let's draw them out."

"If we do this, Mr. President, it means that *he*," Mead pointed to his right, "has to stay at Riverside."

They both followed Mead's pointed finger to look at Robert Kennedy, sitting in the wooden rocking chair as he listened to every word the two had said.

"This is my fight too," RFK angrily replied.

"I know it is, Bobby," Mead said.

"He's right, Bobby," JFK added. "If something happens, you have to be safe."

"What if something *does* happen? What if The Nimayrd kill you, me, our entire family? What if they kill every person in Texas? New York? What do I tell people?"

"You tell them whatever Mead says," JFK answered.

*November 22, 1963*

"That was J. Edgar," Bobby said.

"I'm sorry, Bobby," Mead consoled. "He thought this was the only way."

"We both know it's only a matter of time before they get to me."

"I will do all I can to protect you, Bobby. But you *must* leave the public eye. Come with me to New York tonight. You'll be safe at Riverside. We have to leave…now."

"I can't do that, Mead. Jack brought us out into the open to help people. I can't just abandon what he did—especially now."

Mead shook his head with a combination of understanding and disappointment. He knew that Bobby was right on both points; he couldn't turn away from the fight his brother had started for the people of the United States, and that he would surely meet the same fate.

"I will help you see it through, Bobby," Mead said.

"No, Mead, you go back to New York and protect the others. We both know you can't stay in D.C. We knew the risks when we used Camelot to describe our leadership…we put a target on our backs by taunting The Nimayrd and we paid the price for it…we knew the risks."

*Present Day*

Mead stared off into the distance as he continued to sip his drink. His eyes caught the Grail and his heart sunk into his chest.

"I'm sorry, boys."

*October 20, 1985 – New York City, 5:00 am*

Mead walked the floors around the interior of the Broadway Arcade on the crossing of Broadway and 52nd Street. The lights of the pinball machines were all turned off and Mead relished in the silence and darkness. He whistled softly to himself but abruptly stopped when he thought he heard a noise in the arcade. He stopped whistling and waited to hear more, but the noise died out. He started to whistle again, and the noise became louder, as someone pounded on the glass doors at the entrance to the arcade. Mead left off his happy tune and stepped into the arcade's main entranceway. In that light, Mead's glasses reflected the outside light. It was a young Terrence at the door.

"Good morning, Mr. Mead," Terrence said.

"Good morning, Terrence. What happened?"

"I found it, Mead. It was where you said it would be."

"Where is it?"

"It's at Riverside."

"Let's go have a look, shall we?"

Terrence entered the arcade and the duo moved through the dark to the game *Gauntlet*. Mead tapped the side of the game and the machine moved slowly to the right, opening a staircase to the underground tunnels that led to Riverside. When they entered, the game closed itself back up. Mead and Terrence quickly made their way to underneath 3 Riverside Drive. Terrence chomped on a lit cigar and reached down to the ground to where a blanket was laid. Terrence pulled it away to reveal a long staff, and Mead smiled when he saw the item.

"I can't believe it!" Mead exclaimed.

"Merlin's staff," Terrence affirmed. "I wouldn't believe it if it wasn't here in front of me. We finally have something to protect us and Riverside."

"Terrence, you may have just saved us all," Mead said.

"How does it work?" Terrence wondered.

Mead extended his hand to Terrence, who passed the staff along to the old man. Mead twirled the staff as he looked it over. The power Mead felt in his hands was unquestionable, and he knew what he had to do.

"Stand back," Mead warned.

Terrence walked back behind Mead as the old man straightened the staff upright in his right hand and slammed its bottom into the ground.

"Protect us all, Merlin," Mead intoned.

A kaleidoscope of light shot from the top of the staff and filled the tunnels with a variety of beautiful colors. Mead and Terrence's eyes filled with the light that surrounded them as a force field rose around them and shot upwards to 3 Riverside Drive.

The house was now protected by old magic, a powerful spell cast by the remaining possession of Merlin.

While the duo watched the force field envelop their home, reverberations of the magic being cast rumbled throughout New York.

*Present Day*

"The earthquake of 1985," Mead mumbled to himself in the lounge.

*July 4th, 2000 – 3 Riverside Drive*

"Thomas, we are broken," Mead said. "Terrence's death has left us vulnerable. There's nothing we can do right now."

"There must be something we can do. What do I tell Sam and Mel?" Rogers' voice crackled on the other end of the phone.

"I will send help, Thomas. Stay there, protect them and the baby."

"We have to find him, Mead," Rogers implored. "Get the Grail."

"I dare not do that without a full group, Thomas."

"If you don't do it, we will all be in danger."

The call ended abruptly in Mead's mind, because his next memories were only of him touching the Grail and the deaths of Samuel and Melanie.

Mead's mind returned to the present day and gazed at the Grail. His heart raced with the thoughts of all the negative that could come from his touching the chalice again. The mere thought of it gripped his heart and mind in fear. The Grail had been part of the reason Arthur's rule failed and the Nimayrd came to be, so Mead wanted no part of it. He finished the rest of his port, slammed the glass down on the bar top and sneered at the Grail before walking out of the lounge and down the hallway.

He made it halfway when he realized the Holy Grail was in his hands.

*Moments ago – Riverside Drive*

The young man stroked his full black beard, astonished. "Has it been so long?"

No answer came, but he continued to speak to the mirror.

"Nimuë, hear me now. When Arthur was taken to Avalon to die, I returned Excalibur to you. It was then you told me to keep the Grail safe, and I have. I have never asked you for anything, Nimuë, but I am asking now. We need your help; the boy is worthy of being king. It's a different time now, one where men's hearts are full of hatred. Honor, chivalry, and compassion are things few men display. Weakness has taken over the hearts of men. They believe in false gods; they believe in men without honor or courage. Violence is everywhere. Where peace should be is strife and unrest. The world is crumbling, Nimuë, and you could have stopped it centuries ago. Help me *now*, Nimuë. Help me restore hope in the world. It is time for peace to reign again. Let's put an end to Arthur's madness."

Perceval looked down on the floor at the Holy Grail. He picked it up and venerated the cup of Christ. It had been a long time since he lifted the cup to his lips, bringing life to his body and spirit. Gone was the pain of old age; gone was the soreness of any movement in the vessel he had used for so long. His body felt renewed, his muscles felt powerful.

"This gift has given me life. It has kept me alive all these years, hidden from the Nimayrd. But now, Nimuë, they will know the cup still exists— and they will stop at nothing to kill me and take it."

Perceval picked up a pair of glasses from the ground. There was nothing special about them and somehow represented so much to the knight. He held them in his right hand and clenched a fist around them. The glasses were crushed easily in his grip, and he let the pieces fall to the floor. He held his hand in front of his face, marveling at his renewed strength.

"I'm sorry, old friend," Perceval said. "You served me well all these years, but the time has come to say goodbye."

Perceval grabbed a pink towel off the rack and wrapped it around his waist as he headed toward the bathroom door. He made sure the Grail was in his left hand and he grabbed the door handle with his right hand, took a deep breath, and pulled it open. He looked down at the broken glasses and umbrella on the floor, the last reminder that Mead was gone for good.

## Chapter 5 – Fire & Ice

Allen loaded his backpack with food and water, unsure of how long the trip underground would take. He zipped his backpack closed, placed the straps over his shoulders and quickly moved through the house and down into the tunnels. As Allen paced at the entrance to Riverside, Rogers emerged from the opening.

"You shouldn't be going alone," Rogers cautioned. "You're not 100 percent healthy, Allen."

"I know I'm not, Professor," Allen replied. "But I can't sit here and just let everyone else do things meant to protect *me*. Besides, I won't be alone."

Clarissa came through the opening, wearing black jeans and a black tank top. Her hair was pulled back into a messy bun, and she'd put stud earrings in her ears to avoid the noise that came from her dangles. She reached her Apple Watch to her mouth and sent a text message to her sister.

*"Allen and I are going to the subways, be back later. XO."*

"You're sure you can do this, Allen?" Rogers asked.

"Professor, you know me," Allen responded.

Rogers smiled uneasily and nodded. He then turned his attention to Clarissa.

"Be careful," he said. "168th Street station. It'll take an hour to get there."

"I won't let anything happen to him," Clarissa assured.

Clarissa led Allen through the tunnels and to an access door that opened from just the tunnel side. Allen opened the door and the two found themselves to the left of a subway platform, hidden from the people waiting for the next train.

"Pretty cool, isn't it?" Clarissa said.

"I have lived in New York City most of my young adult life and never imagined any of this was possible. It's like I'm standing on the roof at the bar all over again."

"What do you mean?"

"When I was a freshman at Fordham, we went to a rooftop bar, and it was the happiest I think I've ever been in this city. Joe and Stephanie were alive, we were all so young and carefree."

"I'm sorry, Allen. I really am."

"Yeah, well, me too," Allen lamented.

Silence gripped the duo as they made their way parallel to the tracks. Within the darkness of the subway's tracks, Allen and Clarissa were greeted by the sounds of creatures of the underground: rats, spiders, and any other insects that enjoyed the smell of the three Ps of New York: pizza, peanuts, and pee. They pushed forward despite their shared phobias, knowing this could be their one chance to find the piece to the puzzle The Remains so desperately needed. As they pressed deeper into the gloom of the subway, Allen tripped over something against the wall. He used his cell phone's flashlight to give himself even a little light. Allen shined the light down to see what he'd tripped over.

"Turn that damn light off," the homeless man barked.

Allen quickly turned off the flashlight.

"Is this where you live?" Allen asked.

"No, my penthouse is being remodeled," snipped the man.

"I didn't mean any offense…"

"Come on, Allen," Clarissa pulled. "Let's get out of here."

Allen opened his backpack and pulled out the water and sandwich he had brought along. "Here," Allen offered. "Just a little something until the penthouse is finished."

The homeless man sat up, reached out and took the gifts from Allen. "She said your name is Allen, is that right?"

"Yeah, that's right," Allen replied.

"Thank you, Allen. This is the first full meal I've had in months. The name is Ben, but my friends call me Doc."

Ben reached out his hand. Allen met it with his and the two shared a handshake.

"Young lady," Ben motioned.

"Clarissa," she answered.

"Clarissa—what a lovely name. You've got a good one here. Don't let him go."

Clarissa blushed in the darkness, happy that nobody could see her embarrassment. "We're just friends, but thank you," she giggled.

"Be careful down here you two. Lots of trains and trouble ahead."

"Thank you, Ben," Allen said. "We will be. You take care of yourself."

"Goodbye, friends, and thank you again."

Allen and Clarissa continued, quiet but for the crunch of the ground under their feet, both flustered by their interaction with Ben.

"The opening has to be close," Clarissa said.

"It has to be here somewhere," Allen responded. "This is exactly where Rogers said it would be."

"He was right, you know."

"Well, Professor Rogers is rarely wrong," Allen said as he banged on the wall, stomped on the ground, and looked for any sign of a secret passage.

"Not Rogers…Ben."

Allen wasn't paying attention to what Clarissa said as he continued to search for the opening. "What has Rogers been?" he said, squinting at the wall.

"I said Ben."

"Oh—what was he right about?"

"He was right about you. You're one of the good ones."

"I don't know about all that, I just treat people as they should be, nothing more."

"You really are perfect," Clarissa muttered under her breath.

"What'd you say?" Allen asked, looking her way now.

"I said you're right, the opening has to be close."

"If you're looking for the opening, it's just past that sign on the left," a voice whispered.

Clarissa spun around and punched Ben in the face. Allen turned his flashlight to see the commotion and Clarissa begged forgiveness.

"I am so, so sorry, Ben. Holy hell you scared the shit out of me."

Ben squeezed his nose, but no blood followed. "It's okay, I am…okay," he said.

"Why did you sneak up on me like that?"

"Your voices echo when no trains are coming. Just wanted to help."

Ben moved toward Allen and just past the sign. He put Allen's two hands on the sign and motioned for Allen to pull it toward himself and then let go. Allen followed the directions and the track started to open to their left, revealing a ladder that led another hundred feet further underground. Ben continued to rub his nose.

"You have to hurry," Ben explained. "If a train comes now, it's lights out."

"How do you know?"

"If you get run over by a train, I'm pretty sure you die."

Clarissa rolled her eyes. "How do you know what to do?"

"You wouldn't believe me if I told you."

"Try me," she said.

"I've been down here before."

"Come with us," Clarissa proposed.

"You don't need me down there. Nothing but caves and some animals."

But Allen persisted, sensing the need to have him tag along. "She's right, Ben. Why don't you come with us? We'll get you somewhere comfortable to sleep."

"And leave all this?" Ben joked.

The ground shook suddenly under their feet.

"There's a train coming, better move quick," Allen ordered. He waved Clarissa ahead first, and she descended the ladder. "Now or never, Ben," Allen said with a smile.

"Had to make friends with two adventurous kids, didn't I?"

Ben moved down the ladder next and Allen followed. On the third rung, Allen saw a lever and pulled it to close the track above him. The descent felt like forever, all forty-nine rungs. When they reached the bottom safely, Ben took a lighter out of his pocket and pressed it against a railing on the wall. The flame started small and then moved incredibly fast in a straight line. He used the same method on the other wall to light the railing. The underground area was now completely lit. Allen turned off his iPhone flashlight.

Ben was in his late forties, his appearance ravaged by years on the streets of New York. He had on a long green overcoat, cargo pants with a knife in the left front pocket, and a black button-down under the overcoat. His dark eyes reflected orange in the light of the fire. Subtle wrinkles and dark circles had taken permanent residence under his eyes. His hair was grey but greasy and dirty, and his face hadn't been washed in weeks, covered with a combination of dirt, ash, and exhaust. His ears and hands were blackened by dirt and his teeth needed a good cleaning. His smile, however, was soft and welcoming, and he drank the water Allen gave him. Ben grabbed a pack of cigarettes from his pocket, pulled a cigarette out and raised to his lips, and leaned into the flame to light his smoke. The trio walked along the seemingly never-ending path.

"You really have been here before?" Clarissa asked.

"Believe it or not," Ben started as he inhaled smoke from his cigarette, "I was rich and happy years ago. Then one night coming home from work, I see a guy in a $3000 suit sneaking past the subway platform into the darkness. I was intrigued, so naturally I followed. He pulls that sign, disappears into the track. I wait a few minutes and follow him down here. He knew I was following him, but he let me do the James Bond stealth thing. I come to a fork in the path and picked the wrong way— clearly, not stealthy enough. It led me to a room full of ice, like the funhouse room of mirrors. I'm lost, spinning in circles and the next thing I know, I'm in my bed at home. I went to anyone who would listen, but nobody believed me. The cops laughed, the MTA scoffed at me, then the news people called, and I thought for sure that would be the ticket to proving everyone wrong. I was mistaken. There I was on TV pulling at that damn sign like a madman and it wouldn't budge. The lady on the news called me crazy to millions of New Yorkers. The next morning my supervisor called me in, and they put a temporary psychiatric hold on me. The state suspended my medical license shortly after that. I went from being a well-respected physician to this *lovely* thing you see in front of you."

"I'm so sorry, Ben," Allen said.

"Eh, it's okay, kid," Ben responded. "You just proved to me I'm not crazy. I'd been trying to get back into this place for twenty-two years."

"That's a long time to think you're crazy," Clarissa said.

"I always knew someone would prove me right," Ben said.

The trio came to the fork in the road.

"Which way, Ben?" Allen asked.

"Well, last time I went left, so I guess we go to the rig—"

"Left. We go the same exact way you went before," Clarissa insisted.

"Care to fill me in?" Allen asked.

"You went the right way, Ben; you just didn't belong where you ended up. Lead the way."

Ben followed the fire path to the left as he had years earlier.

"What can you tell us about the room that you remember?" Allen inquired.

"It's been years, but if I remember correctly, there's a set of stairs when you pass under a small stone bridge through an archway. Then it got really cold as you went down the stairs. Then you pass through a tunnel and into the room of ice."

"That's all?" Allen pressed.

"There were some inscriptions on the wall, but that's when the room started spinning," Ben explained.

"Clarissa, anything you can add?"

"Sorry, Allen, I just know it exists. Ben knows more than I do. I can't believe he's seen it."

Allen, Clarissa, and Ben approached the archway under the stone bridge, right where Ben said it would be. As they headed toward the spiral staircase that led further to the depths under New York, Allen was prepared for whatever came next.

"This is it, you two." Ben coughed.

"Let's go, then!" Allen shouted.

As Allen moved forward, he felt a gust of wind against his face. The stairway was lit by the same fire that had guided them to this point, but as Allen hit the fourth step on the staircase, the wind's intensity picked up and blew the fire out. The deeper they descended into the unknown, the more the temperature began to drop. Things became harder to see. Allen's heart pounded as he raced down the spiral stairs in the darkness, against the powerful wind that now blew, holding onto the walls to keep his balance. The three companions moved quickly, hoping to avoid the possibility of any trouble that lurked underground. Finally, they reached the bottom of the stairs and light broke from the end of the tunnel. The gusts of wind dwindled to a breeze, but the tunnel walls were solid blocks of ice. The trio went through the ice tunnel until they came upon a large corridor; on the walls of the corridor were the inscriptions that Ben had spoken of, but Allen couldn't understand any of what was written. The language on the walls was far too ancient.

"Clarissa, can you make any sense of this stuff?"

"I'm definitely the wrong sister in the family for that," she answered.

"This is already lasting longer than the last time I was here," Ben added.

"It's freezing down here." Clarissa shivered.

The columns that separated one set of inscriptions from the other were in a circle around the room, lit up by a ring of fire. In the center of the room, there was a large blue block, with the light focused directly on it. Allen moved closer to the block and realized it was a large cube of ice. Ben and Clarissa both came up and touched the block.

"It's ice," Ben remarked.

"Thank you, Detective," Clarissa quipped. "Allen, what do we do?"

"Wait!" Allen shouted, hunched over to look deeper. "There's a body inside."

There, inside the ice, was a man, frozen solid.

Ben held his lighter to the ice, but to no avail. "It's way too thick for this lighter," Ben realized.

"Stop," Allen demanded. "This feel wrong to either of you?"

"What do you mean?" Clarissa asked.

"This…someone buried down here in ice; what if there's a reason for it?"

"What if this is who you're meant to free?" Clarissa asked.

"What if it's not?" Allen said.

Allen pulled the backpack off his back and unzipped the largest opening. He pulled out a small axe and started to chop the ice with the weapon. But after a few minutes of no progress, the axe head broke and was sent flying against the wall.

"Dammit," Allen said.

Angry and frustrated, Allen leaned against the block of ice, and then let his body slide down it until he was sitting on the ground with his back against the block. As he leaned his head back, his eyes caught writing on the ceiling, reflecting off the light and the block of ice. Just one word was printed on the top of this corridor, separate from all the other inscriptions. He slowly stood again, to try to make out the word, and as he squinted his eyes to focus, he realized it was written in English.

"What is it, Allen?" Clarissa asked.

"Look." Allen pointed.

All three looked up at the same time and then at each other.

"Merlin," they said in unison.

The temperature in the room warmed, and the ice block Allen was seated against faded and gave way to a stone seat behind him.

"What…" Allen ran his hand over the stone. "Clarissa, look at this," he said. But when he got no response, he looked around to find that Clarissa and Ben had disappeared. He shot up straight, swiveling to see that he now stood in an empty room in what felt like a castle tower. The walls and floors were thick, grey stonemasonry so beautiful and well-built; rarely seen in the 21st century. Allen had never laid his eyes on something so different. The room was circular, like the one the three of them had been in just moments earlier.

"Clarissa? Ben?" he shouted.

"*They can't hear you,*" a man's voice echoed.

Allen wasn't afraid; he recognized the voice. It had spoken to him in the subway station not long after the attack in Times Square.

"Merlin, is that you?"

No answer came. Allen circled the room, trying to find the source of the voice, but instead the floor began to give way under his feet, plunging Allen into the darkness below him.

Allen landed in a forest he'd never seen before—the quiet of the night complemented by the fireflies glowing through the dense wood as the full moon shone above. The light from the moon brightened the stars, and as Allen began to walk on the path in front of him, two figures approached.

"Hello," Allen greeted.

But Allen was in someone else's memory now; an intimate viewer of the past.

"My Lady," a man started. "We must stop this madness."

"Listen to reason," begged the young woman. "There isn't time for bickering. We have to free him."

The figures stepped into Allen's line of vision. It was Mead and a young lady; someone Allen hadn't seen before. She was exceedingly tall and pale-skinned with long, curly, strawberry blonde hair. Her eyes were a greyish-blue, but the moonlight accentuated the lightness of her eyes. Her peach dress stretched all the way over her bare feet, and yet, it conformed to her body perfectly. She began to smile, and as she did, the area around the girl and Mead lit up. Allen was mesmerized by her beauty. He had never seen such a woman.

"Vivian, if anyone can free Merlin, it's you, but at what cost?"

*Who is Vivian?* Allen thought to himself.

"Mead, give me the key."

Mead handed the key to Vivian—the same key Allen had held in the lounge at Riverside—as they came to a clearing that led to a lake surrounded by trees and purple schist.

"The Val sans Retour…" Mead said, as he touched one of the purple rocks near the water.

"And the Mirror of Fairies," Vivian said. "It's the only way, isn't it?"

"It is."

Vivian and Mead moved in unison and leaned over the lake to see their reflections, and the water began to swirl upward. They backed up and watched as a doorway made of water emerged from the lake, glistening, and reflecting the white light of the moon. Vivian saw a small keyhole in the door, and she took the key in her hand and entered it into the hole. As they approached the water, both Vivian and Mead dissolved into the water—and a feeling of warmth came over Allen in the room of ice in the present day. Fire swirled as the room started to spin, and Allen grabbed onto the ice block, but his grip weakened when the block started to melt.

"This is what happened last time," Ben warned.

A subtle cracking sound emanated from the disappearing ice block. Rocks chipped off the walls from behind the melting ice, forcing Allen and his companions to dodge debris. Allen took three steps back, pushing Clarissa and Ben behind him. Allen's heart raced with questions; his mind racing with possibilities both good and bad.

When the ice cube had completely melted, leaving its prisoner on the cold ground, cloaked and shivering. There was silence. Sparks of fire surrounded the freezing body that had been in the ice, embracing it with warmth and disappearing in one fluid motion. It was then that the trio noticed the prisoner began to move. Subtle at first—the fingers, slowly down to the elbows; then, more pronounced. The figure slowly stood in the center of the room and turned to face them. They observed as the figure's eyes blinked open, adjusting to the light with a mix of awe and wonder. As the red burns of frostbite faded from the prisoner's face, a flash of white light filled the room, and the red burns of the cold dissipated from the prisoner's face.

He wore a long black cloak, had round, blue eyes and a bald head; his beard was long and grey, and the frame of his body was intimidating despite its weakened state. Without warning, he raised his arms and fire once again engulfed the room. Allen, Clarissa, and Ben were trapped in the center of the room, but none of them were harmed by the flames. The room began to shake, and pieces of the wall crumbled to the ground—the magic that had freed this man was now destroying the very prison that had kept him captive all these years.

"Impossible," Allen said in awe.

"Is it so hard to believe, Allen?" the man asked.

"Was it your voice?" Allen shot back.

"Free me!" the man uttered in the all-too-familiar voice.

"This changes everything," Clarissa said.

"Yes, Ms. Blakemore, it certainly does. You have freed me from Hell, my friends!" Merlin bellowed.

"Holy shit! Merlin is real?" Ben yelled.

"I am as real as you are, Doctor."

"Wait…how do you know who I am?"

"I know all there was, is, and could be," Merlin explained. "All these years stuck in this icy prison, with the vision and knowledge of every event in the world, powerless to help in the fight against the Nimayrd, against Arthur and Morgana. Though, I am forgetting some things…"

"King Arthur?" Ben wondered. "He's evil?"

Merlin shook his head and turned his attention to Arthur's descendant.

"Allen White, I've been waiting for you."

"Me?"

"Did you think all those dreams when you were a boy meant nothing?"

"I never knew what any of them meant, they were just dreams," Allen replied.

"And yet you asked and hoped to have them over and over," Merlin said.

Allen realized that Merlin wasn't kidding when he said he knew everything. The power of the wizard was unchartered territory for a small-town boy living in the big city.

"You heard all of it?" Allen asked.

"I know all you wish and want in life, Allen," Merlin began. "We don't have time to discuss that right now. We have bigger things to face and much to do if we are going to win this war, Allen."

"But Merlin, you're the most powerful wizard of all," Clarissa said. "Only you can put an end to Morgana."

"I wish that were true, Clarissa," Merlin said.

"What do you mean?" Allen worried.

"I'm afraid the staff that rests at Riverside is only part of my power. I am weakened from the captivity and without the weapon of the king, I am no match for Morgana."

"Then we have to find Excalibur," Allen stated.

"To do that, we'll have to get to the Lady of the Lake."

"Does anyone else feel like this isn't happening?" Ben interrupted.

Merlin turned his attention to Ben as he sized up the former physician and thought about what should be done with him.

"I'm sorry, Doctor, but your memory will have to be…altered," Merlin warned.

"'Altered'?" Ben angrily replied. "Save us all the trouble and say 'erased.'"

Allen turned to Clarissa and shook his head no.

"*I'm* sorry, Merlin," Allen said. "You can't do that. He's coming back to Riverside with us."

"Are you sure he can be trusted?" Merlin pressed. "Why is it I don't know you, Doctor? Why can't I remember some things? Was it the ice? What did *she* do to me?"

Clarissa maneuvered herself between Merlin and Ben and spread her arms out wide to shield Ben. "He can be trusted."

"What's Riverside?" Ben whispered into Clarissa's ear.

Clarissa grinned, curled her mouth sideways and whispered back, "It's the penthouse you've been waiting for."

Allen walked ahead of Clarissa and Ben through the underbelly of New York City with Merlin by his side. Merlin, still weakened from the ice, clutched Allen's arm with his left hand for support.

"I am sure you have so many questions, Allen," Merlin said.

"Actually, Mead has been good about answering most of them," Allen responded. "I do have one—who is Vivian?"

Merlin stopped walking. He looked back at Clarissa and Ben and motioned them to pass he and Allen.

"Is everything okay?" Clarissa asked.

"Oh, yes, Clarissa, everything is fine," Merlin replied. "Just a little tired, need to rest for a second. You and the doctor go ahead, we will meet you at Riverside. Tell Mead we will be along."

"Okay," Clarissa agreed. "See you in a bit."

Merlin and Allen watched as Clarissa and Ben disappear into the distance before Allen asked, "What's wrong, Merlin?"

"Nothing, son," Merlin breathed. "I just haven't heard that name in a very long time. Where did you see her?"

"Who is she, Merlin?"

Merlin paused for another moment and looked at Allen before he explained. "She is the woman I love, Allen. And she is the guardian of the Weapon of the King. Vivian is Nimuë."

A stunned Allen stepped back.

"That's right, Allen. She is the one your books all call the Lady of the Lake."

"And she's been waiting for us for a long time," a voice bellowed in the labyrinth.

Allen turned and tried to pinpoint the echo of the voice as he looked to protect a weakened Merlin. The wizard calmed Allen.

"I am here," Merlin said.

"And I am as well," the voice responded.

Perceval stepped into the light of the tunnels from around a corner with a pink towel wrapped around his waist and the Grail in his hands. He walked carefully toward Merlin and Allen and handed the Grail to the seated Merlin. The wizard drank from it and Allen watched as Merlin rose to his feet with renewed strength. Merlin embraced Perceval and placed both his hands onto Perceval's shoulders.

"It's good to see you, my friend," Merlin said.

"This is a miracle, Merlin," Perceval said.

"I told you many years ago that miracles aren't impossible."

"Excuse me," Allen interrupted. "Who are you?"

"Your Majesty." Perceval kneeled. "I am Perceval li Galois, loyal to the one true King, a Knight of the Round Table, and protector of the Holy Grail."

"Please stand up," Allen motioned. "I am not a king. But I still don't understand who *you* are," he said kindly.

Perceval got to his feet and exchanged a big smile with Merlin. The old sage nodded his head up and down.

"Perhaps, Mr. White, you prefer this voice," Perceval's body blurred for a moment and came back into focus as Mr. Mead.

"No way," Allen screamed. "How is that even possible?"

"The Grail," Merlin interjected. "The power of life, youth; the gift of eternity."

"I would love to explain everything to you, Allen," Perceval said. "You have to get Merlin to Riverside and to his staff."

"You're not coming with us, Mea…I'm sorry…Perceval?"

"I have to find Nimuë," he answered. "I have to find Excalibur."

"Arthur will come for us soon," Merlin warned.

"Then I guess I'd better hurry," Perceval replied.

Perceval—clad in nothing but a towel and carrying the Grail—ran into the labyrinth and out of sight, leaving Allen to help Merlin back to

Riverside; the realization coming to him that with the legendary wizard free, the beginning of the end had also arrived.

# Chapter 6 – LIVE/EVIL

Arthur's eyes popped open as he sat on his purple throne. He was in his room of bones in the realm Morgana had created to shield The Nimayrd from the world. His sorceress sister stood nearby watching The Fylorn slowly spin, while Jaxx and Kimo paced around the room.

"The wizard is free, sister," Arthur said.

"I felt it too, brother," she replied. "I don't need The Fylorn to tell me that. Remember, I'm the one who put him in that prison."

"Jaxx, you know what to do," Arthur said.

"Yes, Master," Jaxx snarled.

The mammoth monster waited as Morgana opened The Fylorn. He jumped through the orb and disappeared.

"It shouldn't take very long at all," Morgana whispered.

"And what of the boy?" Arthur asked.

"They must be at Riverside, my King. I cannot get to them anymore."

"Kimo, my friend. Step forward," Arthur said solemnly.

"Yes, Master," Kimo responded, going straightaway to Arthur.

"I saw the hatred in your eyes in Times Square; I know your nature is one of violence and vengeance, it's why we wanted you here with us. It's time to put that energy to good use. Go and gather the Syph army…tell them it is time for another fight…one we will win."

Kimo bowed his head and left the room just as Jaxx returned through The Fylorn. The former king stood up from his chair, anticipation electrifying him inside.

"Well?" Arthur asked.

"It is done, Master," Jaxx answered.

"Perfect. Now for one last thing."

Arthur lifted about fifteen inches off the ground a giant black bag that rested next to his throne and threw it across the floor to Jaxx's feet. The mammoth looked down at the bag and then up to Arthur with a huge grin on his face.

"You know what to do when the time is right," Arthur explained. "Keep it safe until then."

"As you wish, Master," Jaxx bowed.

Jaxx picked up the bag, slung it over his shoulder and left the throne room. Morgana came to stand beside Arthur as he took his seat again.

"The time has come, Morgana. We need to end this."

"Merlin is weak; our time to strike is now," Morgana encouraged. "Once the wizard is dead, nothing can stop us, Arthur."

"The boy can; he must die as well," Arthur said.

"And he will, brother. Kimo is capable."

"No!" Arthur slammed his fist on the throne, breaking one of the skulls on the armrest. "He is mine to kill."

*60 minutes ago*

The man in the black suit and white button-down shirt with black shoes walked along the unpaved dirt road in Clayton, New York. He had long, straight, dirty blonde hair down to the middle of his back. The sun beamed down on the hot July day, but he seemed unbothered by the heat. As he approached the White home, he grew excited. He ran his right hand through his hair, pulling strands off his face as he reached his destination. He held a clipboard under his arm. The White's garage door was open, and Jamie's motorcycle was gone, so the Man in Black realized Lisa might be alone. The front door was wide open, but the screen door was locked. The Man in Black jiggled the handle to confirm this before knocking on the screen door. He could hear James Taylor's "Fire and Rain" playing inside the house, so he banged a little harder on the door and the music stopped.

"Coming!" Lisa shouted.

The Man in Black breathed deep as Lisa approached the door. She was wearing a green and yellow floral sundress, and her smile was warmer than the day. Lisa was barefoot and had a dish towel draped over her left shoulder.

"Can I help you?" Lisa asked.

"Mrs. White? Lisa White?" The Man questioned.

"Yes, that's me…who are you?"

The Man in Black handed Lisa a card.

"My name is Eric DuLac, I'm from the United States Census Department. Our records show you never completed your Census 2020 forms. I was wondering if you had time now to complete this?"

"I'm a little busy at the moment getting things ready for a party," Lisa explained. "Could you come back later this week?"

"It won't take more than five minutes of your time, Mrs. White."

"Okay, Mr. DuLac, come on in."

Lisa unlocked the door and let Eric in. She led him into the kitchen and motioned for him to have a seat.

"Please, make yourself at home. Can I get you anything to drink?"

"A glass of water would be great if it's not too much trouble."

"No problem at all."

Lisa opened the cupboard to the left of the sink, the one with pictures of the family on it, and took out Allen's favorite glass, a royal blue pint glass. She filled the glass with cold water and gave it to the seated DuLac, who took a sip before he placed the glass on the table.

"Okay if I keep working while we talk?" Lisa asked, turning her attention back to the carrots she was cutting before he arrived.

"Oh, absolutely, Mrs. White," DuLac said. "Will your husband be home soon as well? We like to talk to both members of the household, but it's not necessary."

"He should be back momentarily, but who knows with him," she laughed.

"So, Mrs. White, how long have you lived here?"

"We've been in this house almost twenty-five years now," Lisa replied. "It'll be twenty-five years in October."

"Just you and your husband?"

"Our son, as well."

"You husband's name is Jamie, and your son is…"

"Allen."

"And he lives here?"

"When he isn't at school, yes."

"Where does he go to school?"

"Fordham University."

"That's in New York City, right?"

"Yes, that's right; the Bronx."

"Very good. You must be very proud."

"Oh, incredibly. He's a great young man, always has been."

DuLac wrote down Lisa's answers as he listened intently. He stopped to take another sip of his water as Lisa chopped cucumbers on the cutting board. As she neared the end of a cucumber, she accidentally nicked her finger with the knife. A few drops of blood fell to the kitchen floor as Lisa turned to rinse the wound in the sink. The faint sound of a Harley Davidson could be heard echoing on the quiet summer day. Lisa turned the faucet on and placed her finger under the cold water.

"That's Jamie on his way back," Lisa explained. "He should be here in a couple of minutes."

Lisa turned away from the sink toward the table and bumped into DuLac.

"Are you okay?" he asked. "Let me take a look, I'm first aid certified."

"I'm fine, just a little spilled blood."

DuLac dropped to a knee and wiped the droplets of blood with his finger. He stood up as he brought his blood-covered finger to his mouth and tasted the blood.

"Oh, but a little spilled blood can go a long way," DuLac said.

Lisa backed away from DuLac with fear in her heart. DuLac closed his eyes and rotated his neck in a circular motion. Lisa could hear the bones of DuLac's neck as they cracked. When DuLac opened his eyes, they glowed red. Lisa's mouth opened to scream, but the terror rendered her mute. DuLac's body convulsed as his skin smoldered and began to fall off. Lisa froze in fear as DuLac's appearance gave way to the mammoth Jaxx.

"You taste nothing like your son," Jaxx snickered. "Did you really think you'd be protected here forever?"

Jamie's motorcycle grew louder coming down the dirt road – startling Jaxx and pushing Lisa to act. She took a chance and attempted to drive the weapon into Jaxx's chest. He grabbed her hand before it crashed down on him, knocking the knife to the floor. Jaxx used his gigantic hand to smother Lisa's face, leaving her incapacitated in his grip while he snatched the knife off the floor and drove it into her side. He twisted the blade. Lisa collapsed to the ground as blood soaked through her shirt and seeped onto the kitchen floor. Jaxx ripped the knife from Lisa's side and straddled her as she used her remaining energy to fight him off; Jaxx simply laughed at her.

The motorcycle stopped in the driveway and the noise cut off. Jaxx brought his index finger to his lips and taunted Lisa to be quiet as she lay dying. Gripping the knife with both hands, he drew back his arms and drove the knife into Lisa's chest with all his force.

"Honey, I'm back," Jamie called from the front door. "They didn't have any Pinot, so I got a Chardonnay, I hope that's okay."

Jamie stopped short in the kitchen when he saw Jaxx, then looked down to see the mammoth was standing over his wife's body. A puddle of blood spread across the kitchen floor. With a pained, raging cry, Jamie held the wine bottle as a weapon and attacked the murderer. He was no match for Jaxx, who grabbed Jamie by the throat and slammed him into the puddle on the floor. Jaxx flipped Jamie over in one quick move and smeared his face into his dead wife's blood.

"Why did you do this?" Jamie begged; his voice muffled.

"Why not?" Jaxx snarled. "You can thank your son for this."

"Please, I'll do anything, just leave Allen alone," Jamie pleaded as he choked on his wife's blood.

"It's too late, the boy will die soon enough. But first, he suffers."

"May God have mercy on your soul," Jamie screamed. "You're a monster."

"You have no idea."

Jaxx turned Jamie back over and looked at his prey. He leaned into Jamie's chest and sniffed him and then licked the blood off his face.

"Your fear is amazing," Jaxx moaned.

Then Jaxx drove his elbow down into Jamie's neck and crushed Jamie's windpipe on impact.

Jaxx stood up and hovered as Jamie's hands scrambled at his own neck, a wasted effort to try and save himself from death. Jamie crawled to Lisa just as The Fylorn appeared in the Whites' kitchen. Jaxx stepped through the orb and back into the dark realm of Arthur.

Jaxx listened to Arthur and Morgana's conversation, and his right forearm warmed; he looked down to see the crimson of The Fylorn circling his arm. Two new tattoos formed in its path—Jamie and Lisa's faces—and they joined a plethora of other faces on Jaxx's body. A new tattoo for each life he extinguished.

*504 A.D. – Three years after Morgana saved Arthur's life*

Smoke rose from the fireplace as the cold of winter settled in on the countryside. Outside the small log cabin, the freshly fallen snow offered calm. The sun disappeared only moments before and the growing quiet of night was disturbed only by the occasional sound of an animal in the distance. Inside the cabin, a man wrapped in a raggedy grey blanket huddled in front of the fire to keep warm. His hair was black and curly, his eyes were a soft shade of brown. He carried scars on his neck that extended down to his chest. He wore a simple, knee-length woolen tunic, as most Anglo-Saxon men did in the fifth and sixth centuries. He rubbed his hands together and extended them as close to the flames as he could without burning his fingers, stopping to toss another piece of wood into the fire. The embers danced in the air as the man marveled at their beauty. His tranquility was interrupted by a knock at the door. He stood up and moved through the shadows cast by the orange firelight in the one-room cabin. The man opened the door and was greeted by two figures, both cloaked in long, black, elegant robes.

"We seek shelter from the cold," a woman said, her body visibly shivering under the cloak.

"Please, come in, share in my fire," the man of the house said.

"Thank you for your kindness," the woman replied.

"You are most welcome, friends."

"Ha, you are no friend to me," a man's voice said from under his cloak.

The unmistakable laugh of Morgana filled the cabin and echoed in the night. The sorceress removed her cloak and confirmed her existence while the cloaked man revealed himself.

"Arthur?!" the man exclaimed. "I thought you were dead! I mourned for you."

Lancelot kneeled before Arthur and kissed the former monarch's hand. Arthur quickly drew back his hand.

"Spare me the groveling, Lancelot," Arthur snapped. "All that has happened to me and to this country lays at your feet. You did this."

"You're wro—"

"You betrayed me, Lancelot. You bedded my wife, you left the Round Table in a time of war, and you hide now, like a *rat*," Arthur sneered, eyes blazing as much as the fire.

Arthur pulled a dagger from under his cloak and teased it against Lancelot's jugular vein.

"Hmmmm," Morgana thought. "He could prove useful, brother."

Arthur stared at his sister and hesitated, and then eased the dagger away from Lancelot's throat. "Why couldn't you just leave her alone?"

"I loved her; but you knew that."

"Look at everything we lost because of your love."

"Nobody told you to make up for my mistake by going after the Grail. You could've just left me in exile—Mordred wouldn't have come after us all."

"*Us?* How dare you talk like you bore the pain of losing all of Camelot."

"I was part of the Round Table too, or have you forgotten?"

"Who could forget *Sir Lancelot?* So brave…so honorable…"

"I'm sorry, Arthur; forgive me, please."

"Why would I do that when I can just kill you here and now?"

"Forgive me, my King," Lancelot cried. "The shame and guilt of my actions are punishment enough. Please let me live. I will spend the rest of my life doing your bidding to show you how sorry I truly feel."

"Swear it to me, Lancelot. Swear you will follow my every command for as long as you shall live."

"I swear it, Arthur," Lancelot looked up from the floor. "I will be a faithful knight from now until my dying day."

"We are no longer bound by the rules of knights and kings," Arthur explained.

Morgana grabbed the dagger from Arthur's hand and waved the knife around in a circle on Lancelot's wooden table. Slowly, the chalice of blood appeared on the table. Arthur reverently lifted the cup with both hands, as he remained standing above Lancelot.

"Drink, old friend, and you shall be reborn as one of us again—this time in the darkness; and trust me, it feels so much better than the light." Arthur encouraged; any signs of the chivalrous monarch gone for good.

Arthur extended the chalice to Lancelot, who did not hesitate to drink, his guilt over the destruction of Camelot his great motivator.

"You were the strongest of us all, Lancelot," Arthur remembered. "You will be the strongest of us for eternity."

Lancelot convulsed as the blood of Arthur and Morgana overtook his mind and body. His tunic began to rip, and Lancelot's muscles expanded as his body transformed. Lancelot's skin became impenetrable, his mind focused on obedience; his eyes went from the soft blue hue to all black with crimson streaks. After a few tortured moments, the massive man rose to his feet. Morgana clapped with excitement at their creation and Arthur looked proudly over his former best friend.

"From this day forth, Lancelot is dead," Arthur proclaimed. "Henceforth, you will be known as Jaxx."

"Yes, Master," Jaxx answered.

*March 27, 1884 – Cannes, French Riviera*

Jaxx sneaked into La Villa Nevada, fully aware that Prince Leopold, Duke of Albany had been sent there by his mother, Queen Victoria for his protection. The villa was property of the Royal Family, and its beautiful Art Deco architecture made it the perfect getaway for the royals. It overlooked the vast Mediterranean Sea and village of Cannes and was guarded extensively outside and inside.

Her Majesty had become suspicious of the rumors she'd heard that Arthur had survived all these years—rumors told to her by her son Leopold's friend, Alice Liddell. Young Alice had confided in the Queen that the book Lewis Carroll wrote was in fact Carroll's discovery of the "Arthur Lives" conspiracy during his time in Oxford. Carroll's knowledge came from his curiosity about the Oxford murder of a young girl in the 1200s. Carroll stumbled upon what he called "the dwelling": a land of such vastness and evil it was indescribable to most. Carroll told Alice about his time in this place and the mad tyrant he'd witnessed slaughtering two Britons. Alice convinced him to write it all down, but it became a children's story, treated as nothing more than fiction.

Arthur didn't care about killing Carroll because most people thought he was insane and didn't believe his rantings. Arthur wanted to send a message to the Queen, however, so he sent Jaxx to kill her youngest son to silence her. Jaxx dispatched the eight guards outside La Villa Nevada and strolled inside. Jaxx killed seven more royal guards before heading to Leopold's bedroom. Jaxx entered the room and the Leopold resigned himself to the reality of death.

"It's true then," Leopold said. "Arthur lives?"

"Arthur has always lived," Jaxx growled.

"Mr. Carroll was right. I'll be damned," Leopold confirmed. "Alice?"

"The girl lives," Jaxx answered.

"I never got to tell her how much I loved her."

"And you never will," Jaxx stalked closer to Leopold, ready to strike him down.

"You remember love, don't you?"

Jaxx stopped; for a moment it seemed to the prince that he might've reached beyond the abomination before him…but he was wrong. "Love is what created the monster you see before you."

"So, Mr. Carroll was right again; you *are* Lancelot."

"Lancelot died a long time ago," Jaxx retorted. "He paid the price for his actions."

"And what of your actions since? Who pays that price?"

"Today, dear Prince, it is you. A new face for my collection."

Jaxx showed off the tattoos on his body to Leopold, and the prince tried once more to reason with the mammoth.

Leopold swallowed hard, chilled by the faces of the dead. "Lancelot was a protector," he said quietly. "A healer, a good knight, and an even better man. How could you turn your back on all the good?"

"There *was* no good!" Jaxx shouted.

Leopold reached to his nightstand and pulled a book to his lap in the bed. He opened to a page he'd marked and began reading.

"'Today I told the King how Lancelot saved my life on the road back from London,'" Leopold read. "'Arthur seemed genuinely grateful in his praise of Lancelot. This young knight has saved a great many people from horrible fates. It is as if God himself sent this bastion of light as a beacon, for all of us to mold ourselves to be. He is unshakeable, unwavering in his loyalty, and the greatest swordsman I have ever seen. We are all lucky to have a man with his honor and courage living amongst us.' Signed, Queen Guinevere." Leopold looked up imploringly at the mammoth. "You say there was no good—but the woman you love saw nothing but good in you."

Jaxx listened intently to the words, his lips quivering for a split second before he had heard enough. He reached over and closed the book. The prince closed his eyes. Jaxx took the book and placed it in his pocket. He then drew his knife out of its sheath on his belt.

"I will make this quick," Jaxx promised.


*November 22, 1963*

As the motorcade made its way through Dallas, Texas, Lee Harvey Oswald set his rifle scope from his perch in the depository. Oswald knew his task was to create chaos, and he fired his gun without a second thought. At the same moment, from the grassy knoll, Jaxx appeared through The Fylorn, undetected. He fired the shot that killed President John F. Kennedy, smiled and walked back through The Fylorn.


*July 1, 2000*

Terrence lit his cigar inside the arcade doorway as the rain drenched

New York. He put his lighter back in his pocket and puffed on the cigar. It was unseasonably warm for the beginning of April in New York, but Terrence just pulled up the collar on his jacket to keep himself dry. After walking for three blocks, Terrence tossed his cigar into the street and stopped on the corner of Broadway and 49th to get a hot dog and soda, getting momentary relief under the vendor's umbrella.

"Dog with the works and a coke, please," Terrence said to the vendor—a middle-aged man with greying hair and a grey moustache. He wore a New York Mets hat, and his apron was covered in ketchup and mustard, right down to his jeans and blue Reeboks. His white t-shirt showed off his tattoo of Felix the Cat.

The vendor prepared the hot dog and placed it in a carrying tray. He reached down into the cart's attached mini-freezer and grabbed a can of Coca-Cola. He put the tray and the drink on the customer side of the cart.

"Dollar-fifty, Mack," the vendor replied.

Terrence handed the vendor a twenty-dollar bill and walked away, placing the soda can in the tray.

"Uh, Mack, your change!" the vendor shouted.

"Keep the change," Terrence yelled.

Terrence took two big bites of his hot dog as he waited for the street sign to change from DON'T WALK to WALK. A little mustard and some relish fell into the tray, but he finished the hot dog before the sign changed, opened the soda, and began to drink. He tossed the tray into the trash can on the corner and started crossing the street when he felt the chill of someone watching him. Terrence chugged the rest of the soda and kept walking. He looked back at the hot dog cart, and the city stopped for a heartbeat as he caught eyes with the vendor. The hot dog vendor's eyes turned pitch black, and he shoved his cart aside and stalked after Terrence. Terrence turned and ran, pushing through a sea of umbrellas on 48th Street. He made it to 47th as the light changed, keeping the vendor at bay for two minutes. Terrence raced to a payphone and called Riverside. As soon as he hung up, the vendor slammed him against the door of the phone booth.

Terrence focused on the Felix the Cat tattoo, the one thing that was still entirely the vendor's. His teeth were as yellow as mustard, his breath hotter than the July heat, and reeked of onions. The vendor shook his head wildly, almost fighting off what Terrence knew was behind the sight and smell before him. "You should have stayed in the arcade, fat man."

"Just do it, already," Terrence demanded.

Jaxx drew back his hand, a pair of hot dog tongs in his fist, and drove them into Terrence's chest.

*August 1, 2008 – Los Angeles, California*

"Right away, Mr. Blakemore," the teenage valet in the red bomber jacket and black dress slacks said.

Moments later, Howard Blakemore's Mercedes SUV pulled up to the curb. The young driver came around to open the door for Johanna, and Howard handed him a fifty-dollar bill. The kid pulled out a Sharpie and valet tag from his jacket pocket.

"Mrs. Blakemore," the valet said. "I'm sorry to bother you but my mother is a huge fan of your work. Would you be able to sign this for me?"

"Absolutely, sweetheart." Johanna smiled.

The kid beamed through his braces. Johanna took the Sharpie and paper and signed an autograph before handing it back to him.

"Thank you so much, Mrs. Blakemore," the kid said as he closed the passenger door. "Thank you both so much."

Johanna waved goodbye from inside the car, happy to be at an event where the paparazzi never showed up. Howard slowly pulled away from the curb and into the streets of Los Angeles.

"I love these things, Howard. No pressure, no vultures."

"I guess we'll just have to have more of them, honey."

"What do you mean?"

"Well, I talked to Steve, and he thinks we should make a run for Sacramento."

"Governor Blakemore?" she laughed. "Howard, you can't be serious."

"I told Steve that 'd run it by you and the girls before I decided on anything," Howard assured, reaching out his hand to touch Johanna's face.

"I'm not worried about Kay—she'll follow you anywhere. But Clarissa? You think voters are tough to sway…good luck, Howard."

"I know, I told Steve the same thing," he smirked. "It could be big for us."

"Being governor or Clarissa's tantrum?"

The couple laughed as the car navigated through Mulholland Drive.

As the Mercedes came around a curve, a vehicle with its hazard lights on caught Howard's attention. He slowed the Mercedes and pulled over behind the vehicle, a red sedan with its hood propped open. He placed his car in park and unlocked the doors.

"I'll be right back, love."

Before Howard could open the door, someone opened Johanna's door and pulled her out into the dirt.

"Howard, help me!" she screamed.

Howard jumped out of the Mercedes and was knocked out from behind. When he regained consciousness, Howard's eyes opened to Johanna being terrorized by Jaxx. Howard was seated on the ground and handcuffed to a street sign.

"So nice of you to join us, Mr. District Attorney," Jaxx said.

"Let her go, Jaxx, you son of a bitch, she has nothing to do with this."

"She knew when she married you what she was getting into, Howard. This is what happens to all of you. I don't know what she ever saw in you." Jaxx pointed a gun at Johanna's chest…but then second guessed himself. "Saw in you…" he mumbled. "Hmmmm…"

Jaxx moved the gun to Johanna's eyes and pulled the trigger twice. Johanna's eyes were replaced with two gaping holes in her face. Howard could only watch as his wife was brutally murdered. Out of The Fylorn came The Master. He stood over a tearful Howard.

"See, Howard, you politicians are all the same. You claim to protect the innocent and punish the guilty, but it's you who are guilty. You and your little band of friends are guilty of trying to bring down a force you don't even comprehend. Didn't your little friend tell you we are invincible? You should have never revolted against us, Howard. You will lose. Jaxx, kill him—and make it hurt."

"With pleasure, Master," Jaxx agreed.

The next morning, Howard and Johanna's bodies were found on the side of the road. Howard had been tortured—his tongue cut out, his fingers all broken, his eyelids charred to blackness. He had two screws through the back of his skull. Whatever information the Nimayrd had sought, Howard Blakemore died without giving anything away.

*Present Day*

Jaxx walked through the wide-open space of their realm with the bag over his shoulder. He was followed by Arthur and Morgana. It was painfully quiet in all the areas that usually rumbled with the sounds of the Syphs. The trio came upon the gigantic hallway, ceilings hundreds of feet high, a cavernous expanse created by Arthur and Morgana. Kimo had seen this hallway his first night in the realm, but now he stood in front of an army of evil, proud of his accomplishment. Morgana waved her arms and the endless room lit up column by column.

"My friends, today we go to New York, together. Today we end The Remains forever!" Arthur decreed. "Kill them all."

Morgana created a Fylorn tunnel and the Syphs prepared their attack. She clapped her hands together and Arthur, Morgana, Jaxx, and Kimo disappeared into the orb.

# Chapter 7 – The Lady of the Lake

Perceval left Allen and Merlin and went the opposite way from where Merlin was freed moments earlier. Perceval felt in his gut that he was on the right path to find Nimuë. He understood that the only way to get to her was the Grail. His immortality was tied to her, and hers to the cup.

In the depths of the underground labyrinth, Perceval came upon a pool of water, about as big as a jacuzzi. He dipped the Grail into the water and filled the cup. Perceval then gulped down the water and half-prayed, half-wished for a miracle.

"Please, My Lady."

The pool expanded before Perceval's eyes. The ground cracked and separated, and a waterfall formed. Perceval leaned over the top of the waterfall and looked down to see the waterfall had a maelstrom at its end.

"A leap of faith on faith alone," Perceval whispered to himself.

Perceval closed his eyes and gripped the Grail tight before he crossed his hands to his chest and launched himself into the water. The maelstrom swirled uncontrollably in the underground of New York City as the water engulfed Perceval. The ground that had broken returned to its form and the pool of water was restored.

"You told me 1600 years ago that this day would come," Perceval remembered. "You said the King would rise again."

*501 A.D. - Camlann*

Perceval smiled as Nimuë reached her hand out of the water and grabbed Excalibur. As the red sun started to descend after the bloody war at Camlann, the last flickers of light reflected off Perceval's armor and the Grail. When he turned to walk away, Nimuë revealed herself on the battlefield. She was as beautiful as many men had imagined; Perceval stood awed by her beauty. With each step she took, Perceval grew more and more nervous. She was statuesque, a moving piece of art that men and women could behold and never know the true depths of the beauty. In a light peach dress that hugged her curves, her golden hair settled on her shoulders.

"Sir Perceval, come forward," she said. "Don't be afraid."

The young knight nervously approached Nimuë. She sensed the apprehension and reached out and took his hand in both of her hands. She locked eyes with Perceval and smiled.

"You were meant to survive this war, Perceval. You are the keeper of the Grail now. This cannot be taken lightly for several reasons; but with this responsibility comes a gift, young knight."

"What gift?" Perceval wondered.

"Immortality."

Perceval bowed his head in thought. *Immortality? What would I even do? Would I be stuck on this land? What about everyone else?* "I don't want to live forever, My Lady Nimuë," Perceval refused.

"You must, Perceval. You are all that's left. As the red sun sets on this dark moment in history, evil forces plot."

"Mordred and Morgana are dead," Perceval insisted.

"No, Perceval, Morgana is not dead. She has defeated Merlin. As we speak, she makes her way to Avalon."

"How is this possible, My Lady?"

"Merlin's staff is lost, the great sword Excalibur is returned to me, and Arthur is dead."

"The King lost his way, My Lady," Perceval said, his eyes searching Nimuë's for sympathy.

"Arthur no longer wanted to be King, my friend. He forsook the very vows you swore to uphold; the great temptation was his undoing."

"What do I have to do?" Perceval asked.

"Before night falls, you must drink from the Grail. It will protect you, shield you from all manner of evil, and hide your true form from the world around you. The children of the Knights of the Round Table will be in danger—you must do all you can to hide them and their children after that. Morgana will come for them; her bloodlust is stronger now that her son was killed. It will take some years for her to regain her full strength, but she will come back with murder in her heart. Send the children to the corners of the Earth. Keep the son of Arthur by your side."

"My Lady?"

"The Queen is pregnant. See that the Lady Guinevere drinks from that cup before a fortnight has passed."

"How long will I have to protect those who remain?"

"For as long as you can, Perceval. When those who remain are at full strength, it is only then that Merlin can be free again; for now, even my power cannot help the one I love."

"When will the new king retake his throne?"

"When the people need him the most, young knight."

"Then I swear to see this through," Perceval declared.

The young Perceval, the last man of the Round Table left standing after the great war, sipped from the Holy Grail as Nimuë returned to the depths of the water that surrounded Camlann.

*501 AD*

"Are you sure?" Guinevere asked.

"I swear it, My Queen," Perceval answered.

"I have always trusted you, Perceval, so I will do what it is you ask of me."

"Thank you, My Queen."

"I am no longer the Queen," Guinevere insisted. "That life is behind me."

"None of us blamed you for the things that happened, My Lady," Perceval assured. "We all saw what Arthur had become; we all watched his descent into madness. His death was brought on by his greed."

"I laid with a man who was not my husband," Guinevere confessed. "I loved Lancelot, and I loved Arthur. Both were good men, and both are dead because of me."

"I'm sorry, My Lady. I truly am. But you are not to blame for their deaths. The blame lies within for both."

Guinevere raised the Grail to her lips and drank from the cup of Christ. She placed the cup back down on the wooden table in the convent, her full lips stained red.

"We will make this right for those that remain, Perceval."

"Yes, My Lady, we will."

*1250 A.D.*

Perceval—now fully disguised as Mead—sat in the saddle atop the horse as it galloped with great speed in the night. He directed the mare to go right at a fork in the road. The path followed alongside a stream and through a village, and Perceval slowed the horse as they approached a house on his left that was surrounded by farmland.

"*Keep going,*" the voice called out from the stream.

Perceval saw a hole in the roof—the house crisp black from the fire that killed Eldon and Emma. He encouraged the horse to keep moving down the path. Four hours later, in the deep of the night, Perceval walked alongside his horse. The man and his animal companion came upon a large oak tree at another fork in the road. Tired from the long journey, Perceval first calmed his horse and then slumped against the tree, eyes closed before he hit the ground. As he slept, a voice masked by the darkness jolted him awake.

"Is that you?" Perceval whispered in Mead's soft voice.

"Yes, I'm here," the voice murmured back as Amra emerged from behind an oak tree.

"What of the baby?"

"She's safe."

"And the others?"

A long, silent moment happened as Perceval waited on an answer. The quiet gave Perceval the answer he dreaded.

"I'm sorry, Amra. Emma and Eldon were good people."

"My daughter lived her way. But we both know it's only a matter of when, not if, that they find me."

"We can keep you safe, Amra."

"No, Mead, you can't. Jaxx was there; the beast can smell my blood. You have to go, now."

"I won't leave you to die, Amra."

"You have to, old friend. Go!"

*1492 – Captain's Quarters, Santa Maria – Somewhere in the Atlantic Ocean*
Mead poured himself a glass of Port Wine as he discussed the future with the captain of the Santa Maria—Christopher Columbus. The infamous explorer was seated with his hands connected behind his head and a smug smile that ran across his face.

"How did you find this new world?" Columbus asked.

"It's a long story, Captain. Perhaps someday I can tell it to you."

"Perhaps, Mr. Mead. Now tell me again of these people that live on our new land."

"The thing you have to understand, Master Columbus, as I've explained before, is that this isn't *our* new land we venture toward; these people have been here a very long time," Mead explained. "There are families living there and they won't take kindly to your expansionist ideals. If you come with violence, you will be met with violence."

Columbus snickered at Mead as he looked around the room at all the weapons at his disposal, a smug grin gleaming from his face. "Mr. Mead, you can see we are more than ready for violence. If these savages want to war with us, we will take what is theirs by force. This is God's will, and it shall be done."

"I beg you to consider a peaceful alternative," Mead pleaded. "These people are innocent."

"No man is innocent that would stand in the way of a king," Columbus rationalized. "These people will all bow to the divine ruler, Ferdinand."

"I have known tyrants before, Master Columbus. They all end up dead from their own greed."

Columbus didn't like that warning from Mead; he jumped to his feet and threw his glass against the wall, shattering shards throughout the cabin. "I agreed to captain this vessel for you, Mr. Mead," Columbus shouted. "You said it would lead to a new world, one free of the constraints across Europe. When I told Isabella and Ferdinand of this journey, I assured them of riches beyond their wildest dreams. You speak of greed and yet you are ignorant to the reality of the world. These people you look to protect stand between the crown and money. They will meet the fate that many before them have met; be careful you don't meet the same fate for defying the crown."

"I answer to one crown," Mead mumbled as he calmly finished his port.

*July 24, 1981 – Point Pleasant Beach, New Jersey*
It was a dreadfully hot summer day on Jenkinson's Boardwalk at Point Pleasant Beach in New Jersey. Mead had spent most of the day standing in the ocean as he attempted time and again to draw out Nimuë. He was discouraged, frustrated, and defeated by the lack of contact with Nimuë beyond the voice he heard the night he saw Amra. He readied to leave the water when he heard a much different voice.

"Help!" a young boy shouted. "Somebody please, help!"

Mead looked out into the ocean and saw the young boy struggling to stay afloat. The current was getting stronger. The old man dived headfirst into the Atlantic Ocean and swam as fast as he could, but the boy had sunk into the water. Mead could feel the water gaining strength with each slap against his face, nearly pulling him under too, but he fought the current and submerged. Mead came back up, both sputtering and gasping, the boy in his right arm. Two lifeguards met Mead in the water and helped him get the boy back to shore. When they reached the sand, the boy coughed up some water and regained his breath. After resting a few minutes, the child mustered the courage to speak to his elderly rescuer.

"Thanks, mister," the boy said. "You saved my life."

The kid was wildly unremarkable at first glance. A scrawny, dark-skinned, gap-toothed boy who didn't know how to swim; but there was a glow about this kid that Mead couldn't ignore.

"How old are you, kid?" Mead asked.

"Nine-and-a-half," the kid boasted.

"Where are your parents?"

"My dad was supposed to come with me, but he had to work."

"And your mother?"

"She moved to Las Vegas, but that's okay," the kid responded.

"Why's that?" Mead wondered.

"Dad said she had to 'go, go, dance.'"

Mead turned his head away from the kid to try and contain the laughter that was about to jump out of his body. The kid reached out and grabbed Mead's shoulder with his hand and shook the old man.

"You okay, mister?"

"Mead is the name. I'm quite alright, thank you."

"Well, okay, Mead. I'm going to go find my dad," the child said as he readied to sprint away down the beach.

"What'd you say your name was?"

"Thomas," the kid answered. "Thomas Rogers."


*Present Day*

Perceval laughed to himself as he continued to fall through the maelstrom in the waterfall. The same waterfall he leapt into after drinking from the Grail. Just as he began another trip down memory lane, he reached the bottom of the never-ending drop. Perceval stood on a soft ground—what felt like sand or grass—in the vastness of the falls and looked up to see nothing but the brightness of the moon. His nakedness was now covered in a light blue tunic. The bright green tint of the water to his left was only accented by the moonlight. There was an overwhelming smell of saltwater in the air, as if his memory of saving Rogers all those years ago had just happened.

"It's a strong memory you have of Thomas," Nimuë said.

Completely dry, the long dormant Lady of the Lake rose from the lagoon and stepped out onto the wet rock where Perceval waited. Her light dress looked the same as it did over a millennium earlier, her beauty still unmatched.

"He certainly exceeded the first impressions you had of him, my brave knight."

"Thomas is my oldest friend, My Lady."

"And here I thought *I* was your oldest friend," she teased.

"My Lady, you heard my prayers."

"Your words have echoed in my waters for a very long time, Perceval. I am sorry I have not come to you before now. I was shielded for many years from the world."

"Where have you been, Nimuë?" worried Perceval.

"The sword of the King controls when I appear, good knight. It has taken until now for Excalibur to *let me* return to you."

"Allen, Merlin, and now you, My Lady. All of you here now, each from different hidden corners of the universe. What do you need me to do?"

Nimuë smiled at the loyalty of Perceval after all this time and his eagerness to get right to doing what needed to be done.

"This is the chance you have waited over 1500 years for, Perceval. I have gone to great lengths to help Allen. I sent visions of me, visions of *us* with the key to Allen to help him unlock the mystery. I even used my old name, Vivian. The Master is helpless against us now that Allen is ready."

"The Master? Nimuë, that name was nothing more than a device that concealed a terrible truth—Arthur *lives*. *He* is the evil lord by Morgana's side."

"Impossible," Nimuë said as she stumbled backward. "How could that be true? I should have felt him."

"I don't know, My Lady. But Allen needs our help; the young man is special, you've seen it."

"I have…but Perceval…how is *he* alive?"

"My best guess is that whatever Morgana did kept him hidden from you; no longer tied to you and the land, but to her."

"Perceval," Nimuë fretted. "What if Excalibur remains loyal to Arthur? What if that evil…*thing*…gets control of the great weapon?"

"Then God help us all, My Lady. Arthur already has an endless army of brainless Syphs that greatly outnumber us. If he gets his hand on that sword…this world will fall."

The Lady of the Lake placed her hand over her heart. The news that Arthur was alive devastated her; she had seen so much good in him when Merlin came to her after Uther's death. She watched as King Arthur created a world of equals, fulfilling the promise of his capacity for good. She also saw the downfall of Camelot and Arthur's hunger for power, his mind twisted by his sister, Morgana. But in this moment, all she could think about was Merlin's return.

*501 A.D. – England*

He leaned against a tree and stroked her hair, humming a tune as her head rested in his lap. She momentarily opened her blue eyes and stared up at him, her right arm holding his side. They normally cherished these moments together, but this romantic interlude felt different. He looked down at her and caught her gaze—and saw his moment to break the tension.

"What are you thinking, my love?" Merlin asked.

"Let's leave this world and be done with the power of men and women who are unworthy, Merlin," Nimuë begged.

"We both know that cannot happen. We are tied to that sword. You know what happened when Arthur nearly destroyed that weapon, the pain it caused us both. I fear if Excalibur is destroyed…that we will cease to exist."

"We can be free in another world, Merlin. We can take the sword with us."

"We leave them all to die if we do that."

Nimuë sat up and stared intently into Merlin's eyes. "What do we have to do, my love?" she asked.

"It's up to you now, dear Nimuë. Morgana is stronger than anything I have ever encountered. I can't defeat her."

"You can't die, either, Merlin," she reminded him.

"No, I cannot die. But I can be neutralized. I have dreamed of the days to come and the hell that we will pay for letting Arthur send his men after the Grail."

"He holds the sword; he commands those tied to it. What could we have done to convince him otherwise?"

"I don't know, Nimuë. The King is weak, both body and mind right now. The Round Table is all but destroyed, and Mordred has declared war on anyone with allegiance to his father."

"What of the Queen? Lancelot?"

"Guinevere has chosen a new path, one that will keep her protected for some time. Sir Lancelot has disappeared."

"Surely you can see with your magic where he is?" Nimuë supposed.

"Healing Excalibur has cost me a great deal of my power," Merlin said. "The ability to conjure has…momentarily left me."

Nimuë's chest filled with a tinge of fear hearing that Merlin was temporarily powerless. *We're no match for them.* She looked away for a moment and then turned with certainty in her face and determination in her eyes as she looked directly at Merlin, her demeanor and voice stern.

"It truly is up to me," Nimuë accepted. "What must I do?"

"When Arthur dies, the mighty Excalibur must return to you. You're the only being alive that can protect that sword from Morgana. We both know she will stop at nothing to see Mordred hoist Excalibur and take the throne for himself."

"I understand," she agreed. "It will be safe with me."

"What little power I have left, I give to you, my love," Merlin offered.

Nimuë jerked her body back a little as her eyes widened. "I am no sorceress, Merlin. I wouldn't know what to do with your power."

"This power is specific," Merlin said. "You'll have the ability to project yourself into the dreams of the king. If Mordred takes the throne, you will see what he's thinking in the depths of his subconscious. You'll know what makes the boy vulnerable."

"How do I get this power?" she asked, her face overflowing with curiosity.

"It's simple," Merlin explained with a smile. "Kiss me."


*Present Day*

"Where is Excalibur, My Lady?" Perceval asked, wringing his hands.

Nimuë smiled softly and reached for Perceval's hands with hers— not just to calm him—but to help calm her.

"I have kept the sword safe for over a millennium, Perceval. It is hidden in the depths of this lagoon."

"The time has come, Nimuë; Excalibur must be returned to the king."

"Then you must come with me."

Nimuë let go of Perceval's hands and she gracefully dove into the lagoon. Perceval looked around the underground cave of waterfalls. He breathed deep and jumped in after her, unafraid of what awaited underwater.

Perceval quickly found that he could breathe normally, and his eyes could remain open while he followed Nimuë as she descended further underwater. The little lagoon they'd stood beside moments ago disappeared as Nimuë revealed the depths of her home to Perceval. All around them, Perceval could see the shapes of what he thought were people. He tried to swim toward one of the figures, but Nimuë grabbed him by the hand and increased her speed, bringing them both to the floor of the body of water. As Nimuë's feet touched the bottom, a path of round white pebbles formed under her feet and the water pushed to each side of the duo, fashioning walls that stretched high, far beyond what Perceval's eyes could see. Out of the walls of water walked men, women, and children, all created and surrounded by water.

"Who are they?" Perceval asked.

"These are my children," Nimuë responded. "Crafted to help me protect the weapon of the king."

"This is incredible," Perceval remarked.

"This way, good knight."

The people of the water marveled at Perceval, pointing, murmuring and smiling, and he returned the admiration. Perceval's head swiveled in every direction at Nimuë's children whispering to each other as he passed. As they came to the end of the path, one of Nimuë's children—a woman with the likeness of Nimuë outlined by water—joined the duo and escorted them through a waterfall doorway. When they exited the other end, snowflakes dropped onto Perceval's tunic and melted. Perceval lifted his head to the sky and held out his arms, smiling at the snowfall.

"Absolutely incredible," he laughed.

The ground was completely covered by untouched snow. Perceval considered his surroundings and knew he had been to this place in his early life, long before he even met Arthur. He turned to Nimuë with a bewildered look in his eyes.

"It was the only way to keep the sword hidden," she explained.

"Morgana would have found it otherwise."

As Perceval moved through the snow, he could hear the crunch of hard-packed snow but couldn't feel the coldness. Perceval came upon a courtyard. A white church with a tall cross on its steeple stood in the center of the courtyard. The sun shined down on the opposite side of the church, creating shadows where Perceval stood. Perceval quickly ran to the other side and came upon a slab of stone with an anvil on top of it. And stuck in the anvil, Excalibur.

"Excalibur," he beamed.

Tears welled in Perceval's eyes as he reached out to touch the handle of the sword.

"We both know the only place Morgana would never have looked is the past," Nimuë offered. "The old magic of the water made this place, a moment frozen in time."

Perceval gripped the sword tightly and understood the gravity of what he was ready to do.

"Whoso pulleth out this sword of this stone and anvil…" he started.

"…is rightwise King," Nimuë finished. "I was there the night Merlin cast that spell; I was there when this sword was born into the world."

Nimuë placed a hand on Perceval's shoulder and gently moved him back from the stone. She reached down with her hand and slowly slid Excalibur out of the stone and into her grip. The hilt resembled a capital 'I' with gold on the horizontal portion of the hilt and silver that twisted on the vertical grip itself.

The Lady of the Lake thought about the day the sword was created, a little sad at the thought of the cost they had paid all these years.

"The idea was to have this sword act as a bridge between your world and ours, Perceval," she explained. "All of our power in one weapon."

"You made the mistake of thinking humans, no matter how honorable they seem, aren't driven by their thirst for power, revenge, and more power."

"After Uther, we knew the only way to protect the land was to hide the sword. But Merlin's guilt over Uther's betrayal left us with only one option. We never could have predicted he would go to that courtyard," Nimuë said. "Especially not on the day Merlin collected Arthur. We should have known then Morgana's potential for darkness. I still have no doubt she twisted the fates in her favor that day—Merlin was powerless, and I was trapped in my underwater world, left to spectate."

Perceval nodded in sympathy. "We've all been given a chance to make this right again, My Lady," Perceval proposed. "That sword may tip the fates back in our favor."

"Let's go get this to the rightwise king." Nimuë said with joy, anticipation, hope.

"My Lady, we are ready," the woman said.

"Ready for what?" Perceval asked.

"My dear Perceval." Nimuë's warmth was palpable. "You say you're outnumbered, that Arthur and Morgana have an army of Syphs ready to destroy you all. Look around you, Perceval; *we* have an army capable of helping in this fight. You are *not* alone. Adair, ready our people."

"Something is wrong, Mother," Adair warned. "I can sense—"

"I feel it too, Adair."

"What is it, Nimuë?" Perceval asked.

"They're here, brave knight. The Nimayrd has entered the human world. Their attack has begun."

# ABOUT THE AUTHOR

Lennie DiFino has been crafting creative content since 1997 as a writer, copywriter, and content creator. Starting at the New York State Fair, Lennie moved on to WWE, where he served as a Multimedia Producer, contributing to the weekly shows and developing popular features like "Top 25". He also authored the "Where Are They Now?" series and crafted interview questions for icons like John Cena.

Lennie holds a Bachelor's in English and a Master's in Adolescent Education from Le Moyne College, with extensive studies in Arthurian Legend and History, Victorian Literature, and Creative Writing at the University of Oxford – where he began his journey with *Whispers of Excalibur*.

His creative inspirations and passions include David Lynch, *Lord of the Rings*, and many more. Lennie's blend of academic insight, pop culture savvy, and real-world experience defines his writing and content creation.

Lennie currently resides in New York where he is a devoted father of two; Lennie balances his creative pursuits with family time.

You can visit his website at: lenniedifino.com.